The Philo Vance
Murder Cases: 1

The Philo Vance Murder Cases: 1

The Benson Murder Case &
The 'Canary' Murder Case

S. S. Van Dine

LEONAUR

The Philo Vance Murder Cases: 1—The Benson Murder Case
& The 'Canary' Murder Case
by S. S. Van Dine

Published by Leonaur Ltd

Material original to this edition and this editorial selection
copyright © 2010 Leonaur Ltd

ISBN: 978-0-85706-425-7 (hardcover)
ISBN: 978-0-85706-426-4 (softcover)

http://www.leonaur.com

Publisher's Notes

The views expressed in this book are not necessarily
those of the publisher.

Contents

The Benson Murder Case   7

The 'Canary' Murder Case   231

The Benson
Murder Case

"Mr. Mason," he said, "I wish to thank you for my life."
"Sir," said Mason, "I had no interest in your life. The adjustment of your problem was the only thing of interest to me."

—*Randolph Mason: Corrector of Destinies*

Introductory

If you will refer to the municipal statistics of the City of New York, you will find that the number of unsolved major crimes during the four years that John F.-X. Markham was district attorney, was far smaller than under any of his predecessors' administrations. Markham projected the district attorney's office into all manner of criminal investigations; and, as a result, many abstruse crimes on which the police had hopelessly gone aground were eventually disposed of.

But although he was personally credited with the many important indictments and subsequent convictions that he secured, the truth is that he was only an instrument in many of his most famous cases. The man who actually solved them and supplied the evidence for their prosecution was in no way connected with the city's administration and never once came into the public eye.

At that time I happened to be both legal advisor and personal friend of this other man, and it was thus that the strange and amazing facts of the situation became known to me. But not until recently have I been at liberty to make them public. Even now I am not permitted to divulge the man's name, and for that reason I have chosen, arbitrarily, to refer to him throughout these *ex officio* reports as Philo Vance.

It is, of course, possible that some of his acquaintances may, through my revelations, be able to guess his identity; and if such should prove the case, I beg of them to guard that knowledge; for though he has now gone to Italy to live and has given me permission to record the exploits of which he was the unique central character, he has very emphatically imposed his anonymity upon me; and I should not like to feel that, through any lack of discretion or delicacy, I have been the cause of his secret becoming generally known.

The present chronicle has to do with Vance's solution of the notorious Benson murder which, due to the unexpectedness of the crime, the prominence of the persons involved, and the startling evidence adduced, was invested with an interest rarely surpassed in the annals of New York's criminal history.

This sensational case was the first of many in which Vance figured as a kind of *amicus curiae* in Markham's investigations.

S. S. Van Dine
New York

Characters of the Book

Philo Vance

John F.-X. Markham *District Attorney of New York County*

Alvin H. Benson *Well-known Wall Street broker and man-about-town, who was mysteriously murdered in his home*

Major Anthony Benson *Brother of the murdered man*

Mrs. Anna Platz *Housekeeper for Alvin Benson*

Muriel St. Clair *A young singer*

Captain Philip Leacock *Miss St. Clair's fiancé*

Leander Pfyfe *Intimate friend of Alvin Benson's*

Mrs. Paula Banning *A friend of Leander Pfyfe's*

Elsie Hoffman *Secretary of the firm of Benson and Benson*

Colonel Bigsby Ostrander *A retired army officer*

William H. Moriarty *An alderman, Borough of the Bronx*

Jack Prisco *Elevator boy at the Chatham Arms*

George G. Stitt *Of the firm of Stitt and McCoy, Public Accountants*

Maurice Dinwiddie *Assistant District Attorney*

Chief Inspector O'Brien *Of the Police Department of New York City*

William M. Moran *Commanding Officer of the Detective Bureau*

Ernest Heath *Sergeant of the Homicide Bureau*

Burke *Detective of the Homicide Bureau*

Snitkin *Detective of the Homicide Bureau*

Emery *Detective of the Homicide Bureau*

Ben Hanlon *Commanding Officer of Detectives assigned to District Attorney's office*

Phelps *Detective assigned to District Attorney's office*

Tracy *Detective assigned to District Attorney's office*

Springer *Detective assigned to District Attorney's office*

Higginbotham *Detective assigned to District Attorney's office*
Captain Carl Hagedorn *Firearms expert*
Dr. Doremus *Medical Examiner*
Francis Swacker *Secretary to the District Attorney*
Currie *Vance's valet*

CHAPTER 1

Philo Vance at Home

Friday, June 14; 8:30 a.m.

It happened that, on the morning of the momentous June the four-teenth when the discovery of the murdered body of Alvin H. Benson created a sensation which, to this day, has not entirely died away, I had breakfasted with Philo Vance in his apartment. It was not unusual for me to share Vance's luncheons and dinners, but to have breakfast with him was something of an occasion. He was a late riser, and it was his habit to remain incommunicado until his midday meal.

The reason for this early meeting was a matter of business—or, rather, of aesthetics. On the afternoon of the previous day Vance had attended a preview of Vollard's collection of Cézanne watercolours at the Kessler Galleries and, having seen several pictures he particularly wanted, he had invited me to an early breakfast to give me instruc-tions regarding their purchase.

A word concerning my relationship with Vance is necessary to clarify my role of narrator in this chronicle. The legal tradition is deeply imbedded in my family, and when my preparatory-school days were over, I was sent, almost as a matter of course, to Harvard to study law. It was there I met Vance, a reserved, cynical, and caustic freshman who was the bane of his professors and the fear of his fel-low classmen. Why he should have chosen me, of all the students at the university, for his extrascholastic association, I have never been able to understand fully. My own liking for Vance was simply ex-plained: he fascinated and interested me, and supplied me with a novel kind of intellectual diversion. In his liking for me, however, no such basis of appeal was present. I was (and am now) a com-monplace fellow, possessed of a conservative and rather conventional mind. But, at least, my mentality was not rigid, and the ponderosity of the legal procedure did not impress me greatly—which is why, no doubt, I had little taste for my inherited profession—; and it is possible that these traits found certain affinities in Vance's unconscious mind. There is, to be sure, the less consoling explanation that I appealed to Vance as a kind of foil, or anchorage, and that he sensed in my nature a complementary antithesis to his own. But whatever the explanation, we were much together; and, as the years went by, that association ripened into an inseparable friendship.

Upon graduation I entered my father's law firm—Van Dine and Davis—and after five years of dull apprenticeship I was taken into the firm as the junior partner. At present I am the second Van Dine of Van Dine, Davis, and Van Dine, with offices at 120 Broadway. At about the time my name first appeared on the letterheads of the firm, Vance returned from Europe, where he had been living during my legal novitiate, and, an aunt of his having died and made him her principal beneficiary, I was called upon to discharge the technical obligations involved in putting him in possession of his inherited property.

This work was the beginning of a new and somewhat unusual relationship between us. Vance had a strong distaste for any kind of business transaction, and in time I became the custodian of all his monetary interests and his agent at large. I found that his affairs were various enough to occupy as much of my time as I cared to give to legal matters, and as Vance was able to indulge the luxury of having a personal legal factotum, so to speak, I permanently closed my desk at the office and devoted myself exclusively to his needs and whims.

If, up to the time when Vance summoned me to discuss the purchase of the Cézannes, I had harboured any secret or repressed regrets for having deprived the firm of Van Dine, Davis, and Van Dine of my modest legal talents, they were permanently banished on that eventful morning; for, beginning with the notorious Benson murder, and extending over a period of nearly four years, it was my privilege to be a spectator of what I believe was the most amazing series of criminal cases that ever passed before the eyes of a young lawyer. Indeed, the grim dramas I witnessed during that period constitute one of the most astonishing secret documents in the police history of this country.

Of these dramas Vance was the central character. By an analytical and interpretative process which, as far as I know, has never before been applied to criminal activities, he succeeded in solving many of the important crimes on which both the police and the district attorney's office had hopelessly fallen down.

Due to my peculiar relations with Vance it happened that not only did I participate in all the cases with which he was connected but I was also present at most of the informal discussions concerning them which took place between him and the district attorney; and, being of methodical temperament, I kept a fairly complete record of them. In addition, I noted down (as accurately as memory permitted) Vance's unique psychological methods of determining guilt, as he explained them from time to time. It is fortunate that I performed this gratuitous labour of accumulation and transcription, for now that circumstances have unexpectedly rendered possible my making the cases public, I am able to present them in full detail and with all their various sidelights and succeeding steps—a task that would be impossible were it not for my numerous clippings and *adversaria*.

Fortunately, too, the first case to draw Vance into its ramifications was that of Alvin Benson's murder. Not only did it prove one of the most famous of New York's causes *célèbres*, but it gave Vance an excellent opportunity of displaying his rare talents of deductive reasoning, and, by its nature and magnitude, aroused his interest in a branch of activity which heretofore had been alien to his temperamental promptings and habitual predilections.

The case intruded upon Vance's life suddenly and unexpectedly, although he himself had, by a casual request made to the district attorney over a month before, been the involuntary agent of this destruction of his normal routine. The thing, in fact, burst upon us before we had quite finished our breakfast on that mid-June morning, and put an end temporarily to all business connected with the purchase of the Cézanne paintings. When, later in the day, I visited the Kessler Galleries, two of the watercolours that Vance had particularly desired had been sold; and I am convinced that, despite his success in the unravelling of the Benson murder mystery and his saving of at least one innocent person from arrest, he has never to this day felt entirely compensated for the loss of those two little sketches on which he had set his heart.

As I was ushered into the living room that morning by Currie, a rare old English servant who acted as Vance's butler, valet, majordomo and, on occasions, specialty cook, Vance was sitting in a large armchair, attired in a *surah* silk dressing gown and grey suede slippers, with Vollard's book on Cézanne open across his knees.

"Forgive my not rising, Van." He greeted me casually. "I have the whole weight of the modern evolution in art resting on my legs. Furthermore, this plebeian early rising fatigues me, y'know."

He riffled the pages of the volume, pausing here and there at a reproduction.

"This chap Vollard," he remarked at length, "has been rather liberal with our art-fearing country. He has sent a really goodish collection of his Cézannes here. I viewed 'em yesterday with the proper reverence and, I might add, unconcern, for Kessler was watching me; and I've marked the ones I want you to buy for me as soon as the gallery opens this morning."

He handed me a small catalogue he had been using as a bookmark.

"A beastly assignment, I know," he added, with an indolent smile. "These delicate little smudges with all their blank paper will prob'ly be meaningless to your legal mind—they're so unlike a neatly typed brief, don't y'know. And you'll no doubt think some of 'em are hung upside-down—one of 'em is, in fact, and even Kessler doesn't know it. But don't fret, Van old dear. They're very beautiful and valuable little knickknacks, and rather inexpensive when one considers what they'll be bringing in a few years. Really an excellent investment for some money-loving soul, y'know—inf'nitely better than that Lawyer's Equity Stock over which you grew so eloquent at the time of my dear Aunt Agatha's death."*

Vance's one passion (if a purely intellectual enthusiasm may be called a passion) was art—not art in its narrow, personal aspects, but in its broader, more universal significance. And art was not only his dominating interest but his chief diversion. He was something of an authority on Japanese and Chinese prints; he knew tapestries and ceramics; and once I heard him give an impromptu causerie to a few guests on Tanagra figurines, which, had it been transcribed, would have made a most delightful and instructive monograph.

Vance had sufficient means to indulge his instinct for collecting, and possessed a fine assortment of pictures and *objets d'art*. His collection was heterogeneous only in its superficial characteristics: every piece he owned embodied some principle of form or line that related it to all the others. One who knew art could feel the unity and consistency in all the items with which he surrounded himself, however widely separated they were in point of time or *métier* or surface appeal. Vance, I have always felt, was one of those rare human beings, a collector with a definite philosophic point of view.

His apartment in East Thirty-eighth Street—actually the two top floors of an old mansion, beautifully remodelled and in part rebuilt to secure spacious rooms and lofty ceilings—was filled, but not crowded,

---

* As a matter of fact, the same watercolours that Vance obtained for $250 and $300 were bringing three times as much four years later.

with rare specimens of oriental and occidental, ancient and modern, art. His paintings ranged from the Italian primitives to Cézanne and Matisse; and among his collection of original drawings were works as widely separated as those of Michelangelo and Picasso. Vance's Chinese prints constituted one of the finest private collections in this country. They included beautiful examples of the work of Ririomin, Rianchu, Jinkomin, Kakei, and Mokkei.

"The Chinese," Vance once said to me, "are the truly great artists of the East. They were the men whose work expressed most intensely a broad philosophic spirit. By contrast the Japanese were superficial. It's a long step between the little more than decorative *souci* of a Hokusai and the profoundly thoughtful and conscious artistry of a Ririomin. Even when Chinese art degenerated under the Manchus, we find in it a deep philosophic quality—a spiritual *sensibilité*, so to speak. And in the modern copies of copies—what is called the *bunjinga* style—we still have pictures of profound meaning."

Vance's catholicity of taste in art was remarkable. His collection was as varied as that of a museum. It embraced a black-figured amphora by Amasis, a proto-Corinthian vase in the Aegean style, Koubatcha and Rhodian plates, Athenian pottery, a sixteenth-century Italian holy water stoup of rock crystal, pewter of the Tudor period (several pieces bearing the double-rose hallmark), a bronze plaque by Cellini, a triptych of Limoges enamel, a Spanish *retable* of an altarpiece by Vallfogona, several Etruscan bronzes, an Indian Greco Buddhist, a statuette of the Goddess Kuan Yin from the Ming Dynasty, a number of very fine Renaissance woodcuts, and several specimens of Byzantine, Carolingian, and early French ivory carvings.

His Egyptian treasures included a gold jug from Zakazik, a statuette of the Lady Nai (as lovely as the one in the Louvre), two beautifully carved steles of the First Theban Age, various small sculptures comprising rare representations of Hapi and Amset, and several Arrentine bowls carved with Kalathiskos dancers. On top of one of his embayed Jacobean bookcases in the library, where most of his modern paintings and drawings were hung, was a fascinating group of African sculpture—ceremonial masks and statuette fetishes from French Guinea, the Sudan, Nigeria, the Ivory Coast, and the Congo.

A definite purpose has animated me in speaking at such length about Vance's art instinct, for, in order to understand fully the melodramatic adventures which began for him on that June morning, one must have a general idea of the man's penchants and inner promptings. His interest in art was an important—one might almost say the dominant—factor in his personality. I have never met a man quite like him—a man so apparently diversified and yet so fundamentally consistent.

Vance was what many would call a dilettante. But the designation does him injustice. He was a man of unusual culture and brilliance. An aristocrat by birth and instinct, he held himself severely aloof from the common world of men. In his manner there was an indefinable contempt for inferiority of all kinds. The great majority of those with whom he came in contact regarded him as a snob. Yet there was in his condescension and disdain no trace of spuriousness. His snobbishness was intellectual as well as social. He detested stupidity even more, I believe, than he did vulgarity or bad taste. I have heard him on several occasions quote Fouché's famous line: *C'est plus qu'un crime; c'est une faute.* And he meant it literally.

Vance was frankly a cynic, but he was rarely bitter; his was a flippant, Juvenalian cynicism. Perhaps he may best be described as a bored and supercilious, but highly conscious and penetrating, spectator of life. He was keenly interested in all human reactions; but it was the interest of the scientist, not the humanitarian. Withal he was a man of rare personal charm. Even people who found it difficult to admire him found it equally difficult not to like him. His somewhat quixotic mannerisms and his slightly English accent and inflection—a heritage of his postgraduate days at Oxford—impressed those who did not know him well as affectations. But the truth is, there was very little of the poseur about him.

He was unusually good-looking, although his mouth was ascetic and cruel, like the mouths on some of the Medici portraits;* moreover, there was a slightly derisive hauteur in the lift of his eyebrows. Despite the aquiline severity of his lineaments, his face was highly sensitive. His forehead was full and sloping—it was the artist's, rather than the scholar's, brow. His cold grey eyes were widely spaced. His nose was straight and slender, and his chin narrow but prominent, with an unusually deep cleft. When I saw John Barrymore recently in Hamlet, I was somehow reminded of Vance; and once before, in a scene of Caesar and Cleopatra played by Forbes- Robertson, I received a similar impression.

---

* I am thinking particularly of Bronzino's portraits of Pietro de' Medici and Cosimo de' Medici, in the National Gallery, and of Vasari's medallion portrait of Lorenzo de' Medici in the Vecchio Palazzo, Florence.

Once when Vance was suffering from sinusitis, he had an X-ray photograph of his head made; and the accompanying chart described him as a "marked *dolichocephalic*" and a "disharmonious Nordic." It also contained the following data:—cephalic index 75; nose, *leptorhine*, with an index of 48; facial angle, 85 deg.; vertical index, 72; upper facial index, 54; interpupilary width, 67; chin, *masognathous*, with an index of 103; *sella turcica*, abnormally large.

Vance was slightly under six feet, graceful, and giving the impression of sinewy strength and nervous endurance. He was an expert fencer and had been the captain of the university's fencing team. He was mildly fond of outdoor sports and had a knack of doing things well without any extensive practice. His golf handicap was only three; and one season he had played on our championship polo team against England. Nevertheless, he had a positive antipathy to walking and would not go a hundred yards on foot if there was any possible means of riding.

In his dress he was always fashionable—scrupulously correct to the smallest detail—yet unobtrusive. He spent considerable time at his clubs; his favourite was the Stuyvesant, because, as he explained to me, its membership was drawn largely from the political and commercial ranks, and he was never drawn into a discussion which required any mental effort. He went occasionally to the more modern operas and was a regular subscriber to the symphony concerts and chamber music recitals.

Incidentally, he was one of the most unerring poker players I have ever seen. I mention this fact not merely because it was unusual and significant that a man of Vance's type should have preferred so democratic a game to bridge or chess, for instance, but because his knowledge of the science of human psychology involved in poker had an intimate bearing on the chronicles I am about to set down.

Vance's knowledge of psychology was indeed uncanny. He was gifted with an instinctively accurate judgment of people, and his study and reading had coordinated and rationalized this gift to an amazing extent. He was well grounded in the academic principles of psychology, and all his courses at college had either centred about this subject or been subordinated to it. While I was confining myself to a restricted area of torts and contracts, constitutional and common law, equity, evidence, and pleading, Vance was reconnoitring the whole field of cultural endeavour. He had courses in the history of religions, the Greek classics, biology, civics, and political economy, philosophy, anthropology, literature, theoretical

and experimental psychology, and ancient and modern languages.*
But it was, I think, his courses under Münsterberg and William
James that interested him the most.

Vance's mind was basically philosophical—that is, philosophical in
the more general sense. Being singularly free from the conventional
sentimentalities and current superstitions, he could look beneath the
surface of human acts into actuating impulses and motives. Moreover,
he was resolute both in his avoidance of any attitude that savoured of
credulousness and in his adherence to cold, logical exactness in his
mental processes.

"Until we can approach all human problems," he once remarked,
"with the clinical aloofness and cynical contempt of a doctor examining a guinea pig strapped to a board, we have little chance of getting
at the truth."

Vance led an active, but by no means animated, social life—a concession to various family ties. But he was not a social animal—I cannot remember ever having met a man with so undeveloped a gre-
garious instinct—and when he went forth into the social world, it
was generally under compulsion. In fact, one of his "duty" affairs had
occupied him on the night before that memorable June breakfast;
otherwise, we would have consulted about the Cézannes the evening
before; and Vance groused a good deal about it while Currie was serving our strawberries and eggs Benedictine. Later on I was to give
profound thanks to the God of Coincidence that the blocks had been
arranged in just that pattern; for had Vance been slumbering peacefully at nine o'clock when the district attorney called, I would probably have missed four of the most interesting and exciting years of my
life; and many of New York's shrewdest and most desperate criminals
might still be at large.

Vance and I had just settled back in our chairs for our second
cup of coffee and a cigarette when Currie, answering an impetuous
ringing of the front door bell, ushered the district attorney into the
living room.

---

* "Culture," Vance said to me shortly after I had met him, "is polyglot; and the knowledge of many tongues is essential to an understanding of the world's intellectual
and aesthetic achievements. Especially are the Greek and Latin classics vitiated by
translation." I quote the remark here because his omnivorous reading in languages
other than English, coupled with his amazingly retentive memory, had a tendency to
affect his own speech. And while it may appear to some that his speech was at times
pedantic, I have tried, throughout these chronicles to quote him literally, in the hope
of presenting a portrait of the man as he was.

"By all that's holy!" he exclaimed, raising his hands in mock astonishment. "New York's leading *flâneur* and art connoisseur is up and about!"

"And I am suffused with blushes at the disgrace of it," Vance replied.

It was evident, however, that the district attorney was not in a jovial mood. His face suddenly sobered. "Vance, a serious thing has brought me here. I'm in a great hurry and merely dropped by to keep my promise. . . . The fact is, Alvin Benson has been murdered."

Vance lifted his eyebrows languidly. "Really, now," he drawled. "How messy! But he no doubt deserved it. In any event, that's no reason why you should repine. Take a chair and have a cup of Currie's incomp'rable coffee." And before the other could protest, he rose and pushed a bell-button.

Markham hesitated a second or two.

"Oh, well. A couple of minutes won't make any difference. But only a gulp." And he sank into a chair facing us.

CHAPTER 2

At the Scene of the Crime

Friday, June 14; 9 a.m.

John F.-X. Markham, as you remember, had been elected district attorney of New York County on the Independent Reform Ticket during one of the city's periodical reactions against Tammany Hall. He served his four years and would probably have been elected to a second term had not the ticket been hopelessly split by the political juggling of his opponents. He was an indefatigable worker and projected the district attorney's office into all manner of criminal and civil investigations. Being utterly incorruptible, he not only aroused the fervid admiration of his constituents but produced an almost unprecedented sense of security in those who had opposed him on partisan lines.

He had been in office only a few months when one of the newspapers referred to him as the Watch Dog; and the sobriquet clung to him until the end of his administration. Indeed, his record as a successful prosecutor during the four years of his incumbency was such a remarkable one that even today it is not infrequently referred to in legal and political discussions.

Markham was a tall, strongly built man in the middle forties, with a clean-shaven, somewhat youthful face which belied his uniformly grey hair. He was not handsome according to conventional standards, but he had an unmistakable air of distinction, and was possessed of an amount of social culture rarely found in our latter-day political office-holders. Withal he was a man of brusque and vindictive temperament; but his brusqueness was an incrustation on a solid foundation of good breeding, not—as is usually the case—the roughness of substructure showing through an inadequately superimposed crust of gentility.

When his nature was relieved of the stress of duty and care, he was the most gracious of men. But early in my acquaintance with him I had seen his attitude of cordiality suddenly displaced by one of grim authority. It was as if a new personality—hard, indomitable, symbolic of eternal justice—had in that moment been born in Markham's body. I was to witness this transformation many times before our association ended. In fact, this very morning, as he sat opposite to me in Vance's living room, there was more than a hint of it in the aggressive sternness of his expression; and I knew that he was deeply troubled over Alvin Benson's murder.

He swallowed his coffee rapidly and was setting down the cup, when Vance, who had been watching him with quizzical amusement, remarked, "I say, why this sad preoccupation over the passing of one Benson? You weren't, by any chance, the murderer, what?"

Markham ignored Vance's levity. "I'm on my way to Benson's. Do you care to come along? You asked for the experience, and I dropped in to keep my promise."

I then recalled that several weeks before at the Stuyvesant Club, when the subject of the prevalent homicides in New York was being discussed, Vance had expressed a desire to accompany the district attorney on one of his investigations, and that Markham had promised to take him on his next important case. Vance's interest in the psychology of human behaviour had prompted the desire, and his friendship with Markham, which had been of long standing, had made the request possible.

"You remember everything, don't you?" Vance replied lazily. "An admirable gift, even if an uncomfortable one." He glanced at the clock on the mantel, it lacked a few minutes of nine. "But what an indecent hour! Suppose someone should see me."

Markham moved forward impatiently in his chair. "Well, if you think the gratification of your curiosity would compensate you for the disgrace of being seen in public at nine o'clock in the morning, you'll have to hurry. I certainly won't take you in dressing gown and bedroom slippers. And I most certainly won't wait over five minutes for you to get dressed."

"Why the haste, old dear?" Vance asked, yawning. "The chap's dead, don't y'know; he can't possibly run away."

"Come, get a move on, you orchid," the other urged. "This affair is no joke. It's damned serious, and from the looks of it, it's going to cause an ungodly scandal. What are you going to do?"

"Do? I shall humbly follow the great avenger of the common people," returned Vance, rising and making an obsequious bow.

He rang for Currie and ordered his clothes brought to him.

"I'm attending a levee which Mr. Markham is holding over a corpse and I want something rather spiffy. Is it warm enough for a silk suit?. . . . And a lavender tie, by all means."

"I trust you won't also wear your green carnation," grumbled Markham.

"Tut! Tut!" Vance chided him. "You've been reading Mr. Hitchens. Such heresy in a district attorney! Anyway, you know full well I never wear *boutonnieres*. The decoration has fallen into disrepute. The only remaining devotees of the practice are roués and saxophone players. . . . But tell me about the departed Benson."

Vance was now dressing, with Currie's assistance, at a rate of speed I had rarely seen him display in such matters. Beneath his bantering pose I recognized the true eagerness of the man for a new experience and one that promised such dramatic possibilities for his alert and observing mind.

"You knew Alvin Benson casually, I believe," the district attorney said. "Well, early this morning his housekeeper phoned the local precinct station that she had found him shot through the head, fully dressed and sitting in his favourite chair in his living room. The message, of course, was put through at once to the telegraph bureau at headquarters, and my assistant on duty notified me immediately. I was tempted to let the case follow the regular police routine. But half an hour later Major Benson, Alvin's brother, phoned me and asked me, as a special favour, to take charge. I've known the major for twenty years and I couldn't very well refuse. So I took a hurried breakfast and started for Benson's house. He lived in West Forty-eighth Street; and as I passed your corner I remembered your request and dropped by to see if you cared to go along."

"Most consid'rate," murmured Vance, adjusting his four-in-hand before a small polychrome mirror by the door. Then he turned to me. "Come, Van. We'll all gaze upon the defunct Benson. I'm sure some of Markham's sleuths will unearth the fact that I detested the bounder and accuse me of the crime; and I'll feel safer, don't y'know, with legal talent at hand. . . . No objections—eh, what, Markham?"

"Certainly not," the other agreed readily, although I felt that he would rather not have had me along. But I was too deeply interested in the affair to offer any ceremonious objections and I followed Vance and Markham downstairs.

As we settled back in the waiting taxicab and started up Madison Avenue, I marvelled a little, as I had often done before, at the strange friendship of these two dissimilar men beside me—Markham forthright, conventional, a trifle austere, and over serious in his dealings with life; and Vance casual, mercurial, debonair, and whimsically cynical in the face of the grimmest realities. And yet this temperamental diversity seemed, in some wise, the very cornerstone of their friendship; it was as if each saw in the other some unattainable field of experience and sensation that had been denied himself. Markham represented to Vance the solid and immutable realism of life, whereas Vance symbolized for Markham the carefree, exotic, gypsy spirit of intellectual adventure. Their intimacy, in fact, was even greater than showed on the surface; and despite Markham's exaggerated deprecations of the other's attitudes and opinions, I believe he respected Vance's intelligence more profoundly than that of any other man he knew.

As we rode uptown that morning Markham appeared preoccupied and gloomy. No word had been spoken since we left the apartment; but as we turned west into Forty-eighth Street Vance asked; "What is the social etiquette of these early-morning murder functions, aside from removing one's hat in the presence of the body?"

"You keep your hat on," growled Markham.

"My word! Like a synagogue, what? Most int'restin'! Perhaps one takes off one's shoes so as not to confuse the footprints."

"No," Markham told him. "The guests remain fully clothed—in which the function differs from the ordinary evening affairs of your smart set."

"My *dear* Markham!"—Vance's tone was one of melancholy reproof—"The horrified moralist in your nature is at work again. That remark of yours was pos'tively Epworth Leaguish."

Markham was too abstracted to follow up Vance's badinage. "There are one or two things," he said soberly, "that I think I'd better warn you about. From the looks of it, this case is going to cause considerable noise, and there'll be a lot of jealousy and battling for honours. I won't be fallen upon and caressed affectionately by the police for coming in at this stage of the game; so be careful not to rub their bristles the wrong way. My assistant, who's there now, tells me he thinks the inspector has put Heath in charge. Heath's a sergeant in the homicide bureau and is undoubtedly convinced at the present moment that I'm taking hold in order to get the publicity."

"Aren't you his technical superior?" asked Vance.

"Of course; and that makes the situation just so much more delicate.... I wish to God the major hadn't called me up."

"*Eheu!*" sighed Vance. "The world is full of Heaths. Beastly nuisances."

"Don't misunderstand me," Markham hastened to assure him. "Heath is a good man—in fact, as good a man as we've got. The mere fact that he was assigned to the case shows how seriously the affair is regarded at headquarters. There'll be no unpleasantness about my taking charge, you understand; but I want the atmosphere to be as halcyon as possible. Heath'll resent my bringing along you two chaps as spectators, anyway; so I beg of you, Vance, emulate the modest violet."

"I prefer the blushing rose, if you don't mind," Vance protested. "However, I'll instantly give the hypersensitive Heath one of my choicest Régie cigarettes with the rose-petal tips."

"If you do," smiled Markham, "he'll probably arrest you as a suspicious character."

We had drawn up abruptly in front of an old brownstone residence on the upper side of Forty-eighth Street, near Sixth Avenue. It was a house of the better class, built on a twenty-five foot lot in a day when permanency and beauty were still matters of consideration among the city's architects. The design was conventional, to accord with the other houses in the block, but a touch of luxury and individuality was to be seen in its decorative copings and in the stone carvings about the entrance and above the windows.

There was a shallow paved areaway between the street line and the front elevation of the house; but this was enclosed in a high iron railing, and the only entrance was by way of the front door, which was about six feet above the street level at the top of a flight of ten broad stone stairs. Between the entrance and the right-hand wall were two spacious windows covered with heavy iron grilles.

A considerable crowd of morbid onlookers had gathered in front of the house; and on the steps lounged several alert-looking young men whom I took to be newspaper reporters. The door of our taxicab was opened by a uniformed patrolman who saluted Markham with exaggerated respect and ostentatiously cleared a passage for us through the gaping throng of idlers. Another uniformed patrolman stood in the little vestibule and, on recognizing Markham, held the outer door open for us and saluted with great dignity.

"*Ave, Caesar, te salutamus,*" whispered Vance, grinning.

"Be quiet," Markham grumbled. "I've got troubles enough without your garbled questions."

As we passed through the massive carved-oak front door into the main hallway we were met by Assistant District Attorney Dinwiddie, a serious, swarthy young man with a prematurely lined face, whose appearance gave one the impression that most of the woes of humanity were resting upon his shoulders.

"Good morning, Chief," he greeted Markham, with eager relief. "I'm damned glad you've got here. This case'll rip things wide open. Cut-and-dried murder, and not a lead."

Markham nodded gloomily and looked past him into the living room. "Who's here?" he asked.

"The whole works, from the chief inspector down," Dinwiddie told him, with a hopeless shrug, as if the fact boded ill for all concerned.

At that moment a tall, massive, middle-aged man with a pink complexion and a closely cropped white moustache, appeared in the doorway of the living room. On seeing Markham he came forward stiffly with outstretched hand. I recognized him at once as Chief Inspector O'Brien, who was in command of the entire police department. Dignified greetings were exchanged between him and Markham, and then Vance and I were introduced to him. Inspector O'Brien gave us each a curt, silent nod and turned back to the living room, with Markham, Dinwiddie, Vance, and myself following.

The room, which was entered by a wide double door about ten feet down the hall, was a spacious one, almost square, and with high ceilings. Two windows gave on the street; and on the extreme right of the north wall, opposite to the front of the house, was another window opening on a paved court. To the left of this window were the sliding doors leading into the dining room at the rear.

The room presented an appearance of garish opulence. About the walls hung several elaborately framed paintings of race horses and a number of mounted hunting trophies. A highly coloured oriental rug covered nearly the entire floor. In the middle of the east wall, facing the door, was an ornate fireplace and carved marble mantel. Placed diagonally in the corner on the right stood a walnut upright piano with copper trimmings. Then there was a mahogany bookcase with glass doors and figured curtains, a sprawling tapestried davenport, a squat Venetian *tabouret* with inlaid mother-of-pearl, a teakwood stand containing a large brass samovar, and a *buhl*-topped centre table nearly six feet long. At the side of the table nearest the hallway, with its back to the front windows, stood a large wicker lounge chair with a high, fan-shaped back.

In this chair reposed the body of Alvin Benson.

Though I had served two years at the front in the World War and had seen death in many terrible guises, I could not repress a strong sense of revulsion at the sight of this murdered man. In France death

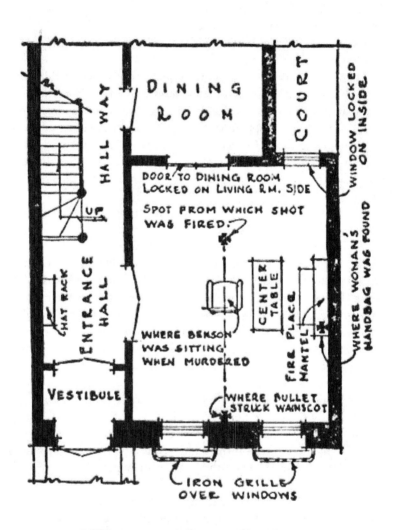

DINING ROOM

COURT

WINDOW LOCKED ON INSIDE

HALL WAY

UP

DOOR TO DINING ROOM.
LOCKED ON LIVING R.M. SIDE

SPOT FROM WHICH SHOT
WAS FIRED:

WHERE WOMAN'S HANDBAG WAS FOUND

ENTRANCE HALL

HAT RACK

CENTER TABLE

FIRE PLACE MANTEL

WHERE BENSON
WAS SITTING
WHEN MURDERED

VESTIBULE

WHERE BULLET
STRUCK WAINSCOT

IRON GRILLE
OVER WINDOWS

WEST 48TH. STREET

had seemed an inevitable part of my daily routine, but here all the organisms of environment were opposed to the idea of fatal violence. The bright June sunshine was pouring into the room, and through the open windows came the continuous din of the city's noises, which, for all their cacophony, are associated with peace and security and the orderly social processes of life.

Benson's body was reclining in the chair in an attitude so natural that one almost expected him to turn to us and ask why we were intruding upon his privacy. His head was resting against the chair's back. His right leg was crossed over his left in a position of comfortable relaxation. His right arm was resting easily on the centre table, and his left arm lay along the chair's arm. But that which most strikingly gave his attitude its appearance of naturalness was a small book which he held in his right hand with his thumb still marking the place where he had evidently been reading.*

He had been shot through the forehead from in front; and the small circular bullet mark was now almost black as a result of the coagulation of the blood. A large dark spot on the rug at the rear of the chair indicated the extent of the haemorrhage caused by the grinding passage of the bullet through his brain. Had it not been for these grisly indications, one might have thought that he had merely paused momentarily in his reading to lean back and rest.

He was attired in an old smoking jacket and red felt bedroom slippers but still wore his dress trousers and evening shirt, though he was collarless, and the neckband of the shirt had been unbuttoned as if for comfort. He was not an attractive man physically, being almost completely bald and more than a little stout. His face was flabby, and the puffiness of his neck was doubly conspicuous without its confining collar. With a slight shudder of distaste I ended my brief contemplation of him and turned to the other occupants of the room.

Two burly fellows with large hands and feet, their black felt hats pushed far back on their heads, were minutely inspecting the iron grillwork over the front windows. They seemed to be giving particular attention to the points where the bars were cemented into the masonry; and one of them had just taken hold of a grille with both hands and was shaking it, simian-wise, as if to test its strength. Another man, of medium height and dapper appearance, with a small blond moustache, was bending over in front of the grate looking intently, so

---

* The book was O. Henry's *Strictly Business*, and the place at which it was being held open was, curiously enough, the story entitled "A Municipal Report."

it seemed, at the dusty gas logs. On the far side of the table a thickset man in blue serge and a derby hat, stood with arms akimbo scrutinizing the silent figure in the chair. His eyes, hard and pale blue, were narrowed, and his square *prognathous* jaw was rigidly set. He was gazing with rapt intensity at Benson's body, as though he hoped, by the sheer power of concentration, to probe the secret of the murder.

Another man, of unusual mien, was standing before the rear window, with a jeweller's magnifying glass in his eye, inspecting a small object held in the palm of his hand. From pictures I had seen of him I knew he was Captain Carl Hagedorn, the most famous firearms expert in America. He was a large, cumbersome, broad-shouldered man of about fifty; and his black, shiny clothes were several sizes too large for him. His coat hitched up behind, and in front hung halfway down to his knees; and his trousers were baggy and lay over his ankles in grotesquely comic folds. His head was round and abnormally large, and his ears seemed sunken into his skull. His mouth was entirely hidden by a scraggly, grey-shot moustache, all the hairs of which grew downward, forming a kind of lambrequin to his lips. Captain Hagedorn had been connected with the New York Police Department for thirty years, and though his appearance and manner were ridiculed at headquarters, he was profoundly respected. His word on any point pertaining to firearms and gunshot wounds was accepted as final by headquarters men.

In the rear of the room, near the dining room door, stood two other men talking earnestly together. One was Inspector William M. Moran, commanding officer of the detective bureau; the other, Sergeant Ernest Heath of the homicide bureau, of whom Markham had already spoken to us.

As we entered the room in the wake of Chief Inspector O'Brien everyone ceased his occupation for a moment and looked at the district attorney in a spirit of uneasy, but respectful, recognition. Only Captain Hagedorn, after a cursory squint at Markham, returned to the inspection of the tiny object in his hand, with an abstracted unconcern which brought a faint smile to Vance's lips.

Inspector Moran and Sergeant Heath came forward with stolid dignity; and after the ceremony of handshaking (which I later observed to be a kind of religious rite among the police and the members of the district attorney's staff), Markham introduced Vance and me and briefly explained our presence. The inspector bowed pleasantly to indicate his acceptance of the intrusion, but I noticed that Heath ignored Markham's explanation and proceeded to treat us as if we were nonexistent.

Inspector Moran was a man of different quality from the others in the room. He was about sixty, with white hair and a brown moustache, and was immaculately dressed. He looked more like a successful Wall Street broker of the better class than a police official.*

"I've assigned Sergeant Heath to the case, Mr. Markham," he explained in a low, well-modulated voice. "It looks as though we are in for a bit of trouble before it's finished. Even the chief inspector thought it warranted his lending the moral support of his presence to the preliminary rounds. He has been here since eight o'clock."

Inspector O'Brien had left us immediately upon entering the room and now stood between the front windows, watching the proceedings with a grave, indecipherable face.

"Well, I think I'll be going," Moran added. "They had me out of bed at seven thirty, and I haven't had any breakfast yet. I won't be needed anyway now that you're here. . . . Good morning." And again he shook hands.

When he had gone, Markham turned to the assistant district attorney.

"Look after these two gentlemen, will you, Dinwiddie? They're babes in the wood and want to see how these affairs work. Explain things to them while I have a little confab with Sergeant Heath."

Dinwiddie accepted the assignment eagerly. I think he was glad of the opportunity to have someone to talk to by way of venting his pent-up excitement.

As the three of us turned rather instinctively toward the body of the murdered man—he was, after all, the hub of this tragic drama—I heard Heath say in a sullen voice:

"I suppose you'll take charge now, Mr. Markham."

Dinwiddie and Vance were talking together, and I watched Markham with interest after what he had told us of the rivalry between the police department and the district attorney's office.

Markham looked at Heath with a slow, gracious smile and shook his head. "No, Sergeant," he replied. "I'm here to work with you, and I want that relationship understood from the outset. In fact, I wouldn't be here now if Major Benson hadn't phoned me and asked me to lend a hand. And I particularly want my name kept out of it. It's pretty generally known—and if it isn't, it will be—that the major

---

* Inspector Moran (as I learned later) had once been the president of a large upstate bank that had failed during the panic of 1907, and during the Gaynor Administration had been seriously considered for the post of Police Commissioner.

is an old friend of mine; so, it will be better all round if my connection with the case is kept quiet."

Heath murmured something I did not catch, but I could see that he had, in large measure, been placated. He, in common with all other men who were acquainted with Markham, knew his word was good; and he personally liked the district attorney.

"If there's any credit coming from this affair," Markham went on, "the police department is to get it; therefore I think it best for you to see the report. . . . And, by the way," he added good- naturedly, "if there's any blame coming, you fellows will have to bear that, too."

"Fair enough," assented Heath.

"And now, Sergeant, let's get to work," said Markham.

CHAPTER 3

A Lady's Handbag

Friday, June 14; 9:30 a.m.

The district attorney and Heath walked up to the body and stood regarding it.

"You see," Heath explained; "he was shot directly from the front. A pretty powerful shot, too, for the bullet passed through the head and struck the woodwork over there by the window." He pointed to a place on the wainscot a short distance from the floor near the drapery of the window nearest the hallway. "We found the expelled shell, and Captain Hagedorn's got the bullet."

He turned to the firearms expert. "How about it, Captain? Anything special?"

Hagedorn raised his head slowly and gave Heath a myopic frown. Then, after a few awkward movements, he answered with unhurried precision. "A forty-five army bullet—Colt automatic."

"Any idea how close to Benson the gun was held?" asked Markham.

"Yes, sir, I have," Hagedorn replied, in his ponderous monotone. "Between five and six feet—probably."

Heath snorted. "'Probably,'" he repeated to Markham with good-natured contempt. "You can bank on it if the captain says so.... You see, sir, nothing smaller than a forty-four or forty-five will stop a man, and these steel-capped army bullets go through a human skull like it was cheese. But in order to carry straight to the woodwork the gun had to be held pretty close; and, as there aren't any powder marks on the face, it's a safe bet to take the captain's figures as to distance."

At this point we heard the front door open and close, and Dr. Doremus, the chief medical examiner, accompanied by his assistant, bustled in. He shook hands with Markham and Inspector O'Brien, and gave Heath a friendly salutation.

35

"Sorry I couldn't get here sooner," he apologized.

He was a nervous man with a heavily seamed face and the manner of a real estate salesman.

"What have we got here?" he asked, in the same breath, making a wry face at the body in the chair.

"You tell us, Doc," retorted Heath.

Dr. Doremus approached the murdered man with a callous indifference indicative of a long process of hardening. He first inspected the face closely. He was, I imagine, looking for powder marks. Then he glanced at the bullet hole in the forehead and at the ragged wound in the back of the head. Next he moved the dead man's arm, bent the fingers, and pushed the head a little to the side. Having satisfied himself as to the state of rigor mortis, he turned to Heath.

"Can we get him on the settee there?"

Heath looked at Markham inquiringly. "All through, sir?"

Markham nodded, and Heath beckoned to the two men at the front windows and ordered the body placed on the davenport. It retained its sitting posture, due to the hardening of the muscles after death, until the doctor and his assistant straightened out the limbs. The body was then undressed, and Dr. Doremus examined it carefully for other wounds. He paid particular attention to the arms; and he opened both hands wide and scrutinized the palms. At length he straightened up and wiped his hands on a large coloured silk handkerchief.

"Shot through the left frontal," he announced. "Direct angle of fire. Bullet passed completely through the skull. Exit wound in the left occipital region—base of skull. You found the bullet, didn't you? He was awake when shot, and death was immediate—probably never knew what hit him. . . . He's been dead about—well, I should judge, eight hours, maybe longer."

"How about twelve thirty for the exact time?" asked Heath.

The doctor looked at his watch.

"Fits O.K. . . . Anything else?"

No one answered, and after a slight pause the chief inspector spoke. "We'd like a post-mortem report today, Doctor."

"That'll be all right," Dr. Doremus answered, snapping shut his medical case and handing it to his assistant. "But get the body to the mortuary as soon as you can."

After a brief handshaking ceremony, he went out hurriedly.

Heath turned to the detective who had been standing by the

table when we entered. "Burke, you phone headquarters to call for the body, and tell 'em to get a move on. Then go back to the office and wait for me."

Burke saluted and disappeared.

Heath then addressed one of the two men who had been inspecting the grilles of the front windows. "How about that ironwork, Snitkin?"

"No chance, Sergeant," was the answer. "Strong as a jail—both of 'em. Nobody never got in through those windows."

"Very good," Heath told him. "Now you two fellows chase along with Burke."

When they had gone, the dapper man in the blue serge suit and derby, whose sphere of activity had seemed to be the fireplace, laid two cigarette butts on the table.

"I found these under the gas logs, Sergeant," he explained unenthusiastically. "Not much, but there's nothing else laying around."

"All right, Emery." Heath gave the butts a disgruntled look. "You needn't wait, either. I'll see you at the office later."

Hagedorn came ponderously forward. "I guess I'll be getting along, too," he rumbled. "But I'm going to keep this bullet awhile. It's got some peculiar rifling marks on it. You don't want it specially, do you, Sergeant?"

Heath smiled tolerantly. "What'll I do with it, Captain? You keep it. But don't you dare lose it."

"I won't lose it," Hagedorn assured him, with stodgy seriousness; and, without so much as a glance at either the district attorney or the chief inspector, he waddled from the room with a slightly rolling movement which suggested that of some huge amphibious mammal.

Vance, who was standing beside me near the door, turned and followed Hagedorn into the hall. The two stood talking in low tones for several minutes. Vance appeared to be asking questions, and although I was not close enough to hear their conversation, I caught several words and phrases—"trajectory," "muzzle velocity," "angle of fire," "impetus," "impact," "deflection," and the like—and wondered what on earth had prompted this strange interrogation.

As Vance was thanking Hagedorn for his information Inspector O'Brien entered the hall. "Learning fast?" he asked, smiling patronizingly at Vance. Then, without waiting for a reply: "Come along, Captain; I'll drive you downtown."

Markham heard him. "Have you got room for Dinwiddie, too, Inspector?"

"Plenty, Mr. Markham."

The three of them went out.

Vance and I were now left alone in the room with Heath and the district attorney, and, as if by common impulse, we all settled ourselves in chairs, Vance taking one near the dining room door directly facing the chair in which Benson had been murdered.

I had been keenly interested in Vance's manner and actions from the moment of his arrival at the house. When he had first entered the room he had adjusted his monocle carefully—an act which, despite his air of passivity, I recognized as an indication of interest. When his mind was alert and he wished to take on external impressions quickly, he invariably brought out his monocle. He could see adequately enough without it, and his use of it, I had observed, was largely the result of an intellectual dictate. The added clarity of vision it gave him seemed subtly to affect his clarity of mind.*

At first he had looked over the room incuriously and watched the proceedings with bored apathy; but during Heath's brief questioning of his subordinates, an expression of cynical amusement had appeared on his face. Following a few general queries to Assistant District Attorney Dinwiddie, he had sauntered, with apparent aimlessness, about the room, looking at the various articles and occasionally shifting his gaze back and forth between different pieces of furniture. At length he had stooped down and inspected the mark made by the bullet on the wainscot; and once he had gone to the door and looked up and down the hall.

The only thing that had seemed to hold his attention to any extent was the body itself. He had stood before it for several minutes, studying its position, and had even bent over the outstretched arm on the table as if to see just how the dead man's hand was holding the book. The crossed position of the legs, however, had attracted him most, and he had stood studying them for a considerable time. Finally, he had returned his monocle to his waistcoat pocket and joined Dinwiddie and me near the door, where he had stood, watching Heath and the other detectives with lazy indifference, until the departure of Captain Hagedorn.

The four of us had no more than taken seats when the patrolman stationed in the vestibule appeared at the door. "There's a man from the local precinct station here, sir," he announced, "who wants to see the officer in charge. Shall I send him in?"

---

* Vance's eyes were slightly bifocal. His right eye was 1.2 astigmatic, whereas his left eye was practically normal.

Heath nodded curtly, and a moment later a large red-faced Irishman, in civilian clothes, stood before us. He saluted Heath, but on recognizing the district attorney, made Markham the recipient of his report.

"I'm Officer McLaughlin, sir—West Forty-seventh Street station," he informed us; "and I was on duty on this beat last night. Around midnight, I guess it was, there was a big grey Cadillac standing in front of this house—I noticed it particular, because it had a lot of fishing tackle sticking out the back, and all of its lights were on. When I heard of the crime this morning, I reported the car to the station sergeant, and he sent me around to tell you about it."

"Excellent," Markham commented; and then, with a nod, referred the matter to Heath.

"May be something in it," the latter admitted dubiously. "How long would you say the car was here, Officer?"

"A good half hour anyway. It was here before twelve, and when I come back at twelve thirty or thereabouts, it was still here. But the next time I come by, it was gone."

"You saw nothing else? Nobody in the car, or anyone hanging around who might have been the owner?"

"No, sir, I did not."

Several other questions of a similar nature were asked him; but nothing more could be learned, and he was dismissed.

"Anyway," remarked Heath, "the car story will be good stuff to hand the reporters."

Vance had sat through the questioning of McLaughlin with drowsy inattention—I doubt if he even heard more than the first few words of the officer's report—and now, with a stifled yawn, he rose and, sauntering to the centre table, picked up one of the cigarette butts that had been found in the fireplace. After rolling it between his thumb and forefinger and scrutinizing the tip, he ripped the paper open with his thumbnail and held the exposed tobacco to his nose.

Heath, who had been watching him gloweringly, leaned suddenly forward in his chair.

"What are you doing there?" he demanded, in a tone of surly truculence.

Vance lifted his eyes in decorous astonishment.

"Merely smelling of the tobacco," he replied, with condescending unconcern. "It's rather mild, y'know, but delicately blended."

The muscles in Heath's cheeks worked angrily. "Well, you'd better put it down, sir," he advised. Then he looked Vance up and down. "Tobacco expert?" he asked, with ill-disguised sarcasm.

"Oh, dear no." Vance's voice was dulcet. "My specialty is scarab-cartouches of the Ptolemaic dynasties."

Markham interposed diplomatically. "You really shouldn't touch anything around here, Vance, at this stage of the game. You never know what'll turn out to be important. Those cigarette stubs may quite possibly be significant evidence."

"Evidence?" repeated Vance sweetly. "My word! You don't say, really! Most amusin'!"

Markham was plainly annoyed; and Heath was boiling inwardly but made no further comment; he even forced a mirthless smile. He evidently felt that he had been a little too abrupt with this friend of the district attorney's, however much the friend might have deserved being reprimanded.

Heath, however, was no sycophant in the presence of his superiors. He knew his worth and lived up to it with his whole energy, discharging the tasks to which he was assigned with a dogged indifference to his own political wellbeing. This stubbornness of spirit, and the solidity of character it implied, were respected and valued by the men over him.

He was a large, powerful man but agile and graceful in his movements, like a highly trained boxer. He had hard blue eyes, remarkably bright and penetrating, a small nose, a broad, oval chin, and a stern, straight mouth with lips that appeared always compressed. His hair, which, though he was well along in his forties, was without a trace of greyness, was cropped about the edges and stood upright in a short bristly pompadour. His voice had an aggressive resonance, but he rarely blustered. In many ways he accorded with the conventional notion of what a detective is like. But there was something more to the man's personality, an added capability and strength, as it were; and as I sat watching him that morning I felt myself unconsciously admiring him, despite his very obvious limitations.

"What's the exact situation, Sergeant?" Markham asked. "Dinwiddie gave me only the barest facts."

Heath cleared his throat. "We got the word a little before seven. Benson's housekeeper, a Mrs. Platz, called up the local station and reported that she'd found him dead, and asked that somebody be sent over at once. The message, of course, was relayed to headquarters. I wasn't there at the time, but Burke and Emery were on duty, and after notifying Inspector Moran, they came on up here. Several of the men from the local station were already on the job doing the usual nosing about. When the inspector had got here and looked the situation over, he telephoned me to hurry along. When I arrived, the local men had gone, and three more men from the homicide bureau had joined Burke and Emery. The inspector also phoned Captain Hagedorn—he thought the case big enough to call him in on it at once—and the captain had just got here when you arrived. Mr. Dinwiddie had come in right after the inspector and phoned you at once. Chief Inspector O'Brien came along a little ahead of me. I questioned the Platz woman right off; and my men were looking the place over when you showed up."

"Where's this Mrs. Platz now?" asked Markham.

"Upstairs being watched by one of the local men. She lives in the house."

"Why did you mention the specific hour of twelve thirty to the doctor?"

"Platz told me she heard a report at that time, which I thought might have been the shot. I guess now it *was* the shot—it checks up with a number of things."

"I think we'd better have another talk with Mrs. Platz," Markham suggested. "But first: did you find anything suggestive in the room here—anything to go on?"

Heath hesitated almost imperceptibly; then he drew from his coat pocket a woman's handbag and a pair of long white kid gloves, and tossed them on the table in front of the district attorney.

"Only these," he said. "One of the local men found them on the end of the mantel over there."

After a casual inspection of the gloves Markham opened the handbag and turned its contents out onto the table. I came forward and looked on, but Vance remained in his chair, placidly smoking a cigarette.

The handbag was of fine gold mesh with a catch set with small sapphires. It was unusually small and obviously designed only for evening wear. The objects which it had held, and which Markham was now inspecting, consisted of a flat watered-silk cigarette case, a small gold phial of Roger and Gallet's Fleurs d'Amour perfume, a *cloisonné* vanity compact, a short delicate cigarette holder of inlaid amber, a gold-cased lipstick, a small embroidered French linen handkerchief with *M. St. C.* monogrammed in the corner, and a Yale latchkey.

"This ought to give us a good lead," said Markham, indicating the handkerchief. "I suppose you went over the articles carefully, Sergeant."

Heath nodded. "Yes, and I imagine the bag belongs to the woman Benson was out with last night. The housekeeper told me he had an appointment and went out to dinner in his dress clothes. She didn't hear Benson when he came back, though. Anyway, we ought to be able to run down 'M. St. C.' without much trouble."

Markham had taken up the cigarette case again, and as he held it upside down a little shower of loose dried tobacco fell onto the table.

Heath stood up suddenly. "Maybe those cigarettes came out of that case," he suggested. He picked up the intact butt and looked at it. "It's a lady's cigarette, all right. It looks as though it might have been smoked in a holder, too."

"I beg to differ with you, Sergeant," drawled Vance. "You'll forgive me, I'm sure. But there's a bit of lip rouge on the end of the cigarette. It's hard to see, on account of the gold tip."

Heath looked at Vance sharply; he was too much surprised to be resentful. After a closer inspection of the cigarette, he turned again to Vance.

"Perhaps you could also tell us from these tobacco grains, if the cigarettes came from this case," he suggested, with gruff irony.

"One never knows, does one?" Vance replied, indolently rising.

Picking up the case, he pressed it wide open and tapped it on the table. Then he looked into it closely, and a humorous smile twitched the corners of his mouth. Putting his forefinger deep into the case, he drew out a small cigarette which had evidently been wedged flat along the bottom of the pocket.

"My olfact'ry gifts won't be necess'ry now," he said. "It is apparent even to the naked eye that the cigarettes are, to speak loosely, identical—eh what, Sergeant?"

Heath grinned good-naturedly. "That's one on us, Mr. Markham." And he carefully put the cigarette and the stub in an envelope, which he marked and pocketed.

"You now see, Vance," observed Markham, "the importance of those cigarette butts."

"Can't say that I do," responded the other. "Of what possible value is a cigarette butt? You can't smoke it, y'know."

"It's evidence, my dear fellow," explained Markham patiently. "One knows that the owner of this bag returned with Benson last night and remained long enough to smoke two cigarettes."

Vance lifted his eyebrows in mock amazement. "One does, does one? Fancy that, now."

"It only remains to locate her," interjected Heath.

"She's a rather decided brunette, at any rate—if that fact will facilitate your quest any," said Vance easily; "though why you should desire to annoy the lady, I can't for the life of me imagine—really I can't, don't y'know."

"Why do you say she's a brunette?" asked Markham.

"Well, if she isn't," Vance told him, sinking listlessly back in his chair, "then she should consult a cosmetician as to the proper way to make up. I see she uses 'Rachel' powder and Guerlain's dark lipstick. And it simply isn't done among blondes, old dear."

"I defer, of course, to your expert opinion," smiled Markham. Then, to Heath: "I guess we'll have to look for a brunette, Sergeant."

"It's all right with me," agreed Heath jocularly. By this time, I think, he had entirely forgiven Vance for destroying the cigarette butt.

CHAPTER 4

The Housekeeper's Story
Friday, June 14; 11 a.m.

"Now," suggested Markham, "suppose we take a look over the house. I imagine you've done that pretty thoroughly already, Sergeant, but I'd like to see the layout. Anyway, I don't want to question the housekeeper until the body has been removed."

Heath rose. "Very good, sir. I'd like another look myself."

The four of us went into the hall and walked down the passageway to the rear of the house. At the extreme end, on the left, was a door leading downstairs to the basement; but it was locked and bolted.

"The basement is only used for storage now," Heath explained; "and the door which opens from it into the street areaway is boarded up. The Platz woman sleeps upstairs—Benson lived here alone, and there's plenty of spare room in the house—and the kitchen is on this floor."

He opened a door on the opposite side of the passageway, and we stepped into a small, modern kitchen. Its two high windows, which gave into the paved rear yard at a height of about eight feet from the ground, were securely guarded with iron bars, and, in addition, the sashes were closed and locked. Passing through a swinging door, we entered the dining room, which was directly behind the living room. The two windows here looked upon a small stone court, really no more than a deep air-well between Benson's house and the adjoining one; and these also were iron-barred and locked.

We now re-entered the hallway and stood for a moment at the foot of the stairs leading above.

"You can see, Mr. Markham," Heath pointed out, "that whoever shot Benson must have gotten in by the front door. There's no other way he could have entered. Living alone, I guess Benson was a little touchy on the subject of burglars. The only window that wasn't barred was the rear one in the living room; and that was shut and locked. Anyway, it only leads into the inside court. The front windows of the living room have that ironwork over them; so they couldn't have been used even to shoot through, for Benson was shot from the opposite direction. . . . It's pretty clear the gunman got in the front door."

"Looks that way," said Markham.

"And pardon me for saying so," remarked Vance, "but Benson let him in."

"Yes?" retorted Heath unenthusiastically. "Well, we'll find all that out later, I hope."

"Oh, doubtless," Vance dryly agreed.

We ascended the stairs and entered Benson's bedroom, which was directly over the living room. It was severely but well furnished and in excellent order. The bed was made, showing it had not been slept in that night; and the window shades were drawn. Benson's dinner jacket and white piqué waistcoat were hanging over a chair. A winged collar and a black bowtie were on the bed, where they had evidently been thrown when Benson had taken them off on returning home. A pair of low evening shoes were standing by the bench at the foot of the bed. In a glass of water on the night table was a platinum plate of four false teeth; and a toupee of beautiful workmanship was lying on the chiffonier.

This last item aroused Vance's special interest. He walked up to it and regarded it closely.

"Most int'restin'," he commented. "Our departed friend seems to have worn false hair; did you know that, Markham?"

"I always suspected it," was the indifferent answer.

Heath, who had remained standing on the threshold, seemed a little impatient.

"There's only one other room on this floor," he said, leading the way down the hall. "It's also a bedroom—for guests, so the house-keeper explained."

Markham and I looked in through the door, but Vance remained lounging against the balustrade at the head of the stairs. He was manifestly uninterested in Alvin Benson's domestic arrangements; and when Markham and Heath and I went up to the third floor, he sauntered down into the main hallway. When at length we descended from our tour of inspection he was casually looking over the titles in Benson's bookcase.

We had just reached the foot of the stairs when the front door opened and two men with a stretcher entered. The ambulance from the Department of Welfare had arrived to take the corpse to the Morgue; and the brutal, businesslike way in which Benson's body was covered up, lifted onto the stretcher, carried out and shoved into the wagon, made me shudder. Vance, on the other hand; after the merest fleeting glance at the two men, paid no attention to them. He had found a volume with a beautiful Humphrey-Milford binding, and was absorbed in its Roger Payne tooling and powdering.

"I think an interview with Mrs. Platz is indicated now," said Markham; and Heath went to the foot of the stairs and gave a loud, brisk order.

Presently a grey-haired, middle-aged woman entered the living room accompanied by a plainclothesman smoking a large cigar. Mrs. Platz was of the simple, old-fashioned, motherly type, with a calm, benevolent countenance. She impressed me as highly capable, and as a woman given little to hysteria—an impression strengthened by her attitude of passive resignation. She seemed, however, to possess that taciturn shrewdness that is so often found among the ignorant.

"Sit down, Mrs. Platz." Markham greeted her kindly. "I'm the district attorney, and there are some questions I want to ask you."

She took a straight chair by the door and waited, gazing nervously from one to the other of us. Markham's gentle, persuasive voice, though, appeared to encourage her; and her answers became more and more fluent.

The main facts that transpired from a quarter-of-an-hour's examination may be summed up as follows:

Mrs. Platz had been Benson's housekeeper for four years and was the only servant employed. She lived in the house, and her room was on the third, or top, floor in the rear.

On the afternoon of the preceding day Benson had returned from his office at an unusually early hour—around four o'clock—announcing to Mrs. Platz that he would not be home for dinner that evening. He had remained in the living room, with the hall door closed, until half past six and had then gone upstairs to dress.

He had left the house about seven o'clock but had not said where he was going. He had remarked casually that he would return in fairly good season but had told Mrs. Platz she need not wait up for him— which was her custom whenever he intended bringing guests home. This was the last she had seen him alive. She had not heard him when he returned that night.

She had retired about half past ten and, because of the heat, had left the door ajar. She had been awakened some time later by a loud deto-

46

nation. It had startled her, and she had turned on the light by her bed, noting that it was just half past twelve by the small alarm clock she used for rising. It was, in fact, the early hour which had reassured her. Benson, whenever he went out for the evening, rarely returned home before two, and this fact, coupled with the stillness of the house, had made her conclude that the noise which had aroused her had been merely the backfiring of an automobile in Forty-ninth Street. Consequently, she had dismissed the matter from her mind, and gone back to sleep.

At seven o'clock the next morning she came downstairs as usual to begin her day's duties and, on her way to the front door to bring in the milk and cream, had discovered Benson's body. All the shades in the living room were down.

At first she thought Benson had fallen asleep in his chair, but when she saw the bullet hole and noticed that the electric lights had been switched off, she knew he was dead. She had gone at once to the telephone in the hall and, asking the operator for the police station, had reported the murder. She had then remembered Benson's brother, Major Anthony Benson, and had telephoned him also. He had arrived at the house almost simultaneously with the detectives from the West Forty-seventh Street station. He had questioned her a little, talked with the plainclothesmen, and gone away before the men from headquarters arrived.

"And now, Mrs. Platz," said Markham, glancing at the notes he had been making, "one or two more questions, and we won't trouble you further. . . . Have you noticed anything in Mr. Benson's actions lately that might lead you to suspect that he was worried—or, let us say, in fear of anything happening to him?"

"No sir," the woman answered readily. "It looked like he was in special good humour for the last week or so."

"I notice that most of the windows on this floor are barred. Was he particularly afraid of burglars, or of people breaking in?"

"Well—not exactly," was the hesitant reply. "But he did use to say as how the police were no good—begging your pardon, sir—and how a man in this city had to look out for himself if he didn't want to get held up."

Markham turned to Heath with a chuckle. "You might make a special note of that for your files, Sergeant." Then to Mrs. Platz: "Do you know of anyone who had a grudge against Mr. Benson?"

"Not a soul, sir," the housekeeper answered emphatically. "He was a queer man in many ways, but everybody seemed to like him. He was all the time going to parties or giving parties. I just can't see why anybody'd want to kill him."

Markham looked over his notes again. "I don't think there's anything else for the present. . . . How about it, Sergeant? Anything further you want to ask?"

Heath pondered a moment. "No, I can't think of anything more just now. . . . But you, Mrs. Platz," he added, turning a cold glance on the woman, "will stay here in this house till you're given permission to leave. We'll want to question you later. But you're not to talk to anyone else—understand? Two of my men will be here for a while yet."

Vance, during the interview, had been jotting down something on the fly-leaf of a small pocket address book and as Heath was speaking he tore out the page and handed it to Markham. Markham glanced at it frowningly and pursed his lips. Then after a few moments' hesitation, he addressed himself again to the housekeeper.

"You mentioned, Mrs. Platz, that Mr. Benson was liked by everyone. Did you yourself like him?"

The woman shifted her eyes to her lap. "Well, sir," she replied reluctantly, "I was only working for him and I haven't got any complaint about the way he treated me."

Despite her words, she gave the impression that she either disliked Benson extremely or greatly disapproved of him. Markham, however, did not push the point.

"And, by the way, Mrs. Platz," he said next, "did Mr. Benson keep any firearms about the house? For instance, do you know if he owned a revolver?"

For the first time during the interview, the woman appeared agitated, even frightened.

"Yes, sir, I—think he did," she admitted, in an unsteady voice.

"Where did he keep it?"

The woman glanced up apprehensively and rolled her eyes slightly as if weighing the advisability of speaking frankly. Then she replied in a low voice, "In that hidden drawer there in the centre table. You—you use that little brass button to open it with."

Heath jumped up, and pressed the button she had indicated. A tiny, shallow drawer shot out; and in it lay a Smith and Wesson thirty- eight revolver with an inlaid pearl handle. He picked it up, broke the carriage, and looked at the head of the cylinder.

"Full," he announced laconically.

An expression of tremendous relief spread over the woman's features, and she sighed audibly.

Markham has risen and was looking at the revolver over Heath's shoulder.

"You'd better take charge of it, Sergeant," he said; "though I don't see exactly how it fits in with the case."

He resumed his seat and, glancing at the notation Vance had given him, turned again to the housekeeper.

"One more question, Mrs. Platz. You said Mr. Benson came home early and spent his time before dinner in this room. Did he have any callers during that time?"

I was watching the woman closely, and it seemed to me that she quickly compressed her lips. At any rate, she sat up a little straighter in her chair before answering.

"There wasn't no one, as far as I know."

"But surely you would have known if the bell rang," insisted Markham. "You would have answered the door, wouldn't you?"

"There wasn't no one," she repeated, with a trace of sullenness.

"And last night—did the doorbell ring at all after you had retired?"

"No, sir."

"You would have heard it, even if you'd been asleep?"

"Yes, sir. There's a bell just outside my door, the same as in the kitchen. It rings in both places. Mr. Benson had it fixed that way."

Markham thanked her and dismissed her. When she had gone, he looked at Vance questioningly. "What idea did you have in your mind when you handed me those questions?"

"I might have been a bit presumptuous, y'know," said Vance; "but when the lady was extolling the deceased's popularity, I rather felt she was overdoing it a bit. There was an unconscious implication of antithesis in her eulogy, which suggested to me that she herself was not ardently enamoured of the gentleman."

"And what put the notion of firearms into your mind?"

"That query," explained Vance, "was a corollary of your own questions about barred windows and Benson's fear of burglars. If he was in a funk about housebreakers or enemies, he'd be likely to have weapons at hand—eh, what?"

"Well, anyway, Mr. Vance," put in Heath, "your curiosity unearthed a nice little revolver that's probably never been used."

"By the bye, Sergeant," returned Vance, ignoring the other's good-humoured sarcasm, "just what do you make of that nice little revolver?"

"Well, now," Heath replied, with ponderous facetiousness, "I deduct that Mr. Benson kept a pearl-handled Smith and Wesson in a secret drawer of his centre table."

"You don't say—really!" exclaimed Vance in mock admiration. "Pos'tively illuminatin'!"

Markham broke up this raillery. "Why did you want to know about visitors, Vance? There obviously hadn't been anyone here."

"Oh, just a whim of mine. I was assailed by an impulsive yearning to hear what La Platz would say."

Heath was studying Vance curiously. His first impressions of the man were being dispelled, and he had begun to suspect that beneath the other's casual and debonair exterior there was something of a more solid nature than he had at first imagined. He was not altogether satisfied with Vance's explanations to Markham and seemed to be endeavouring to penetrate to his real reasons for supplementing the district attorney's interrogation of the housekeeper. Heath was astute, and he had the worldly man's ability to read people; but Vance, being different from the men with whom he usually came in contact, was an enigma to him.

At length he relinquished his scrutiny and drew up his chair to the table with a spirited air.

"And now, Mr. Markham," he said crisply, "we'd better outline our activities so as not to duplicate our efforts. The sooner I get my men started, the better."

Markham assented readily. "The investigation is entirely up to you, Sergeant. I'm here to help wherever I'm needed."

"That's very kind of you, sir," Heath returned. "But it looks to me as though there'd be enough work for all parties. . . . Suppose I get to work on running down the owner of the handbag, and send some men out scouting among Benson's night-life cronies—I can pick up some names from the housekeeper, and they'll be a good starting point. And I'll get after that Cadillac, too. . . . Then we ought to look into his lady friends—I guess he had enough of 'em."

"I may get something out of the major along that line," supplied Markham. "He'll tell me anything I want to know. And I can also look into Benson's business associates through the same channel."

"I was going to suggest that you could do that better than I could," Heath rejoined. "We ought to run into something pretty quick that'll give us a line to go on. And I've got an idea that when we locate the lady he took to dinner last night and brought back here, we'll know a lot more than we do now."

"Or a lot less," murmured Vance.

Heath looked up quickly and grunted with an air of massive petulance.

"Let me tell you something, Mr. Vance," he said, "since I understand you want to learn something about these affairs: when anything goes seriously wrong in this world, it's pretty safe to look for a woman in the case."

"Ah, yes," smiled Vance. "*Cherchez la femme*—an aged notion. Even the Romans laboured under the superstition. They expressed it with *Dux femina facti.*"

"However they expressed it," retorted Heath, "they had the right idea. And don't let 'em tell you different."

Again Markham diplomatically intervened.

"That point will be settled very soon, I hope. . . . And now, Sergeant, if you've nothing else to suggest, I'll be getting along. I told Major Benson I'd see him at lunchtime; and I may have some news for you by tonight."

"Right," assented Heath. "I'm going to stick around here awhile and see if there's anything I overlooked. I'll arrange for a guard outside and also for a man inside to keep an eye on the Platz woman. Then I'll see the reporters and let them in on the disappearing Cadillac and Mr. Vance's mysterious revolver in the secret drawer. I guess that ought to hold 'em. If I find out anything, I'll phone you."

When he had shaken hands with the district attorney, he turned to Vance. "Good-bye, sir," he said pleasantly, much to my surprise, and to Markham's, too, I imagine. "I hope you learned something this morning."

"You'd be pos'tively dumfounded, Sergeant, at all I did learn," Vance answered carelessly.

Again I noted the look of shrewd scrutiny in Heath's eyes; but in a second it was gone. "Well, I'm glad of that," was his perfunctory reply.

Markham, Vance, and I went out, and the patrolman on duty hailed a taxicab for us.

"So that's the way our lofty gendarmerie approaches the mysterious wherefores of criminal enterprise—eh?" mused Vance, as we started on our way across town. "Markham, old dear, how do those robust lads ever succeed in running down a culprit?"

"You have witnessed only the barest preliminaries," Markham explained. "There are certain things that must be done as a matter of routine—*ex abundantia cautelae*, as we lawyers say."

"But, my word!—such technique!" sighed Vance. "Ah, well, *quantum est in rubus inane!* as we laymen say."

"You don't think much of Heath's capacity, I know"—Markham's voice was patient—"but he's a clever man and one that it's very easy to underestimate."

"I daresay," murmured Vance. "Anyway, I'm deuced grateful to you, and all that, for letting me behold the solemn proceedings. I've been vastly amused, even if not uplifted. Your official Aesculapius rather appealed to me, y'know—such a brisk, unemotional chap, and utterly unimpressed with the corpse. He really should have taken up crime in a serious way, instead of studying medicine."

Markham lapsed into gloomy silence and sat looking out of the window in troubled meditation until we reached Vance's house.

"I don't like the looks of things," he remarked, as we drew up to the curb. "I have a curious feeling about this case."

Vance regarded him a moment from the corner of his eye. "See here, Markham," he said with unwonted seriousness; "haven't you any idea who shot Benson?"

Markham forced a faint smile, "I wish I had. Crimes of wilful murder are not so easily solved. And this case strikes me as a particularly complex one."

"Fancy, now!" said Vance, as he stepped out of the machine. "And I thought it extr'ordin'rily simple."

CHAPTER 5

Gathering Information
Saturday, June 15; forenoon

You will remember the sensation caused by Alvin Benson's murder. It was one of those crimes that appeal irresistibly to the popular imagination. Mystery is the basis of all romance, and about the Benson case there hung an impenetrable aura of mystery. It was many days before any definite light was shed on the circumstances surrounding the shooting; but numerous *ignes fatui* arose to beguile the public's imagination, and wild speculations were heard on all sides.

Alvin Benson, while not a romantic figure in any respect, had been well known; and his personality had been a colourful and spectacular one. He had been a member of New York's wealthy bohemian social set—an avid sportsman, a rash gambler, and professional man-about- town; and his life, led on the borderland of the demimonde, had contained many highlights. His exploits in the nightclubs and cabarets had long supplied the subject matter for exaggerated stories and comments in the various local papers and magazines which batten on Broadway's scandalmongers.

Benson and his brother, Anthony, had, at the time of the former's sudden death, been running a brokerage office at 21 Wall Street, under the name of Benson and Benson. Both were regarded by the other brokers of the Street as shrewd businessmen, though perhaps a shade unethical when gauged by the constitution and bylaws of the New York Stock Exchange. They were markedly contrasted as to temperament and taste and saw little of each other outside the office. Alvin Benson devoted his entire leisure to pleasure-seeking and was a regular patron of the city's leading cafés; whereas Anthony Benson, who was the older and had served as a major in the late war, followed a sedate and conventional existence, spending most of his evenings quietly at his clubs. Both, however, were popular in their respective circles, and between them they had built up a large clientele.

The glamour of the financial district had much to do with the manner in which the crime was handled by the newspapers. Moreover, the murder had been committed at a time when the metropolitan press was experiencing a temporary lull in sensationalism; and the story was spread over the front pages of the papers with a prodigality rarely encountered in such cases.* Eminent detectives throughout the country were interviewed by enterprising reporters. Histories of famous unsolved murder cases were revived; and clairvoyants and astrologers were engaged by the Sunday editors to solve the mystery by various metaphysical devices. Photographs and detailed diagrams were the daily accompaniments of these journalistic outpourings.

The Benson case from the outset had proved a trying and difficult one from the police standpoint. Within an hour of the time that Vance and I had left the scene of the crime a systematic investigation had been launched by the men of the homicide bureau in charge of Sergeant Heath. Benson's house was again gone over thoroughly, and all his private correspondence read; but nothing was brought forth that could throw any light on the tragedy. No weapon was found aside from Benson's own Smith and Wesson; and though all the window grilles were again inspected, they were found to be secure, indicating that the murderer had either let himself in with a key or else been admitted by Benson. Heath, by the way, was unwilling to admit this latter possibility despite Mrs. Platz's positive assertion that no other person besides herself and Benson had a key.

Because of the absence of any definite clue, other than the handbag and the gloves, the only proceeding possible was the interrogating of Benson's friends and associates in the hope of uncovering some fact

---

* Even the famous Elwell case, which came several years later and bore certain points of similarity to the Benson case, created no greater sensation, despite the fact that Elwell was more widely known than Benson, and the persons involved were more prominent socially. Indeed, the Benson case was referred to several times in descriptions of the Elwell case; and one anti-administration paper regretted editorially that John F.-X. Markham was no longer district attorney of New York. In all the news stories the grey Cadillac and the pearl-handled Smith and Wesson were featured. There were pictures of Cadillac cars, "touched up" and reconstructed to accord with Patrolman McLaughlin's description, some of them even showing the fishing tackle protruding from the tonneau. A photograph of Benson's centre table had been taken, with the secret drawer enlarged and reproduced in an "inset." One Sunday magazine went so far as to hire an expert cabinetmaker to write a dissertation on secret compartments in furniture.

which would furnish a trail. It was by this process also that Heath hoped to establish the identity of the owner of the handbag. A special effort was therefore made to ascertain where Benson had spent the evening; but though many of his acquaintances were questioned, and the cafés where he habitually dined were visited, no one could at once be found who had seen him that night; nor, as far as it was possible to learn, had he mentioned to anyone his plans for the evening. Furthermore, no general information of a helpful nature came to light immediately, although the police pushed their inquiry with the utmost thoroughness. Benson apparently had no enemies; he had not quarrelled seriously with anyone; and his affairs were reported in their usual orderly shape.

Major Anthony Benson was naturally the principal person looked to for information, because of his intimate knowledge of his brother's affairs; and it was in this connection that the district attorney's office did its chief functioning at the beginning of the case. Markham had lunched with Major Benson the day the crime was discovered, and though the latter had shown a willingness to cooperate—even to the detriment of his brother's character—his suggestions were of little value. He explained to Markham that, though he knew most of his brother's associates, he could not name anyone who would have any reason for committing such a crime or anyone who, in his opinion, would be able to help in leading the police to the guilty person. He admitted frankly, however, that there was a side to his brother's life with which he was unacquainted and regretted that he was unable to suggest any specific way of ascertaining the hidden facts. But he intimated that his brother's relations with women were of a somewhat unconventional nature; and he ventured the opinion that there was a bare possibility of a motive being found in that direction.

Pursuant of the few indefinite and unsatisfactory suggestions of Major Benson, Markham had immediately put to work two good men from the detective division assigned to the district attorney's office, with instructions to confine their investigations to Benson's women acquaintances so as not to appear in any way to be encroaching upon the activities of the central office men. Also, as a result of Vance's apparent interest in the housekeeper at the time of the interrogation, he had sent a man to look into the woman's antecedents and relationships.

Mrs. Platz, it was learned, had been born in a small Pennsylvania town, of German parents both of whom were dead; and had been a widow for over sixteen years. Before coming to Benson, she had been with one family for twelve years and had left the position only because her mistress had given up housekeeping and moved into a hotel. Her former employer, when questioned, said she thought there had been a daughter but had never seen the child and knew nothing of it. In these facts there was nothing to take hold of, and Markham had merely filed the report as a matter of form.

Heath had instigated a citywide search for the grey Cadillac, although he had little faith in its direct connection with the crime; and in this the newspapers helped considerably by the extensive advertising given the car. One curious fact developed that fired the police with the hope that the Cadillac might indeed hold some clue to the mystery. A street cleaner, having read or heard about the fishing tackle in the machine, reported the finding of two jointed fishing rods, in good condition, at the side of one of the drives in Central Park near Columbus Circle. The question was: were these rods part of the equipment Patrolman McLaughlin had seen in the Cadillac? The owner of the car might conceivably have thrown them away in his flight; but, on the other hand, they might have been lost by someone else while driving through the park. No further information was forthcoming, and on the morning of the day following the discovery of the crime the case, so far as any definite progress toward a solution was concerned, had taken no perceptible forward step.

That morning Vance had sent Currie out to buy him every available newspaper; and he had spent over an hour perusing the various accounts of the crime. It was unusual for him to glance at a newspaper, even casually, and I could not refrain from expressing my amazement at his sudden interest in a subject so entirely outside his normal routine.

"No, Van old dear," he explained languidly, "I am not becoming sentimental or even human, as that word is erroneously used today. I can not say with Terence, 'Homo sum, humani nihil a me alienum puto,' because I regard most things that are called human as decidedly alien to myself. But, y'know, this little flurry in crime has proved rather int'restin', or, as the magazine writers say, intriguing—beastly word! . . . Van, you really should read this precious interview with Sergeant Heath. He takes an entire column to say, 'I know nothing.' A priceless lad! I'm becoming pos'tively fond of him."

"It may be," I suggested, "that Heath is keeping his true knowledge from the papers as a bit of tactical diplomacy."

"No," Vance returned, with a sad wag of the head, "no man has so little vanity that he would delib'rately reveal himself to the world as a creature with no perceptible powers of human reasoning—as he does in all these morning journals—for the mere sake of bringing one murderer to justice. That would be martyrdom gone mad."

"Markham, at any rate, may know or suspect something that hasn't been revealed," I said.

Vance pondered a moment. "That's not impossible," he admitted. "He has kept himself modestly in the background in all this journalistic palaver. Suppose we look into the matter more thoroughly—eh, what?"

Going to the telephone, he called the district attorney's office, and I heard him make an appointment with Markham for lunch at the Stuyvesant Club.

"What about that Nadelmann statuette at Stieglitz's," I asked, remembering the reason for my presence at Vance's that morning.

"I ain't* in the mood for Greek simplifications today," he answered, turning again to his newspapers.

To say that I was surprised at his attitude is to express it mildly. In all my association with him I had never known him to forgo his enthusiasm for art in favour of any other divertisement; and heretofore anything pertaining to the law and its operations had failed to interest him. I realized, therefore that something of an unusual nature was at work in his brain and I refrained from further comment.

Markham was a little late for the appointment at the club, and Vance and I were already at our favourite corner table when he arrived.

"Well, my good Lycurgus," Vance greeted him, "aside from the fact that several new and significant clues have been unearthed and that the public may expect important developments in the very near future, and all that sort of tosh, how are things really going?"

Markham smiled. "I see you have been reading the newspapers. What do you think of the accounts?"

"Typical, no doubt," replied Vance. "They carefully and painstakingly omit nothing but the essentials."

"Indeed?" Markham's tone was jocular. "And what, may I ask, do you regard as the essentials of the case?"

"In my foolish amateur way," said Vance, "I looked upon dear Alvin's toupee as a rather conspicuous essential, don't y'know." "Benson, at any rate, regarded it in that light, I imagine. . . . Anything else?"

---

*Vance, who had lived many years in England, frequently said "ain't"—a contraction which is regarded there more leniently than in this country. He also pronounced ate as if it were spelled et; and I can not remember his ever using the word "stomach" or "bug," both of which are under the social ban in England.

"Well, there was the collar and the tie on the chiffonier."

"And," added Markham chaffingly, "don't overlook the false teeth in the tumbler."

"You're pos'tively coruscatin'!" Vance exclaimed. "Yes, they, too, were an essential of the situation. And I'll warrant the incomp'rable Heath didn't even notice them. But the other Aristotles present were equally sketchy in their observations."

"You weren't particularly impressed by the investigation yesterday, I take it," said Markham.

"On the contrary," Vance assured him, "I was impressed to the point of stupefaction. The whole proceedings constituted a masterpiece of absurdity. Everything relevant was sublimely ignored. There were at least a dozen *points de départ*, all leading in the same direction, but not one of them apparently was even noticed by any of the officiating *pourparleurs*. Everybody was too busy at such silly occupations as looking for cigarette ends and inspecting the ironwork at the windows. Those grilles, by the way, were rather attractive—Florentine design."

Markham was both amused and ruffled.

"One's pretty safe with the police, Vance," he said. "They get there eventually."

"I simply adore your trusting nature," murmured Vance. "But confide in me: what do you know regarding Benson's murderer?"

Markham hesitated. "This is, of course, in confidence," he said at length; "but this morning, right after you phoned, one of the men I had put to work on the amatory end of Benson's life reported that he had found the woman who left her handbag and gloves at the house that night—the initials on the handkerchief gave him the clue. And he dug up some interesting facts about her. As I suspected, she was Benson's dinner companion that evening. She's an actress—musical comedy, I believe. Muriel St. Clair by name."

"Most unfortunate," breathed Vance. "I was hoping, y'know, your myrmidons wouldn't discover the lady. I haven't the pleasure of her acquaintance or I'd send her a note of commiseration. . . . Now, I presume, you'll play the *juge d'instruction* and chivvy her most horribly, what?"

"I shall certainly question her, if that's what you mean."

Markham's manner was preoccupied, and during the rest of the lunch we spoke but little.

As we sat in the club's lounge room later having our smoke, Major Benson, who had been standing dejectedly at a window close by, caught sight of Markham and came over to us. He was a full-faced man of about fifty, with grave, kindly features and a sturdy, erect body.

He greeted Vance and me with a casual bow and turned at once to the district attorney. "Markham, I've been thinking things over constantly since our lunch yesterday," he said, "and there's one other suggestion I think I might make. There's a man named Leander Pfyfe who was very close to Alvin; and it's possible he could give you some helpful information. His name didn't occur to me yesterday, for he doesn't live in the city; he's on Long Island somewhere—Port Washington, I think. It's just an idea. The truth is, I can't seem to figure out anything that makes sense in this terrible affair."

He drew a quick, resolute breath, as if to check some involuntary sign of emotion. It was evident that the man, for all his habitual passivity of nature, was deeply moved.

"That's a good suggestion, Major," Markham said, making a notation on the back of a letter. "I'll get after it immediately."

Vance, who, during this brief interchange, had been gazing unconcernedly out of the window, turned and addressed himself to the major. "How about Colonel Ostrander? I've seen him several times in the company of your brother."

Major Benson made a slight gesture of depreciation.

"Only an acquaintance. He'd be of no value." Then he turned to Markham. "I don't imagine it's time even to hope that you've run across anything."

Markham took his cigar from his mouth and turning it about in his fingers, contemplated it thoughtfully.

"I wouldn't say that," he remarked, after a moment. "I've managed to find out whom your brother dined with Thursday night; and I know that this person returned home with him shortly after midnight." He paused as if deliberating the wisdom of saying more. Then: "The fact is, I don't need a great deal more evidence than I've got already to go before the grand jury and ask for an indictment."

A look of surprised admiration flashed in the major's sombre face.

"Thank God for that, Markham!" he said. Then, setting his heavy jaw, he placed his hand on the district attorney's shoulder. "Go the limit—for my sake!" he urged. "If you want me for anything, I'll be here at the club till late."

With this he turned and walked from the room.

"It seems a bit cold-blooded to bother the major with questions so soon after his brother's death," commented Markham. "Still, the world has got to go on."

Vance stifled a yawn. "Why—in Heaven's name?" he murmured listlessly.

CHAPTER 6

Vance Offers an Opinion
Saturday, June 15; 2 p.m.

We sat for a while smoking in silence, Vance gazing lazily out into Madison Square, Markham frowning deeply at the faded oil portrait of old Peter Stuyvesant that hung over the fireplace.

Presently Vance turned and contemplated the district attorney with a faintly sardonic smile.

"I say, Markham," he drawled; "it has always been a source of amazement to me how easily you investigators of crime are misled by what you call clues. You find a footprint, or a parked automobile, or a monogrammed handkerchief, and then dash off on a wild chase with your eternal *Ecce signum!* 'Pon my word, it's as if you chaps were all under the spell of shillin' shockers. Won't you ever learn that crimes can't be solved by deductions based merely on material clues and circumst'ntial evidence?"

I think Markham was as much surprised as I at this sudden criticism; yet we both knew Vance well enough to realize that, despite his placid and almost flippant tone, there was a serious purpose behind his words.

"Would you advocate ignoring all the tangible evidence of a crime?" asked Markham, a bit patronizingly.

"Most emphatically," Vance declared calmly. "It's not only worthless but dangerous. . . . The great trouble with you chaps, d' ye see, is that you approach every crime with a fixed and unshakable assumption that the criminal is either half-witted or a colossal bungler. I say, has it never by any chance occurred to you that if a detective could see a clue, the criminal would also have seen it and would either have concealed it or disguised it, if he had not wanted it found? And have you never paused to consider that anyone clever enough to plan and execute a successful crime these days is, ipso facto, clever enough to manufacture whatever clues suit his purpose? Your detective seems wholly unwilling to admit that the surface appearance of a crime may be delib'rately deceptive or that the clues may have been planted for the def'nite purpose of misleading him."

"I'm afraid," Markham pointed out, with an air of indulgent irony, "that we'd convict very few criminals if we were to ignore all indicatory evidence, cogent circumstances, and irresistible inferences. . . . As a rule, you know, crimes are not witnessed by outsiders."

"That's your fundamental error, don't y'know,"Vance observed impassively. "Every crime is witnessed by outsiders, just as is every work of art. The fact that no one sees the criminal, or the artist, actu'lly at work, is wholly incons'quential. The modern investigator of crime would doubtless refuse to believe that Rubens painted the Descent from the Cross in the Cathedral at Antwerp if there was sufficient circumst'ntial evidence to indicate that he had been away on diplomatic business, for instance, at the time it was painted. And yet, my dear fellow, such a conclusion would be prepost'rous. Even if the inf'rences to the contr'ry were so irresistible as to be legally overpowering, the picture itself would prove conclusively that Rubens did paint it. Why? For the simple reason, d' ye see, that no one but Rubens could have painted it. It bears the indelible imprint of his personality and genius—and his alone."

"I'm not an aesthetician," Markham reminded him, a trifle testily. "I'm merely a practical lawyer and when it comes to determining the authorship of a crime, I prefer tangible evidence to metaphysical hypotheses."

"Your pref'rence, my dear fellow," Vance returned blandly, "will inev'tably involve you in all manner of embarrassing errors."

He slowly lit another cigarette and blew a wreath of smoke toward the ceiling. "Consider, for example, your conclusions in the present murder case," he went on, in his emotionless drawl. "You are labouring under the grave misconception that you know the person who prob'bly killed the unspeakable Benson. You admitted as much to the major; and you told him you had nearly enough evidence to ask for an indictment. No doubt, you do possess a number of what the learned Solons of today regard as convincing clues. But the truth is, don't y'know, you haven't your eye on the guilty person at all. You're about to bedevil some poor girl who had nothing whatever to do with the crime."

Markham swung about sharply.

"So!" he retorted. "I'm about to bedevil an innocent person, eh?

Since my assistants and I are the only ones who happen to know what evidence we hold against her, perhaps you will explain by what occult process you acquired your knowledge of this person's innocence."

"It's quite simple, y'know," Vance replied, with a quizzical twitch of the lips. "You haven't your eye on the murderer for the reason that the person who committed this particular crime was sufficiently shrewd and perspicacious to see to it that no evidence which you or the police were likely to find would even remotely indicate his guilt."

He had spoken with the easy assurance of one who enunciates an obvious fact—a fact which permits of no argument.

Markham gave a disdainful laugh. "No lawbreaker," he asserted oracularly, "is shrewd enough to see all contingencies. Even the most trivial event has so many intimately related and serrated points of contact with other events which precede and follow, that it is a known fact that every criminal—however long and carefully he may plan—leaves some loose end to his preparations, which in the end betrays him."

"A known fact?" Vance repeated. "No, my dear fellow—merely a conventional superstition, based on the childish idea of an implacable, avenging Nemesis. I can see how this esoteric notion of the inev'tability of divine punishment would appeal to the popular imagination, like fortune-telling and Ouija boards, don't y'know; but—my word!—it desolates me to think that you, old chap, would give credence to such mystical moonshine."

"Don't let it spoil your entire day," said Markham acridly.

"Regard the unsolved, or successful, crimes that are taking place every day," Vance continued, disregarding the other's irony, "—crimes which completely baffle the best detectives in the business, what? The fact is, the only crimes that are ever solved are those planned by stupid people. That's why, whenever a man of even mod'rate sagacity decides to commit a crime, he accomplishes it with but little diff'culty and fortified with the pos'tive assurance of his immunity to discovery."

"Undetected crimes," scornfully submitted Markham, "result, in the main, from official bad luck, not from superior criminal cleverness."

"Bad luck"—Vance's voice was almost dulcet—"is merely a defensive and self-consoling synonym for inefficiency. A man with ingenuity and brains is not harassed by bad luck. . . . No, Markham old dear; unsolved crimes are simply crimes which have been intelligently planned and executed. And, d' ye see, it happens that the Benson murder falls into that categ'ry. Therefore, when, after a few hours' investigation, you say you're pretty sure who committed it, you must pardon me if I take issue with you."

He paused and took a few meditative puffs on his cigarette. "The factitious and casuistic methods of deduction you chaps pursue are apt to lead almost anywhere. In proof of which assertion I point triumphantly to the unfortunate young lady whose liberty you are now plotting to take away."

Markham, who had been hiding his resentment behind a smile of tolerant contempt, now turned on Vance and fairly glowered.

"It so happens—and I'm speaking ex cathedra," he proclaimed defiantly, "that I come pretty near having the goods on your 'unfortunate young lady.'"

Vance was unmoved. "And yet, y'know," he observed dryly, "no woman could possibly have done it."

I could see that Markham was furious. When he spoke he almost spluttered.

"A woman couldn't have done it, eh—no matter what the evidence?"

"Quite so," Vance rejoined placidly; "not if she herself swore to it and produced a tome of what you scions of the law term, rather pompously, incontrovertible evidence."

"Ah!" There was no mistaking the sarcasm of Markham's tone. "I am to understand, then, that you even regard confessions as valueless?"

"Yes, my dear Justinian," the other responded, with an air of complacency; "I would have you understand precisely that. Indeed, they are worse than valueless—they're downright misleading. The fact that occasionally they may prove to be correct—like woman's prepost'rously overrated intuition—renders them just so much more unreliable."

Markham grunted disdainfully.

"Why should any person confess something to his detriment unless he felt that the truth had been found out or was likely to be found out?"

"'Pon my word, Markham, you astound me! Permit me to murmur, *privatissime et gratis*, into your innocent ear that there are many other presumable motives for confessing. A confession may be the result of fear, or duress, or expediency, or mother-love, or chivalry, or what the psychoanalysts call the inferiority complex, or delusions, or a mistaken sense of duty, or a perverted egotism, or sheer vanity, or any other of a hundred causes. Confessions are the most treach'rous and unreliable of all forms of evidence; and even the silly and unscientific law repudiates them in murder cases unless substantiated by other evidence."

"You are eloquent; you wring me," said Markham. "But if the law threw out all confessions and ignored all material clues, as you appear to advise, then society might as well close down all its courts and scrap all its jails."

"A typical non sequitur of legal logic," Vance replied.

"But how would you convict the guilty, may I ask?"

"There is one infallible method of determining human guilt and responsibility," Vance explained; "but as yet the police are as blissfully unaware of its possibilities as they are ignorant of its operations. The truth can be learned only by an analysis of the psychological factors of a crime and an application of them to the individual. The only real clues are psychological—not material. Your truly profound art expert, for instance, does not judge and authenticate pictures by an inspection of the under-painting and a chemical analysis of the pigments, but by studying the creative personality revealed in the picture's conception and execution. He asks himself: Does this work of art embody the qualities of form and technique and mental attitude that made up the genius—namely, the personality—of Rubens, or Michelangelo, or Veronese, or Titian, or Tintoretto, or whoever may be the artist to whom the work has been tentatively credited."

"My mind is, I fear," Markham confessed, "still sufficiently primitive to be impressed by vulgar facts; and in the present instance—unfortunately for your most original and artistic analogy—I possess quite an array of such facts, all of which indicate that a certain young woman is the—shall we say?—creator of the criminal opus entitled *The Murder of Alvin Benson.*"

Vance shrugged his shoulders almost imperceptibly.

"Would you mind telling me—in confidence, of course—what these facts are?"

"Certainly not," Markham acceded. "*Imprimis*: the lady was in the house at the time the shot was fired."

Vance affected incredibility. "Eh—my word! She was actu'lly there? Most extr'ordin'ry!"

"The evidence of her presence is unassailable," pursued Markham. "As you know, the gloves she wore at dinner and the handbag she carried with her were both found on the mantel in Benson's living room."

"Oh!" murmured Vance, with a faintly deprecating smile. "It was not the lady, then, but her gloves and bag which were present—a minute and unimportant distinction, no doubt, from the legal point of view. . . . Still," he added, "I deplore the inability of my layman's untutored mind to accept the two conditions as identical. My trousers are at the dry cleaners; therefore, I am at the dry cleaners, what?"

Markham turned on him with considerable warmth.

"Does it mean nothing in the way of evidence, even to your layman's mind, that a woman's intimate and necessary articles, which she has carried throughout the evening, are found in her escort's quarters the following morning?"

"In admitting that it does not," Vance acknowledged quietly, "I no doubt expose a legal perception lamentably inefficient."

"But since the lady certainly wouldn't have carried these particular objects during the afternoon, and since she couldn't have called at the house that evening during Benson's absence without the housekeeper knowing it, how, may one ask, did these articles happen to be there the next morning if she herself did not take them there late that night?"

"'Pon my word, I haven't the slightest notion," Vance rejoined. "The lady, herself could doubtless appease your curiosity. But there are any number of possible explanations, y'know. Our departed Chesterfield might have brought them home in his coat pocket—women are eternally handing men all manner of gewgaws and bundles to carry for 'em, with the cooing request: 'Can you put this in your pocket for me?' . . . Then again, there is the possibility that the real murderer secured them in some way and placed them on the mantel delib'rately to mislead the *Polizei*. Women, don't y'know, never put their belongings in such neat, out-of-the-way places as mantels and hat-racks. They invariably throw them down on your fav'rite chair or your centre table."

"And, I suppose," Markham interjected, "Benson also brought the lady's cigarette butts home in his pocket?"

"Stranger things have happened," returned Vance equably; "though I sha'n't accuse him of it in this instance. . . . The cigarette butts may, y'know, be evidence of a previous *conversazione*."

"Even your despised Heath," Markham informed him, "had sufficient intelligence to ascertain from the housekeeper that she sweeps out the grate every morning."

Vance sighed admiringly. "You're *so* thorough, aren't you? . . . But, I say, that can't be, by any chance, your only evidence against the lady?"

"By no means," Markham assured him. "But, despite your superior distrust, it's good corroboratory evidence nevertheless."

"I daresay," Vance agreed, "seeing with what frequency innocent persons are condemned in our courts. . . . But tell me more."

Markham proceeded with an air of quiet self-assurance. "My man learned, first, that Benson dined alone with this woman at the Marseilles, a little bohemian restaurant in West Fortieth Street; secondly, that they quarrelled; and thirdly, that they departed at midnight, entering a taxicab together. . . . Now, the murder was committed at twelve-thirty; but since the lady lives on Riverside Drive, in the Eighties, Benson couldn't possibly have accompanied her home—which obviously he would have done had he not taken her to his own house—and returned by the time the shot was fired. But we have further proof pointing to her being at Benson's. My man learned, at the woman's apartment house, that actually she did not get home until shortly after one. Moreover, she was without gloves and handbag and had to be let in to her rooms with a passkey, because, as she explained, she had lost hers. As you remember, we found the key in her bag. And—to clinch the whole matter—the smoked cigarettes in the grate corresponded to the one you found in her case."

Markham paused to relight his cigar.

"So much for that particular evening," he resumed. "As soon as I learned the woman's identity this morning, I put two more men to work on her private life. Just as I was leaving the office this noon the men phoned in their reports. They had learned that the woman has a fiancé, a chap named Leacock, who was a captain in the army, and who would be likely to own just such a gun as Benson was killed with. Furthermore, this Captain Leacock lunched with the woman the day of the murder and also called on her at her apartment the morning after."

Markham leaned slightly forward, and his next words were emphasized by the tapping of his fingers on the arm of the chair.

"As you see, we have the motive, the opportunity, and the means. . . . Perhaps you will tell me now that I possess no incriminating evidence."

"My dear Markham," Vance affirmed calmly, "you haven't brought out a single point which could not easily be explained away by any bright schoolboy." He shook his head lugubriously. "And on such evidence people are deprived of their life and liberty! 'Pon my word, you alarm me. I tremble for my personal safety."

Markham was nettled.

"Would you be so good as to point out, from your dizzy pinnacle of sapience, the errors in my reasoning?"

"As far as I can see," returned Vance evenly, "your particularization concerning the lady is innocent of reasoning. You've simply taken several un-affined facts and jumped to a false conclusion. I happen to know the conclusion is false because all the psychological indications of the crime contradict it—that is to say, the only real evidence in the case points unmistakably in another direction."

He made a gesture of emphasis, and his tone assumed an unwonted gravity.

"And if you arrest any woman for killing Alvin Benson, you will simply be adding another crime—a crime of delib'rate and unpardonable stupidity—to the one already committed. And between shooting a bounder like Benson and ruining an innocent woman's reputation, I'm inclined to regard the latter as the more reprehensible."

I could see a flash of resentment leap into Markham's eyes; but he did not take offence. Remember: these two men were close friends; and, for all their divergency of nature, they understood and respected each other. Their frankness—severe and even mordant at times—was, indeed, a result of that respect.

There was a moment's silence; then Markham forced a smile. "You fill me with misgivings," he averred mockingly; but, despite the lightness of his tone, I felt that he was half in earnest. "However, I hadn't exactly planned to arrest the lady just yet."

"You reveal commendable restraint," Vance complimented him. "But I'm sure you've already arranged to ballyrag the lady and perhaps trick her into one or two of those contradictions so dear to every lawyer's heart—just as if any nervous or high-strung person could help indulging in apparent contradictions while being cross-questioned as a suspect in a crime they had nothing to do with. . . . To 'put 'em on the grill'—a most accurate designation. So reminiscent of burning people at the stake, what?"

"Well, I'm most certainly going to question her," replied Markham firmly, glancing at his watch. "And one of my men is escorting her to the office in half an hour; so I must break up this most delightful and edifying chat."

"You really expect to learn something incriminating by interrogating her?" asked Vance. "Y' know, I'd jolly well like to witness your humiliation. But I presume your heckling of suspects is a part of the legal *arcana.*"

Markham had risen and turned toward the door, but at Vance's words he paused and appeared to deliberate. "I can't see any particular objection to your being present," he said, "if you really care to come."

I think he had an idea that the humiliation of which the other had spoken would prove to be Vance's own; and soon we were in a taxicab headed for the Criminal Courts Building.

CHAPTER 7

Reports and an Interview
Saturday, June 15; 3 p.m.

We entered the ancient building, with its discoloured marble pillars and balustrades and its old-fashioned iron scrollwork, by the Franklin Street door and went directly to the district attorney's office on the fourth floor. The office, like the building, breathed an air of former days. Its high ceilings, its massive golden-oak woodwork, its elaborate low-hung chandelier of bronze and china, its dingy bay walls of painted plaster, and its four high narrow windows to the south—all bespoke a departed era in architecture and decoration.

On the floor was a large velvet carpet-rug of dingy brown; and the windows were hung with velour draperies of the same colour. Several large, comfortable chairs stood about the walls and before the long oak table in front of the district attorney's desk. This desk, directly under the windows and facing the room, was broad and flat, with carved uprights and two rows of drawers extending to the floor. To the right of the high-backed swivel desk-chair, was another table of carved oak. There were also several filing cabinets in the room and a large safe. In the centre of the east wall a leather-covered door, decorated with large brass nail heads, led into a long narrow room, between the office and the waiting room, where the district attorney's secretary and several clerks had their desks. Opposite to this door was another one opening into the district attorney's inner sanctum; and still another door, facing the windows, gave on the main corridor.

Vance glanced over the room casually.

"So this is the matrix of municipal justice—eh, what?" He walked to one of the windows and looked out upon the grey circular tower of the Tombs opposite. "And there, I take it, are the oubliettes where the victims of our law are incarc'rated so as to reduce the competition of criminal activity among the remaining citizenry. A most distressin' sight, Markham."

The district attorney had sat down at his desk and was glancing at several notations on his blotter.

"There are a couple of my men waiting to see me," he remarked, without looking up; "so, if you'll be good enough to take a chair over here, I'll proceed with my humble efforts to undermine society still further."

He pressed a button under the edge of his desk, and an alert young man with thick-lensed glasses appeared at the door.

"Swacker, tell Phelps to come in," Markham ordered. "And also tell Springer, if he's back from lunch, that I want to see him in a few minutes."

The secretary disappeared, and a moment later a tall, hawk-faced man, with stoop shoulders and an awkward, angular gait, entered.

"What news?" asked Markham.

"Well, Chief," the detective replied in a low, grating voice, "I just found out something I thought you could use right away. After I reported this noon, I ambled around to this Captain Leacock's house, thinking I might learn something from the houseboys, and ran into the captain coming out. I tailed along; and he went straight up to the lady's house on the Drive and stayed there over an hour. Then he went back home, looking worried."

Markham considered a moment.

"It may mean nothing at all, but I'm glad to know it anyway. St. Clair'll be here in a few minutes, and I'll find out what she has to say. There's nothing else for today. . . . Tell Swacker to send Tracy in."

Tracy was the antithesis of Phelps. He was short, a trifle stout, and exuded an atmosphere of studied suavity. His face was rotund and genial; he wore a *pince nez*; and his clothes were modish and fitted him well.

"Good-morning, Chief." He greeted Markham in a quiet, ingratiating tone. "I understand the St. Clair woman is to call here this afternoon, and there are a few things I've found out that may assist in your questioning."

He opened a small notebook and adjusted his *pince nez*.

"I thought I might learn something from her singing teacher, an Italian formerly connected with the Metropolitan but now running a sort of choral society of his own. He trains aspiring prima donnas in their roles with a chorus and settings, and Miss St. Clair is one of his pet students. He talked to me without any trouble; and it seems he knew Benson well. Benson attended several of St. Clair's rehearsals and sometimes called for her in a taxicab. Rinaldo—that's the man's name—thinks he had a bad crush on the girl. Last winter when she sang at the Criterion in a small part, Rinaldo was back stage coaching, and Benson sent her enough hothouse flowers to fill the star's dressing room and have some left over. I tried to find out if Benson was playing 'angel' for her, but Rinaldo either didn't know or pretended he didn't." Tracy closed his notebook and looked up. "That any good to you Chief?"

"First-rate," Markham told him. "Keep at work along that line and let me hear from you again about this time Monday."

Tracy bowed, and as he went out the secretary again appeared at the door. "Springer's here now, sir," he said. "Shall I send him in?"

Springer proved to be a type of detective quite different from either Phelps or Tracy. He was older, and had the gloomy capable air of a hardworking bookkeeper in a bank. There was no initiative in his bearing, but one felt that he could discharge a delicate task with extreme competency.

Markham took from his pocket the envelope on which he had noted the name given him by Major Benson.

"Springer, there's a man down on Long Island that I want to interview as soon as possible. It's in connection with the Benson case, and I wish you'd locate him and get him up here as soon as possible. If you can find him in the telephone book, you needn't go down personally. His name is Leander Pfyfe, and he lives, I think, at Port Washington."

Markham jotted down the name on a card and handed it to the detective. "This is Saturday, so if he comes to town tomorrow, have him ask for me at the Stuyvesant Club. I'll be there in the afternoon."

When Springer had gone, Markham again rang for his secretary and gave instructions that the moment Miss St. Clair arrived she was to be shown in.

"Sergeant Heath is here," Swacker informed him, "and wants to see you if you're not too busy."

Markham glanced at the clock over the door. "I guess I'll have time. Send him in."

Heath was surprised to see Vance and me in the district attorney's office, but after greeting Markham with the customary handshake, he turned to Vance with a good-natured smile.

"Still acquiring knowledge, Mr. Vance?"

"Can't say that I am, Sergeant," returned Vance lightly. "But I'm learning a number of most int'restin' errors. . . . How goes the sleuthin'?"

Heath's face became suddenly serious.

"That's what I'm here to tell the chief about." He addressed himself to Markham. "This case is a jawbreaker, sir. My men and myself have talked to a dozen of Benson's cronies, and we can't worm a single fact of any value out of 'em. They either don't know anything or they're giving a swell imitation of a lot of clams. They all appear to be greatly shocked—bowled over, floored, flabbergasted—by the news of the shooting. And have they got any idea as to why or how it happened? They'll tell the world they haven't. You know the line of talk: Who'd want to shoot good old Al? Nobody could've done it but a burglar who didn't know good old Al. If he'd known good old Al, even the burglar wouldn't have done it. . . . Hell! I felt like killing off a few of those birds myself so they could go and join their good old Al."

"Any news of the car?" asked Markham.

Heath grunted his disgust. "Not a word. And that's funny, too, seeing all the advertising it got. Those fishing rods are the only thing we've got. . . . The inspector, by the way, sent me the *post-mortem* report this morning; but it didn't tell us anything we didn't know. Translated into human language, it said Benson died from a shot in the head, with all his organs sound. It's a wonder, though, they didn't discover that he'd been poisoned with a Mexican bean or bit by an African snake, or something, so's to make the case a little more intrikkit than it already is."

"Cheer up, Sergeant," Markham exhorted him. "I've had a little better luck. Tracy ran down the owner of the handbag and found out she'd been to dinner with Benson that night. He and Phelps also learned a few other supplementary facts that fit in well; and I'm expecting the lady here at any minute. I'm going to find out what she has to say for herself."

An expression of resentment came into Heath's eyes as the district attorney was speaking, but he erased it at once and began asking questions. Markham gave him every detail and also informed him of Leander Pfyfe.

"I'll let you know immediately how the interview comes out," he concluded.

As the door closed on Heath, Vance looked up at Markham with a sly smile.

"Not exactly one of Nietzsche's *Übermenschen*—eh, what? I fear the subtleties of this complex world bemuse him a bit, y'know. . . . And he's so disappointin'. I felt pos'tively elated when the bustling lad with the thick glasses announced his presence. I thought surely he wanted to tell you he had jailed at least six of Benson's murderers."

"Your hopes run too high, I fear," commented Markham.

"And yet, that's the usual procedure—if the headlines in our great moral dailies are to be credited. I always thought that the moment a crime was committed the police began arresting people promiscuously—to maintain the excitement, don't y'know. Another illusion gone! . . . Sad, sad," he murmured. "I sha'n't forgive our Heath; he has betrayed my faith in him."

At this point Markham's secretary came to the door and announced the arrival of Miss St. Clair.

I think we were all taken a little aback at the spectacle presented by this young woman as she came slowly into the room with a firm graceful step, and with her head held slightly to one side in an attitude of supercilious inquiry. She was small and strikingly pretty, although "pretty" is not exactly the word with which to describe her. She possessed that faintly exotic beauty that we find in the portraits of the Carracci, who sweetened the severity of Leonardo and made it at once intimate and decadent. Her eyes were dark and widely spaced; her nose was delicate and straight, and her forehead broad. Her full sensuous lips were almost sculpturesque in their linear precision, and her mouth wore an enigmatic smile, or hint of a smile. Her rounded, firm chin was a bit heavy when examined apart from the other features, but not in the ensemble. There was poise and a certain strength of character in her bearing; but one sensed the potentialities of powerful emotions beneath her exterior calm. Her clothes harmonized with her personality; they were quiet and apparently in the conventional style, but a touch of colour and originality here and there conferred on them a fascinating distinction.

Markham rose and bowing, with formal courtesy, indicated a comfortable upholstered chair directly in front of his desk. With a barely perceptible nod, she glanced at the chair and then seated herself in a straight armless chair standing next to it.

"You won't mind, I'm sure," she said, "if I choose my own chair for the inquisition."

Her voice was low and resonant—the speaking voice of the highly trained singer. She smiled as she spoke, but it was not a cordial smile; it was cold and distant, yet somehow indicative of levity.

"Miss St. Clair," began Markham, in a tone of polite severity, "the murder of Mr. Alvin Benson has intimately involved yourself. Before taking any definite steps, I have invited you here to ask you a few questions. I can, therefore, advise you quite honestly that frankness will best serve your interests."

72

He paused, and the woman looked at him with an ironically questioning gaze. "Am I supposed to thank you for your generous advice?"

Markham's scowl deepened as he glanced down at a typewritten page on his desk.

"You are probably aware that your gloves and handbag were found in Mr. Benson's house the morning after he was shot."

"I can understand how you might have traced the handbag to me," she said; "but how did you arrive at the conclusion that the gloves were mine?"

Markham looked up sharply. "Do you mean to say the gloves are not yours?"

"Oh, no." She gave him another wintry smile. "I merely wondered how you knew they belonged to me, since you couldn't have known either my taste in gloves or the size I wore."

"They're your gloves, then?"

"If they are Tréfousse, size five-and-three-quarters, of white kid and elbow length, they are certainly mine. And I'd so like to have them back, if you don't mind."

"I'm sorry," said Markham, "but it is necessary that I keep them for the present."

She dismissed the matter with a slight shrug of the shoulders. "Do you mind if I smoke?" she asked.

Markham instantly opened a drawer of his desk and took out a box of Benson and Hedges cigarettes.

"I have my own, thank you," she informed him. "But I would so appreciate my holder. I've missed it horribly."

Markham hesitated. He was manifestly annoyed by the woman's attitude. "I'll be glad to lend it to you," he compromised; and reaching into another drawer of his desk, he laid the holder on the table before her.

"Now, Miss St. Clair," he said, resuming his gravity of manner, "will you tell me how these personal articles of yours happened to be in Mr. Benson's living room?"

"No, Mr. Markham, I will not," she answered.

"Do you realize the serious construction your refusal places upon the circumstances?"

"I really hadn't given it much thought." Her tone was indifferent.

"It would be well if you did," Markham advised her. "Your position is not an enviable one; and the presence of your belongings in Mr. Benson's room is, by no means, the only thing that connects you directly with the crime."

The woman raised her eyes inquiringly, and again the enigmatic smile appeared at the corners of her mouth. "Perhaps you have sufficient evidence to accuse me of the murder?"

Markham ignored this question. "You were well acquainted with Mr. Benson, I believe?"

"The finding of my handbag and gloves in his apartment might lead one to assume as much, mightn't it?" she parried.

"He was, in fact, much interested in you?" persisted Markham.

She made a moue and sighed. "Alas, yes! Too much for my peace of mind. . . . Have I been brought here to discuss the attentions this gentleman paid me?"

Again Markham ignored her query. "Where were you, Miss St. Clair, between the time you left the Marseilles at midnight and the time you arrived home—which, I understand, was after one o'clock?"

"You are simply wonderful!" she exclaimed. "You seem to know everything. . . . Well, I can only say that during that time I was on my way home."

"Did it take you an hour to go from Fortieth Street to Eighty-first and Riverside Drive?"

"Just about, I should say—a few minutes more or less, perhaps."

"How do you account for that?" Markham was becoming impatient.

"I can't account for it," she said, "except by the passage of time. Time does fly, doesn't it, Mr. Markham?"

"By your attitude you are only working detriment to yourself," Markham warned her, with a show of irritation. "Can you not see the seriousness of your position? You are known to have dined with Mr. Benson, to have left the restaurant at midnight, and to have arrived at your own apartment after one o'clock. At twelve-thirty, Mr. Benson was shot; and your personal articles were found in the same room the morning after."

"It looks terribly suspicious, I know," she admitted, with whimsical seriousness. "And I'll tell you this, Mr. Markham: if my thoughts could have killed Mr. Benson, he would have died long ago. I know I shouldn't speak ill of the dead—there's a saying about it beginning 'de mortuis,' isn't there?—but the truth is, I had reason to dislike Mr. Benson exceedingly."

"Then, why did you go to dinner with him?"

"I've asked myself the same question a dozen times since," she confessed dolefully. "We women are such impulsive creatures—always doing things we shouldn't. . . . But I know what you're thinking: if I had intended to shoot him, that would have been a natural preliminary. Isn't that what's in your mind? I suppose all murderesses do go to dinner with their victims first."

While she spoke she opened her vanity case and looked at her reflection in its mirror. She daintily adjusted several imaginary stray ends of her abundant dark brown hair, and touched her arched eyebrows gently with her little finger as if to rectify some infinitesimal disturbance in their pencilled contour. Then she tilted her head, regarded herself appraisingly, and returned her gaze to the district attorney only as she came to the end of her speech. Her actions had perfectly conveyed to her listeners the impression that the subject of the conversation was, in her scheme of things, of secondary importance to her personal appearance. No words could have expressed her indifference so convincingly as had her little pantomime.

Markham was becoming exasperated. A different type of district attorney would no doubt have attempted to use the pressure of his office to force her into a more amenable frame of mind. But Markham shrank instinctively from the bludgeoning, threatening methods of the ordinary public prosecutor, especially in his dealings with women. In the present case, however, had it not been for Vance's strictures at the club, he would no doubt have taken a more aggressive stand. But it was evident he was labouring under a burden of uncertainty superinduced by Vance's words and augmented by the evasive deportment of the woman herself.

After a moment's silence he asked grimly, "You did considerable speculating through the firm of Benson and Benson, did you not?"

A faint ring of musical laughter greeted this question. "I see that the dear major has been telling tales. . . . Yes, I've been gambling most extravagantly. And I had no business to do it. I'm afraid I'm avaricious."

"And is it not true that you've lost heavily of late—that, in fact, Mr. Alvin Benson called upon you for additional margin and finally sold out your securities?"

"I wish to Heaven it were not true," she lamented, with a look of simulated tragedy. Then: "Am I supposed to have done away with Mr. Benson out of sordid revenge or as an act of just retribution?" She smiled archly and waited expectantly, as if her question had been part of a guessing game.

Markham's eyes hardened as he coldly enunciated his next words.

"Is it not a fact that Captain Philip Leacock owned just such a pistol as Mr. Benson was killed with—a forty-five army Colt automatic?"

At the mention of her fiancé's name she stiffened perceptibly and caught her breath. The part she had been playing fell from her, and a faint flush suffused her cheeks and extended to her forehead. But almost immediately she had reassumed her role of playful indifference.

"I never inquired into the make or calibre of Captain Leacock's firearms," she returned carelessly.

"And is it not a fact," pursued Markham's imperturbable voice, "that Captain Leacock lent you his pistol when he called at your apartment on the morning before the murder?"

"It's most ungallant of you, Mr. Markham," she reprimanded him coyly, "to inquire into the personal relations of an engaged couple; for I am betrothed to Captain Leacock—though you probably know it already."

Markham stood up, controlling himself with effort.

"Am I to understand that you refuse to answer any of my questions, or to endeavour to extricate yourself from the very serious position you are in?"

She appeared to consider. "Yes," she said slowly, "I haven't anything I care especially to say just now."

Markham leaned over and rested both hands on the desk. "Do you realize the possible consequences of your attitude?" he asked ominously. "The facts I know regarding your connection with the case, coupled with your refusal to offer a single extenuating explanation, give me more grounds than I actually need to order your being held."

I was watching her closely as he spoke, and it seemed to me that her eyelids drooped involuntarily the merest fraction of an inch. But she gave no other indication of being affected by the pronouncement, and merely looked at the district attorney with an air of defiant amusement.

Markham, with a sudden contraction of the jaw, turned and reached toward a bell button beneath the edge of his desk. But, in doing so, his glance fell upon Vance; and he paused indecisively. The look he had encountered on the other's face was one of reproachful amazement; not only did it express complete surprise at his apparent decision but it stated, more eloquently than words could have done, that he was about to commit an act of irreparable folly.

There were several moments of tense silence in the room. Then calmly and unhurriedly Miss St. Clair opened her vanity case and powdered her nose. When she had finished, she turned a serene gaze upon the district attorney.

"Well, do you want to arrest me now?" she asked.

Markham regarded her for a moment, deliberating. Instead of answering at once, he went to the window and stood for a full minute looking down upon the Bridge of Sighs which connects the Criminal Courts Building with the Tombs.

"No, I think not today," he said slowly.

He stood awhile longer in absorbed contemplation; then, as if shaking off his mood of irresolution, he swung about and confronted the woman.

"I'm not going to arrest you—yet," he reiterated, a bit harshly. "But I'm going to order you to remain in New York for the present. And if you attempt to leave, you *will* be arrested. I hope that is clear."

He pressed a button, and his secretary entered.

"Swacker, please escort Miss St. Clair downstairs, and call a taxicab for her. . . . Then you can go home yourself."

She rose and gave Markham a little nod.

"You were very kind to lend me my cigarette holder," she said pleasantly, laying it on his desk.

Without another word, she walked calmly from the room.

The door had no more than closed behind her when Markham pressed another button. In a few moments the door leading into the outer corridor opened, and a white-haired, middle-aged man appeared.

"Ben," ordered Markham hurriedly, "have that woman that Swacker's taking downstairs followed. Keep her under surveillance and don't let her get lost. She's not to leave the city—understand? It's the St. Clair woman Tracy dug up."

When the man had gone, Markham turned and stood glowering at Vance.

"What do you think of your innocent young lady now?" he asked, with an air of belligerent triumph.

"Nice gel—eh, what?" replied Vance blandly. "Extr'ordin'ry control. And she's about to marry a professional milit'ry man! Ah, well. *De gustibus.* . . . Y' know, I was afraid for a moment you were actu'lly going to send for the manacles. And if you had, Markham old dear, you'd have regretted it to your dying day."

Markham studied him for a few seconds. He knew there was something more than a mere whim beneath Vance's certitude of manner; and it was this knowledge that had stayed his hand when he was about to have the woman placed in custody.

"Her attitude was certainly not conducive to one's belief in her innocence," Markham objected. "She played her part damned cleverly, though. But it was just the part a shrewd woman, knowing herself guilty, would have played."

"I say, didn't it occur to you," asked Vance, "that perhaps she didn't care a farthing whether you thought her guilty or not?—that, in fact, she was a bit disappointed when you let her go?"

"That's hardly the way I read the situation," returned Markham. "Whether guilty or innocent, a person doesn't ordinarily invite arrest."

"By the bye," asked Vance, "where was the fortunate swain during the hour of Alvin's passing?"

"Do you think we didn't check up on that point?" Markham spoke with disdain. "Captain Leacock was at his own apartment that night from eight o'clock on."

"Was he, really?" airily retorted Vance. "A most model young fella!"

Again Markham looked at him sharply. "I'd like to know what weird theory has been struggling in your brain today," he mused. "Now that I've let the lady go temporarily—which is what you obviously wanted me to do—and have stultified my own better judgment in so doing, why not tell me frankly what you've got up your sleeve?"

"'Up my sleeve?' Such an inelegant metaphor! One would think I was a prestidig'tator, what?"

Whenever Vance answered in this fashion, it was a sign that he wished to avoid making a direct reply; and Markham dropped the matter.

"Anyway," he submitted, "you didn't have the pleasure of witnessing my humiliation, as you prophesied."

Vance looked up in simulated surprise. "Didn't I, now?" Then he added sorrowfully, "Life is so full of disappointments, y'know."

CHAPTER 8

Vance Accepts a Challenge
Saturday, June 15; 4 p.m.

After Markham had telephoned Heath the details of the interview, we returned to the Stuyvesant Club. Ordinarily the district attorney's office shuts down at one o'clock on Saturdays; but today the hour had been extended because of the importance attaching to Miss St. Clair's visit.

Markham had lapsed into an introspective silence which lasted until we were again seated in the alcove of the club's lounge-room. Then he spoke irritably.

"Damn it! I shouldn't have let her go. . . . I still have a feeling she's guilty."

Vance assumed an air of gushing credulousness.

"Oh, really? I daresay you're *so* psychic. Been that way all your life, no doubt. And haven't you had lots and lots of dreams that came true? I'm sure you've often had a phone call from someone you were thinking about at the moment. A delectable gift. Do you read palms, also? . . . Why not have the lady's horoscope cast?"

"I have no evidence as yet," Markham retorted, "that your belief in her innocence is founded on anything more substantial than your impressions."

"Ah, but it is," averred Vance. "I *know* she's innocent. Furthermore, I know that no woman could possibly have fired the shot."

"Don't get the erroneous idea in your head that a woman couldn't have manipulated a forty-five army Colt."

"Oh, that?" Vance dismissed the notion with a shrug. "The material indications of the crime don't enter into my calculations, y'know—I leave 'em entirely to you lawyers and the lads with the bulging deltoids. I have other, and surer, ways of reaching conclusions. That's why

I told you that if you arrested any woman for shooting Benson, you'd be blundering most shamefully."

Markham grunted indignantly. "And yet you seem to have repudiated all processes of deduction whereby the truth may be arrived at. Have you, by any chance, entirely renounced your faith in the operations of the human mind?"

"Ah, there speaks the voice of God's great common people!" exclaimed Vance. "Your mind is so typical, Markham. It works on the principle that what you don't know isn't knowledge, and that, since you don't understand a thing there is no explanation. A comfortable point of view. It relieves one from all care and uncertainty. Don't you find the world a very sweet and wonderful place?"

Markham adopted an attitude of affable forbearance. "You spoke at lunchtime, I believe, of one infallible method of detecting crime. Would you care to divulge this profound and priceless secret to a mere district attorney?"

Vance bowed with exaggerated courtesy.*

"Delighted, I'm sure," he returned. "I referred to the science of individual character and the psychology of human nature. We all do things, d' ye see, in a certain individual way, according to our temp'raments. Every human act, no matter how large or how small, is a direct expression of a man's personality and bears the inev'table impress of his nature. Thus, a musician, by looking at a sheet of music, is able to tell at once whether it was composed, for example, by Beethoven, or Schubert, or Debussy, or Chopin. And an artist, by looking at a canvas, knows immediately whether it is a Corot, a Harpignies, a Rembrandt, or a Franz Hals. And just as no two faces are exactly alike, so no two natures are exactly alike; the combination of ingredients which go to make up our personalities, varies in each individual. That is why, when twenty artists, let us say, sit down to paint the same subject, each one conceives and executes it in a different manner. The result in each case is a distinct and unmistakable expression of the personality of the painter who did it. . . . It's really rather simple, don't y'know."

"Your theory, doubtless, would be comprehensible to an artist," said Markham, in a tone of indulgent irony. "But its metaphysical refinements are, I admit, considerably beyond the grasp of a vulgar worldling like myself."

---

* The following conversation in which Vance explains his psychological methods of criminal analysis, is, of course, set down from memory. However, a proof of this passage was sent to him with a request that he revise and alter it in whatever manner he chose; so that, as it now stands, it describes Vance's theory in practically his own words.

"'The mind inclined to what is false rejects the nobler course,'" murmured Vance, with a sigh.

"There is," argued Markham, "a slight difference between art and crime."

"Psychologically, old chap, there's none," Vance amended evenly. "Crimes possess all the basic factors of a work of art—approach, conception, technique, imagination, attack, method, and organization. Moreover, crimes vary fully as much in their manner, their aspects, and their general nature, as do works of art. Indeed, a carefully planned crime is just as direct an expression of the individual as is a painting, for instance. And therein lies the one great possibility of detection. Just as an expert aesthetician can analyze a picture and tell you who painted it, or the personality and temp'rament of the person who painted it, so can the expert psychologist analyze a crime and tell you who committed it—that is, if he happens to be acquainted with the person—or else can describe to you, with almost mathematical surety, the criminal's nature and character. . . . And that, my dear Markham, is the only sure and inev'table means of determining human guilt. All others are mere guesswork, unscientific, uncertain, and—perilous."

Throughout this explanation Vance's manner had been almost casual; yet the very serenity and assurance of his attitude conferred upon his words a curious sense of authority. Markham had listened with interest, though it could be seen that he did not regard Vance's theorizing seriously.

"Your system ignores motive altogether," he objected.

"Naturally," Vance replied, "since it's an irrelevant factor in most crimes. Every one of us, my dear chap, has just as good a motive for killing at least a score of men as the motives which actuate ninety-nine crimes out of a hundred. And, when anyone is murdered, there are dozens of innocent people who had just as strong a motive for doing it as had the actual murderer. Really, y'know, the fact that a man has a motive is no evidence whatever that he's guilty—such motives are too universal a possession of the human race. Suspecting a man of murder because he has a motive is like suspecting a man of running away with another man's wife because he has two legs. The reason that some people kill and others don't, is a matter of temp'rament—of individual psychology. It all comes back to that. . . . And another thing: when a person does possess a real motive—something tremendous and overpowering—he's pretty apt to keep it to himself, to hide it and guard it carefully—eh, what? He may even have disguised the motive through years of preparation; or the mo-

81

tive may have been born within five minutes of the crime through the unexpected discovery of facts a decade old. . . . So, d' ye see, the absence of any apparent motive in a crime might be regarded as more incriminating than the presence of one."

"You are going to have some difficulty in eliminating the idea of *cui bono* from the consideration of crime."

"I daresay," agreed Vance. "The idea of cui bono is just silly enough to be impregnable. And yet, many persons would be benefited by almost anyone's death. Kill Sumner, and, on that theory, you could arrest the entire membership of the Authors' League."

"Opportunity, at any rate," persisted Markham, "is an insuperable factor in crime—and by opportunity, I mean that affinity of circumstances and conditions which make a particular crime possible, feasible, and convenient for a particular person."

"Another irrelevant factor," asserted Vance. "Think of the opportunities we have every day to murder people we dislike! Only the other night I had ten insuff'rable bores to dinner in my apartment—a social devoir. But I refrained—with consid'rable effort, I admit—from putting arsenic in the Pontet Canet. The Borgias and I, y'see, merely belong in different psychological categ'ries. On the other hand, had I been resolved to do murder, I would—like those resourceful *cinque-cenio* patricians—have created my own opportunity. . . . And there's the rub:—one can either make an opportunity or disguise the fact that he had it, with false alibis and various other tricks. You remember the case of the murderer who called the police to break into his victim's house before the latter had been killed, saying he suspected foul play, and who then preceded the policemen indoors and stabbed the man as they were trailing up the stairs."*

"Well, what of actual proximity, or presence—the proof of a person being on the scene of the crime at the time it was committed?"

"Again misleading," Vance declared. "An innocent person's presence is too often used as a shield by the real murderer, who is actu'lly absent. A clever criminal can commit a crime from a distance through an agency that is present. Also, a clever criminal can arrange an alibi and then go to the scene of the crime disguised and unrecognized. There are far too many convincing ways of being present when one is believed to be absent—and *vice versa*. . . . But we can never part

---

* I don't know what case Vance was referring to; but there are several instances of this device on record, and writers of detective fiction have often used it. The latest instance is to be found in G. K. Chesterton's *The Innocence of Father Brown*, in the story entitled "The Wrong Shape."

from our individualities and our natures. And that is why all crime inev'tably comes back to human psychology—the one fixed, undisguisable basis of deduction."

"It's a wonder to me," said Markham, "in view of your theories, that you don't advocate dismissing nine-tenths of the police force and installing a gross or two of those psychological machines so popular with the Sunday Supplement editor."

Vance smoked a minute meditatively.

"I've read about 'em. Int'restin' toys. They can no doubt indicate a certain augmented emotional stress when the patient transfers his attention from the pious platitudes of Dr. Frank Crane to a problem in spherical trigonometry. But if an innocent person were harnessed up to the various tubes, galvanometers, electromagnets, glass plates, and brass knobs of one of these apparatuses, and then quizzed about some recent crime, your indicat'ry needle would cavort about like a Russian dancer as a result of sheer nervous panic on the patient's part."

Markham smiled patronizingly.

"And I suppose the needle would remain static with a guilty person in contact?"

"Oh, on the contr'ry," Vance's tone was unruffled. "The needle would bob up and down just the same—but not *because* he was guilty. If he was stupid, for instance, the needle would jump as a result of his resentment at a seemingly newfangled third-degree torture. And if he was intelligent, the needle would jump because of his suppressed mirth at the puerility of the legal mind for indulging in such nonsense."

"You move me deeply," said Markham. "My head is spinning like a turbine. But there are those of us poor worldlings who believe that criminality is a defect of the brain."

"So it is," Vance readily agreed. "But unfortunately the entire human race possesses the defect. The virtuous ones haven't, so to speak, the courage of their defects. . . . However, if you were referring to a criminal type, then, alas! we must part company. It was Lombrosco, that darling of the yellow journals, who invented the idea of the congenital criminal. Real scientists like DuBois, Karl Pearson, and Goring have shot his idiotic theories full of holes."*

"I am floored by your erudition," declared Markham, as he sig-

---

* It was Pearson and Goring who, about twenty years ago, made an extensive investigation and tabulation of professional criminals in England, the results of which showed (1) that criminal careers began mostly between the ages of 16 and 21; (2) that over ninety percent of criminals were mentally normal; and (3) that more criminals had criminal older brothers than criminal fathers.

nalled to a passing attendant and ordered another cigar. "I console myself, however, with the fact that, as a rule, murder will leak out."

Vance smoked his cigarette in silence, looking thoughtfully out through the window up at the hazy June sky.

"Markham," he said at length, "the number of fantastic ideas extant about criminals is pos'tively amazing. How a sane person can subscribe to that ancient hallucination that 'murder will out' is beyond me. It rarely 'outs,' old dear. And, if it did 'out,' why a homicide bureau? Why all this whirlin'-dervish activity by the police whenever a body is found? . . . The poets are to blame for this bit of lunacy. Chaucer probably started it with his '*Mordre wol out,*' and Shakespeare helped it along by attributing to murder a miraculous organ that speaks in lieu of a tongue. It was some poet, too, no doubt, who conceived the fancy that carcasses bleed at the sight of the murderer. . . . Would you, as the great Protector of the Faithful, dare tell the police to wait calmly in their offices, or clubs, or favourite beauty parlours—or wherever policemen do their waiting—until a murder 'outs'? Poor dear!—if you did, they'd ask the governor for your detention as *particeps criminis*, or apply for a *de lunatico inquirendo.*"*

Markham grunted good-naturedly. He was busy cutting and lighting his cigar.

"I believe you chaps have another hallucination about crime," continued Vance, "namely, that the criminal always returns to the scene of the crime. This weird notion is even explained on some recondite and misty psychological ground. But, I assure you, psychology teaches no such prepost'rous doctrine. If ever a murderer returned to the body of his victim for any reason other than to rectify some blunder he had made, then he is a subject for Broadmoor—or Bloomingdale. . . . How easy it would be for the police if this fanciful notion were true! They'd merely have to sit down at the scene of the crime, play bezique or Mah Jongg until the murderer returned, and then escort him to the Bastille, what? The true psychological instinct

---

* Sir Basil Thomson, K.C.B., former Assistant Commissioner of Metropolitan Police, London, writing in the *Saturday Evening Post* several years after this conversation, said: "Take, for example, the proverb that *murder will out,* which is employed whenever one out of many thousands of undiscovered murderers is caught through a chance coincidence that captures the popular imagination. It is because murder will not out that the pleasant shock of surprise when it does out calls for a proverb to enshrine the phenomenon. The poisoner who is brought to justice has almost invariably proved to have killed other victims without exciting suspicion until he has grown careless."

in anyone having committed a punishable act is to get as far away from the scene of it as the limits of this world will permit."[*]

"In the present case, at any rate," Markham reminded him, "we are neither waiting inactively for the murder to out, nor sitting in Benson's living room trusting to the voluntary return of the criminal."

"Either course would achieve success as quickly as the one you are now pursuing,"Vance said.

"Not being gifted with your singular insight," retorted Markham, "I can only follow the inadequate processes of human reasoning."

"No doubt," Vance agreed commiseratingly. "And the results of your activities thus far force me to the conclusion that a man with a handful of legalistic logic can successfully withstand the most obst'nate and heroic assaults of ordin'ry common sense."

Markham was piqued. "Still harping on the St. Clair woman's innocence, eh? However, in view of the complete absence of any tangible evidence pointing elsewhere, you must admit I have no choice of courses."

"I admit nothing of the kind," Vance told him, "for, I assure you, there is an abundance of evidence pointing elsewhere. You simply failed to see it."

"You think so!"Vance's nonchalant cocksureness had at last overthrown Markham's equanimity. "Very well, old man; I hereby enter an emphatic denial to all your fine theories; and I challenge you to produce a single piece of this evidence which you say exists."

He threw his words out with asperity, and gave a curt, aggressive gesture with his extended fingers, to indicate that, as far as he was concerned, the subject was closed.

Vance, too, I think, was pricked a little.

"Y'know, Markham old dear, I'm no avenger of blood or vindicator of the honour of society. The role would bore me."

Markham smiled loftily but made no reply.

Vance smoked meditatively for a while. Then, to my amazement, he turned calmly and deliberately to Markham, and said in a quiet, matter-of-fact voice, "I'm going to accept your challenge. It's a bit alien to my tastes; but the problem, y'know, rather appeals to me; it presents the same diff'culties as the Concert Champêtre affair—a question of disputed authorship, as it were."[**]

---

[*] In "Popular Fallacies About Crime", *Saturday Evening Post*, April 21, 1923, p. 8, Sir Basil Thomson also upheld this point of view.

[**] For years the famous Concert Champêtre in the Louvre was officially attributed to Titian. Vance, however, took it upon himself to convince the Curator, M. Lepelletier, that it was a Giorgione, with the result that the painting is now credited to that artist.

Markham abruptly suspended the motion of lifting his cigar to his lips. He had scarcely intended his challenge literally; it had been uttered more in the nature of a verbal defiance; and he scrutinized Vance a bit uncertainly. Little did he realize that the other's casual acceptance of his unthinking and but half-serious challenge was to alter the entire criminal history of New York.

"Just how do you intend to proceed?" he asked.

Vance waved his hand carelessly. "Like Napoleon, *je m'en gage, et puis je vois*. However, I must have your word that you'll give me every possible assistance and will refrain from all profound legal objections."

Markham pursed his lips. He was frankly perplexed by the unexpected manner in which Vance had met his defiance. But immediately he gave a good-natured laugh, as if, after all, the matter was of no serious consequence.

"Very well," he assented. "You have my word. . . . And now what?"

After a moment Vance lit a fresh cigarette and rose languidly. "First," he announced, "I shall determine the exact height of the guilty person. Such a fact will, no doubt, come under the head of indicat'ry evidence—eh, what?"

Markham stared at him incredulously.

"How, in Heaven's name, are you going to do that?"

"By those primitive deductive methods to which you so touchingly pin your faith," he answered easily. "But come; let us repair to the scene of the crime."

He moved toward the door, Markham reluctantly following in a state of perplexed irritation. "But you know the body was removed," the latter protested; "and the place by now has no doubt been straightened up."

"Thank Heaven for that!" murmured Vance. "I'm not particularly fond of corpses; and untidiness, y'know, annoys me frightfully."

As we emerged into Madison Avenue, he signalled to the commissionaire for a taxicab, and without a word, urged us into it.

"This is all nonsense," Markham declared ill-naturedly, as we started on our journey uptown. "How do you expect to find any clues now? By this time everything has been obliterated."

"Alas, my dear Markham," lamented Vance, in a tone of mock solicitude, "how woefully deficient you are in philosophic theory! If anything, no matter how inf'nitesimal, could really be obliterated, the universe, y'know, would cease to exist—the cosmic problem would be solved, and the Creator would write *Q.E.D.* across an empty firmament. Our only chance of going on with this illusion we call Life, d' ye see, lies in the fact that consciousness is like an inf'nite decimal point. Did you, as a child, ever try to complete the decimal one-third by filling a whole sheet of paper with the numeral three? You always had the fraction one-third left, don't y'know. If you could have eliminated the smallest one-third, after having set down ten thousand threes, the problem would have ended. So with life, my dear fellow. It's only because we can't erase or obliterate anything that we go on existing."

He made a movement with his fingers, putting a sort of tangible period to his remarks, and looked dreamily out of the window up at the fiery film of sky.

Markham had settled back into his corner and was chewing morosely at his cigar. I could see he was fairly simmering with impotent anger at having let himself be goaded into issuing his challenge. But there was no retreating now. As he told me afterward, he was fully convinced he had been dragged forth out of a comfortable chair on a patent and ridiculous fool's errand.

CHAPTER 9

The Height of the Murderer
Saturday, June 15; 5 p.m.

When we arrived at Benson's house, a patrolman leaning somnolently against the iron paling of the areaway came suddenly to attention and saluted. He eyed Vance and me hopefully, regarding us no doubt as suspects being taken to the scene of the crime for questioning by the district attorney. We were admitted by one of the men from the homicide bureau who had been in the house on the morning of the investigation.

Markham greeted him with a nod.

"Everything going all right?"

"Sure," the man replied good-naturedly. "The old lady's as meek as a cat—and a swell cook."

"We want to be alone for a while, Sniffin," said Markham, as we passed into the living room.

"The gastronome's name is Snitkin, not Sniffin," Vance corrected him, when the door had closed on us.

"Wonderful memory," muttered Markham churlishly.

"A failing of mine," said Vance. "I suppose you are one of those rare persons who never forget a face but just can't recall names, what?"

But Markham was in no mood to be twitted. "Now that you've dragged me here, what are you going to do?" He waved his hand depreciatingly and sank into a chair with an air of contemptuous abdication.

The living room looked much the same as when we saw it last, except that it had been put neatly in order. The shades were up, and the late afternoon light was flooding in profusely. The ornateness of the room's furnishings seemed intensified by the glare.

Vance glanced about him and gave a shudder. "I'm half inclined to turn back," he drawled. "It's a clear case of justifiable homicide by an outraged interior decorator."

"My dear aesthete," Markham urged impatiently, "be good enough to bury your artistic prejudices and to proceed with your problem... . Of course," he added, with a malicious smile, "if you fear the result, you may still withdraw and thereby preserve your charming theories in their present virgin state."

"And permit you to send an innocent maiden to the chair!" exclaimed Vance, in mock indignation. *"Fie, fie! La politesse* alone forbids my withdrawal. May I never have to lament, with Prince Henry, that 'to my shame I have a truant been to chivalry.'"

Markham set his jaw and gave Vance a ferocious look. "I'm beginning to think that, after all, there is something in your theory that every man has some motive for murdering another."

"Well," replied Vance cheerfully, "now that you have begun to come round to my way of thinking, do you mind if I send Mr. Snitkin on an errand?"

Markham sighed audibly and shrugged his shoulders. "I'll smoke during the *opéra bouffe,* if it won't interfere with your performance."

Vance went to the door and called Snitkin.

"I say, would you mind going to Mrs. Platz and borrowing a long tape measure and a ball of string. . . . The district attorney wants them," he added, giving Markham a sycophantic bow.

"I can't hope that you're going to hang yourself, can I?" asked Markham. Vance gazed at him reprovingly. "Permit me," he said sweetly, "to command Othello to your attention:

'How poor are they that have not patience! What wound did ever heal but by degrees?'

Or—to descend from a poet to a platitudinarian—let me present for your consid'ration a pentameter from Longfellow: 'All things come round to him who will but wait.' Untrue, of course, but consolin'. Milton said it much better in his 'They also serve——.' But Cervantes said it best: 'Patience and shuffle the cards.' Sound advice, Markham—and advice expressed rakishly, as all good advice should be. . . . To be sure, patience is a sort of last resort—a practice to adopt when there's nothing else to do. Still, like virtue, it occasionally rewards the practitioner; although I'll admit that, as a rule, it is—again like virtue—bootless. That is to say, it is its own reward. It has, however, been swathed in many verbal robes. It is *'sorrows's slave,'* and the *'sov'reign o'er transmuted ills,'* as well as *'all the passion of great hearts.'* Rousseau wrote, *La patience est amère mais son fruit est doux.* But perhaps your legal taste runs to Latin. *Superanda omnis fortuna ferendo est,* quoth Vergil. And Horace also spoke on the subject. *Durum!* said he, *sed levius fit patientia——*"

"Why the hell doesn't Snitkin come?" growled Markham.

Almost as he spoke the door opened, and the detective handed Vance the tape measure and string.

"And now, Markham, for your reward!"

Bending over the rug Vance moved the large wicker chair into the exact position it had occupied when Benson had been shot. The position was easily determined, for the impressions of the chair's castors on the deep nap of the rug were plainly visible. He then ran the string through the bullet hole in the back of the chair and directed me to hold one end of it against the place where the bullet had struck the wainscot. Next he took up the tape measure and, extending the string through the hole, measured a distance of five feet and six inches along it, starting at the point which corresponded to the location of Benson's forehead as he sat in the chair. Tying a knot in the string to indicate the measurement, he drew the string taut, so that it extended in a straight line from the mark on the wainscot, through the hole in the back of the chair, to a point five feet and six inches in front of where Benson's head had rested.

"This knot in the string," he explained, "now represents the exact location of the muzzle of the gun that ended Benson's career. You see the reasoning—eh, what? Having two points in the bullet's course—namely, the hole in the chair and the mark on the wainscot—and also knowing the approximate vertical line of explosion, which was between five and six feet from the gentleman's skull, it was merely necess'ry to extend the straight line of the bullet's course to the vertical line of explosion in order to ascertain the exact point at which the shot was fired."

"Theoretically very pretty," commented Markham; "though why you should go to so much trouble to ascertain this point in space I can't imagine. . . . Not that it matters, for you have overlooked the possibility of the bullet's deflection."

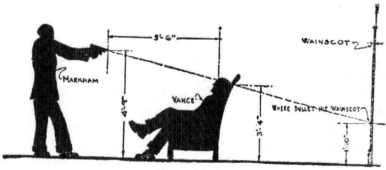

Diagram of shooting.

"Forgive me for contradicting you,"—Vance smiled—"but yesterday morning I questioned Captain Hagedorn at some length and learned that there had been no deflection of the bullet. Hagedorn had inspected the wound before we arrived; and he was really pos'tive on that point. In the first place, the bullet struck the frontal bone at such an angle as to make deflection practically impossible even had the pistol been of smaller calibre. And in the second place, the pistol with which Benson was shot was of so large a bore—a point-forty-five—and the muzzle velocity was so great, that the bullet would have taken a straight course even had it been held at a greater distance from the gentleman's brow."

"And how," asked Markham, "did Hagedorn know what the muzzle velocity was?"

"I was inquis'tive on that point myself," answered Vance; "and he explained that the size and character of the bullet and the expelled shell told him the whole tale. That's how he knew the gun was an army Colt automatic—I believe he called it a U.S. Government Colt—and not the ordinary Colt automatic. The weight of the bullets of these two pistols is slightly different: the ordinary Colt bullet weighs 200 grains, whereas the army Colt bullet weighs 230 grains. Hagedorn, having a hypersensitive tactile sense, was able, I presume, to distinguish the diff'rence at once, though I didn't go into his physiological gifts with him—my reticent nature, you understand. . . . However, he could tell it was a forty-five army Colt automatic bullet; and knowing this, he knew that the muzzle velocity was 809 feet, and that the striking energy was 329—which gives a six-inch penetration in white pine at a distance of twenty- five yards. . . . An amazin' creature, this Hagedorn. Imagine having one's head full of such entrancing information! The old mysteries of why a man should take up the bass fiddle as a life work and where all the pins go are babes' conundrums compared with the one of why a human being should devote his years to the idiosyncrasies of bullets."

"The subject is not exactly an enthralling one," said Markham wearily; "so, for the sake of argument, let us admit that you have now found the precise point of the gun's explosion. Where do we go from there?"

"While I hold the string on a straight line," directed Vance, "be good enough to measure the exact distance from the floor to the knot. Then my secret will be known."

"This game doesn't enthral me, either," Markham protested. "I'd much prefer 'London Bridge'"

Nevertheless he made the measurement.

"Four feet, eight and a half inches," he announced indifferently.

Vance laid a cigarette on the rug at a point directly beneath the knot.

"We now know the exact height at which the pistol was held when it was fired. . . . You grasp the process by which this conclusion was reached, I'm sure."

"It seems rather obvious," answered Markham.

Vance again went to the door and called Snitkin.

"The district attorney desires the loan of your gun for a moment," he said. "He wishes to make a test."

Snitkin stepped up to Markham and held out his pistol wonderingly. "The safety's on, sir. Shall I shift it?"

Markham was about to refuse the weapon when Vance interposed. "That's quite all right. Mr. Markham doesn't intend to fire it—I hope."

When the man had gone, Vance seated himself in the wicker chair and placed his head in juxtaposition with the bullet hole.

"Now, Markham," he requested, "will you please stand on the spot where the murderer stood, holding the gun directly above that cigarette on the floor, and aim delib'rately at my left temple. . . . Take care," he cautioned, with an engaging smile, "not to pull the trigger, or you will never learn who killed Benson."

Reluctantly Markham complied. As he stood taking aim Vance asked me to measure the height of the gun muzzle from the floor.

The distance was four feet and nine inches.

"Quite so," he said, rising. "Y'see, Markham, you are five feet, eleven inches tall; therefore the person who shot Benson was very nearly your own height—certainly not under five feet, ten. . . . That, too, is rather obvious, what?"

His demonstration had been simple and clear. Markham was frankly impressed; his manner had become serious. He regarded Vance for a moment with a meditative frown; then he said, "That's all very well; but the person who fired the shot might have held the pistol relatively higher than I did."

"Not tenable," returned Vance. "I've done too much shooting myself not to know that when an expert takes delib'rate aim with a pistol at a small target, he does it with a stiff arm and with a slightly raised shoulder, so as to bring the sight on a straight line between his eye and the object at which he aims. The height at which one holds a revolver, under such conditions, pretty accurately determines his own height."

"Your argument is based on the assumption that the person who killed Benson was an expert taking deliberate aim at a small target?"

"Not an assumption, but a fact," declared Vance. "Consider: had the person not been an expert shot, he would not—at a distance of five or six feet—have selected the forehead but a larger target—namely, the breast. And having selected the forehead, he most certainly took delib'rate aim, what? Furthermore, had he not been an expert shot, and had he pointed the gun at the breast without taking delib'rate aim, he would, in all prob'bility, have fired more than one shot."

Markham pondered. "I'll grant that, on the face of it, your theory sounds plausible," he conceded at length. "On the other hand, the guilty man could have been almost any height over five feet, ten; for certainly a man may crouch as much as he likes and still take deliberate aim."

"True," agreed Vance. "But don't overlook the fact that the murderer's position, in this instance, was a perfectly natural one. Otherwise, Benson's attention would have been attracted, and he would not have been taken unawares. That he was shot unawares was indicated by his attitude. Of course, the assassin might have stooped a little without causing Benson to look up. . . . Let us say, therefore, that the guilty person's height is somewhere between five feet, ten, and six feet, two. Does that appeal to you?"

Markham was silent.

"The delightful Miss St. Clair, y'know," remarked Vance, with a japish smile, "can't possibly be over five feet, five or six."

Markham grunted and continued to smoke abstractedly.

"This Captain Leacock, I take it," said Vance, "is over six feet—eh, what?"

Markham's eyes narrowed. "What makes you think so?"

"You just told me, don't y'know."

"I told you!"

"Not in so many words," Vance pointed out. "But after I had shown you the approximate height of the murderer, and it didn't correspond at all to that of the young lady you suspected, I knew your active mind was busy looking around for another possibility. And, as the lady's *inamorato* was the only other possibility on your horizon, I concluded that you were permitting your thoughts to play about the captain. Had he, therefore, been the stipulated height, you would have said nothing; but when you argued that the murderer might have stooped to fire the shot, I decided that the captain was inord'nately tall. . . . Thus, in the pregnant silence that emanated from you, old dear, your spirit held sweet communion with mine and told me that the gentleman was a six-footer no less."

"I see that you include mind reading among your gifts," said Markham. "I now await an exhibition of slate writing."

His tone was irritable, but his irritation was that of a man reluctant to admit the alteration of his beliefs. He felt himself yielding to Vance's guiding rein, but he still held stubbornly to the course of his own previous convictions.

"Surely you don't question my demonstration of the guilty person's height?" asked Vance mellifluously.

"Not altogether," Markham replied. "It seems colourable enough. . . . But why, I wonder, didn't Hagedorn work the thing out, if it was so simple?"

"Anaxagoras said that those who have occasion for a lamp supply it with oil. A profound remark, Markham—one of those seemingly simple quips that contain a great truth. A lamp without oil, y'know, is useless. The police always have plenty of lamps—every variety, in fact—but no oil, as it were. That's why they never find anyone unless it's broad daylight."

Markham's mind was now busy in another direction, and he rose and began to pace the floor. "Until now I hadn't thought of Captain Leacock as the actual agent of the crime."

"Why hadn't you thought of him? Was it because one of your sleuths told you he was at home like a good boy that night?"

"I suppose so." Markham continued pacing thoughtfully. Then suddenly he swung about. "That wasn't it, either. It was the amount of damning circumstantial evidence against the St. Clair woman. . . . And, Vance, despite your demonstration here today, you haven't explained away any of the evidence against her. Where was she between twelve and one? Why did she go with Benson to dinner? How did her handbag get here? And what about those burned cigarettes of hers in the grate?—they're the obstacle, those cigarette butts; and I can't admit that your demonstration wholly convinces me—despite the fact that it IS convincing—as long as I've got the evidence of those cigarettes to contend with, for that evidence is also convincing."

"My word!" sighed Vance. "You're in a pos'tively ghastly predic'ment. However, maybe I can cast illumination on those disquietin' cigarette butts." Once more he went to the door and, summoning Snitkin, returned the pistol. "The district attorney thanks you," he said. "And will you be good enough to fetch Mrs. Platz. We wish to chat with her."

Turning back to the room, he smiled amiably at Markham. "I desire to do all the conversing with the lady this time, if you don't mind. There are potentialities in Mrs. Platz which you entirely overlooked when you questioned her yesterday."

Markham was interested, though sceptical. "You have the floor," he said.

CHAPTER 10

Eliminating a Suspect
Saturday, June 15, 5:30 p.m.

When the housekeeper entered, she appeared even more composed than when Markham had first questioned her. There was something at once sullen and indomitable in her manner, and she looked at me with a slightly challenging expression. Markham merely nodded to her, but Vance stood up and indicated a low tufted Morris chair near the fireplace, facing the front windows. She sat down on the edge of it, resting her elbows on its broad arms.

"I have some questions to ask you, Mrs. Platz," Vance began, fixing her sharply with his gaze; "and it will be best for everyone if you tell the whole truth. You understand me—eh, what?"

The easygoing, half-whimsical manner he had taken with Markham had disappeared. He stood before the woman, stern and implacable.

At his words she lifted her head. Her face was blank, but her mouth was set stubbornly, and a smouldering look in her eyes told of a suppressed anxiety.

Vance waited a moment and then went on, enunciating each word with distinctness.

"At what time, on the day Mr. Benson was killed, did the lady call here?"

The woman's gaze did not falter, but the pupils of her eyes dilated. "There was nobody here."

"Oh, yes, there was, Mrs. Platz." Vance's tone was assured. "What time did she call?"

"Nobody was here, I tell you," she persisted.

Vance lit a cigarette with interminable deliberation, his eyes resting steadily on hers. He smoked placidly until her gaze dropped. Then he stepped nearer to her, and said firmly, "If you tell the truth, no harm

95

will come to you. But if you refuse any information you will find yourself in trouble. The withholding of evidence is a crime, y'know, and the law will show you no mercy."

He made a sly grimace at Markham, who was watching the proceedings with interest.

The woman now began to show signs of agitation. She drew in her elbows, and her breathing quickened. "In God's name, I swear it!—there wasn't anybody here." A slight hoarseness gave evidence of her emotion.

"Let us not invoke the Deity," suggested Vance carelessly. "What time was the lady here?"

She set her lips stubbornly, and for a whole minute there was silence in the room. Vance smoked quietly, but Markham held his cigar motionless between his thumb and forefinger in an attitude of expectancy.

Again Vance's impassive voice demanded: "What time was she here?"

The woman clinched her hands with a spasmodic gesture, and thrust her head forward.

"I tell you—I swear it—"

Vance made a peremptory movement of his hand and smiled coldly. "It's no go," he told her. "You're acting stupidly. We're here to get the truth—and you're going to tell us."

"I've told you the truth."

"Is it going to be necess'ry for the district attorney here to order you placed in custody?"

"I've told you the truth," she repeated.

Vance crushed out his cigarette decisively in an ash receiver on the table.

"Right-o, Mrs. Platz. Since you refuse to tell me about the young woman who was here that afternoon, I'm going to tell you about her."

His manner was easy and cynical, and the woman watched him suspiciously.

"Late in the afternoon of the day your employer was shot the doorbell rang. Perhaps you had been informed by Mr. Benson that he was expecting a caller, what? Anyhow, you answered the door and admitted a charming young lady. You showed her into this room . . . and—what do you think, my dear Madam!—she took that very chair on which you are resting so uncomfortably."

He paused and smiled tantalizingly.

"Then," he continued, "you served tea to the young lady and Mr. Benson. After a bit she departed, and Mr. Benson went upstairs to dress for dinner. . . . Y' see, Mrs. Platz, I happen to know."

He lit another cigarette.

"Did you notice the young lady particularly? If not, I'll describe her to you. She was rather short—petite is the word. She had dark hair and dark eyes and she was dressed quietly."

A change had come over the woman. Her eyes stared; her cheeks were now grey; and her breathing had become audible.

"Now, Mrs. Platz," demanded Vance sharply, "what have you to say?"

She drew a deep breath. "There wasn't anybody here," she said doggedly. There was something almost admirable in her obstinacy.

Vance considered a moment. Markham was about to speak but evidently thought better of it and sat watching the woman fixedly.

"Your attitude is understandable," Vance observed finally. "The young lady, of course, was well known to you, and you had a personal reason for not wanting it known she was here."

At these words she sat up straight, a look of terror in her face. "I never saw her before!" she cried, then stopped abruptly.

"Ah!" Vance gave her an amused leer. "You had never seen the young lady before—eh, what? . . . That's quite possible. But it's immaterial. She's a nice girl, though, I'm sure—even if she did have a dish of tea with your employer alone in his home."

"Did she tell you she was here?" The woman's voice was listless. The reaction to her tense obduracy had left her apathetic.

"Not exactly," Vance replied. "But it wasn't necess'ry. I knew without her informing me. . . . Just when did she arrive, Mrs. Platz?"

"About a half hour after Mr. Benson got here from the office." She had at last given over all denials and evasions. "But he didn't expect her—that is, he didn't say anything to me about her coming; and he didn't order tea until after she came."

Markham thrust himself forward. "Why didn't you tell me she'd been here when I asked you yesterday morning?"

The woman cast an uneasy glance about the room.

"I rather fancy," Vance intervened pleasantly, "that Mrs. Platz was afraid you might unjustly suspect the young lady."

She grasped eagerly at his words. "Yes sir—that was all. I was afraid you might think she—did it. And she was such a quiet, sweet-looking girl. . . . That was the only reason, sir."

"Quite so," agreed Vance consolingly. "But tell me: did it not shock you to see such a quiet, sweet-looking young lady smoking cigarettes?"

Her apprehension gave way to astonishment. "Why—yes, sir, it did. . . . But she wasn't a bad girl—I could tell that. And most girls smoke nowadays. They don't think anything of it, like they used to."

"You're quite right," Vance assured her. "Still young ladies really shouldn't throw their cigarettes in tiled, gas-log fireplaces, should they, now?"

The woman regarded him uncertainly; she suspected him of jesting. "Did she do that?" She leaned over and looked into the fireplace. "I didn't see any cigarettes there this morning."

"No, you wouldn't have," Vance informed her. "One of the district attorney's sleuths, d' ye see, cleaned it all up nicely for you yesterday."

She shot Markham a questioning glance. She was not sure whether Vance's remark was to be taken seriously; but his casualness of manner and pleasantness of voice tended to put her at ease.

"Now that we understand each other, Mrs. Platz," he was saying, "was there anything else you particularly noticed when the young lady was here? You will be doing her a good service by telling us, because both the district attorney and I happen to know she is innocent."

She gave Vance a long, shrewd look, as if appraising his sincerity. Evidently the results of her scrutiny were favourable, for her answer left no doubt as to her complete frankness.

"I don't know if it'll help, but when I came in with the toast, Mr. Benson looked like he was arguing with her. She seemed worried about something that was going to happen and asked him not to hold her to some promise she'd made. I was only in the room a minute and I didn't hear much. But just as I was going out he laughed and said it was only a bluff and that nothing was going to happen."

She stopped and waited anxiously. She seemed to fear that her revelation might, after all, prove injurious rather than helpful to the girl.

"Was that all?" Vance's tone indicated that the matter was of no consequence.

The woman demurred.

"That was all I heard; but . . . there was a small blue box of jewellery sitting on the table."

"My word!—a box of jewellery! Do you know whose it was?"

"No, sir, I don't. The lady hadn't brought it, and I never saw it in the house before."

"How did you know it was jewellery?"

"When Mr. Benson went upstairs to dress, I came in to clear the tea things away, and it was still sitting on the table."

Vance smiled. "And you played Pandora and took a peep—eh, what? Most natural—I'd have done it myself."

He stepped back and bowed politely.

"That will be all, Mrs. Platz. . . . And you needn't worry about the young lady. Nothing is going to happen to her."

When she had left us, Markham leaned forward and shook his cigar at Vance. "Why didn't you tell me you had information about the case unknown to me?"

"My dear chap!" Vance lifted his eyebrows in protestation. "To what do you refer specifically?"

"How did you know this St. Clair woman had been here in the afternoon?"

"I didn't; but I surmised it. There were cigarette butts of hers in the grate; and, as I knew she hadn't been here on the night Benson was shot, I thought it rather likely she had been here earlier in the day. And since Benson didn't arrive from his office until four, I whispered into my ear that she had called sometime between four and the hour of his departure for dinner. . . . An element'ry syllogism, what?"

"How did you know she wasn't here that night?"

"The psychological aspects of the crime left me in no doubt. As I told you, no woman committed it—my metaphysical hypotheses again; but never mind. . . . Furthermore, yesterday morning I stood on the spot where the murderer stood and sighted with my eye along the line of fire, using Benson's head and the mark on the wainscot as my points of coinc'dence. It was evident to me then, even without measurements, that the guilty person was rather tall."

"Very well. . . . But how did you know she left here that afternoon before Benson did?" persisted Markham.

"How else could she have changed into an evening gown? Really, y'know, ladies don't go about *décolletées* in the afternoon."

"You assume, then, that Benson himself brought her gloves and handbag back here that night?"

"Someone did—and it certainly wasn't Miss St. Clair."

"All right," conceded Markham. "And what about this Morris chair?—how did you know she sat in it?"

"What other chair could she have sat in and still thrown her cigarettes into the fireplace? Women are notoriously poor shots, even if they were given to hurling their cigarette stubs across the room."

"That deduction is simple enough," admitted Markham. "But suppose you tell me how you know she had tea here unless you were privy to some information on the point?"

"It pos'tively shames me to explain it. But the humiliating truth is that I inferred the fact from the condition of yon samovar. I noted yesterday that it had been used and had not been emptied or wiped off."

Markham nodded with contemptuous elation.

"You seem to have sunk to the despised legal level of material clues."

"That's why I'm blushing so furiously. . . . However, psychological deductions alone do not determine facts in *esse*, but only in *posse*. Other conditions must, of course, be considered. In the present instance the indications of the samovar served merely as the basis for an assumption, or guess, with which to draw out the housekeeper."

"Well, I won't deny that you succeeded," said Markham. "I'd like to know, though, what you had in mind when you accused the woman of a personal interest in the girl. That remark certainly indicated some pre-knowledge of the situation."

Vance's face became serious.

"Markham, I give you my word," he said earnestly, "I had nothing in mind. I made the accusation, thinking it was false, merely to trap her into a denial. And she fell into the trap. But—deuce take it!—I seemed to hit some nail squarely on the head, what? I can't for the life of me imagine why she was frightened. But it really doesn't matter."

"Perhaps not," agreed Markham, but his tone was dubious. "What do you make of the box of jewellery and the disagreement between Benson and the girl?"

"Nothing yet. They don't fit in, do they?"

He was silent a moment. Then he spoke with unusual seriousness. "Markham, take my advice and don't bother with these side issues. I'm telling you the girl had no part in the murder. Let her alone—you'll be happier in your old age if you do."

Markham sat scowling, his eyes in space. "I'm convinced that you *think* you know something."

"*Cogito, ergo sum*," murmured Vance. "Y'know, the naturalistic philosophy of Descartes has always rather appealed to me. It was a departure from universal doubt and a seeking for positive knowledge in self-consciousness. Spinoza in his pantheism, and Berkeley in his idealism, quite misunderstood the significance of their precursor's favourite enthymeme. Even Descartes' errors were brilliant. His method of reasoning, for all its scientific inaccuracies, gave new signif'cation to the symbols of the analyst. The mind, after all, if it is to function effectively, must combine the mathematical precision of a natural science with such pure speculations as astronomy. For instance, Descartes' doctrine of Vortices—"

"Oh, be quiet," growled Markham. "I'm not insisting that you reveal your precious information. So why burden me with a dissertation on seventeenth-century philosophy?"

"Anyhow, you'll admit, won't you," asked Vance lightly, "that, in elim'nating those disturbing cigarette butts, so to speak, I've elim'nated Miss St. Clair as a suspect?"

Markham did not answer at once. There was no doubt that the developments of the past hour had made a decided impression upon him. He did not underestimate Vance, despite his persistent opposition; and he knew that, for all his flippancy, Vance was fundamentally serious. Furthermore, Markham had a finely developed sense of justice. He was not narrow, even though obstinate at times; and I have never known him to close his mind to the possibilities of truth, however opposed to his own interests. It did not, therefore, surprise me in the least when, at last, he looked up with a gracious smile of surrender.

"You've made your point," he said; "and I accept it with proper humility. I'm most grateful to you."

Vance walked indifferently to the window and looked out. "I am happy to learn that you are capable of accepting such evidence as the human mind could not possibly deny."

I had always noticed, in the relationship of these two men, that whenever either made a remark that bordered on generosity, the other answered in a manner which ended all outward show of sentiment. It was as if they wished to keep this more intimate side of their mutual regard hidden from the world.

Markham therefore ignored Vance's thrust. "Have you perhaps any enlightening suggestions, other than negative ones, to offer as to Benson's murderer?" he asked.

"Rather!" said Vance. "No end of suggestions."

"Could you spare me a good one?" Markham imitated the other's playful tone.

Vance appeared to reflect. "Well, I should advise that, as a beginning, you look for a rather tall man, cool-headed, familiar with firearms, a good shot, and fairly well known to the deceased—a man who was aware that Benson was going to dinner with Miss St. Clair, or who had reason to suspect the fact."

Markham looked narrowly at Vance for several moments.

"I think I understand. . . . Not a bad theory, either. You know, I'm going to suggest immediately to Heath that he investigate more thoroughly Captain Leacock's activities on the night of the murder."

"Oh, by all means," said Vance carelessly, going to the piano.

Markham watched him with an expression of puzzled interrogation. He was about to speak when Vance began playing a rollicking French café song which opens, I believe, with *"Ils sont dans les vignes les moineaux."*

CHAPTER 11

A Motive and a Threat

Sunday, June 16; afternoon

The following day, which was Sunday, we lunched with Markham at the Stuyvesant Club. Vance had suggested the appointment the evening before; for, as he explained to me, he wished to be present in case Leander Pfyfe should arrive from Long Island.

"It amuses me tremendously," he had said, "the way human beings delib'rately complicate the most ordin'ry issues. They have a downright horror of anything simple and direct. The whole modern commercial system is nothing but a colossal mechanism for doing things in the most involved and roundabout way. If one makes a ten- cent purchase at a department store nowadays, a complete history of the transaction is written out in triplicate, checked by a dozen floorwalkers and clerks, signed and countersigned, entered into innum'rable ledgers with various coloured inks, and then elab'rately secreted in steel filing cabinets. And not content with all this superfluous *chinoiserie*, our businessmen have created a large and expensive army of efficiency experts whose sole duty it is to complicate and befuddle this system still further. . . . It's the same with everything else in modern life. Regard that insup'rable mania called golf. It consists merely of knocking a ball into a hole with a stick. But the devotees of this pastime have developed a unique and distinctive livery in which to play it. They concentrate for twenty years on the correct angulation of their feet and the proper method of entwining their fingers about the stick. Moreover, in order to discuss the pseudo-intr'cacies of this idiotic sport, they've invented an outlandish vocabulary which is unintelligible even to an English scholar."

He pointed disgustedly at a pile of Sunday newspapers.

"Then here's this Benson murder—a simple and incons'quential affair. Yet the entire machinery of the law is going at high pressure and blowing off jets of steam all over the community, when the matter could be settled quietly in five minutes with a bit of intelligent thinking."

At lunch, however, he did not refer to the crime; and, as if by tacit agreement, the subject was avoided. Markham had merely mentioned casually to us as we went into the dining room that he was expecting Heath a little later.

The sergeant was waiting for us when we retired to the lounge room for our smoke, and by his expression it was evident he was not pleased with the way things were going.

"I told you, Mr. Markham," he said, when he had drawn up our chairs, "that this case was going to be a tough one. . . . Could you get any kind of a lead from the St. Clair woman?"

Markham shook his head.

"She's out of it." And he recounted briefly the happenings at Benson's house the preceding afternoon.

"Well, if you're satisfied," was Heath's somewhat dubious comment, "that's good enough for me. But what about this Captain Leacock?"

"That's what I asked you here to talk about," Markham told him. "There's no direct evidence against him, but there are several suspicious circumstances that tend to connect him with the murder. He seems to meet the specifications as to height; and we mustn't overlook the fact that Benson was shot with just such a gun as Leacock would be likely to possess. He was engaged to the girl, and a motive might be found in Benson's attentions to her."

"And ever since the big scrap," supplemented Heath, "these Army boys don't think anything of shooting people. They got used to blood on the other side."

"The only hitch," resumed Markham, "is that Phelps, who had the job of checking up on the captain, reported to me that he was home that night from eight o'clock on. Of course, there may be a loophole somewhere, and I was going to suggest that you have one of your men go into the matter thoroughly and see just what the situation is. Phelps got his information from one of the hall-boys; and I think it might be well to get hold of the boy again and apply a little pressure. If it was found that Leacock was not at home at twelve- thirty that night, we might have the lead you've been looking for."

"I'll attend to it myself," said Heath. "I'll go round there tonight, and if this boy knows anything, he'll spill it before I'm through with him."

We had talked but a few minutes longer when a uniformed attendant bowed deferentially at the district attorney's elbow and announced
that Mr. Pfyfe was calling.

Markham requested that his visitor be shown into the lounge
room, and then added to Heath, "You'd better remain, and hear what
he has to say."

Leander Pfyfe was an immaculate and exquisite personage. He approached us with a mincing gate of self-approbation. His legs, which
were very long and thin, with knees that seemed to bend slightly inward, supported a short bulging torso; and his chest curved outward in
a generous arc, like that of a pouter pigeon. His face was rotund, and
his jowls hung in two loops over a collar too tight for comfort. His
blond sparse hair was brushed back sleekly; and the ends of his narrow,
silken moustache were waxed into needle-points. He was dressed in
light grey summer flannels and wore a pale turquoise-green silk shirt,
a vivid foulard tie, and grey suede Oxfords. A strong odour of oriental
perfume was given off by the carefully arranged batiste handkerchief
in his breast pocket.

He greeted Markham with viscid urbanity and acknowledged his
introduction to us with a patronizing bow. After posing himself in a
chair the attendant placed for him, he began polishing a gold- rimmed
eyeglass which he wore on a ribbon, and fixed Markham with a melancholy gaze.

"A very sad occasion, this," he sighed.

"Realizing your friendship for Mr. Benson," said Markham, "I deplore the necessity of appealing to you at this time. It was very good
of you, by the way, to come to the city today."

Pfyfe made a mildly deprecating movement with his carefully
manicured fingers. He was, he explained with an air of ineffable self-
complacency, only too glad to discommode himself to give aid to
servants of the public. A distressing necessity, to be sure; but his manner conveyed unmistakably that he knew and recognized the obligations attaching to the dictum of noblesse oblige and was prepared to
meet them.

He looked at Markham with a self-congratulatory air, and his
eyebrows queried: "What can I do for you?" though his lips did not
move.

"I understand from Major Anthony Benson," Markham said, "that
you were very close to his brother and therefore might be able to tell
us something of his personal affairs, or private social relationships, that
would indicate a line of investigation."

Pfyfe gazed sadly at the floor. "Ah, yes. Alvin and I were very close—we were, in fact, the most intimate of friends. You can not imagine how broken up I was at hearing of the dear fellow's tragic end." He gave the impression that here was a modern instance of Aeneas and Achates. "And I was deeply grieved at not being able to come at once to New York to put myself at the service of those that needed me."

"I'm sure it would have been a comfort to his other friends," remarked Vance, with cool politeness. "But in the circumst'nces you will be forgiven."

Pfyfe blinked regretfully. "Ah, but I shall never forgive myself—though I cannot hold myself altogether blameworthy. Only the day before the tragedy I had started on a trip to the Catskills. I had even asked dear Alvin to go along; but he was too busy." Pfyfe shook his head as if lamenting the incomprehensible irony of life. "How much better—ah, how infinitely much better—if only—"

"You were gone a very short time," commented Markham, interrupting what promised to be a homily on perverse providence.

"True," Pfyfe indulgently admitted. "But I met with a most unfortunate accident." He polished his eyeglass a moment. "My car broke down, and I was necessitated to return."

"What road did you take?" asked Heath.

Pfyfe delicately adjusted his eyeglass and regarded the sergeant with an intimation of boredom.

"My advice, Mr.—ah—Sneed—"

"Heath," the other corrected him surlily.

"Ah, yes—Heath.... My advice, Mr. Heath, is that if you are contemplating a motor trip to the Catskills, you apply to the Automobile Club of America for a roadmap. My choice of itinerary might very possibly not suit you."

He turned back to the district attorney with an air that implied he preferred talking to an equal.

"Tell me, Mr. Pfyfe," Markham asked; "did Mr. Benson have any enemies?"

The other appeared to think the matter over. "No-o. Not one, I should say, who would actually have killed him as a result of animosity."

"You imply nevertheless that he had enemies. Could you not tell us a little more?"

Pfyfe passed his hand gracefully over the tips of his golden moustache and then permitted his index-finger to linger on his cheek in an attitude of meditative indecision.

"Your request, Mr. Markham,"—he spoke with pained reluctance—"brings up a matter which I hesitate to discuss. But perhaps it is best that I confide in you—as one gentleman to another. Alvin, in common with many other admirable fellows, had a—what shall I say?—a weakness let me put it that way—for the fair sex."

He looked at Markham, seeking approbation for his extreme tact in stating an indelicate truth.

"You understand," he continued, in answer to the other's sympathetic nod, "Alvin was not a man who possessed the personal characteristics that women hold attractive. (I somehow got the impression that Pfyfe considered himself as differing radically from Benson in this respect.) Alvin was aware of his physical deficiency, and the result was—I trust you will understand my hesitancy in mentioning this distressing fact—but the result was that Alvin used certain—ah—methods in his dealings with women, which you and I could never bring ourselves to adopt. Indeed—though it pains me to say it—he often took unfair advantage of women. He used underhand methods, as it were."

He paused, apparently shocked by this heinous imperfection of his friend and by the necessity of his own seemingly disloyal revelation.

"Was it one of these women whom Benson had dealt with unfairly that you had in mind?" asked Markham.

"No—not the woman herself," Pfyfe replied; "but a man who was interested in her. In fact, this man threatened Alvin's life. You will appreciate my reluctance in telling you this; but my excuse is that the threat was made quite openly. There were several others besides myself who heard it."

"That, of course, relieves you from any technical breach of confidence," Markham observed.

Pfyfe acknowledged the other's understanding with a slight bow.

"It happened at a little party of which I was the unfortunate host," he confessed modestly.

"Who was the man?" Markham's tone was polite but firm.

"You will comprehend my reticence. . . ." Pfyfe began. Then, with an air of righteous frankness, he leaned forward. "It might prove unfair to Alvin to withhold the gentleman's name. . . . He was Captain Philip Leacock."

He allowed himself the emotional outlet of a sigh.

"I trust you won't ask me for the lady's name."

"It won't be necessary," Markham assured him. "But I'd appreciate your telling us a little more of the episode."

Pfyfe complied with an expression of patient resignation.

"Alvin was considerably taken with the lady in question and showed her many attentions which were, I am forced to admit, unwelcome. Captain Leacock resented these attentions; and at the little affair to which I had invited him and Alvin some unpleasant and, I must say, unrefined words passed between them. I fear the wine had been flowing too freely, for Alvin was always punctilious—he was a man, indeed, skilled in the niceties of social intercourse; and the captain, in an outburst of temper, told Alvin that, unless he left the lady strictly alone in the future, he would pay with his life. The captain even went so far as to draw a revolver halfway out of his pocket."

"Was it a revolver or an automatic pistol?" asked Heath.

Pfyfe gave the district attorney a faint smile of annoyance, without deigning even to glance at the sergeant.

"I misspoke myself; forgive me. It was not a revolver. It was, I believe, an automatic army pistol—though, you understand, I didn't see it in its entirety."

"You say there were others who witnessed the altercation?"

"Several of my guests were standing about," Pfyfe explained; "but, on my word, I couldn't name them. The fact is, I attached little importance to the threat—indeed, it had entirely slipped my memory until I read the account of poor Alvin's death. Then I thought at once of the unfortunate incident and said to myself: Why not tell the district attorney. . .?"

"Thoughts that breathe and words that burn," murmured Vance, who had been sitting through the interview in oppressive boredom.

Pfyfe once more adjusted his eyeglass and gave Vance a withering look.

"I beg your pardon, sir?"

Vance smiled disarmingly. "Merely a quotation from Gray. Poetry appeals to me in certain moods, don't y'know. . . . Do you, by any chance, know Colonel Ostrander?"

Pfyfe looked at him coldly, but only a vacuous countenance met his gaze. "I am acquainted with the gentleman," he replied haughtily.

"Was Colonel Ostrander present at this delightful little social affair of yours?" Vance's tone was artlessly innocent.

"Now that you mention it, I believe he was," admitted Pfyfe, and lifted his eyebrows inquisitively.

But Vance was again staring disinterestedly out of the window.

Markham, annoyed at the interruption, attempted to re-establish the conversation on a more amiable and practical basis. But Pfyfe, though loquacious, had little more information to give. He insisted constantly on bringing the talk back to Captain Leacock, and, despite his eloquent protestations, it was obvious he attached more importance to the threat than he chose to admit. Markham questioned him for fully an hour but could learn nothing else of a suggestive nature.

When Pfyfe rose to go, Vance turned from his contemplation of the outside world and, bowing affably, let his eyes rest on the other with ingenuous good nature.

"Now that you are in New York, Mr. Pfyfe, and were so unfortunate as to be unable to arrive earlier, I assume that you will remain until after the investigation."

Pfyfe's studied and habitual calm gave way to a look of oily astonishment. "I hadn't contemplated doing so."

"It would be most desirable if you could arrange it," urged Markham; though I am sure he had no intention of making the request until Vance suggested it.

Pfyfe hesitated and then made an elegant gesture of resignation. "Certainly I shall remain. When you have further need of my services, you will find me at the Ansonia."

He spoke with exalted condescension and magnanimously conferred upon Markham a parting smile. But the smile did not spring from within. It appeared to have been adjusted upon his features by the unseen hands of a sculptor; and it affected only the muscles about his mouth.

When he had gone, Vance gave Markham a look of suppressed mirth.

"'Elegancy, facility, and golden cadence.' . . . But put not your faith in poesy, old dear. Our Ciceronian friend is an unmitigated fashioner of deceptions."

"If you're trying to say that he's a smooth liar," remarked Heath, "I don't agree with you. I think that story about the captain's threat is straight goods."

"Oh, that! Of course, it's true. . . . And, y'know, Markham, the knightly Mr. Pfyfe was frightfully disappointed when you didn't insist on his revealing Miss St. Clair's name. This Leander, I fear, would never have swum the Hellespont for a lady's sake."

"Whether he's a swimmer or not," said Heath impatiently, "he's given us something to go on."

Markham agreed that Pfyfe's recital had added materially to the case against Leacock.

"I think I'll have the captain down to my office tomorrow, and question him," he said.

A moment later Major Benson entered the room, and Markham invited him to join us.

"I just saw Pfyfe get into a taxi," he said, when he had sat down. "I suppose you've been asking him about Alvin's affairs. . . . Did he help you any?"

"I hope so, for all our sakes," returned Markham kindly. "By the way, Major, what do you know about a Captain Philip Leacock?"

Major Benson lifted his eyes to Markham's in surprise. "Didn't you know? Leacock was one of the captains in my regiment—a first-rate man. He knew Alvin pretty well, I think; but my impression is they didn't hit it off very chummily. . . . Surely you don't connect him with this affair?"

Markham ignored the question. "Did you happen to attend a party of Pfyfe's the night the captain threatened your brother?"

"I went, I remember, to one or two of Pfyfe's parties," said the major. "I don't, as a rule, care for such gatherings, but Alvin convinced me it was a good business policy."

He lifted his head and frowned fixedly into space, like one searching for an elusive memory.

"However, I don't recall—By George! Yes, I believe I do. . . . But if the instance I am thinking of is what you have in mind, you can dismiss it. We were all a little moist that night."

"Did you see the gun?" pursued Heath.

The major pursed his lips. "Now that you mention it, I think he did make some motion of the kind."

"Did you see the gun?" pursued Heath.

"No, I can't say that I did."

Markham put the next question. "Do you think Captain Leacock capable of the act of murder?"

"Hardly," Major Benson answered with emphasis. "Leacock isn't cold-blooded. The woman over whom the tiff occurred is more capable of such an act than he is."

A short silence followed, broken by Vance.

"What do you know, Major, about this glass of fashion and mould of form, Pfyfe? He appears a rare bird. Has he a history, or is his presence his life's document?"

"Leander Pfyfe," said the major, "is a typical specimen of the modern young do-nothing—I say young, though I imagine he's around forty. He was pampered in his upbringing—had everything he wanted, I believe; but he became restless and followed several different fads till he tired of them. He was two years in South Africa hunting big game and, I think, wrote a book recounting his adventures. Since then he has done nothing that I know of. He married a wealthy shrew some years ago—for her money, I imagine. But the woman's father controls the purse strings and holds him down to a rigid allowance. . . . Pfyfe's a waster and an idler, but Alvin seemed to find some attraction in the man."

The major's words had been careless in inflection and undeliberated, like those of a man discussing a neutral matter; but all of us, I think, received the impression that he had a strong personal dislike for Pfyfe.

"Not a ravishing personality, what?" remarked Vance. "And he uses far too much Jicky."

"Still," supplied Heath, with a puzzled frown, "a fellow's got to have a lot of nerve to shoot big game. . . . And, speaking of nerve, I've been thinking that the guy who shot your brother, Major, was a mighty cool-headed proposition. He did it from the front when his man was wide awake and with a servant upstairs. That takes nerve."

"Sergeant, you're pos'tively brilliant!" exclaimed Vance.

CHAPTER 12

The Owner of a Colt .45

Monday, June 17; forenoon

Though Vance and I arrived at the district attorney's office the following morning a little after nine, the captain had been waiting twenty minutes; and Markham directed Swacker to send him in at once.

Captain Philip Leacock was a typical army officer, very tall—fully six feet, two inches—clean-shaven, straight, and slender. His face was grave and immobile; and he stood before the district attorney in the erect, earnest attitude of a soldier awaiting orders from his superior officer.

"Take a seat, Captain," said Markham, with a formal bow. "I have asked you here, as you probably know, to put a few questions to you concerning Mr. Alvin Benson. There are several points regarding your relationship with him which I want you to explain."

"Am I suspected of complicity in the crime?" Leacock spoke with a slight southern accent.

"That remains to be seen," Markham told him coldly. "It is to determine that point that I wish to question you."

The other sat rigidly in his chair and waited.

Markham fixed him with a direct gaze.

"You recently made a threat on Mr. Alvin Benson's life, I believe."

Leacock started, and his fingers tightened over his knees. But before he could answer, Markham continued: "I can tell you the occasion on which the threat was made—it was at a party given by Mr. Leander Pfyfe."

Leacock hesitated, then thrust forward his jaw. "Very well, sir; I admit I made the threat. Benson was a cad—he deserved shooting. . . . That night he had become more obnoxious than usual. He'd been drinking too much—and so had I, I reckon."

He gave a twisted smile and looked nervously past the district attorney out of the window.

"But I didn't shoot him, sir. I didn't even know he'd been shot until I read the paper next day."

"He was shot with an army Colt, the kind you fellows carried in the war," said Markham, keeping his eyes on the man.

"I know," Leacock replied. "The papers said so."

"You have such a gun, haven't you, Captain?"

Again the other hesitated. "No, sir." His voice was barely audible.

"What became of it?"

The man glanced at Markham and then quickly shifted his eyes. "I—I lost it . . . in France."

Markham smiled faintly.

"Then how do you account for the fact that Mr. Pfyfe saw the gun the night you made the threat?"

"Saw the gun?" He looked blankly at the district attorney.

"Yes, saw it and recognized it as an army gun," persisted Markham, in a level voice. "Also, Major Benson saw you make a motion as if to draw a gun."

Leacock drew a deep breath, and set his mouth doggedly.

"I tell you sir, I haven't a gun. . . . I lost it in France."

"Perhaps you didn't lose it, Captain. Perhaps you lent it to someone."

"I didn't sir!" the words burst from his lips.

"Think a minute, Captain. . . . Didn't you lend it to someone?"

"No—I did not!"

"You paid a visit—yesterday—to Riverside Drive. . . . Perhaps you took it there with you."

Vance had been listening closely. "Oh, deuced clever!" he now murmured in my ear.

Captain Leacock moved uneasily. His face, even with its deep coat of tan, seemed to pale, and he sought to avoid the implacable gaze of his questioner by concentrating his attention upon some object on the table. When he spoke his voice, heretofore truculent, was coloured by anxiety.

"I didn't have it with me. . . . And I didn't lend it to anyone."

Markham sat leaning forward over the desk, his chin on his hand, like a minatory graven image. "It may be you lent it to someone prior to that morning."

"Prior to . . . ?" Leacock looked up quickly and paused, as if analyzing the other's remark.

Markham took advantage of his perplexity.

"Have you lent your gun to anyone since you returned from France?"

"No, I've never lent it—" he began, but suddenly halted and flushed. Then he added hastily, "How could I lend it? I just told you, sir—"

"Never mind that!" Markham cut in. "So you had a gun, did you, Captain? . . . Have you still got it?"

Leacock opened his lips to speak but closed them again tightly.

Markham relaxed and leaned back in his chair.

"You were aware, of course, that Benson had been annoying Miss St. Clair with his attentions?"

At the mention of the girl's name the captain's body became rigid; his face turned a dull red, and he glared menacingly at the district attorney. At the end of a slow, deep inhalation he spoke through clenched teeth.

"Suppose we leave Miss St. Clair out of this." He looked as though he might spring at Markham.

"Unfortunately, we can't." Markham's words were sympathetic but firm. "Too many facts connect her with the case. Her handbag, for instance, was found in Benson's living room the morning after the murder."

"That's a lie, sir!"

Markham ignored the insult.

"Miss St. Clair herself admits the circumstance." He held up his hand, as the other was about to answer. "Don't misinterpret my mentioning the fact. I am not accusing Miss St. Clair of having anything to do with the affair. I'm merely endeavouring to get some light on your own connection with it."

The captain studied Markham with an expression that clearly indicated he doubted these assurances. Finally he set his mouth and announced with determination: "I haven't anything more to say on the subject, sir."

"You knew, didn't you," continued Markham, "that Miss St. Clair dined with Benson at the Marseilles on the night he was shot?"

"What of it?" retorted Leacock sullenly.

"And you knew, didn't you, that they left the restaurant at midnight, and that Miss St. Clair did not reach home until after one?"

A strange look came into the man's eyes. The ligaments of his neck tightened, and he took a deep, resolute breath. But he neither glanced at the district attorney nor spoke.

"You know, of course," pursued Markham's monotonous voice, "that Benson was shot at half past twelve?" He waited, and for a whole minute there was silence in the room.

"You have nothing more to say, Captain?" he asked at length; "no further explanations to give me?"

Leacock did not answer. He sat gazing imperturbably ahead of him; and it was evident he had sealed his lips for the time being.

Markham rose.

"In that case, let us consider the interview at an end."

The moment Captain Leacock had gone, Markham rang for one of his clerks.

"Tell Ben to have that man followed. Find out where he goes and what he does. I want a report at the Stuyvesant Club tonight."

When we were alone, Vance gave Markham a look of half-bantering admiration.

"Ingenious, not to say artful. . . . But, y'know, your questions about the lady were shocking bad form."

"No doubt," Markham agreed. "But it looks now as if we were on the right track. Leacock didn't create an impression of unassailable innocence."

"Didn't he?" asked Vance. "Just what were the signs of his assailable guilt?"

"You saw him turn white when I questioned him about the weapon. His nerves were on edge—he was genuinely frightened."

Vance sighed. "What a perfect ready-made set of notions you have, Markham! Don't you know that an innocent man, when he comes under suspicion, is apt to be more nervous than a guilty one, who, to begin with, had enough nerve to commit the crime and, secondly, realizes that any show of nervousness is regarded as guilt by you lawyer chaps? 'My strength is as the strength of ten because my heart is pure' is a mere Sunday school pleasantry. Touch almost any innocent man on the shoulder and say 'You're arrested,' and his pupils will dilate, he'll break out in a cold sweat, the blood will rush from his face, and he'll have tremors and *dyspnea*. If he's a *hystérique*, or a cardiac neurotic, he'll probably collapse completely. It's the guilty person who, when thus accosted, lifts his eyebrows in bored surprise and says, 'You don't mean it, really—here have a cigar.'"

"The hardened criminal may act as you say," Markham conceded; "but an honest man who's innocent doesn't go to pieces, even when accused."

Vance shook his head hopelessly. "My dear fellow, Crile and Voronoff might have lived in vain for all of you. Manifestations of fear are the result of glandular secretions—nothing more. All they prove is that the person's thyroid is undeveloped or that his adrenals are subnormal.

A man accused of a crime, or shown the bloody weapon with which it was committed, will either smile serenely, or scream, or have hysterics, or faint, or appear disint'rested according to his hormones and irrespective of his guilt. Your theory, d' ye see, would be quite all right if everyone had the same amount of the various internal secretions. But they haven't. . . . Really, y' know, you shouldn't send a man to the electric chair simply because he's deficient in endocrines. It isn't cricket."

Before Markham could reply, Swacker appeared at the door and said Heath had arrived.

The sergeant, beaming with satisfaction, fairly burst into the room. For once he forgot to shake hands. "Well, it looks like we've got hold of something workable. I went to this Captain Leacock's apartment house last night, and here's the straight of it:—Leacock was at home the night of the thirteenth all right; but shortly after midnight he went out, headed west—get that!—and he didn't return till about quarter of one!"

"What about the hall-boy's original story?" asked Markham.

"That's the best part of it. Leacock had the boy fixed. Gave him money to swear he hadn't left the house that night. What do you think of that, Mr. Markham? Pretty crude—huh? . . . The kid loosened up when I told him I was thinking of sending him up the river for doing the job himself." Heath laughed unpleasantly. "And he won't spill anything to Leacock, either."

Markham nodded his head slowly.

"What you tell me, Sergeant, bears out certain conclusions I arrived at when I talked to Captain Leacock this morning. Ben put a man on him when he left here, and I'm to get a report tonight. Tomorrow may see this thing through. I'll get in touch with you in the morning, and if anything's to be done, you understand, you'll have the handling of it."

When Heath had left us, Markham folded his hands behind his head and leaned back contentedly.

"I think I've got the answer," he said. "The girl dined with Benson and returned to his house afterward. The captain, suspecting the fact, went out, found her there, and shot Benson. That would account not only for her gloves and handbag but for the hour it took her to go from the Marseilles to her home. It would also account for her attitude here Saturday and for the captain's lying about the gun. . . . There. I believe, I have my case. The smashing of the captain's alibi about clinches it."

"Oh, quite," said Vance airily. "'Hope springs exulting on triumphant wing.'"

Markham regarded him a moment. "Have you entirely forsworn human reason as a means of reaching a decision? Here we have an admitted threat, a motive, the time, the place, the opportunity, the conduct, and the criminal agent."

"Those words sound strangely familiar," Vance smiled. "Didn't most of 'em fit the young lady also? . . . And you really haven't got the criminal agent, y'know. But it's no doubt floating about the city somewhere. A mere detail, however."

"I may not have it in my hand," Markham countered. "But with a good man on watch every minute, Leacock won't find much opportunity of disposing of the weapon."

Vance shrugged indifferently.

"In any event, go easy," he admonished. "My humble opinion is that you've merely unearthed a conspiracy."

"Conspiracy? . . . Good Lord! What kind?"

"A conspiracy of circumst'nces, don't y'know."

"I'm glad, at any rate, it hasn't to do with international politics," returned Markham good-naturedly.

He glanced at the clock. "You won't mind if I get to work? I've a dozen things to attend to and a couple of committees to see. . . . Why don't you go across the hall and have a talk with Ben Hanlon and then come back at twelve thirty? We'll have lunch together at the Bankers' Club. Ben's our greatest expert on foreign extradition and has spent most of his life chasing about the world after fugitives from justice. He'll spin you some good yarns."

"How perfectly fascinatin'!" exclaimed Vance, with a yawn. But instead of taking the suggestion, he walked to the window and lit a cigarette. He stood for a while puffing at it, rolling it between his fingers, and inspecting it critically.

"Y'know, Markham," he observed, "everything's going to pot these days. It's this silly democracy. Even the nobility is degen'rating. These Régie cigarettes, now; they've fallen off frightfully. There was a time when no self-respecting potentate would have smoked such inferior tobacco."

Markham smiled. "What's the favour you want to ask?"

"Favour? What has that to do with the decay of Europe's aristocracy?"

"I've noticed that whenever you want to ask a favour which you consider questionable etiquette, you begin with a denunciation of royalty."

"Observin' fella," commented Vance dryly. Then he, too, smiled. "Do you mind if I invite Colonel Ostrander along to lunch?"

Markham gave him a sharp look. "Bigsby Ostrander, you mean? . . . Is he the mysterious colonel you've been asking people about for the past two days?"

"That's the lad. Pompous ass and that sort of thing. Might prove a bit edifyin', though. He's the papa of Benson's crowd, so to speak; knows all parties. Regular old scandalmonger."

"Have him along, by all means," agreed Markham. Then he picked up the telephone. "Now I'm going to tell Ben you're coming over for an hour or so."

CHAPTER 13

The Gray Cadillac

Monday, June 17; 12:30 p.m.

When, at half past twelve, Markham, Vance, and I entered the Grill of the Bankers' Club in the Equitable Building, Colonel Ostrander was already at the bar engaged with one of Charlie's prohibition clam-broth-and-Worcestershire-sauce cocktails. Vance had telephoned him immediately upon our leaving the district attorney's office, requesting him to meet us at the club; and the colonel had seemed eager to comply.

"Here is New York's gayest dog," said Vance, introducing him to Markham (I had met him before); "a sybarite and a hedonist. He sleeps till noon, and makes no appointments before tiffin-time. I had to knock him up and threaten him with your official ire to get him downtown at this early hour."

"Only too pleased to be of any service," the colonel assured Markham grandiloquently. "Shocking affair! Gad! I couldn't credit it when I read it in the papers. Fact is, though—I don't mind sayin' it—I've one or two ideas on the subject. Came very near calling you up myself, sir."

When we had taken our seats at the table, Vance began interrogating him without preliminaries.

"You know all the people in Benson's set, Colonel. Tell us something about Captain Leacock. What sort of chap is he?"

"Ha! So you have your eye on the gallant captain?"

Colonel Ostrander pulled importantly at his white moustache. He was a large pink-faced man with bushy eyelashes and small blue eyes; and his manner and bearing were those of a pompous light-opera general.

"Not a bad idea. Might possibly have done it. Hot-headed fellow. He's badly smitten with a Miss St. Clair—fine girl, Muriel. And Benson was smitten, too. If I'd been twenty years younger myself—"

"You're too fascinatin' to the ladies, as it is, Colonel," interrupted Vance. "But tell us about the captain."

"Ah, yes—the captain. Comes from Georgia originally. Served in the war—some kind of decoration. He didn't care for Benson—disliked him, in fact. Quick-tempered, single-track-minded sort of person. Jealous, too. You know the type—a product of that tribal etiquette below the Mason and Dixon line. Puts women on a pedestal—not that they shouldn't be put there, God bless 'em! But he'd go to jail for a lady's honour. A shielder of womanhood. Sentimental cuss, full of chivalry; just the kind to blow out a rival's brains:—no questions asked—POP—and it's all over. Dangerous chap to monkey with. Benson was a confounded idiot to bother with the girl when he knew she was engaged to Leacock. Playin' with fire. I don't mind sayin' I was tempted to warn him. But it was none of my affair—I had no business interferin'. Bad taste."

"Just how well did Captain Leacock know Benson?" asked Vance. "By that I mean, how intimate were they?"

"Not intimate at all," the colonel replied.

He made a ponderous gesture of negation, and added, "I should say not! Formal, in fact. They met each other here and there a good deal, though. Knowing 'em both pretty well, I've often had 'em to little affairs at my humble diggin's."

"You wouldn't say Captain Leacock was a good gambler—level-headed and all that?"

"Gambler—huh!" The colonel's manner was heavily contemptuous. "Poorest I ever saw. Played poker worse than a woman. Too excitable—couldn't keep his feelin's to himself. Altogether too rash."

Then, after a momentary pause: "By George! I see what you're aimin' at. . . . And you're dead right. It's rash young puppies just like him that go about shootin' people they don't like."

"The captain, I take it, is quite different in that regard from your friend, Leander Pfyfe," remarked Vance.

The colonel appeared to consider. "Yes and no," he decided. "Pfyfe's a cool gambler—that I'll grant you. He once ran a private gambling place of his own down on Long Island—roulette, monte, baccarat, that sort of thing. And he popped tigers and wild boars in Africa for a while. But Pfyfe's got his sentimental side, and he'd plunge on a pair of deuces with all the betting odds against him. Not a good scientific gambler. Flighty in his impulses, if you understand me. I don't mind admittin', though, that he could shoot a man and forget all about it in five minutes. But he'd need a lot of provocation. . . . He may have had it—you can't tell."

120

"Pfyfe and Benson were rather intimate, weren't they?"

"Very—very. Always saw 'em together when Pfyfe was in New York. Known each other years. Boon companions, as they called 'em in the old days. Actually lived together before Pfyfe got married. An exacting woman, Pfyfe's wife; makes him toe the mark. But loads of money."

"Speaking of the ladies," said Vance, "what was the situation between Benson and Miss St. Clair?"

"Who can tell?" asked the colonel sententiously. "Muriel didn't cotton to Benson—that's sure. And yet . . . women are strange creatures—"

"Oh, no end strange," agreed Vance, a trifle wearily. "But really, y'know, I wasn't prying into the lady's personal relations with Benson. I thought you might know her mental attitude concerning him."

"Ah—I see. Would she, in short, have been likely to take desperate measures against him? . . . Egad! That's an idea!"

The colonel pondered the point.

"Muriel, now, is a girl of strong character. Works hard at her art. She's a singer and, I don't mind tellin' you, a mighty fine one. She's deep, too—deuced deep. And capable. Not afraid of taking a chance. Independent. I myself wouldn't want to be in her path if she had it in for me. Might stick at nothing."

He nodded his head sagely.

"Women are funny that way. Always surprisin' you. No sense of values. The most peaceful of 'em will shoot a man in cold blood without warnin'—"

He suddenly sat up, and his little blue eyes glistened like china. "By gad!" He fairly blurted the ejaculation. "Muriel had dinner alone with Benson the night he was shot—the very night. Saw 'em together myself at the Marseilles."

"You don't say, really!" muttered Vance incuriously. "But I suppose we all must eat. . . . By the bye, how well did you yourself know Benson?"

The colonel looked startled, but Vance's innocuous expression seemed to reassure him.

"I? My dear fellow! I've known Alvin Benson fifteen years. At least fifteen—maybe longer. Showed him the sights in this old town before the lid was put on. A live town it was then. Wide open. Anything you wanted. Gad—what times we had! Those were the days of the old Haymarket. Never thought of toddlin' home till breakfast—"

Vance again interrupted his irrelevancies.

"How intimate are your relations with Major Benson?"

"The major? . . . That's another matter. He and I belong to different schools. Dissimilar tastes. We never hit it off. Rarely see each other."

He seemed to think that some explanation was necessary, for before Vance could speak again, he nodded, "The major, you know, was never one of the boys, as we say. Disapproved of gaiety. Didn't mix with our little set. Considered me and Alvin too frivolous. Serious- minded chap."

Vance ate in silence for a while, then asked in an offhand way, "Did you do much speculating through Benson and Benson?"

For the first time the colonel appeared hesitant about answering. He ostentatiously wiped his mouth with his napkin.

"Oh—dabbled a bit," he at length admitted airily. "Not very lucky, though. . . . We all flirted now and then with the Goddess of Chance in Benson's office."

Throughout the lunch Vance kept plying him with questions along these lines; but at the end of an hour he seemed to be no nearer anything definite than when he began. Colonel Ostrander was voluble, but his fluency was vague and disorganized. He talked mainly in parentheses and insisted on elaborating his answers with rambling opinions, until it was almost impossible to extract what little information his words contained.

Vance, however, did not appear discouraged. He dwelt on Captain Leacock's character and seemed particularly interested in his personal relationship with Benson. Pfyfe's gambling proclivities also occupied his attention, and he let the colonel ramble on tiresomely about the man's gambling house on Long Island and his hunting experiences in South Africa. He asked numerous questions about Benson's other friends but paid scant attention to the answers.

The whole interview impressed me as pointless, and I could not help wondering what Vance hoped to learn. Markham, I was convinced, was equally at sea. He pretended polite interest and nodded appreciatively during the colonel's incredibly drawn-out periods; but his eyes wandered occasionally, and several times I saw him give Vance a look of reproachful inquiry. There was no doubt, however, that Colonel Ostrander knew his people.

When we were back in the district attorney's office, having taken leave of our garrulous guest at the subway entrance, Vance threw himself into one of the easy chairs with an air of satisfaction.

"Most entertainin', what? As an elim'nator of suspects the colonel has his good points."

"Eliminator!" retorted Markham. "It's a good thing he's not connected with the police; he'd have half the community jailed for shooting Benson."

"He *is* a bit bloodthirsty," Vance admitted. "He's determined to get somebody jailed for the crime."

"According to that old warrior, Benson's coterie was a *camorra* of gunmen—not forgetting the women. I couldn't help getting the impression, as he talked, that Benson was miraculously lucky not to have been riddled with bullets long ago."

"It's obvious," commented Vance, "that you overlooked the illuminatin' flashes in the colonel's thunder."

"Were there any?" Markham asked. "At any rate, I can't say that they exactly blinded me by their brilliance."

"And you received no solace from his words?"

"Only those in which he bade me a fond farewell. The parting didn't exactly break my heart. . . . What the old boy said about Leacock, however, might be called a confirmatory opinion. It verified—if verification had been necessary—the case against the captain."

Vance smiled cynically. "Oh, to be sure. And what he said about Miss St. Clair would have verified the case against her, too—last Saturday. Also, what he said about Pfyfe would have verified the case against that *beau sabreur*, if you had happened to suspect him—eh, what?"

Vance had scarcely finished speaking when Swacker came in to say that Emery from the homicide bureau had been sent over by Heath and wished, if possible, to see the district attorney.

When the man entered, I recognized him at once as the detective who had found the cigarette butts in Benson's grate.

With a quick glance at Vance and me, he went directly to Markham. "We've found the grey Cadillac, sir; and Sergeant Heath thought you might want to know about it right away. It's in a small, one-man garage on Seventy-fourth Street near Amsterdam Avenue, and has been there three days. One of the men from the Sixty-eighth Street station located it and phoned in to headquarters; and I hopped uptown at once. It's the right car—fishing tackle and all, except for the rods; so I guess the ones found in Central Park belonged to the car after all; fell out probably. . . . It seems a fellow drove the car into the garage about noon last Friday, and gave the garage- man twenty dollars to keep his mouth shut. The man's a wop and says he don't read the papers. Anyway, he came across pronto when I put the screws on."

The detective drew out a small notebook.

"I looked up the car's number. . . . It's listed in the name of Leander Pfyfe, 24 Elm Boulevard, Port Washington, Long Island."

Markham received this piece of unexpected information with

a perplexed frown. He dismissed Emery almost curtly and sat tapping thoughtfully on his desk.

Vance watched him with an amused smile.

"It's really not a madhouse, y'know," he observed comfortingly. "I say, don't the colonel's words bring you any cheer, now that you know Leander was hovering about the neighbourhood at the time Benson was translated into the Beyond?"

"Damn your old colonel!" snapped Markham. "What interests me at present is fitting this new development into the situation."

"It fits beautifully," Vance told him. "It rounds out the mosaic, so to speak. . . . Are you actu'lly disconcerted by learning that Pfyfe was the owner of the mysterious car?"

"Not having your gift of clairvoyance, I am, I confess, disturbed by the fact."

Markham lit a cigar—an indication of worry. "You, of course," he added, with sarcasm, "knew before Emery came here that it was Pfyfe's car."

"I didn't know," Vance corrected him; "but I had a strong suspicion. Pfyfe overdid his distress when he told us of his breakdown in the Catskills. And Heath's question about his itiner'ry annoyed him frightfully. His hauteur was too melodramatic."

"Your *ex post facto* wisdom is most useful!"

Markham smoked awhile in silence.

"I think I'll find out about this matter."

He rang for Swacker. "Call up the Ansonia," he ordered angrily; "locate Leander Pfyfe, and say I want to see him at the Stuyvesant Club at six o'clock. And tell him he's to be there."

"It occurs to me," said Markham, when Swacker had gone, "that this car episode may prove helpful, after all. Pfyfe was evidently in New York that night, and for some reason he didn't want it known. Why, I wonder? He tipped us off about Leacock's threat against Benson and hinted strongly that we'd better get on the fellow's track. Of course, he may have been sore at Leacock for winning Miss St. Clair away from his friend, and taken this means of wreaking a little revenge on him. On the other hand, if Pfyfe was at Benson's house the night of the murder, he may have some real information. And now that we've found out about the car, I think he'll tell us what he knows."

"He'll tell you something anyway," said Vance. "He's the type of congenital liar that'll tell anybody anything as long as it doesn't involve himself unpleasantly."

"You and the Cumean Sibyl, I presume, could inform me in advance what he's going to tell me."

"I couldn't say as to the Cumean Sibyl, don't y'know," Vance returned lightly; "but speaking for myself, I rather fancy he'll tell you that he saw the impetuous captain at Benson's house that night."

Markham laughed. "I hope he does. You'll want to be on hand to hear him, I suppose."

"I couldn't bear to miss it."

Vance was already at the door, preparatory to going, when he turned again to Markham. "I've another slight favour to ask. Get a dossier on Pfyfe—there's a good fellow. Send one of your innumerable Dogberrys to Port Washington and have the gentleman's conduct and social habits looked into. Tell your emiss'ry to concentrate on the woman question. . . . I promise you, you sha'n't regret it."

Markham, I could see, was decidedly puzzled by this request and half inclined to refuse it. But after deliberating a few moments, he smiled and pressed a button on his desk.

"Anything to humour you," he said. "I'll send a man down at once."

CHAPTER 14

Links in the Chain
Monday, June 17; 6 p.m.

Vance and I spent an hour or so that afternoon at the Anderson Galleries looking at some tapestries which were to be auctioned the next day, and afterward had tea at Sherry's. We were at the Stuyvesant Club a little before six. A few minutes later Markham and Pfyfe arrived; and we went at once into one of the conference rooms.

Pfyfe was as elegant and superior as at the first interview. He wore a rat-catcher suit and Newmarket gaiters of unbleached linen, and was redolent of perfume.

"An unexpected pleasure to see you gentlemen again so soon," he greeted us, like one conferring a blessing.

Markham was far from amiable, and gave him an almost brusque salutation. Vance had merely nodded, and now sat regarding Pfyfe drearily as if seeking to find some excuse for his existence but utterly unable to do so.

Markham went directly to the point. "I've found out, Mr. Pfyfe, that you placed your machine in a garage at noon on Friday and gave the man twenty dollars to say nothing about it."

Pfyfe looked up with a hurt look. "I've been deeply wronged," he complained sadly. "I gave the man fifty dollars."

"I am glad you admit the fact so readily," returned Markham. "You knew, by the newspapers, of course, that your machine was seen outside Benson's house the night he was shot."

"Why else should I have paid so liberally to have its presence in New York kept secret?" His tone indicated that he was pained at the other's obtuseness.

"In that case, why did you keep it in the city at all?" asked Markham. "You could have driven it back to Long Island."

Pfyfe shook his head sorrowfully, a look of commiseration in his eyes. Then he leaned forward with an air of benign patience:—he would be gentle with this dull-witted district attorney, like a fond teacher with a backward child, and would strive to lead him out of the tangle of his uncertainties.

"I am a married man, Mr. Markham." He pronounced the fact as if some special virtue attached to it. "I started on my trip for the Catskills Thursday after dinner, intending to stop a day in New York to make my *adieus* to someone residing here. I arrived quite late—after midnight—and decided to call on Alvin. But when I drove up, the house was dark. So, without even ringing the bell, I walked to Pietro's in Forty-third Street to get a nightcap,—I keep a bit of my own pinch-bottle Haig and Haig there—but, alas! the place was closed, and I strolled back to my car. . . . To think that while I was away poor Alvin was shot!"

He stopped and polished his eyeglass.

"The irony of it! . . . I didn't even guess that anything had happened to the dear fellow—how could I? I drove, all unsuspecting of the tragedy, to a Turkish bath and remained there the night. The next morning I read of the murder; and in the later editions I saw the mention of my car. It was then I became—shall I say worried? But no. *worried* is a misleading word. Let me say, rather, that I became aware of the false position I might be placed in if the car were traced to me. So I drove it to the garage and paid the man to say nothing of its whereabouts, lest its discovery confuse the issue of Alvin's death."

One might have thought, from his tone and the self-righteous way he looked at Markham, that he had bribed the garage man wholly out of consideration for the district attorney and the police.

"Why didn't you continue on your trip?" asked Markham. "That would have made the discovery of the car even less likely."

Pfyfe adopted an air of compassionate surprise.

"With my dearest friend foully murdered? How could one have the heart to seek diversion at such a sad moment? . . . I returned home and informed Mrs. Pfyfe that my car had broken down."

"You might have driven home in your car, it seems to me," observed Markham.

Pfyfe offered a look of infinite forbearance for the other's inspection and took a deep sigh, which conveyed the impression that, though he could not sharpen the world's perceptions, he at least could mourn for its deplorable lack of understanding.

"If I had been in the Catskills away from any source of information, where Mrs. Pfyfe believed me to be, how would I have heard of Alvin's death until, perhaps, days afterward? You see, unfortunately I had not mentioned to Mrs. Pfyfe that I was stopping over in New York. The truth is, Mr. Markham, I had reason for not wishing my wife to know I was in the city. Consequently, if I had driven back at once, she would, I regret to say, have suspected me of breaking my journey. I therefore pursued the course which seemed simplest."

Markham was becoming annoyed at the man's fluent hypocrisy. After a brief silence he asked abruptly, "Did the presence of your car at Benson's house that night have anything to do with your apparent desire to implicate Captain Leacock in the affair?"

Pfyfe lifted his eyebrows in pained astonishment and made a gesture of polite protestation.

"My dear sir!" His voice betokened profound resentment of the other's unjust imputation. "If yesterday you detected in my words an undercurrent of suspicion against Captain Leacock, I can account for it only by the fact that I actually saw the captain in front of Alvin's house when I drove up that night."

Markham shot a curious look at Vance, then said to Pfyfe, "You are sure you saw Leacock?"

"I saw him quite distinctly. And I would have mentioned the fact yesterday had it not involved the tacit confession of my own presence there."

"What if it had?" demanded Markham. "It was vital information, and I could have used it this morning. You were placing your comfort ahead of the legal demands of justice; and your attitude puts a very questionable aspect on your own alleged conduct that night."

"You are pleased to be severe, sir," said Pfyfe with self-pity. "But having placed myself in a false position, I must accept your criticism."

"Do you realize," Markham went on, "that many a district attorney, if he knew what I know about your movements and had been treated the way you've treated me, would arrest you on suspicion?"

"Then I can only say," was the suave response, "that I am most fortunate in my inquisitor."

Markham rose.

"That will be all for today, Mr. Pfyfe. But you are to remain in New York until I give you permission to return home. Otherwise, I will have you held as a material witness."

Pfyfe made a shocked gesture in deprecation of such acerbities and bade us a ceremonious good-afternoon.

When we were alone, Markham looked seriously at Vance. "Your prophecy was fulfilled, though I didn't dare hope for such luck. Pfyfe's evidence puts the final link in the chain against the captain."

Vance smoked languidly.

"I'll admit your theory of the crime is most satisfyin'. But alas! the psychological objection remains. Everything fits, with the one exception of the captain; and he doesn't fit at all. . . . Silly idea, I know. But he has no more business being cast as the murderer of Benson than the *bisonic* Tetrazzini had being cast as the phthisical Mimi."*

"In any other circumstances," Markham answered, "I might defer reverently to your charming theories. But with all the circumstantial and presumptive evidence I have against Leacock, it strikes my inferior legal mind as sheer nonsense to say, 'He just couldn't be guilty because his hair is parted in the middle and he tucks his napkin in his collar.' There's too much logic against it."

"I'll grant your logic is irrefutable—as all logic is, no doubt. You've prob'bly convinced many innocent persons by sheer reasoning that they were guilty."

Vance stretched himself wearily.

"What do you say to a light repast on the roof? The unutt'rable Pfyfe has tired me."

In the summer dining room on the roof of the Stuyvesant Club we found Major Benson sitting alone, and Markham asked him to join us.

"I have good news for you, Major," he said, when we had given our order. "I feel confident I have my man; everything points to him. Tomorrow will see the end, I hope."

The major gave Markham a questioning frown.

"I don't understand exactly. From what you told me the other day, I got the impression there was a woman involved."

Markham smiled awkwardly and avoided Vance's eyes. "A lot of water has run under the bridge since then," he said. "The woman I had in mind was eliminated as soon as we began to check up on her. But in the process I was led to the man. There's little doubt of his guilt. I felt pretty sure about it this morning, and just now I learned that he was seen by a credible witness in front of your brother's house within a few minutes of the time the shot was fired."

"Is there any objection to your telling me who it was?" The major was still frowning.

---

* Obviously a reference to Tetrazzini's performance in La Bohème at the Manhattan Opera House in 1908.

"None whatsoever. The whole city will probably know it tomorrow. . . . It was Captain Leacock."

Major Benson stared at him in unbelief. "Impossible! I simply can't credit it. That boy was with me three years on the other side, and I got to know him pretty well. I can't help feeling there's a mistake somewhere. . . . The police," he added quickly, "have got on the wrong track."

"It's not the police," Markham informed him. "It was my own investigations that turned up the captain."

The major did not answer, but his silence bespoke his doubt.

"Y' know," put in Vance, "I feel the same way about the captain that you do, Major. It rather pleases me to have my impressions verified by one who has known him so long."

"What, then, was Leacock doing in front of the house that night?" urged Markham acidulously.

"He might have been singing carols beneath Benson's window," suggested Vance.

Before Markham could reply, he was handed a card by the head-waiter. When he glanced at it, he gave a grunt of satisfaction and directed that the caller be sent up immediately. Then, turning back to us, he said, "We may learn something more now. I've been expecting this man Higginbotham. He's the detective that followed Leacock from my office this morning."

Higginbotham was a wiry, pale-faced youth with fishy eyes and a shifty manner. He slouched up to the table and stood hesitantly before the district attorney.

"Sit down and report, Higginbotham," Markham ordered. "These gentlemen are working with me on the case."

"I picked up the bird while he was waiting for the elevator," the man began, eyeing Markham craftily. "He went to the subway and rode uptown to Seventy-ninth and Broadway. He walked through Eightieth to Riverside Drive and went in the apartment-house at No. 94. Didn't give his name to the boy—got right in the elevator. He stayed upstairs a coupla hours, come down at one twenty, and hopped a taxi. I picked up another one and followed him. He went down the Drive to Seventy-second, through Central Park, and east on Fifty-ninth. Got out at Avenue A, and walked out on the Queensborough Bridge. About halfway to Blackwell's Island he stood leaning over the rail for five or six minutes. Then he took a small package out of his pocket and dropped it in the river."

"What size was the package?" There was repressed eagerness in Markham's question.

Higginbotham indicated the measurements with his hands.

"How thick was it?"

"Inch or so, maybe."

Markham leaned forward.

"Could it have been a gun—a Colt automatic?"

"Sure, it could. Just about the right size. And it was heavy, too—I could tell by the way he handled it, and the way it hit the water."

"All right." Markham was pleased. "Anything else?"

"No, sir. After he'd ditched the gun, he went home and stayed. I left him there."

When Higginbotham had gone, Markham nodded at Vance with melancholy elation.

"There's your criminal agent. . . . What more would you like?"

"Oh, lots," drawled Vance.

Major Benson looked up, perplexed.

"I don't quite grasp the situation. Why did Leacock have to go to Riverside Drive for his gun?"

"I have reason to think," said Markham, "that he took it to Miss St. Clair the day after the shooting—for safekeeping probably. He wouldn't have wanted it found in his place."

"Might he not have taken it to Miss St. Clair's before the shooting?"

"I know what you mean," Markham answered. (I, too, recalled the major's assertion the day before that Miss St. Clair was more capable of shooting his brother than was the captain.) "I had the same idea myself. But certain evidential facts have eliminated her as a suspect."

"You've undoubtedly satisfied yourself on the point," returned the major; but his tone was dubious. "However, I can't see Leacock as Alvin's murderer."

He paused and laid a hand on the district attorney's arm. "I don't want to appear presumptuous, or unappreciative of all you've done; but I really wish you'd wait a bit before clapping that boy into prison. The most careful and conscientious of us are liable to error. Even facts sometimes lie damnably; and I can't help believing that the facts in this instance have deceived you."

It was plain that Markham was touched by this request of his old friend; but his instinctive fidelity to duty helped him to resist the other's appeal.

"I must act according to my convictions, Major," he said firmly, but with a great kindness.

CHAPTER 15

"Pfyfe—Personal"

Tuesday, June 18; 9 a.m.

The next day—the fourth of the investigation—was an important and, in some ways, a momentous one in the solution of the problem posed by Alvin Benson's murder. Nothing of a definite nature came to light, but a new element was injected into the case; and this new element eventually led to the guilty person.

Before we parted from Markham after our dinner with Major Benson, Vance had made the request that he be permitted to call at the district attorney's office the next morning. Markham, both disconcerted and impressed by his unwonted earnestness, had complied; although, I think, he would rather have made his arrangements for Captain Leacock's arrest without the disturbing influence of the other's protesting presence. It was evident that, after Higginbotham's report, Markham had decided to place the captain in custody and to proceed with his preparation of data for the grand jury.

Although Vance and I arrived at the office at nine o'clock, Markham was already there. As we entered the room, he picked up the telephone receiver and asked to be put through to Sergeant Heath.

At that moment Vance did an amazing thing. He walked swiftly to the district attorney's desk and, snatching the receiver out of Markham's hand, clamped it down on the hook. Then he placed the telephone to one side and laid both hands on the other's shoulders.

Markham was too astonished and bewildered to protest; and before he could recover himself, Vance said in a low, firm voice, which was all the more impelling because of its softness, "I'm not going to let you jail Leacock—that's what I came here for this morning. You're not going to order his arrest as long as I'm in this office and can prevent it by any means whatever. There's only one way you can accomplish this act of unmitigated folly, and that's by summoning your policemen and having me forcibly ejected. And I advise you to call a goodly number of 'em, because I'll give 'em the battle of their bellicose lives!"

The incredible part of this threat was that Vance meant it literally. And Markham knew he meant it.

"If you do call your henchmen," he went on, "you'll be the laughing stock of the city inside of a week; for, by that time, it'll be known who really did shoot Benson. And I'll be a popular hero and a martyr—God save the mark!—for defying the district attorney and offering up my sweet freedom on the altar of truth and justice and that sort of thing. . . ."

The telephone rang, and Vance answered it.

"Not wanted," he said, closing off immediately. Then he stepped back and folded his arms.

At the end of the brief silence Markham spoke, his voice quavering with rage. "If you don't go at once, Vance, and let me run this office myself, I'll have no choice but to call in those policemen."

Vance smiled. He knew Markham would take no such extreme measures. After all, the issue between these two friends was an intellectual one; and though Vance's actions had placed it for a moment on a physical basis, there was no danger of its so continuing.

Markham's belligerent gaze slowly turned to one of profound perplexity. "Why are you so damned interested in Leacock?" he asked gruffly. "Why this irrational insistence that he remain at large?"

"You priceless, inexpressible ass!" Vance strove to keep all hint of affection out of his voice. "Do you think I care particularly what happens to a southern army captain? There are hundreds of Leacocks, all alike—with their square shoulders and square chins, and their knobby clothes, and their totemistic codes of barbaric chivalry. Only a mother could tell 'em apart. . . . I'm int'rested in *you*, old chap. I don't want to see you make a mistake that's going to injure you more than it will Leacock."

Markham's eyes lost their hardness; he understood Vance's motive and forgave him. But he was still firm in his belief of the captain's guilt. He remained thoughtful for some time. Then, having apparently arrived at a decision, he rang for Swacker and asked that Phelps be sent for.

"I've a plan that may nail this affair down tight," he said. "And it'll be evidence that not even you, Vance, can gainsay."

Phelps came in, and Markham gave him instructions.

"Go and see Miss St. Clair at once. Get to her some way, and ask her what was in the package Captain Leacock took away from her apartment yesterday and threw in the East River." He briefly summarized Higginbotham's report of the night before. "Demand that she tell you and intimate that you know it was the gun with which Benson was shot. She'll probably refuse to answer and will tell you to get out. Then go downstairs and wait developments. If she phones, listen in at the switchboard. If she happens to send a note to anyone, intercept it. And if she goes out—which I hardly think likely—follow her and learn what you can. Let me hear from you the minute you get hold of anything."

"I get you, Chief." Phelps seemed pleased with the assignment, and departed with alacrity.

"Are such burglarious and eavesdropping methods considered ethical by your learned profession?" asked Vance. "I can't harmonize such conduct with your other qualities, y'know."

Markham leaned back and gazed up at the chandelier. "Personal ethics don't enter into it. Or, if they do, they are crowded out by greater and graver considerations—by the higher demands of justice. Society must be protected; and the citizens of this county look to me for their security against the encroachments of criminals and evildoers. Sometimes, in the pursuance of my duty, it is necessary to adopt courses of conduct that conflict with my personal instincts. I have no right to jeopardize the whole of society because of an assumed ethical obligation to an individual. . . . You understand, of course, that I would not use any information obtained by these unethical methods, unless it pointed to criminal activities on the part of that individual. And in such case, I would have every right to use it, for the good of the community."

"I daresay you're right," yawned Vance. "But society doesn't int'rest me particularly. And I inf'nitely prefer good manners to righteousness."

As he finished speaking Swacker announced Major Benson, who wanted to see Markham at once.

The major was accompanied by a pretty young woman of about twenty-two with yellow bobbed hair, dressed daintily and simply in light blue *crêpe de Chine*. But for all her youthful and somewhat frivolous appearance, she possessed a reserve and competency of manner that immediately evoked one's confidence.

Major Benson introduced her as his secretary, and Markham placed a chair for her facing his desk.

"Miss Hoffman has just told me something that I think is vital for you to know," said the major; "and I brought her directly to you."

He seemed unusually serious, and his eyes held a look of expectancy coloured with doubt.

"Tell Mr. Markham exactly what you told me, Miss Hoffman."

The girl raised her head prettily and related her story in a capable, well-modulated voice.

"About a week ago—I think it was Wednesday—Mr. Pfyfe called on Mr. Alvin Benson in his private office. I was in the next room, where my typewriter is located. There's only a glass partition between the two rooms, and when anyone talks loudly in Mr. Benson's office, I can hear them. In about five minutes, Mr. Pfyfe and Mr. Benson began to quarrel. I thought it was funny, for they were such good friends; but I didn't pay much attention to it and went on with my typing. Their voices got very loud, though, and I caught several words. Major Benson asked me this morning what the words were; so I suppose you want to know, too. Well, they kept referring to a note; and once or twice a check was mentioned. Several times I caught the word father-in-law, and once Mr. Benson said 'nothing doing.' . . . Then Mr. Benson called me in and told me to get him an envelope marked 'Pfyfe-Personal' out of his private drawer in the safe. I got it for him, but right after that our bookkeeper wanted me for something, so I didn't hear any more. About fifteen minutes later, when Mr. Pfyfe had gone, Mr. Benson called me to put the envelope back. And he told me that if Mr. Pfyfe ever called again, I wasn't, under any circumstances, to let him into the private office unless he himself was there. He also told me that I wasn't to give the envelope to anybody—not even on a written order. . . . And that is all, Mr. Markham."

During her recital I had been as much interested in Vance's actions as in what she had been saying. When first she had entered the room, his casual glance had quickly changed to one of attentive animation, and he had studied her closely. When Markham had placed the chair for her, he had risen and reached for a book lying on the table near her; and, in doing so, he had leaned unnecessarily close to her in order to inspect—or so it appeared to me—the side of her head. And during her story he had continued his observation, at times bending slightly to the right or left to better his view of her. Unaccountable as his actions had seemed, I knew that some serious consideration had prompted the scrutiny.

When she finished speaking, Major Benson reached in his pocket, and tossed a long manila envelope on the desk before Markham.

"Here it is," he said. "I got Miss Hoffman to bring it to me the moment she told me her story."

Markham picked it up hesitantly, as if doubtful of his right to inspect its contents.

"You'd better look at it," the major advised. "That envelope may very possibly have an important bearing on the case."

Markham removed the elastic band and spread the contents of the envelope before him. They consisted of three items—a cancelled check for $10,000 made out to Leander Pfyfe and signed by Alvin Benson; a note for $10,000 to Alvin Benson signed by Pfyfe, and a brief confession, also signed by Pfyfe, saying the check was a forgery. The check was dated March 20th of the current year. The confession and the note were dated two days later. The note—which was for ninety days—fell due on Friday, June 21st, only three days off.

For fully five minutes Markham studied these documents in silence. Their sudden introduction into the case seemed to mystify him. Nor had any of the perplexity left his face when he finally put them back in the envelope.

He questioned the girl carefully and had her repeat certain parts of her story. But nothing more could be learned from her; and at length he turned to the major.

"I'll keep this envelope awhile, if you'll let me. I don't see its significance at present, but I'd like to think it over."

When Major Benson and his secretary had gone, Vance rose and extended his legs.

"À la fin!" he murmured. "'All things journey: sun and moon, morning, noon, and afternoon, night and all her stars.' Videlicet: we begin to make progress.

"What the devil are you driving at?" The new complication of Pfyfe's peccadilloes had left Markham irritable.

"Int'restin' young woman, this Miss Hoffman—eh, what?" Vance rejoined irrelevantly. "Didn't care especially for the deceased Benson. And she fairly detests the aromatic Leander. He has prob'bly told her he was misunderstood by Mrs. Pfyfe and invited her to dinner."

"Well, she's pretty enough," commented Markham indifferently. "Benson, too, may have made advances—which is why she disliked him."

"Oh, absolutely." Vance mused a moment. "Pretty—yes; but misleadin'. She's an ambitious gel and capable, too—knows her business. She's no ball of fluff. She has a solid, honest streak in her—a bit of Teutonic blood, I'd say." He paused meditatively. "Y' know, Markham, I have a suspicion you'll hear from little Miss Katinka again."

"Crystal-gazing, eh?" mumbled Markham.

"Oh, dear no!" Vance was looking lazily out of the window. "But I did enter the silence, so to speak, and indulged in a bit of craniological contemplation."

"I thought I noticed you ogling the girl," said Markham. "But since her hair was bobbed and she had her hat on, how could you analyze the bumps?—if that's the phrase you phrenologists use."

"Forget not Goldsmith's preacher," Vance admonished. "Truth from his lips prevailed, and those who came to scoff remained *et cetera*. . . . To begin with, I'm no phrenologist. But I believe in epochal, racial, and heredit'ry variations in skulls. In that respect I'm merely an old-fashioned Darwinian. Every child knows that the skull of the Piltdown man differs from that of the Cromagnard; and even a lawyer could distinguish an Aryan head from a Ural-Altaic head, or a Maylaic from a Negrillo. And, if one is versed at all in the Mendelian theory, heredit'ry cranial similarities can be detected. . . . But all this erudition is beyond you, I fear. Suffice it to say that, despite the young woman's hat and hair, I could see the contour of her head and the bone structure in her face; and I even caught a glimpse of her ear."

"And thereby deduced that we'd hear from her again," added Markham scornfully.

"Indirectly—yes," admitted Vance. Then, after a pause: "I say, in view of Miss Hoffman's revelation, do not Colonel Ostrander's comments of yesterday begin to take on a phosph'rescent aspect?"

"Look here!" said Markham impatiently. "Cut out these circumlocutions and get to the point."

Vance turned slowly from the window and regarded him pensively. "Markham—I put the question academically—doesn't Pfyfe's forged check, with its accompanying confession and its shortly due note, constitute a rather strong motive for doing away with Benson?"

Markham sat up suddenly. "You think Pfyfe guilty—is that it?"

"Well, here's the touchin' situation: Pfyfe obviously signed Benson's name to a check, told him about it, and got the surprise of his life when his dear old pal asked him for a ninety-day note to cover the amount and also for a written confession to hold over him to insure payment. . . . Now consider the subs'quent facts:—First, Pfyfe called on Benson a week ago and had a quarrel in which the check was mentioned—Damon was prob'bly pleading with Pythias to extend the note and was vulgarly informed that there was 'nothing doing.' Secondly, Benson was shot two days later, less than a week before the note fell due. Thirdly, Pfyfe was at Benson's house the hour of the shooting, and not only lied to you about his whereabouts but bribed a garage owner to keep silent about his car. Fourthly, his explanation, when caught, of his unrewarded search for Haig and Haig was, to say the least, a bit thick. And don't forget that the original tale of his lonely quest for nature's solitudes in the Catskills—with his mysterious stopover in New York to confer a farewell benediction upon some anonymous person—was not all that one could have hoped for in the line of plausibility. Fifthly, he is an impulsive gambler, given to taking chances; and his experiences in South Africa would certainly have familiarized him with firearms. Sixthly, he was rather eager to involve Leacock and did a bit of caddish tale bearing to that end, even informing you that he saw the captain on the spot at the fatal moment. Seventhly—but why bore you? Have I not supplied you with all the factors you hold so dear—what are they now?—motive, time, place, opportunity, conduct? All that's wanting is the criminal agent. But then, the captain's gun is at the bottom of the East River; so you're not very much better off in his case, what?"

Markham had listened attentively to Vance's summary. He now sat in rapt silence gazing down at the desk.

"How about a little chat with Pfyfe before you make any final move against the captain?" suggested Vance.

"I think I'll take your advice," answered Markham slowly, after several minutes' reflection. Then he picked up the telephone. "I wonder if he's at his hotel now."

"Oh, he's there," said Vance. "Watchful waitin' and all that."

Pfyfe was in; and Markham requested him to come at once to the office.

"There's another thing I wish you'd do for me," said Vance, when the other had finished telephoning. "The fact is, I'm longing to know what everyone was doing during the hour of Benson's dissolution— that is, between midnight and one a.m. on the night of the thirteenth, or to speak pedantically, the morning of the fourteenth."

Markham looked at him in amazement.

"Seems silly, doesn't it?" Vance went on blithely. "But you put such faith in alibis—though they do prove disappointin' at times, what? There's Leacock, for instance. If that hall-boy had told Heath to toddle along and sell his violets, you couldn't do a blessed thing to the captain. Which shows, d' ye see, that you're too trustin'. . . . Why not find out where everyone was? Pfyfe and the captain were at Benson's; and they're about the only ones whose whereabouts you've looked into. Maybe there were others hovering around Alvin that night. There may have been a crush of friends and acquaintances on hand—a regular soiree, y'know. . . . Then again, checking up on all these people will supply the desolate sergeant with something to take his mind off his sorrows."

Markham knew, as well as I, that Vance would not have made a suggestion of this kind unless actuated by some serious motive; and for several moments he studied the other's face intently, as if trying to read his reason for this unexpected request.

"Who, specifically," he asked, "is included in your 'everyone'?" He took up his pencil and held it poised above a sheet of paper.

"No one is to be left out," replied Vance. "Put down Miss St. Clair—Captain Leacock—the Major—Pfyfe—Miss Hoffman—"

"Miss Hoffman!"

"Everyone! . . . Have you Miss Hoffman? Now jot down Colonel Ostrander—"

"Look here!" cut in Markham.

"—and I may have one or two others for you later. But that will do nicely for a beginning."

Before Markham could protest further, Swacker came in to say that Heath was waiting outside.

"What about our friend Leacock, sir?" was the sergeant's first question.

"I'm holding that up for a day or so," explained Markham. "I want to have another talk with Pfyfe before I do anything definite." And he told Heath about the visit of Major Benson and Miss Hoffman.

Heath inspected the envelope and its enclosures and then handed them back.

"I don't see anything in that," he said. "It looks to me like a private deal between Benson and this fellow Pfyfe. Leacock's our man; and the sooner I get him locked up, the better I'll feel."

"That may be tomorrow," Markham encouraged him. "So don't feel downcast over this little delay. . . . You're keeping the captain under surveillance, aren't you?"

"I'll say so," grinned Heath.

Vance turned to Markham. "What about that list of names you made out for the sergeant?" he asked ingenuously. "I understood you to say something about alibis."

Markham hesitated, frowning. Then he handed Heath the paper containing the names Vance had called off to him. "As a matter of caution, Sergeant," he said morosely, "I wish you'd get me the alibis of all these people on the night of the murder. It may bring something contributory to light. Verify those you already know, such as Pfyfe's; and let me have the reports as soon as you can."

When Heath had gone, Markham turned a look of angry exasperation upon Vance.

"Of all the confounded troublemakers—" he began.

But Vance interrupted him blandly.

"Such ingratitude! If only you knew it, Markham, I'm your tutelary genius, your *deus ex machina*, your fairy godmother."

CHAPTER 16

Admissions and Suppressions
Tuesday, June 18; afternoon

An hour later Phelps, the operative Markham had sent to 94 Riverside Drive, came in radiating satisfaction.

"I think I've got what you want, Chief." His raucous voice was covertly triumphant. "I went up to the St. Clair woman's apartment and rang the bell. She came to the door herself, and I stepped into the hall and put my questions to her. She sure refused to answer. When I let on I knew the package contained the gun Benson was shot with, she just laughed and jerked the door open. 'Leave this apartment, you vile creature,' she says to me."

He grinned.

"I hurried downstairs, and I hadn't any more than got to the switchboard when her signal flashed. I let the boy get the number and then I stood him to one side and listened in. . . . She was talking to Leacock, and her first words were: 'They know you took the pistol from here yesterday and threw it in the river.' That must've knocked him out, for he didn't say anything for a long time. Then he answered, perfectly calm and kinda sweet: 'Don't worry, Muriel; and don't say a word to anybody for the rest of the day. I'll fix everything in the morning.' He made her promise to keep quiet until tomorrow, and then he said good-bye."

Markham sat awhile digesting the story.

"What impression did you get from the conversation?"

"If you ask me, Chief," said the detective, "I'd lay ten to one that Leacock's guilty and the girl knows it."

Markham thanked him and let him go.

"This sub-Potomac chivalry," commented Vance, "is a frightful nuisance. . . . But aren't we about due to hold polite converse with the genteel Leander?"

Almost as he spoke the man was announced. He entered the room with his habitual urbanity of manner, but for all his suavity, he could not wholly disguise his uneasiness of mind.

"Sit down, Mr. Pfyfe," directed Markham brusquely. "It seems you have a little more explaining to do."

Taking out the manila envelope, he laid its contents on the desk where the other could see them.

"Will you be so good as to tell me about these?"

"With the greatest pleasure," said Pfyfe; but his voice had lost its assurance. Some of his poise, too, had deserted him, and as he paused to light a cigarette I detected a slight nervousness in the way he manipulated his gold match safe.

"I really should have mentioned these before," he confessed, indicating the papers with a delicately inconsequential wave of the hand.

He leaned forward on one elbow, taking a confidential attitude, and as he talked, the cigarette bobbed up and down between his lips.

"It pains me deeply to go into this matter," he began; "but since it is in the interests of truth, I shall not complain.... My—ah—domestic arrangements are not all that one could desire. My wife's father has, curiously enough, taken a most unreasonable dislike to me; and it pleases him to deprive me of all but the meagrest financial assistance, although it is really my wife's money that he refuses to give me. A few months ago I made use of certain funds—ten thousand dollars, to be exact—which, I learned later, had not been intended for me. When my father-in-law discovered my error, it was necessary for me to return the full amount to avoid a misunderstanding between Mrs. Pfyfe and myself—a misunderstanding which might have caused my wife great unhappiness. I regret to say, I used Alvin's name on a check. But I explained it to him at once, you understand, offering him the note and this little confession as evidence of my good faith.... And that is all, Mr. Markham."

"Was that what your quarrel with him last week was about?"

Pfyfe gave him a look of querulous surprise. "Ah, you heard of our little contretemps? ... Yes—we had a slight disagreement as to the—shall I say terms of the transaction?"

"Did Benson insist that the note be paid when due?"

"No—not exactly." Pfyfe's manner became unctuous. "I beg of you, sir, not to press me as to my little chat with Alvin. It was, I assure you, quite irrelevant to the present situation. Indeed, it was of a most personal and private nature." He smiled confidingly. "I will admit, however, that I went to Alvin's house the night he was shot, intending to speak to him about the check; but, as you already know, I found the house dark and spent the night in a Turkish bath."

"Pardon me, Mr. Pfyfe"—it was Vance who spoke—"but did Mr. Benson take your note without security?"

"Of course!" Pfyfe's tone was a rebuke. "Alvin and I, as I have explained, were the closest friends."

"But even a friend, don't y'know," Vance submitted, "might ask for security on such a large amount. How did Benson know that you'd be able to repay him?"

"I can only say that he did know," the other answered, with an air of patient deliberation.

Vance continued to be doubtful. "Perhaps it was because of the confession you had given him."

Pfyfe rewarded him with a look of beaming approval. "You grasp the situation perfectly," he said.

Vance withdrew from the conversation, and though Markham questioned Pfyfe for nearly half an hour, nothing further transpired. Pfyfe clung to his story in every detail and politely refused to go deeper into his quarrel with Benson, insisting that it had no bearing on the case. At last he was permitted to go.

"Not very helpful," Markham observed. "I'm beginning to agree with Heath that we've turned up a mare's nest in Pfyfe's frenzied financial deal."

"You'll never be anything but your own sweet trusting self, will you?" lamented Vance sadly. "Pfyfe has just given you your first intelligent line of investigation, and you say he's not helpful! . . . Listen to me and *nota bene*. Pfyfe's story about the ten thousand dollars is undoubtedly true; he appropriated the money and forged Benson's name to a check with which to replace it. But I don't for a second believe there was no security in addition to the confession. Benson wasn't the type of man—friend or no friend—who'd hand over that amount without security. He wanted his money back, not somebody in jail. That's why I put my oar in and asked about the security. Pfyfe, of course, denied it; but when pressed as to how Benson knew he'd pay the note, he retired into a cloud. I had to suggest the confession as the possible explanation; which showed that something else was in his mind—something he didn't care to mention. And the way he jumped at my suggestion bears out my theory."

"Well, what of it?" Markham asked impatiently.

"Oh, for the gift of tears!" moaned Vance. "Don't you see that there's someone in the background—someone connected with the security? It must be so, y'know; otherwise Pfyfe would have told you the entire tale of the quarrel, if only to clear himself from suspicion. Yet, knowing that his position is an awkward one, he refused to divulge what passed between him and Benson in the office that day.... Pfyfe is shielding someone—and he is not the soul of chivalry, y'know. Therefore, I ask: Why?"

He leaned back and gazed at the ceiling.

"I have an idea, amounting to a cerebral cyclone," he added, "that when we put our hands on that security, we'll also put our hands on the murderer."

At this moment the telephone rang, and when Markham answered it, a look of startled amusement came into his eyes. He made an appointment with the speaker for half past five that afternoon. Then, hanging up the receiver, he laughed outright at Vance.

"Your auricular researches have been confirmed," he said. "Miss Hoffman just called me confidentially on an outside phone to say she has something to add to her story. She's coming here at five thirty."

Vance was unimpressed by the announcement. "I rather imagined she'd telephone during her lunch hour."

Again Markham gave him one of his searching scrutinies. "There's something damned queer going on around here," he observed.

"Oh, quite," returned Vance carelessly. "Queerer than you could possibly imagine."

For fifteen or twenty minutes Markham endeavoured to draw him out; but Vance seemed suddenly possessed of an ability to say nothing with the blandest fluency. Markham finally became exasperated.

"I'm rapidly coming to the conclusion," he said, "that either you had a hand in Benson's murder or you're a phenomenally good guesser."

"There is, y'know, an alternative," rejoined Vance. "It might be that my aesthetic hypotheses and metaphysical deductions, as you call 'em, are working out—eh, what?"

A few minutes before we went to lunch, Swacker announced that Tracy had just returned from Long Island with his report.

"Is he the lad you sent to look into Pfyfe's *affaires du cover*?" Vance asked Markham. "For, if he is, I am all a-flutter."

"He's the man.... Send him in, Swacker."

Tracy entered smiling silkily, his black notebook in one hand, his pince nez in the other.

"I had no trouble learning about Pfyfe," he said. "He's well known in Port Washington—quite a character, in fact—and it was easy to pick up gossip about him."

He adjusted his glasses carefully and referred to his notebook. "He married a Miss Hawthorn in nineteen ten. She's wealthy, but Pfyfe doesn't benefit much by it, because her father sits on the moneybags—"

"Mr. Tracy, I say," interrupted Vance; "never mind the née-Hawthorn and her doting papa—Mr. Pfyfe himself has confided in us about his sad marriage. Tell us, if you can, about Mr. Pfyfe's extra-nuptial affairs. Are there any other ladies?"

Tracy looked inquiringly at the district attorney; he was uncertain as to Vance's *locus standi*. Receiving a nod from Markham, he turned a page in his notebook and proceeded.

"I found one other woman in the case. She lives in New York and often telephones to a drugstore near Pfyfe's house and leaves messages for him. He uses the same phone to call her by. He had made some deal with the proprietor, of course; but I was able to obtain her phone number. As soon as I came back to the city, I got her name and address from Information and made a few inquiries. . . . She's a Mrs. Paula Banning, a widow, and a little fast, I should say; and she lives in an apartment at 268 West Seventy-fifth Street."

This exhausted Tracy's information; and when he went out, Markham smiled broadly at Vance.

"He didn't supply you with very much fuel."

"My word! I think he did unbelievably well," said Vance. "He unearthed the very information we wanted."

"*We* wanted?" echoed Markham. "I have more important things to think about than Pfyfe's amours."

"And yet, y'know, this particular amour of Pfyfe's is going to solve the problem of Benson's murder," replied Vance; and would say no more.

Markham, who had an accumulation of other work awaiting him and numerous appointments for the afternoon, decided to have his lunch served in the office; so Vance and I took leave of him.

We lunched at the Élysée, dropped in at Knoedler's to see an exhibition of French Pointillism, and then went to Aeolian Hall, where a string quartet from San Francisco was giving a program of Mozart. A little before half past five we were again at the district attorney's office, which at that hour was deserted except for Markham.

Shortly after our arrival Miss Hoffman came in and told the rest of her story in direct, businesslike fashion.

"I didn't give you all the particulars this morning," she said; "and I wouldn't care to do so now unless you are willing to regard them as confidential, for my telling you might cost me my position."

"I promise you," Markham assured her, "that I will entirely respect your confidence."

She hesitated a moment and then continued. "When I told Major Benson this morning about Mr. Pfyfe and his brother, he said at once that I should come with him to your office and tell you also. But on the way over, he suggested that I might omit a part of the story. He didn't exactly tell me not to mention it; but he explained that it had nothing to do with the case and might only confuse you. I followed his suggestion; but after I got back to the office, I began thinking it over, and knowing how serious a matter Mr. Benson's death was, I decided to tell you anyway. In case it did have some bearing on the situation, I didn't want to be in the position of having withheld anything from you."

She seemed a little uncertain as to the wisdom of her decision.

"I do hope I haven't been foolish. But the truth is, there was something else besides that envelope which Mr. Benson asked me to bring him from the safe the day he and Mr. Pfyfe had their quarrel. It was a square, heavy package, and, like the envelope, was marked 'Pfyfe-Personal.' And it was over this package that Mr. Benson and Mr. Pfyfe seemed to be quarrelling."

"Was it in the safe this morning when you went to get the envelope for the major?" asked Vance.

"Oh, no. After Mr. Pfyfe left last week, I put the package back in the safe along with the envelope. But Mr. Benson took it home with him last Thursday—the day he was killed."

Markham was but mildly interested in the recital and was about to bring the Interview to a close when Vance spoke up.

"It was very good of you, Miss Hoffman, to take this trouble to tell us about the package; and now that you are here, there are one or two questions I'd like to ask. . . . How did Mr. Alvin Benson and the major get along together?"

She looked at Vance with a curious little smile.

"They didn't get along very well," she said. "They were so different. Mr. Alvin Benson was not a very pleasant person, and not very honourable, I'm afraid. You'd never have thought they were brothers. They were constantly disputing about the business; and they were terribly suspicious of each other."

"That's not unnatural," commented Vance, "seeing how incompatible their temp'raments were. . . . By the bye, how did this suspicion show itself?"

"Well, for one thing, they sometimes spied on each other. You

146

see, their offices were adjoining, and they would listen to each other through the door. I did the secretarial work for both of them, and I often saw them listening. Several times they tried to find out things from me about each other."

Vance smiled at her appreciatively.

"Not a pleasant position for you."

"Oh, I didn't mind it." She smiled back. "It amused me."

"When was the last time you caught either one of them listening?" he asked.

The girl quickly became serious. "The very last day Mr. Alvin Benson was alive, I saw the major standing by the door. Mr. Benson had a caller—a lady—and the major seemed very much interested. It was in the afternoon. Mr. Benson went home early that day—only about half an hour after the lady had gone. She called at the office again later, but he wasn't there, of course, and I told her he had already gone home."

"Do you know who the lady was?" Vance asked her.

"No, I don't," she said. "She didn't give her name."

Vance asked a few other questions, after which we rode uptown in the subway with Miss Hoffman, taking leave of her at Twenty-third Street.

Markham was silent and preoccupied during the trip. Nor did Vance make any comment until we were comfortably relaxed in the easy chairs of the Stuyvesant Club's lounge room. Then, lighting a cigarette lazily, he said, "You grasp the subtle mental processes leading up to my prophecy about Miss Hoffman's second coming—eh, what, Markham? Y'see, I knew friend Alvin had not paid that forged check without security, and I also knew that the tiff must have been about the security, for Pfyfe was not really worrying about being jailed by his alter ego. I rather suspect Pfyfe was trying to get the security back before paying off the note and was told there was 'nothing doing.' . . . Moreover, Little Goldilocks may be a nice girl and all that; but it isn't in the feminine temp'rament to sit next door to an altercation between two such rakes and not listen attentively. I shouldn't care, y'know, to have to decipher the typing she said she did during the episode. I was quite sure she heard more than she told; and I asked myself: Why this curtailment? The only logical answer was: Because the major had suggested it. And since the *gnädiges Fräulein* was a forthright Germanic soul, with an inbred streak of selfish and cautious honesty, I ventured the prognostication that as soon as she was out from under the benev'lent jurisdiction of her tutor, she would tell us the rest in order to save her own skin if the matter should come up later. . . . Not so cryptic when explained, what?"

"That's all very well," conceded Markham petulantly. "But where does it get us?"

"I shouldn't say that the forward movement was entirely imperceptible."

Vance smoked awhile impassively. "You realize, I trust," he said, "that the mysterious package contained the security."

"One might form such a conclusion," agreed Markham. "But the fact doesn't dumbfound me—if that's what you're hoping for."

"And, of course," pursued Vance easily, "your legal mind, trained in the technique of ratiocination, has already identified it as the box of jewels that Mrs. Platz espied on Benson's table that fatal afternoon."

Markham sat up suddenly, then sank back with a shrug.

"Even if it was," he said, "I don't see how that helps us. Unless the major knew the package had nothing to do with the case, he would not have suggested to his secretary that she omit telling us about it."

"Ah! But if the major knew that the package was an irrelevant item in the case, then he must also know something about the case—eh, what? Otherwise, he couldn't determine what was, and what was not, irrelevant. . . . I have felt all along that he knew more than he admitted. Don't forget that he put us on the track of Pfyfe, and also that he was quite pos'tive Captain Leacock was innocent."

Markham thought for several minutes.

"I'm beginning to see what you're driving at," he remarked slowly. "Those jewels, after all, may have an important bearing on the case. . . . I think I'll have a chat with the major about things."

Shortly after dinner at the club that night Major Benson came into the lounge room where we had retired for our smoke; and Markham accosted him at once.

"Major, aren't you willing to help me a little more in getting at the truth about your brother's death?" he asked.

The other gazed at him searchingly; the inflection of Markham's voice belied the apparent casualness of the question.

"God knows it's not my wish to put obstacles in your way," he said, carefully weighing each word. "I'd gladly give you any help I could. But there are one or two things I cannot tell you at this time. . . . If there was only myself to be considered," he added, "it would be different."

"But you do suspect someone?" Vance put the question.

"In a way—yes. I overheard a conversation in Alvin's office one day that took on added significance after his death."

"You shouldn't let chivalry stand in the way," urged Markham. "If your suspicion is unfounded, the truth will surely come out."

"But when I don't *know*, I certainly ought not to hazard a guess," affirmed the major. "I think it best that you solve this problem without me."

Despite Markham's importunities, he would say no more; and shortly afterward he excused himself and went out.

Markham, now profoundly worried, sat smoking restlessly, tapping the arm of his chair with his fingers.

"Well, old bean, a bit involved, what?" commented Vance.

"It's not so damned funny," Markham grumbled. "Everyone seems to know more about the case than the police or the district attorney's office."

"Which wouldn't be so disconcertin' if they all weren't so deuced reticent," supplemented Vance cheerfully. "And the touchin' part of it is that each of 'em appears to be keeping still in order to shield someone else. Mrs. Platz began it; she lied about Benson's having any callers that afternoon because she didn't want to involve his tea companion. Miss St. Clair declined point-blank to tell you anything because she obviously didn't desire to cast suspicion on another. The captain became voiceless the moment you suggested his affianced bride was entangled. Even Leander refused to extricate himself from a delicate situation lest he implicate another. And now the major! . . . Most annoyin'. On the other hand, don't y'know, it's comfortin'—not to say upliftin'—to be dealing exclusively with such noble, self-sacrificin' souls."

"Hell!" Markham put down his cigar and rose. "The case is getting on my nerves. I'm going to sleep on it and tackle it in the morning."

"That ancient idea of sleeping on a problem is a fallacy," said Vance, as we walked out into Madison Avenue, "—an apologia, as it were, for one's not being able to think clearly. Poetic idea, y'know. All poets believe in it—nature's soft nurse, the balm of woe, childhood's *mandragora*, tired nature's sweet restorer, and that sort of thing. Silly notion. When the brain is keyed up and alive, it works far better than when apathetic from the torpor of sleep. Slumber is an anodyne—not a stimulus."

"Well, you sit up and think," was Markham's surly advice.

"That's what I'm going to do," blithely returned Vance; "but not about the Benson case. I did all the thinking I'm going to do along that line four days ago."

CHAPTER 17

The Forged Cheque
Wednesday, June 19; forenoon

We rode downtown with Markham the next morning, and though we arrived at his office before nine o'clock, Heath was already there waiting. He appeared worried, and when he spoke, his voice held an ill-disguised reproof for the district attorney.

"What about this Leacock, Mr. Markham?" he asked. "It looks to me like we'd better grab him quick. We've been tailing him right along; and there's something funny going on. Yesterday morning he went to his bank and spent half an hour in the chief cashier's office. After that he visited his lawyer's and was there over an hour. Then he went back to the bank for another half hour. He dropped in to the Astor Grill for lunch but didn't eat anything—sat staring at the table. About two o'clock he called on the realty agents who have the handling of the building he lives in; and after he'd left, we found out he'd offered his apartment for sublease beginning tomorrow. Then he paid six calls on friends of his and went home. After dinner my man rang his apartment bell and asked for Mr. Hoozitz;—Leacock was packing up! . . . It looks to me like a getaway."

Markham frowned. Heath's report clearly troubled him; but before he could answer, Vance spoke. "Why this perturbation, Sergeant? You're watching the captain. I'm sure he can't slip from your vigilant clutches."

Markham looked at Vance a moment, then turned to Heath. "Let it go at that. But if Leacock attempts to leave the city, nab him."

Heath went out sullenly.

"By the bye, Markham," said Vance; "don't make an appointment for half past twelve today. You already have one, don't y'know. And with a lady."

Markham put down his pen and stared. "What new damned nonsense is this?"

"I made an engagement for you. Called the lady by phone this morning. I'm sure I woke the dear up."

Markham spluttered, striving to articulate his angry protest.

Vance held up his hand soothingly.

"And you simply must keep the engagement. Y' see, I told her it was you speaking; and it would be shocking taste not to appear. . . . I promise, you won't regret meeting her," he added. "Things looked so sadly befuddled last night—I couldn't bear to see you suffering so. Cons'quently, I arranged for you to see Mrs. Paula Banning, Pfyfe's Eloïse, y'know. I'm pos'tive she'll be able to dispel some of this inspissated gloom that's enveloping you."

"See here, Vance!" Markham growled. "I happen to be running this office—" He stopped abruptly, realizing the hopelessness of making headway against the other's blandness. Moreover, I think, the prospect of interviewing Mrs. Paula Banning was not wholly alien to his inclinations. His resentment slowly ebbed, and when he again spoke, his voice was almost matter-of-fact.

"Since you've committed me, I'll see her. But I'd rather Pfyfe wasn't in such close communication with her. He's apt to drop in—with preconcerted unexpectedness."

"Funny," murmured Vance. "I thought of that myself. . . . That's why I phoned him last night that he could return to Long Island."

"You phoned him!"

"Awf'lly sorry and all that," Vance apologized. "But you'd gone to bed. Sleep was knitting up your ravelled sleeve of care; and I couldn't bring myself to disturb you. . . . Pfyfe was so grateful, too. Most touchin'. Said his wife also would be grateful. He was pathetically consid'rate about Mrs. Pfyfe. But I fear he'll need all his velvety forensic powers to explain his absence."

"In what other quarters have you involved me during my absence?" asked Markham acrimoniously.

"That's all," replied Vance, rising and strolling to the window.

He stood looking out, smoking thoughtfully. When he turned back to the room, his bantering air had gone. He sat down facing Markham.

"The major has practically admitted to us," he said, "that he knows more about this affair than he has told. You naturally can't push the point, in view of his hon'rable attitude in the matter. And yet, he's willing for you to find out what he knows, as long as he doesn't tell you himself—that was unquestionably the stand he took last night. Now, I believe there's a way you can find out without calling upon him to go against his principles. . . . You recall Miss Hoffman's story of the eavesdropping; and you also recall that he told you he heard a conversation which, in the light of Benson's murder, became significant. It's quite prob'ble, therefore, that the major's knowledge has to do with something connected with the business of the firm, or at least with one of the firm's clients."

Vance slowly lit another cigarette.

"My suggestion is this: Call up the major and ask permission to send a man to take a peep at his ledger accounts and his purchase and sales books. Tell him you want to find out about the transactions of one of his clients. Intimate that it's Miss St. Clair—or Pfyfe, if you like. I have a strange mediumistic feeling that, in this way, you'll get on the track of the person he's shielding. And I'm also assailed by the premonition that he'll welcome your interest in his ledger."

The plan did not appeal to Markham as feasible or fraught with possibilities; and it was evident he disliked making such a request of Major Benson. But so determined was Vance, so earnestly did he argue his point, that in the end Markham acquiesced.

"He was quite willing to let me send a man," said Markham, hanging up the receiver. "In fact, he seemed eager to give me every assistance."

"I thought he'd take kindly to the suggestion," said Vance. "Y' see, if you discover for yourself whom he suspects, it relieves him of the onus of having tattled."

Markham rang for Swacker. "Call up Stitt and tell him I want to see him here before noon—that I have an immediate job for him."

"Stitt," Markham explained to Vance, "is the head of a firm of public accountants over in the New York Life Building. I use him a good deal on work like this."

Shortly before noon Stitt came. He was a prematurely old young man, with a sharp, shrewd face and a perpetual frown. The prospect of working for the district attorney pleased him.

Markham explained briefly what was wanted, and revealed enough of the case to guide him in his task. The man grasped the situation immediately and made one or two notes on the back of a dilapidated envelope.

Vance also, during the instructions, had jotted down some notations on a piece of paper.

Markham stood up and took his hat.

"Now, I suppose, I must keep the appointment you made for me," he complained to Vance. Then: "Come, Stitt, I'll take you down with us in the judges' private elevator."

"If you don't mind," interposed Vance, "Mr. Stitt and I will forgo the honour and mingle with the commoners in the public lift. We'll meet you downstairs."

Taking the accountant by the arm, he led him out through the main waiting room. It was ten minutes, however, before he joined us. We took the subway to Seventy-second Street and walked up West End Avenue to Mrs. Paula Banning's address. She lived in a small apartment house just around the corner in Seventy-fifth Street. As we stood before her door, waiting for an answer to our ring, a strong odour of Chinese incense drifted out to us.

"Ah! That facilitates matters," said Vance, sniffing. "Ladies who burn joss sticks are invariably sentimental."

Mrs. Banning was a tall, slightly adipose woman of indeterminate age, with straw-coloured hair and a pink-and-white complexion. Her face in repose possessed a youthful and vacuous innocence; but the expression was only superficial. Her eyes, a very light blue, were hard; and a slight puffiness about her cheekbones and beneath her chin attested to years of idle and indulgent living. She was not unattractive, however, in a vivid, flamboyant way; and her manner, when she ushered us into her over furnished and rococo living room, was one of easygoing good-fellowship.

When we were seated and Markham had apologized for our intrusion, Vance at once assumed the role of interviewer. During his opening explanatory remarks he appraised the woman carefully, as if seeking to determine the best means of approaching her for the information he wanted.

After a few minutes of verbal reconnoitring, he asked permission to smoke and offered Mrs. Banning one of his cigarettes, which she accepted. Then he smiled at her in a spirit of appreciative geniality and relaxed comfortably in his chair. He conveyed the impression that he was fully prepared to sympathize with anything she might tell him.

"Mr. Pfyfe strove very hard to keep you entirely out of this affair," said Vance; "and we fully appreciate his delicacy in so doing. But certain circumst'nces connected with Mr. Benson's death have inadvertently involved you in the case; and you can best help us and yourself—and particularly Mr. Pfyfe—by telling us what we want to know and trusting to our discretion and understanding."

He had emphasized Pfyfe's name, giving it a significant intonation;

and the woman had glanced down uneasily. Her apprehension was apparent, and when she looked up into Vance's eyes, she was asking herself: How much does he know? as plainly as if she had spoken the words audibly.

"I can't imagine what you want me to tell you," she said, with an effort at astonishment. "You know that Andy was not in New York that night." (Her designating of the elegant and superior Pfyfe as "Andy" sounded almost like *lèse-majesté*.) "He didn't arrive in the city until nearly nine the next morning."

"Didn't you read in the newspapers about the grey Cadillac that was parked in front of Benson's house?" Vance, in putting the question, imitated her own astonishment.

She smiled confidently. "That wasn't Andy's car. He took the eight o'clock train to New York the next morning. He said it was lucky that he did, seeing that a machine just like his had been at Mr. Benson's the night before."

She had spoken with the sincerity of complete assurance. It was evident that Pfyfe had lied to her on this point.

Vance did not disabuse her; in fact, he gave her to understand that he accepted her explanation and consequently dismissed the idea of Pfyfe's presence in New York on the night of the murder.

"I had in mind a connection of a somewhat diff'rent nature when I mentioned you and Mr. Pfyfe as having been drawn into the case. I referred to a personal relationship between you and Mr. Benson."

She assumed an attitude of smiling indifference.

"I'm afraid you've made another mistake." She spoke lightly. "Mr. Benson and I were not even friends. Indeed, I scarcely knew him."

There was an overtone of emphasis in her denial—a slight eagerness which, in indicating a conscious desire to be believed, robbed her remark of the complete casualness she had intended.

"Even a business relationship may have its personal side," Vance reminded her; "especially when the intermediary is an intimate friend of both parties to the transaction."

She looked at him quickly, then turned her eyes away. "I really don't know what you're talking about," she affirmed; and her face for a moment lost its contours of innocence and became calculating. "You're surely not implying that I had any business dealings with Mr. Benson?"

"Not directly," replied Vance. "But certainly Mr. Pfyfe had business dealings with him; and one of them, I rather imagined, involved you consid'rably."

"Involved me?" She laughed scornfully, but it was a strained laugh.

"It was a somewhat unfortunate transaction, I fear," Vance went on, "—unfortunate in that Mr. Pfyfe was necessitated to deal with Mr. Benson; and doubly unfortunate, y'know, in that he should have had to drag you into it."

His manner was easy and assured, and the woman sensed that no display of scorn or contempt, however well simulated, would make an impression upon him. Therefore, she adopted an attitude of tolerantly incredulous amusement.

"And where did you learn about all this?" she asked playfully.

"Alas! I didn't learn about it," answered Vance, falling in with her manner. "That's the reason, d' ye see, that I indulged in this charming little visit. I was foolish enough to hope that you'd take pity on my ignorance and tell me all about it."

"But I wouldn't think of doing such a thing," she said, "even if this mysterious transaction had really taken place."

"My word!" sighed Vance. "That IS disappointin'. . . . Ah, well. I see that I must tell you what little I know about it and trust to your sympathy to enlighten me further."

Despite the ominous undercurrent of his words, his levity acted like a sedative to her anxiety. She felt that he was friendly, however much he might know about her.

"Am I bringing you news when I tell you that Mr. Pfyfe forged Mr. Benson's name to a check for ten thousand dollars?" he asked.

She hesitated, gauging the possible consequences of her answer. "No, that isn't news. Andy tells me everything."

"And did you also know that Mr. Benson, when informed of it, was rather put out?—that, in fact, he demanded a note and a signed confession before he would pay the check?"

The woman's eyes flashed angrily.

"Yes, I knew that too. And after all Andy had done for him! If ever a man deserved shooting, it was Alvin Benson. He was a dog. And he pretended to be Andy's best friend. Just think of it—refusing to lend Andy the money without a confession! . . . You'd hardly call that a business deal, would you? I'd call it a dirty, contemptible, underhand trick."

She was enraged. Her mask of breeding and good-fellowship had fallen from her; and she poured out vituperation on Benson with no thought of the words she was using. Her speech was devoid of all the ordinary reticences of intercourse between strangers.

Vance nodded consolingly during her tirade.

"Y' know, I sympathize fully with you." The tone in which he made the remark seemed to establish a closer rapprochement.

After a moment he gave her a friendly smile. "But, after all, one could almost forgive Benson for holding the confession, if he hadn't also demanded security."

"What security?"

Vance was quick to sense the change in her tone. Taking advantage of her rage, he had mentioned the security while the barriers of her pose were down. Her frightened, almost involuntary query told him that the right moment had arrived. Before she could gain her equilibrium or dispel the momentary fear which had assailed her, he said, with suave deliberation:

"The day Mr. Benson was shot, he took home with him from the office a small blue box of jewels."

She caught her breath but otherwise gave no outward sign of emotion. "Do you think he had stolen them?"

The moment she had uttered the question, she realized that it was a mistake in technique. An ordinary man might have been momentarily diverted from the truth by it. But by Vance's smile she recognized that he had accepted it as an admission.

"It was rather fine of you, y'know, to lend Mr. Pfyfe your jewels to cover the note with."

At this she threw her head up. The blood had left her face, and the rouge on her cheeks took on a mottled and unnatural hue.

"You say I lent my jewels to Andy! I swear to you—"

Vance halted her denial with a slight movement of the hand and a *coup d'oeil*. She saw that his intention was to save her from the humiliation she might feel later at having made too emphatic and unqualified a statement; and the graciousness of his action, although he was an antagonist, gave her more confidence in him.

She sank back into her chair, and her hands relaxed.

"What makes you think I lent Andy my jewels?"

Her voice was colourless, but Vance understood the question. It was the end of her deceptions. The pause which followed was an amnesty—recognized as such by both. The next spoken words would be the truth.

"Andy had to have them," she said, "or Benson would have put him in jail." One read in her words a strange, self-sacrificing affection for the worthless Pfyfe. "And if Benson hadn't done it, and had merely refused to honour the check, his father-in-law would have done it. . . . Andy is so careless, so unthinking. He does things without weighing the consequences. I am all the time having to hold him down. . . . But this thing has taught him a lesson—I'm sure of it."

I felt that if anything in the world could teach Pfyfe a lesson, it was the blind loyalty of this woman.

"Do you know what he quarrelled about with Mr. Benson in his office last Wednesday?" asked Vance.

"That was all my fault," she explained, with a sigh. "It was getting very near to the time when the note was due, and I knew Andy didn't have all the money. So I asked him to go to Benson and offer him what he had, and see if he couldn't get my jewels back. . . . But he was refused—I thought he would be."

Vance looked at her for a while sympathetically.

"I don't want to worry you any more than I can help," he said; "but won't you tell me the real cause of your anger against Benson a moment ago?"

She gave him an admiring nod. "You're right—I had good reason to hate him." Her eyes narrowed unpleasantly. "The day after he had refused to give Andy the jewels, he called me up—it was in the afternoon—and asked me to have breakfast with him at his house the next morning. He said he was home and had the jewels with him; and he told me—hinted, you understand—that maybe—*maybe* I could have them. That's the kind of beast he was! . . . I telephoned to Port Washington to Andy and told him about it, and he said he'd be in New York the next morning. He got here about nine o'clock, and we read in the paper that Benson had been shot that night."

Vance was silent for a long time. Then he stood up and thanked her.

"You have helped us a great deal. Mr. Markham is a friend of Major Benson's, and, since we have the check and the confession in our possession, I shall ask him to use his influence with the major to permit us to destroy them—very soon."

CHAPTER 18

A Confession

Wednesday, June 19; 1 p.m.

When we were again outside Markham asked, "How in Heaven's name did you know she had put up her jewels to help Pfyfe?"

"My charmin' metaphysical deductions, don't y'know," answered Vance. "As I told you, Benson was not the open handed, big hearted altruist who would have lent money without security; and certainly the impecunious Pfyfe had no collateral worth ten thousand dollars or he wouldn't have forged the check. Ergo: someone lent him the security. Now, who would be so trustin' as to lend Pfyfe that amount of security except a sentimental woman who was blind to his amazin' defects? Y'know, I was just evil-minded enough to suspect there was a Calypso in the life of this Ulysses when he told us of stopping over in New York to murmur *au revoir* to someone. When a man like Pfyfe fails to specify the sex of a person, it is safe to assume the feminine gender. So I suggested that you send a Paul Pry to Port Washington to peer into his trans-matrimonial activities; I felt certain a *bonne amie* would be found. Then, when the mysterious package, which obviously was the security, seemed to identify itself as the box of jewels seen by the inquisitive housekeeper, I said to myself: 'Ah! Leander's misguided Dulcinea has lent him her gewgaws to save him from the yawning dungeon.' Nor did I overlook the fact that he had been shielding someone in his explanation about the check. Therefore, as soon as the lady's name and address were learned by Tracy, I made the appointment for you. . . ."

We were passing the Gothic-Renaissance Schwab residence which extends from West End Avenue to Riverside Drive at Seventy-third Street; and Vance stopped for a moment to contemplate it.

Markham waited patiently. At length Vance walked on.

". . . Y'know, the moment I saw Mrs. Banning, I knew my conclusions were correct. She was a sentimental soul and just the sort of professional good sport who would have handed over her jewels to her amoroso. Also, she was bereft of gems when we called—and a woman of her stamp always wears her jewels when she desires to make an impression on strangers. Moreover, she's the kind that would have jewellery even if the larder was empty. It was therefore merely a question of getting her to talk."

"On the whole, you did very well," observed Markham.

Vance gave him a condescending bow. "Sir Hubert is too generous. But tell me, didn't my little chat with the lady cast a gleam into your darkened mind?"

"Naturally," said Markham. "I'm not utterly obtuse. She played unconsciously into our hands. She believed Pfyfe did not arrive in New York until the morning after the murder, and therefore told us quite frankly that she had phoned him that Benson had the jewels at home. The situation now is: Pfyfe knew they were in Benson's house and was there himself at about the time the shot was fired. Furthermore, the jewels are gone; and Pfyfe tried to cover up his tracks that night."

Vance sighed hopelessly. "Markham, there are altogether too many trees for you in this case. You simply can't see the forest, y'know, because of 'em."

"There is the remote possibility that you are so busily engaged in looking at one particular tree that you are unaware of the others."

A shadow passed over Vance's face. "I wish you were right," he said.

It was nearly half past one, and we dropped into the Fountain Room of the Ansonia Hotel for lunch. Markham was preoccupied throughout the meal, and when we entered the subway later, he looked uneasily at his watch.

"I think I'll go on down to Wall Street and call on the major a moment before returning to the office. I can't understand his asking Miss Hoffman not to mention the package to me. . . . It might not have contained the jewels, after all."

"Do you imagine for one moment," rejoined Vance, "that Alvin told the major the truth about the package? It was not a very cred'table transaction, y'know; and the major most likely would have given him what-for."

Major Benson's explanation bore out Vance's surmise. Markham, in telling him of the interview with Paula Banning, emphasized the jewel episode in the hope that the major would voluntarily mention the package; for his promise to Miss Hoffman prevented him from admitting that he was aware of the other's knowledge concerning it.

The major listened with considerable astonishment, his eyes gradually growing angry. "I'm afraid Alvin deceived me," he said. He looked straight ahead for a moment, his face softening. "And I don't like to think it, now that he's gone. But the truth is, when Miss Hoffman told me this morning about the envelope, she also mentioned a small parcel that had been in Alvin's private safe-drawer; and I asked her to omit any reference to it from her story to you. I knew the parcel contained Mrs. Banning's jewels, but I thought the fact would only confuse matters if brought to your attention. You see, Alvin told me that a judgment had been taken against Mrs. Banning, and that, just before the Supplementary Proceedings, Pfyfe had brought her jewels here and asked him to sequester them temporarily in his safe."

On our way back to the Criminal Courts Building, Markham took Vance's arm and smiled. "Your guessing luck is holding out, I see."

"Rather!" agreed Vance. "It would appear that the late Alvin, like Warren Hastings, resolved to die in the last dyke of prevarication. . . . *Splendide mendax*, what?"

"In any event," replied Markham, "the major has unconsciously added another link in the chain against Pfyfe."

"You seem to be making a collection of chains," commented Vance dryly. "What have you done with the ones you forged about Miss St. Clair and Leacock?"

"I haven't entirely discarded them—if that's what you think," asserted Markham gravely.

When we reached the office, Sergeant Heath was awaiting us with a beatific grin.

"It's all over, Mr. Markham," he announced. "This noon, after you'd gone, Leacock came here looking for you. When he found you were out, he phoned headquarters, and they connected him with me. He wanted to see me—very important, he said; so I hurried over. He was sitting in the waiting room when I came in and he called me over and said: 'I came to give myself up. I killed Benson.' I got him to dictate a confession to Swacker, and then he sighed it. . . . Here it is." He handed Markham a typewritten sheet of paper.

Markham sank wearily into a chair. The strain of the past few days had begun to tell on him. He signed heavily. "Thank God! Now our troubles are ended."

Vance looked at him lugubriously and shook his head.

"I rather fancy, y'know, that your troubles are only beginning," he drawled.

When Markham had glanced through the confession, he handed it to Vance, who read it carefully with an expression of growing amusement.

"Y' know," he said, "this document isn't at all legal. Any judge worthy the name would throw it precip'tately out of court. It's far too simple and precise. It doesn't begin with 'greetings'; it doesn't contain a single 'wherefore-be-it' or 'be-it-known' or 'do-hereby'; it says nothing about 'free will' or 'sound mind' or 'disposin' mem'ry'; and the captain doesn't once refer to himself as 'the party of the first part'. . . . Utterly worthless, Sergeant. If I were you, I'd chuck it."

Heath was feeling too complacently triumphant to be annoyed. He smiled with magnanimous tolerance.

"It strikes you as funny, doesn't it, Mr. Vance?"

"Sergeant, if you knew how inord'nately funny this confession is, you'd pos'tively have hysterics."

Vance then turned to Markham. "Really, y'know, I shouldn't put too much stock in this. It may, however, prove a valuable lever with which to prise open the truth. In fact, I'm jolly glad the captain has gone in for imag'native lit'rature. With this entrancin' fable in our possession, I think we can overcome the major's scruples and get him to tell us what he knows. Maybe I'm wrong, but it's worth trying."

He stepped to the district attorney's desk and leaned over it cajolingly.

"I haven't led you astray yet, old dear; and I'm going to make another suggestion. Call up the major and ask him to come here at once. Tell him you've secured a confession—but don't you dare say whose. Imply it's Miss St. Clair's, or Pfyfe's—or Pontius Pilate's. But urge his immediate presence. Tell him you want to discuss it with him before proceeding with the indictment."

"I can't see the necessity of doing that," objected Markham. "I'm pretty sure to see him at the club tonight and I can tell him then."

"That wouldn't do at all," insisted Vance. "If the major can enlighten us on any point, I think Sergeant Heath should be present to hear him."

"I don't need any enlightenment," cut in Heath.

Vance regarded him with admiring surprise.

"What a wonderful man! Even Goethe cried for *mehr Licht*; and here are you in a state of luminous saturation! . . . Astonishin'!"

"See here, Vance," said Markham: "why try to complicate the matter? It strikes me as a waste of time, besides being an imposition, to ask the major here to discuss Leacock's confession. We don't need his evidence now, anyway."

Despite his gruffness there was a hint of reconsideration in his voice; for though his instinct had been to dismiss the request out of hand, the experiences of the past few days had taught him that Vance's suggestions were not made without an object.

Vance, sensing the other's hesitancy, said, "My request is based on something more than an idle desire to gaze upon the major's rubicund features at this moment. I'm telling you, with all the meagre earnestness I possess, that his presence here now would be most helpful."

Markham deliberated and argued the point at some length. But Vance was so persistent that in the end he was convinced of the advisability of complying. Heath was patently disgusted, but he sat down quietly and sought solace in a cigar.

Major Benson arrived with astonishing promptness, and when Markham handed him the confession, he made little attempt to conceal his eagerness. But as he read it his face clouded, and a look of puzzlement came into his eyes.

At length he looked up, frowning.

"I don't quite understand this; and I'll admit I'm greatly surprised. It doesn't seem credible that Leacock shot Alvin. . . . And yet, I may be mistaken, of course."

He laid the confession on Markham's desk with an air of disappointment, and sank into a chair.

"Do *you* feel satisfied?" he asked.

"I don't see any way around it," said Markham. "If he isn't guilty, why should he come forward and confess? God knows, there's plenty of evidence against him. I was ready to arrest him two days ago."

"He's guilty all right," put in Heath. "I've had my eye on him from the first."

Major Benson did not reply at once; he seemed to be framing his next words.

"It might be—that is, there's the bare possibility—that Leacock had an ulterior motive in confessing."

We all, I think, recognized the thought which his words strove to conceal. "I'll admit," acceded Markham, "that at first I believed Miss St. Clair guilty, and I intimated as much to Leacock. But later I was persuaded that she was not directly involved."

"Does Leacock know this?" the major asked quickly.

Markham thought a moment. "No, I can't say that he does. In fact, it's more than likely he still thinks I suspect her."

"Ah!" The major's exclamation was almost involuntary.

"But what's that got to do with it?" asked Heath irritably. "Do you think he's going to the chair to save her reputation?—Bunk! That sort of thing's all right in the movies, but no man's that crazy in real life."

"I'm not so sure, Sergeant," ventured Vance lazily. "Women are too sane and practical to make such foolish gestures; but men, y'know, have an illim'table capacity for idiocy."

He turned an inquiring gaze on Major Benson.

"Won't you tell us why you think Leacock is playing Sir Galahad?"

But the major took refuge in generalities, and was disinclined even to follow up his original intimation as to the cause of the captain's action. Vance questioned him for some time but was unable to penetrate his reticence.

Heath, becoming restless, finally spoke up. "You can't argue Leacock's guilt away, Mr. Vance. Look at the facts. He threatened Benson that he'd kill him if he caught him with the girl again. The next time Benson goes out with her, he's found shot. Then Leacock hides his gun at her house, and when things begin to get hot, he takes it away and ditches it in the river. He bribes the hall-boy to alibi him; and he's seen at Benson's house at twelve thirty that night. When he's questioned, he can't explain anything. . . . If that ain't an open-and-shut case, I'm a mock-turtle."

"The circumstances are convincing," admitted Major Benson. "But couldn't they be accounted for on other grounds?"

Heath did not deign to answer the question.

"The way I see it," he continued, "is like this: Leacock gets suspicious along about midnight, takes his gun and goes out. He catches Benson with the girl, goes in, and shoots him like he threatened. They're both mixed up in it, if you ask me; but Leacock did the shooting. And now we got his confession. . . . There isn't a jury in the country that wouldn't convict him."

"*Probi et legales homines*—oh, quite!" murmured Vance.

Swacker appeared at the door. "The reporters are clamouring for attention," he announced with a wry face.

"Do they know about the confession?" Markham asked Heath.

"Not yet. I haven't told 'em anything so far—that's why they're clamouring, I guess. But I'll give 'em an earful now, if you say the word."

Markham nodded, and Heath started for the door. But Vance quickly planted himself in the way.

"Could you keep this thing quiet till tomorrow, Markham?" he asked.

Markham was annoyed. "I could if I wanted to—yes. But why should I?"

"For your own sake, if for no other reason. You've got your prize safely locked up. Control your vanity for twenty-four hours. The major and I both know that Leacock's innocent, and by this time tomorrow the whole country'll know it."

Again an argument ensued; but the outcome, like that of the former argument, was a foregone conclusion. Markham had realized for some time that Vance had reason to be convinced of something which as yet he was unwilling to divulge. His opposition to Vance's requests were, I had suspected, largely the result of an effort to ascertain this information; and I was positive of it now as he leaned forward and gravely debated the advisability of making public the captain's confession.

Vance, as heretofore, was careful to reveal nothing; but in the end his sheer determination carried his point; and Markham requested Heath to keep his own council until the next day. The major, by a slight nod, indicated his approbation of the decision.

"You might tell the newspaper lads, though," suggested Vance, "that you'll have a rippin' sensation for 'em tomorrow."

Heath went out, crestfallen and glowering.

"A rash fella, the sergeant—so impetuous!"

Vance again picked up the confession and perused it.

"Now, Markham, I want you to bring your prisoner forth—habeas corpus and that sort of thing. Put him in that chair facing the window, give him one of the good cigars you keep for influential politicians, and then listen attentively while I politely chat with him. . . . The major, I trust, will remain for the interlocut'ry proceedings."

"That request, at least, I'll grant without objections," smiled Markham. "I had already decided to have a talk with Leacock."

He pressed a buzzer, and a brisk, ruddy-faced clerk entered.

"A requisition for Captain Philip Leacock," he ordered.

When it was brought to him, he initialled it. "Take it to Ben, and tell him to hurry."

The clerk disappeared through the door leading to the outer corridor. Ten minutes later a deputy sheriff from the Tombs entered with the prisoner.

CHAPTER 19

Vance Cross-Examines

Wednesday, June 19; 3:30 p.m.

Captain Leacock walked into the room with a hopeless indifference of bearing. His shoulders drooped; his arms hung listlessly. His eyes were haggard like those of a man who had not slept for days. On seeing Major Benson, he straightened a little and, stepping toward him, extended his hand. It was plain that, however much he may have disliked Alvin Benson, he regarded the major as a friend. But suddenly, realizing the situation, he turned away, embarrassed.

The major went quickly to him and touched him on the arm. "It's all right, Leacock," he said softly. "I can't think that you really shot Alvin."

The captain turned apprehensive eyes upon him. "Of course, I shot him." His voice was flat. "I told him I was going to."

Vance came forward and indicated a chair.

"Sit down, Captain. The district attorney wants to hear your story of the shooting. The law, you understand, does not accept murder confessions without corroborat'ry evidence. And since, in the present case, there are suspicions against others than yourself, we want you to answer some questions in order to substantiate your guilt. Otherwise, it will be necess'ry for us to follow up our suspicions."

Taking a seat facing Leacock, he picked up the confession.

"You say here you were satisfied that Mr. Benson had wronged you, and you went to his house at about half past twelve on the night of the thirteenth. . . . When you speak of his wronging you, do you refer to his attentions to Miss St. Clair?"

Leacock's face betrayed a sulky belligerence

"It doesn't matter why I shot him. Can't you leave Miss St. Clair out of it?"

"Certainly," agreed Vance. "I promise you she shall not be brought into it. But we must understand your motive thoroughly."

After a brief silence Leacock said, "Very well, then. That was what I referred to."

"How did you know Miss St. Clair went to dinner with Mr. Benson that night?"

"I followed them to the Marseilles."

"And then you went home?"

"Yes."

"What made you go to Mr. Benson's house later?"

"I got to thinking about it more and more, until I couldn't stand it any longer. I began to see red, and at last I took my Colt and went out, determined to kill him."

A note of passion had crept into his voice. It seemed unbelievable that he could be lying.

Vance again referred to the confession.

"You dictated: 'I went to 87 West Forty-eighth Street and entered the house by the front door.' . . . Did you ring the bell? Or was the front door unlatched?"

Leacock was about to answer but hesitated. Evidently he recalled the newspaper accounts of the housekeeper's testimony in which she asserted positively that the bell had not rung that night.

"What difference does it make?" He was sparring for time.

"We'd like to know—that's all," Vance told him. "But no hurry."

"Well, if it's so important to you: I didn't ring the bell; and the door was unlocked." His hesitancy was gone. "Just as I reached the house, Benson drove up in a taxicab—"

"Just a moment. Did you happen to notice another car standing in front of the house? A grey Cadillac?"

"Why—yes."

"Did you recognize its occupant?"

There was another short silence.

"I'm not sure. I think it was a man named Pfyfe."

"He and Mr. Benson were outside at the same time, then?"

Leacock frowned. "No—not at the same time. There was nobody there when I arrived. . . . I didn't see Pfyfe until I came out a few minutes later."

"He arrived in his car when you were inside—is that it?"

"He must have."

"I see. . . . And now to go back a little: Benson drove up in a taxicab. Then what?"

166

"I went up to him and said I wanted to speak to him. He told me to come inside, and we went in together. He used his latchkey."

"And now, Captain, tell us just what happened after you and Mr. Benson entered the house."

"He laid his hat and stick on the hat-rack, and we walked into the living room. He sat down by the table, and I stood up and said—what I had to say. Then I drew my gun and shot him."

Vance was closely watching the man, and Markham was leaning forward tensely.

"How did it happen that he was reading at the time?"

"I believe he did pick up a book while I was talking. . . . Trying to appear indifferent, I reckon."

"Think now: you and Mr. Benson went into the living room directly from the hall, as soon as you entered the house?"

"Yes."

"Then how do you account for the fact, Captain, that when Mr. Benson was shot, he had on his smoking jacket and slippers?"

Leacock glanced nervously about the room. Before he answered, he wet his lips with his tongue.

"Now that I think of it, Benson did go upstairs for a few minutes first. . . . I guess I was too excited," he added desperately, "to recollect everything."

"That's natural," Vance said sympathetically. "But when he came downstairs, did you happen to notice anything peculiar about his hair?"

Leacock looked up vaguely. "His hair? I—don't understand."

"The colour of it, I mean. When Mr. Benson sat before you under the table lamp, didn't you remark some—difference, let us say—in the way his hair looked?"

The man closed his eyes, as if striving to visualize the scene. "No—I don't remember."

"A minor point," said Vance indifferently. "Did Benson's speech strike you as peculiar when he came downstairs—that is, was there a thickness, or slight impediment of any kind, in his voice?"

Leacock was manifestly puzzled.

"I don't know what you mean," he said. "He seemed to talk the way he always talked."

"And did you happen to see a blue jewel case on the table?"

"I didn't notice."

Vance smoked a moment thoughtfully.

"When you left the room after shooting Mr. Benson, you turned out the lights, of course?"

When no immediate answer came, Vance volunteered the suggestion: "You must have done so, for Mr. Pfyfe says the house was dark when he drove up."

Leacock then nodded an affirmative. "That's right. I couldn't recollect for the moment."

"Now that you remember the fact, just how did you turn them off?"

"I—" he began, and stopped. Then, finally: "At the switch."

"And where is that switch located, Captain?"

"I can't just recall."

"Think a moment. Surely you can remember."

"By the door leading into the hall, I think."

"Which side of the door?"

"How can I tell?" the man asked piteously. "I was too—nervous. . . . But I think it was on the right-hand side of the door."

"The right-hand side when entering or leaving the room?"

"As you go out."

"That would be where the bookcase stands?"

"Yes."

Vance appeared satisfied.

"Now, there's the question of the gun," he said. "Why did you take it to Miss St. Clair?"

"I was a coward," the man replied. "I was afraid they might find it at my apartment. And I never imagined she would be suspected."

"And when she was suspected, you at once took the gun away and threw it into the East River?"

"Yes."

"I suppose there was one cartridge missing from the magazine, too—which in itself would have been a suspicious circumstance."

"I thought of that. That's why I threw the gun away."

Vance frowned. "That's strange. There must have been two guns. We dredged the river, y'know, and found a Colt automatic, but the magazine was full. . . . Are you sure, Captain, that it was *your* gun you took from Miss St. Clair's and threw over the bridge?"

I knew no gun had been retrieved from the river and I wondered what he was driving at. Was he, after all, trying to involve the girl? Markham, too, I could see, was in doubt.

Leacock made no answer for several moments. When he spoke, it was with dogged sullenness.

"There weren't two guns. The one you found was mine. . . . I refilled the magazine myself."

"Ah, that accounts for it." Vance's tone was pleasant and reassuring. "Just one more question, Captain. Why did you come here today and confess?"

Leacock thrust his chin out, and for the first time during the cross-examination his eyes became animated. "Why? It was the only honourable thing to do. You have unjustly suspected an innocent person; and I didn't want anyone else to suffer."

This ended the interview. Markham had no questions to ask; and the deputy sheriff led the captain out.

When the door had closed on him, a curious silence fell over the room. Markham sat smoking furiously, his hands folded behind his head, his eyes fixed on the ceiling. The major had settled back in his chair, and was gazing at Vance with admiring satisfaction. Vance was watching Markham out of the corner of his eye, a drowsy smile on his lips. The expressions and attitudes of the three men conveyed perfectly their varying individual reactions to the interview—Markham troubled, the major pleased, Vance cynical.

It was Vance who broke the silence. He spoke easily, almost lazily. "You see how silly the confession is, what? Our pure and lofty captain is an incredibly poor Munchausen. No one could lie as badly as he did who hadn't been born into the world that way. It's simply impossible to imitate such stupidity. And he did so want us to think him guilty. Very affectin'. He prob'bly imagined you'd merely stick the confession in his shirtfront and send him to the hangman. You noticed, he hadn't even decided how he got into Benson's house that night. Pfyfe's admitted presence outside almost spoiled his impromptu explanation of having entered *bras dessus bras dessous* with his intended victim. And he didn't recall Benson's semi-*négligé* attire. When I reminded him of it, he had to contradict himself and send Benson trotting upstairs to make a rapid change. Luckily, the toupee wasn't mentioned by the newspapers. The captain couldn't imagine what I meant when I intimated that Benson had dyed his hair when changing his coat and shoes.... By the bye, Major, did your brother speak thickly when his false teeth were out?"

"Noticeably so," answered the major. "If Alvin's plate had been removed that night—as I gathered it had been from your question—Leacock would surely have noticed it."

"There were other things he didn't notice," said Vance: "the jewel case, for instance, and the location of the electric light switch."

"He went badly astray on that point," added the major. "Alvin's house is old-fashioned, and the only switch in the room is a pendant one attached to the chandelier."

169

"Exactly," said Vance. "However, his worst break was in connection with the gun. He gave his hand away completely there. He said he threw the pistol into the river largely because of the missing cartridge, and when I told him the magazine was full, he explained that he had refilled it, so I wouldn't think it was anyone else's gun that was found. . . . It's plain to see what's the matter. He thinks Miss St. Clair is guilty, and is determined to take the blame."

"That's my impression," said Major Benson.

"And yet," mused Vance, "the captain's attitude bothers me a little. There's no doubt he had something to do with the crime, else why should he have concealed his pistol the next day in Miss St. Clair's apartment? He's just the kind of silly beggar, d' ye see, who would threaten any man he thought had designs on his fiancée and then carry out the threat if anything happened. And he has a guilty conscience—that's obvious. But for what? Certainly not the shooting. The crime was planned; and the captain never plans. He's the kind that gets an *idée fixe*, girds up his loins, and does the deed in knightly fashion, prepared to take the cons'quences. That sort of chivalry, y'know, is sheer *beau geste*: its acolytes want everyone to know of their valour. And when they go forth to rid the world of a Don Juan, they're always clear-minded. The captain, for instance, wouldn't have overlooked his Lady Fair's gloves and handbag, he would have taken 'em away. In fact, it's just as certain he would have shot Benson as it is he didn't shoot him. That's the beetle in the amber. It's psychologically possible he would have done it, and psychologically impossible he would have done it the way it was done."

He lit a cigarette and watched the drifting spirals of smoke.

"If it wasn't so fantastic, I'd say he started out to do it and found it already done. And yet, that's about the size of it. It would account for Pfyfe's seeing him there, and for his secreting the gun at Miss St. Clair's the next day."

The telephone rang: Colonel Ostrander wanted to speak to the district attorney. Markham, after a short conversation, turned a disgruntled look upon Vance.

"Your bloodthirsty friend wanted to know if I'd arrested anyone yet. He offered to confer more of his invaluable suggestions upon me in case I was still undecided as to who was guilty."

"I heard you thanking him fulsomely for something or other. . . . What did you give him to understand about your mental state?"

"That I was still in the dark."

Markham's answer was accompanied by a sombre, tired smile. It was his way of telling Vance that he had entirely rejected the idea of Captain Leacock's guilt.

The major went to him and held out his hand.

"I know how you feel," he said. "This sort of thing is discouraging; but it's better that the guilty person should escape altogether than that an innocent man should be made to suffer. . . . Don't work too hard, and don't let these disappointments get to you. You'll soon hit on the right solution, and when you do"—his jaw snapped shut, and he uttered the rest of the sentence between clenched teeth—"you'll meet with no opposition from me. I'll help you put the thing over."

He gave Markham a grim smile and took up his hat.

"I'm going back to the office now. If you want me at any time, let me know. I may be able to help you—later on."

With a friendly, appreciative bow to Vance, he went out.

Markham sat in silence for several minutes.

"Damn it, Vance!" he said irritably. "This case gets more difficult by the hour. I feel worn out."

"You really shouldn't take it so seriously, old dear," Vance advised lightly. "It doesn't pay, y' know, to worry over the trivia of existence. 'Nothing's new, And nothing's true, And nothing really matters.'

"Several million johnnies were killed in the war, and you don't let the fact bedevil your phagocytes or inflame your brain cells. But when one rotter is mercifully shot in your district, you lie awake nights perspiring over it, what? My word! You're deucedly inconsistent."

"Consistency—" began Markham; but Vance interrupted him.

"Now don't quote Emerson. I inf'nitely prefer Erasmus. Y' know, you ought to read his Praise of Folly; it would cheer you no end. That goaty old Dutch professor would never have grieved inconsolably over the destruction of Alvin Le Chauve."

"I'm not a *fruges consumere natus* like you," snapped Markham. "I was elected to this office—"

"Oh, quite—'loved I not honour more' and all that," Vance chimed in. "But don't be so sens'tive. Even if the captain has succeeded in bungling his way out of jail, you have at least five possibilities left. There's Mrs. Platz . . . and Pfyfe . . . and Colonel Ostrander . . . and Miss Hoffman . . . and Mrs. Banning.—I say! Why don't you arrest 'em all, one at a time, and get 'em to confess? Heath would go crazy with joy."

Markham was in too crestfallen a mood to resent this chaffing. Indeed, Vance's light-heartedness seemed to buoy him up.

"If you want the truth," he said; "that's exactly what I feel like doing. I am restrained merely by my indecision as to which one to arrest first."

"Stout fella!" Then Vance asked: "What are you going to do with the captain now? It'll break his heart if you release him."

"His heart'll have to break, I'm afraid." Markham reached for the telephone. "I'd better see to the formalities now.

"Just a moment!" Vance put forth a restraining hand. "Don't end his rapturous martyrdom just yet. Let him be happy for another day at least. I've a notion he may be most useful to us, pining away in his lonely cell like the prisoner of Chillon."

Markham put down the telephone without a word. More and more, I had noticed, he was becoming inclined to accept Vance's leadership. This attitude was not merely the result of the hopeless confusion in his mind, though his uncertainty probably influenced him to some extent; but it was due in large measure to the impression Vance had given him of knowing more than he cared to reveal.

"Have you tried to figure out just how Pfyfe and his Turtledove fit into the case?" Vance asked.

"Along with a few thousand other enigmas—yes," was the petulant reply. "But the more I try to reason it out, the more of a mystery the whole thing becomes."

"Loosely put, my dear Markham," criticized Vance. "There are no mysteries originating in human beings, y'know; there are only problems. And any problem originating in one human being can be solved by another human being. It merely requires a knowledge of the human mind, and the application of that knowledge to human acts. Simple, what?"

He glanced at the clock.

"I wonder how your Mr. Stitt is getting along with the Benson and Benson books. I await his report with anticipat'ry excitement."

This was too much for Markham. The wearing-down process of Vance's intimations and veiled innuendoes had at last dissipated his self-control. He bent forward and struck the desk angrily with his hand.

"I'm damned tired of this superior attitude of yours," he complained hotly. "Either you know something or you don't. If you don't know anything, do me the favour of dropping these insinuations of knowledge. If you do know anything, it's up to you to tell me. You've been hinting around in one way or another ever since Benson was shot. If you've got any idea who killed him, I want to know it."

He leaned back and took out a cigar. Not once did he look up as he carefully clipped the end and lit it. I think he was a little ashamed at having given way to his anger.

Vance had sat apparently unconcerned during the outburst. At length he stretched his legs and gave Markham a long contemplative look.

"Y' know, Markham old bean, I don't blame you a bit for your unseemly ebullition. The situation has been most provokin'. But now, I fancy, the time has come to put an end to the *comedietta*. I really haven't been spoofing, y'know. The fact is, I've some most int'restin' ideas on the subject."

He stood up and yawned.

"It's a beastly hot day, but it must be done—eh, what?

'So nigh is grandeur to our dust,

So near is God to man.

When duty whispers low, thou must,

The youth replies, I can.'

"I'm the noble youth, don't y'know. And you're the voice of duty—though you didn't exactly whisper, did you? . . . *Was aber ist deine Pflicht?* And Goethe answered: *Die Forderung des Tages.* But—deuce take it!—I wish the demand had come on a cooler day."

He handed Markham his hat.

"Come, Postume. *To everything there is a season, and a time to every purpose under the heaven.** You are through with the office for today. Inform Swacker of the fact, will you?—there's a dear! We attend upon a lady—Miss St. Clair, no less."

Markham realized that Vance's jesting manner was only the masquerade of a very serious purpose. Also, he knew that Vance would tell him what he knew or suspected only in his own way, and that, no matter how circuitous and unreasonable that way might appear, Vance had excellent reasons for following it. Furthermore, since the unmasking of Captain Leacock's purely fictitious confession, he was in a state of mind to follow any suggestion that held the faintest hope of getting at the truth. He therefore rang at once for Swacker and informed him he was quitting the office for the day.

In ten minutes we were in the subway on our way to 94 Riverside Drive.

---

*This quotation from Ecclesiastes reminds me that Vance regularly read the *Old Testament*. "When I weary of the professional liter'ry man," he once said, "I find stimulation in the majestic prose of the Bible. If the moderns feel that they simply must write, they should be made to spend at least two hours a day with the Biblical historians."

CHAPTER 20

A Lady Explains

Wednesday, June 19; 4:30 p.m.

"The quest for enlightenment upon which we are now embarked," said Vance, as we rode uptown, "may prove a bit tedious. But you must exert your willpower and bear with me. You can't imagine what a ticklish task I have on my hands. And it's not a pleasant one either. I'm a bit too young to be sentimental and yet, d' ye know, I'm half inclined to let your culprit go."

"Would you mind telling me why we are calling on Miss St. Clair?" asked Markham resignedly.

Vance amiably complied. "Not at all. Indeed, I deem it best for you to know. There are several points connected with the lady that need eluc'dation. First, there are the gloves and the handbag. Nor poppy nor *mandragora* shall ever medicine thee to that sweet sleep which thou ow'dst yesterday until you have learned about those articles—eh, what? Then, you recall, Miss Hoffman told us that the major was lending an ear when a certain lady called upon Benson the day he was shot. I suspect that the visitor was Miss St. Clair; and I am rather curious to know what took place in the office that day and why she came back later. Also, why did she go to Benson's for tea that afternoon? And what part did the jewels play in the chit-chat? But there are other items. For example: Why did the captain take his gun to her? What makes him think she shot Benson?—he really believes it, y'know. And why did she think that he was guilty from the first?"

Markham looked sceptical.

"You expect her to tell us all this?"

"My hopes run high," returned Vance. "With her *verray parfit gentil knight* jailed as a self-confessed murderer, she will have nothing to lose by unburdening her soul. . . . But we must have no blustering. Your police brand of aggressive cross-examination will, I assure you, have no effect upon the lady."

"Just how do you propose to elicit your information?"

"With *morbidezza*, as the painters say. Much more refined and gentlemanly, y'know."

Markham considered a moment. "I think I'll keep out of it, and leave the Socratic *elenctus* entirely to you."

"An extr'ordin'rily brilliant suggestion," said Vance.

When we arrived Markham announced over the house telephone that he had come on a vitally important mission; and we were received by Miss St. Clair without a moment's delay. She was apprehensive, I imagine, concerning the whereabouts of Captain Leacock.

As she sat before us in her little drawing room overlooking the Hudson, her face was quite pale, and her hands, though tightly clasped, trembled a little. She had lost much of her cold reserve, and there were unmistakable signs of sleepless worry about her eyes.

Vance went directly to the point. His tone was almost flippant in its lightness: it at once relieved the tension of the atmosphere, and gave an air bordering on inconsequentiality to our visit.

"Captain Leacock has, I regret to inform you, very foolishly confessed to the murder of Mr. Benson. But we are not entirely satisfied with his *bona fides*. We are, alas! awash between Scylla and Charybdis. We can not decide whether the captain is a deep-dyed villain or a *chevalier sans peur et sans reproche*. His story of how he accomplished the dark deed is a bit sketchy; he is vague on certain essential details; and—what's most confusin'—he turned the lights off in Benson's hideous living room by a switch which pos'tively doesn't exist. Cons'quently, the suspicion has crept into my mind that he has concocted this tale of derring-do in order to shield someone whom he really believes guilty."

He indicated Markham with a slight movement of the head.

"The district attorney here does not wholly agree with me. But then, d' ye see, the legal mind is incredibly rigid and unreceptive once it has been invaded by a notion. You will remember that, because you were with Mr. Alvin Benson on his last evening on earth, and for other reasons equally irrelevant and trivial, Mr. Markham actu'lly concluded that you had had something to do with the gentleman's death."

He gave Markham a smile of waggish reproach, and went on: "Since you, Miss St. Clair, are the only person whom Captain Leacock would shield so heroically, and since I, at least, am convinced of your

175

own innocence, will you not clear up for us a few of those points where your orbit crossed that of Mr. Benson? . . . Such information cannot do the captain or yourself any harm, and it very possibly will help to banish from Mr. Markham's mind his lingering doubts as to the captain's innocence."

Vance's manner had an assuaging effect upon the woman; but I could see that Markham was boiling inwardly at Vance's animadversions on him, though he refrained from any interruption.

Miss St. Clair stared steadily at Vance for several minutes.

"I don't know why I should trust you, or even believe you," she said evenly; "but now that Captain Leacock has confessed—I was afraid he was going to, when he last spoke to me—I see no reason why I should not answer your questions. . . . Do you truly think he is innocent?"

The question was like an involuntary cry; her pent-up emotion had broken through her carapace of calm.

"I truly do," Vance avowed soberly. "Mr. Markham will tell you that before we left his office, I pleaded with him to release Captain Leacock. It was with the hope that your explanations would convince him of the wisdom of such a course that I urged him to come here."

Something in his tone and manner seemed to inspire her confidence.

"What do you wish to ask me?" she asked.

Vance cast another reproachful glance at Markham, who was restraining his outraged feelings only with difficulty; and then turned back to the woman.

"First of all, will you explain how your gloves and handbag found their way into Mr. Benson's house? Their presence there has been preying most distressin'ly on the district attorney's mind."

She turned a direct, frank gaze upon Markham.

"I dined with Mr. Benson at his invitation. Things between us were not pleasant, and when we started for home, my resentment of his attitude increased. At Times Square I ordered the chauffeur to stop—I preferred returning home alone. In my anger and my haste to get away, I must have dropped my gloves and bag. It was not until Mr. Benson had driven off that I realized my loss, and having no money, I walked home. Since my things were found in Mr. Benson's house, he must have taken them there himself."

"Such was my own belief," said Vance. "And—my word!—it's a deucedly long walk out here, what?"

He turned to Markham with a tantalizing smile.

"Really, y'know, Miss St. Clair couldn't have been expected to reach here before one."

Markham, grim and resolute, made no reply.

"And now," pursued Vance, "I should love to know under what circumst'nces the invitation to dinner was extended."

A shadow darkened her face, but her voice remained even.

"I had been losing a lot of money through Mr. Benson's firm, and suddenly my intuition told me that he was purposely seeing to it that I did lose, and that he could, if he desired, help me to recoup." She dropped her eyes. "He had been annoying me with his attentions for some time; and I didn't put any despicable scheme past him. I went to his office and told him quite plainly what I suspected. He replied that if I'd dine with him that night, we could talk it over. I knew what his object was, but I was so desperate I decided to go anyway, hoping I might plead with him."

"And how did you happen to mention to Mr. Benson the exact time your little dinner party would terminate?"

She looked at Vance in astonishment but answered unhesitatingly. "He said something about making a gay night of it; and then I told him—very emphatically—that if I went, I would leave him sharply at midnight, as was my invariable rule on all parties. . . . You see," she added, "I study very hard at my singing, and going home at midnight, no matter what the occasion, is one of the sacrifices—or rather, re-strictions—I impose on myself."

"Most commendable and most wise!" commented Vance. "Was this fact generally known among your acquaintances?"

"Oh, yes. It even resulted in my being nicknamed Cinderella."

"Specifically, did Colonel Ostrander and Mr. Pfyfe know it?"

"Yes."

Vance thought a moment.

"How did you happen to go to tea at Mr. Benson's home the day of the murder, if you were to dine with him that night?"

A flush stained her cheeks. "There was nothing wrong in that," she declared. "Somehow, after I had left Mr. Benson's office, I revolted against my decision to dine with him, and I went to his house—I had gone back to the office first, but he had left—to make a final appeal and to beg him to release me from my promise. But he laughed the matter off and, after insisting that I have tea, sent me home in a taxicab to dress for dinner. He called for me about half past seven."

"And when you pleaded with him to release you from your prom-ise, you sought to frighten him by recalling Captain Leacock's threat; and he said it was only a bluff."

Again the woman's astonishment was manifest. "Yes," she murmured.

Vance gave her a soothing smile.

"Colonel Ostrander told me he saw you and Mr. Benson at the Marseilles."

"Yes, and I was terribly ashamed. He knew what Mr. Benson was and had warned me against him only a few days before."

"I was under the impression the colonel and Mr. Benson were good friends."

"They were—up to a week ago. But the colonel lost more money than I did in a stock pool which Mr. Benson engineered recently, and he intimated to me very strongly that Mr. Benson had deliberately misadvised us to his own benefit. He didn't even speak to Mr. Benson that night at the Marseilles."

"What about these rich and precious stones that accompanied your tea with Mr. Benson?"

"Bribes," she answered; and her contemptuous smile was a more eloquent condemnation of Benson than if she had resorted to the bitterest castigation. "The gentleman sought to turn my head with them. I was offered a string of pearls to wear to dinner, but I declined them. And I was told that if I saw things in the right light—or some such charming phrase—I could have jewels just like them for my very, very own—perhaps even those identical ones, on the twenty-first."

"Of course—the twenty-first." Vance grinned. "Markham, are you listening? On the twenty-first Leander's note falls due, and if it's not paid, the jewels are forfeited."

He addressed himself again to Miss St. Clair.

"Did Mr. Benson have the jewels with him at dinner?"

"Oh, no! I think my refusal of the pearls rather discouraged him."

Vance paused, looking at her with ingratiating cordiality.

"Tell us now, please, of the gun episode—in your own words, as the lawyers say, hoping to entangle you later."

But she evidently feared no entanglement.

"The morning after the murder Captain Leacock came here and said he had gone to Mr. Benson's house about half past twelve with the intention of shooting him. But he had seen Mr. Pfyfe outside and, assuming he was calling, had given up the idea and gone home. I feared that Mr. Pfyfe had seen him, and I told him it would be safer to bring his pistol to me and to say, if questioned, that he'd lost it in France. . . . You see, I really thought he had shot Mr. Benson and was—well, lying like a gentleman, to spare my feelings. Then, when he took the pistol from me with the purpose of throwing it away altogether, I was even more certain of it."

She smiled faintly at Markham.

"That was why I refused to answer your questions. I wanted you to think that maybe I had done it, so you'd not suspect Captain Leacock."

"But he wasn't lying at all," said Vance.

"I know now that he wasn't. And I should have known it before. He'd never have brought the pistol to me if he'd been guilty."

A film came over her eyes.

"And—poor boy!—he confessed because he thought that I was guilty."

"That's precisely the harrowin' situation," nodded Vance. "But where did he think you had obtained a weapon?"

"I know many army men, friends of his and of Major Benson's. And last summer at the mountains I did considerable pistol practice for the fun of it. Oh, the idea was reasonable enough."

Vance rose and made a courtly bow.

"You've been most gracious—and most helpful," he said. "Y' see, Mr. Markham had various theories about the murder. The first, I believe, was that you alone were the Madam Borgia. The second was that you and the captain did the deed together—à quatre mains, as it were. The third was that the captain pulled the trigger a cappella. And the legal mind is so exquisitely developed that it can believe in several conflicting theories at the same time. The sad thing about the present case is that Mr. Markham still leans toward the belief that both of you are guilty, individually and collectively. I tried to reason with him before coming here; but I failed. Therefore, I insisted upon his hearing from your own charming lips your story of the affair."

He went up to Markham, who sat glaring at him with lips compressed.

"Well, old chap," he remarked pleasantly, "surely you are not going to persist in your obsession that either Miss St. Clair or Captain Leacock is guilty, what? . . . And won't you relent and unshackle the captain as I begged you to?"

He extended his arms in a theatrical gesture of supplication.

Markham's wrath was at the breaking point, but he got up deliberately and, going to the woman, held out his hand. "Miss St. Clair," he said kindly—and again I was impressed by the bigness of the man—, "I wish to assure you that I have dismissed the idea of your guilt, and also Captain Leacock's, from what Mr. Vance terms my incredibly rigid and unreceptive mind. . . . I forgive him, however, because he has saved me from doing you a very grave injustice. And I will see that you have your captain back as soon as the papers can be signed for his release."

As we walked out onto Riverside Drive, Markham turned savagely on Vance.

"So! *I* was keeping her precious captain locked up, and *you* were pleading with me to let him go! You know damned well I didn't think either one of them was guilty—you—you lounge lizard!"

Vance sighed. "Dear me! Don't you want to be of any help at all in this case?" he asked sadly.

"What good did it do you to make an ass of me in front of that woman?" spluttered Markham. "I can't see that you got anywhere, with all your tomfoolery."

"What!" Vance registered utter amazement. "The testimony you've heard today is going to help immeasurably in convicting the culprit. Furthermore, we now know about the gloves and handbag, and who the lady was that called at Benson's office, and what Miss St. Clair did between twelve and one, and why she dined alone with Alvin, and why she first had tea with him, and how the jewels came to be there, and why the captain took her his gun and then threw it away, and why he confessed. . . . My word! Doesn't all this knowledge soothe you? It rids the situation of so much debris."

He stopped and lit a cigarette.

"The really important thing the lady told us was that her friends knew she invariably departed at midnight when she went out of an evening. Don't overlook or belittle that point, old dear; it's most pert'nent. I told you long ago that the person who shot Benson knew she was dining with him that night."

"You'll be telling me next you know who killed him," Markham scoffed.

Vance sent a ring of smoke circling upward.

"I've known all along who shot the blighter."

Markham snorted derisively.

"Indeed! And when did this revelation burst upon you?"

"Oh, not more than five minutes after I entered Benson's house that first morning," replied Vance.

"Well, well! Why didn't you confide in me and avoid all these trying activities?"

"Quite impossible," Vance explained jocularly. "You were not ready to receive my apocryphal knowledge. It was first necess'ry to lead you patiently by the hand out of the various dark forests and morasses into which you insisted upon straying. You're so dev'lishly unimag'native, don't y'know."

A taxicab was passing and he hailed it.

"Eighty-seven West Forty-eighth Street," he directed.

Then he took Markham's arm confidingly. "Now for a brief chat with Mrs. Platz. And then—then I shall pour into your ear all my maidenly secrets."

CHAPTER 21

Sartorial Revelations
Wednesday, June 19, 5:30 p.m.

The housekeeper regarded our visit that afternoon with marked uneasiness. Though she was a large, powerful woman, her body seemed to have lost some of its strength, and her face showed signs of prolonged anxiety. Snitkin informed us, when we entered, that she had carefully read every newspaper account of the progress of the case and had questioned him interminably on the subject.

She entered the living room with scarcely an acknowledgment of our presence and took the chair Vance placed for her like a woman resigning herself to a dreaded but inevitable ordeal. When Vance looked at her keenly, she gave him a frightened glance and turned her face away, as if, in the second their eyes met, she had read his knowledge of some secret she had been jealously guarding.

Vance began his questioning without prelude or protasis.

"Mrs. Platz, was Mr. Benson very particular about his toupee—that is, did he often receive his friends without having it on?"

The woman appeared relieved. "Oh, no, sir—never."

"Think back, Mrs. Platz. Has Mr. Benson never, to your knowledge, been in anyone's company without his toupee?"

She was silent for some time, her brows contracted.

"Once I saw him take off his wig and show it to Colonel Ostrander, an elderly gentleman who used to call here very often. But Colonel Ostrander was an old friend of his. He told me they lived together once."

"No one else?"

Again she frowned thoughtfully. "No," she said, after several minutes.

"What about the tradespeople?"

"He was very particular about them. . . . And strangers, too," she

182

added. "When he used to sit in here in hot weather without his wig, he always pulled the shade on that window." She pointed to the one nearest the hallway. "You can look in it from the steps."

"I'm glad you brought up that point," said Vance. "And anyone standing on the steps could tap on the window or the iron bars, and attract the attention of anyone in this room?"

"Oh, yes, sir—easily. I did it myself once, when I went on an errand and forgot my key."

"It's quite likely, don't you think, that the person who shot Mr. Benson obtained admittance that way?"

"Yes, sir." She grasped eagerly at the suggestion.

"The person would have had to know Mr. Benson pretty well to tap on the window instead of ringing the bell. Don't you agree with me, Mrs. Platz?"

"Yes, sir." Her tone was doubtful; evidently the point was a little beyond her.

"If a stranger had tapped on the window, would Mr. Benson have admitted him without his toupee?"

"Oh, no—he wouldn't have let a stranger in."

"You are sure the bell didn't ring that night?"

"Positive, sir." The answer was very emphatic.

"Is there a light on the front steps?"

"No, sir."

"If Mr. Benson had looked out of the window to see who was tapping, could he have recognized the person at night?"

The woman hesitated. "I don't know—I don't think so."

"Is there any way you can see through the front door who is outside without opening it?"

"No, sir. Sometimes I wished there was."

"Then, if the person knocked on the window, Mr. Benson must have recognized the voice?"

"It looks that way, sir."

"And you're certain no one could have got in without a key?"

"How could they? The door locks by itself."

"It's the regulation spring lock, isn't it?"

"Yes, sir."

"Then it must have a catch you can turn off so that the door will open from either side even though it's latched."

"It did have a catch like that," she explained, "but Mr. Benson had it fixed so's it wouldn't work. He said it was too dangerous—I might go out and leave the house unlocked."

183

Vance stepped into the hallway, and I heard him opening and shutting the front door.

"You're right, Mrs. Platz," he observed, when he came back. "Now tell me: are you quite sure no one had a key?"

"Yes, sir. No one but me and Mr. Benson had a key."

Vance nodded his acceptance of her statement.

"You said you left your bedroom door open on the night Mr. Benson was shot. . . . Do you generally leave it open?"

"No, I 'most always shut it. But it was terrible close that night."

"Then it was merely an accident you left it open?"

"As you might say."

"If your door had been closed as usual, could you have heard the shot, do you think?"

"If I'd been awake, maybe. Not if I was sleeping, though. They got heavy doors in these old houses, sir."

"And they're beautiful, too," commented Vance.

He looked admiringly at the massive mahogany double door that opened into the hall.

"Y'know, Markham, our so-called civ'lization is nothing more than the persistent destruction of everything that's beautiful and enduring, and the designing of cheap makeshifts. You should read Oswald Spengler's *Untergang des Abendlands*—a most penetratin' document. I wonder some enterprisin' publisher hasn't embalmed it in our native argot.* The whole history of this degen'rate era we call modern civ'lization can be seen in our woodwork. Look at that fine old door, for instance, with its bevelled panels and ornamented bolection, and its Ionic pilasters and carved lintel. And then compare it with the flat, flimsy, machine-made, shellacked boards which are turned out by the thousand today. Sic transit. . . ."

He studied the door for some time; then turned abruptly back to Mrs. Platz, who was eyeing him curiously and with mounting apprehension.

"What did Mr. Benson do with the box of jewels when he went out to dinner?" he asked.

"Nothing, sir," she answered nervously. "He left them on the table there."

"Did you see them after he had gone?"

"Yes; and I was going to put them away. But I decided I'd better not touch them."

---

* The book—or a part of it—has, I believe, been recently translated into English.

"And nobody came to the door, or entered the house, after Mr. Benson left?"

"No, sir."

"You're quite sure?"

"I'm positive, sir."

Vance rose, and began to pace the floor. Suddenly, just as he was passing the woman, he stopped and faced her.

"Was your maiden name Hoffman, Mrs. Platz?"

The thing she had been dreading had come. Her face paled, her eyes opened wide, and her lower lip drooped a little.

Vance stood looking at her, not unkindly. Before she could regain control of herself, he said, "I had the pleasure of meeting your charmin' daughter recently."

"My daughter. . .?" the woman managed to stammer.

"Miss Hoffman, y'know—the attractive young lady with the blond hair. Mr. Benson's secret'ry."

The woman sat erect and spoke through clamped teeth. "She's not my daughter."

"Now, now, Mrs. Platz!" Vance chided her, as if speaking to a child. "Why this foolish attempt at deception? You remember how worried you were when I accused you of having a personal interest in the lady who was here to tea with Mr. Benson? You were afraid I thought it was Miss Hoffman. . . . But why should you be anxious about her, Mrs. Platz? I'm sure she's a very nice girl. And you really can't blame her for preferring the name of Hoffman to that of Platz. Platz means generally a place, though it also means a crash or an explosion; and sometimes a Platz is a bun or a yeast cake. But a Hoffman is a courtier—much nicer than being a yeast cake, what?"

He smiled engagingly, and his manner had a quieting effect upon her.

"It isn't that, sir," she said, looking at him appealingly. "I made her take the name. In this country any girl who's smart can get to be a lady if she's given a chance. And—"

"I understand perfectly," Vance interposed pleasantly. "Miss Hoffman is clever, and you feared that the fact of your being a housekeeper, if it became known, would stand in the way of her success. So you elim'nated yourself, as it were, for her welfare. I think it was very generous of you. . . . Your daughter lives alone?"

"Yes, sir—in Morningside Heights. But I see her every week." Her voice was barely audible.

"Of course—as often as you can, I'm sure. . . . Did you take the position as Mr. Benson's housekeeper because she was his secret'ry?"

She looked up, a bitter expression in her eyes. "Yes, sir—I did. She told me the kind of man he was; and he often made her come to the house here in the evenings to do extra work."

"And you wanted to be here to protect her?"

"Yes, sir—that was it."

"Why were you so worried the morning after the murder, when Mr. Markham here asked you if Mr. Benson kept any firearms around the house?" The woman shifted her gaze. "I—wasn't worried."

"Yes, you were, Mrs. Platz. And I'll tell you why. You were afraid we might think Miss Hoffman shot him."

"Oh, no, sir, I wasn't!" she cried. "My girl wasn't even here that night—I swear it!—she wasn't here. . . ."

She was badly shaken; the nervous tension of a week had snapped, and she looked helplessly about her.

"Come, come, Mrs. Platz," pleaded Vance consolingly. "No one believes for a moment that Miss Hoffman had a hand in Mr. Benson's death."

The woman peered searchingly into his face. At first she was loath to believe him—it was evident that fear had long been preying on her mind—and it took him fully a quarter of an hour to convince her that what he had said was true. When, finally, we left the house, she was in a comparatively peaceful state of mind.

On our way to the Stuyvesant Club Markham was silent, completely engrossed with his thoughts. It was evident that the new facts educed by the interview with Mrs. Platz troubled him considerably.

Vance sat smoking dreamily, turning his head now and then to inspect the buildings we passed. We drove east through Forty-eighth Street, and when we came abreast of the New York Bible Society House, he ordered the chauffeur to stop and insisted that we admire it.

"Christianity," he remarked, "has almost vindicated itself by its architecture alone. With few exceptions, the only buildings in this city that are not eyesores are the churches and their allied structures. The American aesthetic credo is: Whatever's big is beautiful. These depressin' gargantuan boxes with rectangular holes in 'em, which are called skyscrapers, are worshiped by Americans simply because they're huge. A box with forty rows of holes is twice as beautiful as a box with twenty rows. Simple formula, what? . . . Look at this little five-story affair across the street. It's inf'nitely lovelier—and more impressive, too—than any skyscraper in the city. . . ."

Vance referred but once to the crime during our ride to the club and then only indirectly.

"Kind hearts, y'know, Markham, are more than coronets. I've done a good deed today and I feel pos'tively virtuous. *Frau* Platz will *schlafen* much better tonight. She has been frightfully upset about little Gretchen. She's a doughty old soul; motherly and all that. And she couldn't bear to think of the future Lady Vere de Vere being suspected. . . . Wonder why she worried so?" And he gave Markham a sly look.

Nothing further was said until after dinner, which we ate in the Roof Garden. We had pushed back our chairs, and sat looking out over the treetops of Madison Square.

"Now, Markham," said Vance, "give over all prejudices, and consider the situation judiciously—as you lawyers euphemistically put it. . . . To begin with, we now know why Mrs. Platz was so worried at your question regarding firearms and why she was upset by my ref'rence to her personal int'rest in Benson's tea companion. So, those two mysteries are elim'nated. . . ."

"How did you find out about her relation to the girl?" interjected Markham.

"'Twas my ogling did it." Vance gave him a reproving look. "You recall that I 'ogled' the young lady at our first meeting—but I forgive you. . . . And you remember our little discussion about cranial idiosyncrasies? Miss Hoffman, I noticed at once, possessed all the physical formations of Benson's housekeeper. She was *brachycephalic*; she had over-articulated cheekbones, an *orthognathous* jaw, a low, flat *parietal* structure, and a *mesorrhinian* nose. . . . Then I looked for her ear, for I had noted that Mrs. Platz had the pointed, lobeless, 'satyr' ear—sometimes called the Darwin ear. These ears run in families; and when I saw that Miss Hoffman's were of the same type, even though modified, I was fairly certain of the relationship. But there were other similarities—in pigment, for instance, and in height—both are tall, y'know. And the central masses of each were very large in comparison with the peripheral masses; the shoulders were narrow and the wrists and ankles small, while the hips were bulky. . . . That Hoffman was Platz's maiden name was only a guess. But it didn't matter."

Vance adjusted himself more comfortably in his chair.

"Now for your judicial considerations. . . . First, let us assume that at a little before half past twelve on the night of the thirteenth the villain came to Benson's house, saw the light in the living room, tapped on the window, and was instantly admitted. . . . What, would you say, do these assumptions indicate regarding the visitor?"

187

"Merely that Benson was acquainted with him," returned Markham. "But that doesn't help us any. We can't extend the *sus. per coll.* to everybody the man knew."

"The indications go much further than that, old chap," Vance retorted. "They show unmistakably that Benson's murderer was a most intimate crony, or, at least, a person before whom he didn't care how he looked. The absence of the toupee, as I once suggested to you, was a prime essential of the situation. A toupee, don't y'know, is the sartorial *sine qua non* of every middle-aged Beau Brummel afflicted with baldness. You heard Mrs. Platz on the subject. Do you think for a second that Benson, who hid his hirsute deficiency even from the grocer's boy, would visit with a mere acquaintance thus bereft of his crowning glory? And besides being thus denuded, he was without his full complement of teeth. Moreover, he was without collar or tie, and attired in an old smoking jacket and bedroom slippers! Picture the spectacle, my dear fellow. . . . A man does not look fascinatin' without his collar and with his shirt-band and gold stud exposed. Thus attired, he is the equiv'lent of a lady in curl papers. . . . How many men do you think Benson knew with whom he would have sat down to a *tête-à-tête* in this undress condition?"

"Three or four, perhaps," answered Markham. "But I can't arrest them all."

"I'm sure you would if you could. But it won't be necess'ry."

Vance selected another cigarette from his case and went on. "There are other helpful indications, y'know. For instance, the murderer was fairly well acquainted with Benson's domestic arrangements. He must have known that the housekeeper slept a good distance from the living room and would not be startled by the shot if her door was closed as usual. Also, he must have known there was no one else in the house at that hour. And another thing: don't forget that his voice was perfectly familiar to Benson. If there had been the slightest doubt about it, Benson would not have let him in, in view of his natural fear of housebreakers and with the captain's threat hanging over him."

"That's a tenable hypothesis. . . . What else?"

"The jewels, Markham—those orators of love. Have you thought of them? They were on the centre table when Benson came home that night; and they were gone in the morning. Wherefore, it seems inev'table that the murderer took 'em—eh, what? . . . And may they not have been one reason for the murderer's coming there that night? If so, who of Benson's most intimate *personae gratae* knew of their presence in the house? And who wanted 'em particularly?"

"Exactly, Vance." Markham nodded his head slowly. "You've hit it.

I've had an uneasy feeling about Pfyfe right along. I was on the point of ordering his arrest today when Heath brought word of Leacock's confession; and then, when that blew up, my suspicions reverted to him. I said nothing this afternoon because I wanted to see where your ideas had led you. What you've been saying checks up perfectly with my own notions. Pfyfe's our man—"

He brought the front legs of his chair down suddenly.

"And now, damn it, you've let him get away from us!"

"Don't fret, old dear," said Vance. "He's safe with Mrs. Pfyfe, I fancy. And anyhow, your friend, Mr. Ben Hanlon, is well versed in retrieving fugitives. . . . Let the harassed Leander alone for the moment. You don't need him tonight—and tomorrow you won't want him."

Markham wheeled about.

"What's that! I won't want him? And why, pray?"

"Well," Vance explained indolently, "he hasn't a congenial and lovable nature, has he? And he's not exactly an object of blindin' beauty. I shouldn't want him around me more than was necess'ry, don't y'know. . . . Incidentally, he's not guilty."

Markham was too nonplussed to be exasperated. He regarded Vance searchingly for a full minute.

"I don't follow you," he said. "If you think Pfyfe's innocent, who, in God's name, do you think is guilty?"

Vance glanced at his watch.

"Come to my house tomorrow for breakfast and bring those alibis you asked Heath for; and I'll tell you who shot Benson."

Something in his tone impressed Markham. He realized that Vance would not have made so specific a promise unless he was confident of his ability to keep it. He knew Vance too well to ignore, or even minimize, his statement.

"Why not tell me now?" he asked.

"Awf'lly sorry, y'know," apologized Vance; "but I'm going to the Philharmonic's 'special' tonight. They're playing César Franck's D-Minor, and Stransky's temp'rament is em'nently suited to its diatonic sentimentalities. . . . You'd better come along, old man. Soothin' to the nerves and all that."

"Not me!" grumbled Markham. "What I need is a brandy-and-soda"

He walked down with us to the taxicab.

"Come at nine tomorrow," said Vance, as we took our seats. "Let the office wait a bit. And don't forget to phone Heath for those alibis."

Then, just as we started off, he leaned out of the car. "And I say, Markham: how tall would you say Mrs. Platz is?"

CHAPTER 22

Vance Outlines a Theory

Thursday, June 20, 9 a.m.

Markham came to Vance's apartment at promptly nine o'clock the next morning. He was in a bad humour.

"Now, see here, Vance," he said, as soon as he was seated at the table, "I want to know what was the meaning of your parting words last night."

"Eat your melon, old dear," said Vance. "It comes from northern Brazil and is very delicious. But don't devitalize its flavour with pepper or salt. An amazin' practice, that, though not as amazin' as stuffing a melon with ice cream. The American does the most dumbfoundin' things with ice cream. He puts it on pie; he puts it in soda water; he encases it in hard chocolate like a bonbon; he puts it between sweet biscuits and calls the result an ice cream sandwich; he even uses it instead of whipped cream in a Charlotte Russe. . . ."

"What I want to know—" began Markham; but Vance did not permit him to finish.

"It's surprisin', y'know, the erroneous ideas people have about melons. There are only two species, the muskmelon and the watermelon. All breakfast melons—like cantaloupes, citrons, nutmegs, Cassabas, and honeydews—are varieties of the muskmelon. But people have the notion, d' ye see, that cantaloupe is a generic term. Philadelphians call all melons cantaloupes; whereas this type of muskmelon was first cultivated in Cantalupo, Italy. . . ."

"Very interesting," said Markham, with only partly disguised impatience. "Did you intend by your remark last night—"

"And after the melon, Currie has prepared a special dish for you. It's my own gustat'ry *chef-d'oeuvre*—with Currie's collaboration, of course. I've spent months on its conception—composing and organizing it, so to speak. I haven't named it yet; perhaps you can suggest a fitting appellation. . . . To achieve this dish, one first chops up a hard-boiled egg and mixes it with grated Port du Salut cheese, adding a *soupçon* of tarragon. This paste is then enclosed in a filet of white perch, like a French pancake. It is tied with silk, rolled in a specially prepared almond batter, and cooked in sweet butter. That, of course, is the barest outline of its manufacture, with all the truly exquisite details omitted."

"It sounds appetizing." Markham's tone was devoid of enthusiasm. "But I didn't come here for a cooking lesson."

"Y' know, you underestimate the importance of your ventral pleasures," pursued Vance. "Eating is the one infallible guide to a people's intellectual advancement, as well as the inev'table gauge of the individual's temp'rament. The savage cooked and ate like a savage. In the early days of the human race mankind was cursed with one vast epidemic of indigestion. There's where his devils and demons and ideas of hell came from: they were the nightmares of his dyspepsia. Then, as man began to master the technique of cooking, he became civilized; and when he achieved the highest pinnacles of the culin'ry art, he also achieved the highest pinnacles of cultural and intellectual glory. When the art of the gourmet retrogressed, so did man. The tasteless, standardized cookery of America is typical of our decadence. A perfectly blended soup, Markham, is more ennoblin' than Beethoven's C-Minor Symphony. . . ."

Markham listened stolidly to Vance's chatter during breakfast. He made several attempts to bring up the subject of the crime, but Vance glibly ignored each essay. It was not until Currie had cleared away the dishes that he referred to the object of Markham's visit.

"Did you bring the alibi reports?" was his first question.

Markham nodded. "And it took me two hours to find Heath after you'd gone last night."

"Sad," breathed Vance.

He went to the desk and took a closely written double sheet of foolscap from one of the compartments.

"I wish you'd glance this over and give me your learned opinion," he said, handing the paper to Markham. "I prepared it last night after the concert."

I later took possession of the document and filed it with my other notes and papers pertaining to the Benson case. The following is a verbatim copy:

HYPOTHESIS
Mrs. Anna Platz shot and killed Alvin Benson on the night of June 13th.

PLACE
She lived in the house and admitted being there at the time the shot was fired.

OPPORTUNITY
She was alone in the house with Benson.

All the windows were either barred or locked on the inside. The front door was locked. There was no other means of ingress.

Her presence in the living room was natural; she might have entered ostensibly to ask Benson a domestic question.

Her standing directly in front of him would not necessarily have caused him to look up. Hence, his reading attitude.

Who else could have come so close to him for the purpose of shooting him without attracting his attention?

He would not have cared how he appeared before his housekeeper. He had become accustomed to being seen by her without his teeth and toupee and in négligé condition.

Living in the house, she was able to choose a propitious moment for the crime.

TIME
She waited up for him. Despite her denial, he might have told her when he would return.

When he came in alone and changed to his smoking jacket, she knew he was not expecting any late visitors.

She chose a time shortly after his return because it would appear that he had brought someone home with him, and that this other person had killed him.

MEANS
She used Benson's own gun. Benson undoubtedly had more than one; for he would have been more likely to keep a gun in his bedroom than in his living room; and since a Smith and Wesson was found in the living room, there probably was another in the bedroom.

Being his housekeeper, she knew of the gun upstairs. After

he had gone down to the living room to read, she secured it and took it with her, concealed under her apron.

She threw the gun away or hid it after the shooting. She had all night in which to dispose of it.

She was frightened when asked what firearms Benson kept about the house, for she was not sure whether or not we knew of the gun in the bedroom.

MOTIVE

She took the position of housekeeper because she feared Benson's conduct toward her daughter. She always listened when her daughter came to his house at night to work.

Recently she discovered that Benson had dishonourable intentions and believed her daughter to be in imminent danger.

A mother who would sacrifice herself for her daughter's future, as she has done, would not hesitate at killing to save her.

And there are the jewels. She has them hidden and is keeping them for her daughter. Would Benson have gone out and left them on the table? And if he had put them away, who but she, familiar with the house and having plenty of time, could have found them?

CONDUCT

She lied about St. Clair's coming to tea, explaining later that she knew St. Clair could not have had anything to do with the crime. Was this feminine intuition? No. She could know St. Clair was innocent only because she herself was guilty. She was too motherly to want an innocent person suspected.

She was markedly frightened yesterday when her daughter's name was mentioned, because she feared the discovery of the relationship might reveal her motive for shooting Benson.

She admitted hearing the shot, because, if she had denied it, a test might have proved that a shot in the living room would have sounded loudly in her room; and this would have aroused suspicion against her. Does a person, when awakened, turn on the lights and determine the exact hour? And if she had heard a report which sounded like a shot being fired in the house, would she not have investigated or given an alarm?

When first interviewed, she showed plainly she disliked Benson.

Her apprehension has been pronounced each time she has been questioned.

She is the hard-headed, shrewd, determined German type, who could both plan and perform such a crime.

HEIGHT

She is about five feet, ten inches tall—the demonstrated height of the murderer.

Markham read this *précis* through several times—he was fully fifteen minutes at the task—and when he had finished, he sat silent for ten minutes more. Then he rose and walked up and down the room.

"Not a fancy legal document, that," remarked Vance. "But I think even a grand juror could understand it. You, of course, can rearrange and elab'rate it, and bedeck it with innum'rable meaningless phrases and recondite legal idioms."

Markham did not answer at once. He paused by the French windows and looked down into the street. Then he said, "Yes, I think you've made out a case. . . . Extraordinary! I've wondered from the first what you were getting at; and your questioning of Platz yesterday impressed me as pointless. I'll admit it never occurred to me to suspect her. Benson must have given her good cause."

He turned and came slowly toward us, his head down, his hands behind him.

"I don't like the idea of arresting her. . . . Funny I never thought of her in connection with it."

He stopped in front of Vance.

"And you yourself didn't think of her at first, despite your boast that you knew who did it after you'd been in Benson's house five minutes."

Vance smiled mirthfully and sprawled in his chair.

Markham became indignant. "Damn it! You told me the next day that no woman could have done it, no matter what evidence was adduced, and harangued me about art and psychology and God knows what."

"Quite right," murmured Vance, still smiling. "No woman did it."

"No woman did it!" Markham's gorge was rising rapidly.

"Oh, dear no!"

He pointed to the sheet of paper in Markham's hand.

"That's just a bit of spoofing, don't y'know. . . . Poor old Mrs. Platz!—she's as innocent as a lamb."

Markham threw the paper on the table and sat down. I had never seen him so furious; but he controlled himself admirably.

"Y' see, my dear old bean," explained Vance, in his unemotional drawl, "I had an irresistible longing to demonstrate to you how utterly silly your circumst'ntial and material evidence is. I'm rather proud, y'know, of my case against Mrs. Platz. I'm sure you could convict her on the strength of it. But, like the whole theory of your exalted law, it's wholly specious and erroneous. . . . Circumst'ntial evidence, Markham, is the utt'rest tommyrot imag'nable. Its theory is not unlike that of our present-day democracy. The democratic theory is that if you accumulate enough ignorance at the polls, you produce intelligence; and the theory of circumst'ntial evidence is that if you accumulate a sufficient number of weak links, you produce a strong chain."

"Did you get me here this morning," demanded Markham coldly, "to give me a dissertation on legal theory?"

"Oh, no," Vance blithely assured him. "But I simply must prepare you for the acceptance of my revelation; for I haven't a scrap of material or circumst'ntial evidence against the guilty man. And yet, Markham, I know he's guilty as well as I know you're sitting in that chair planning how you can torture and kill me without being punished."

"If you have no evidence, how did you arrive at your conclusion?" Markham's tone was vindictive.

"Solely by psychological analysis—by what might be called the science of personal possibilities. A man's psychological nature is as clear a brand to one who can read it as was Hester Prynne's scarlet letter. . . . I never read Hawthorne, by the bye. I can't abide the New England temp'rament."

Markham set his jaw, and gave Vance a look of arctic ferocity.

"You expect me to go into court, I suppose, leading your victim by the arm, and say to the judge, 'Here's the man that shot Alvin Benson. I have no evidence against him, but I want you to sentence him to death because my brilliant and sagacious friend, Mr. Philo Vance, the inventor of stuffed perch, says this man has a wicked nature.'"

Vance gave an almost imperceptible shrug.

"I sha'n't wither away with grief if you don't even arrest the guilty man. But I thought it no more than humane to tell you who he was, if only to stop you from chivvying all these innocent people."

"All right—tell me, and let me get on about my business."

I don't believe there was any longer a question in Markham's mind that Vance actually knew who had killed Benson. But it was not until considerably later in the morning that he fully understood why Vance had kept him for days upon tenterhooks. When at last he did understand it, he forgave Vance; but at the moment he was angered to the limit of his control.

"There are one or two things that must be done before I can reveal the gentleman's name," Vance told him. "First, let me have a peep at those alibis."

Markham took from his pocket a sheaf of typewritten pages and passed them over.

Vance adjusted his monocle and read through them carefully. Then he stepped out of the room; and I heard him telephoning. When he returned, he reread the reports. One in particular he lingered over, as if weighing its possibilities.

"There's a chance, y'know," he murmured at length, gazing indecisively into the fireplace.

He glanced at the report again.

"I see here," he said, "that Colonel Ostrander, accompanied by a Bronx alderman named Moriarty, attended the Midnight Follies at the Piccadilly Theatre in Forty-seventh Street on the night of the thirteenth, arriving there a little before twelve and remaining through the performance, which was over about half past two a.m. . . . Are you acquainted with this particular alderman?"

Markham's eyes lifted sharply to the other's face. "I've met Mr. Moriarty. What about him?" I thought I detected a note of suppressed excitement in his voice.

"Where do Bronx aldermen loll about in the forenoons?" asked Vance.

"At home, I should say. Or possibly at the Samoset Club. . . . Sometimes they have business at City Hall."

"My word!—such unseemly activity for a politician! . . . Would you mind ascertaining if Mr. Moriarty is at home or at his club. If it's not too much bother, I'd like to have a brief word with him."

Markham gave Vance a penetrating gaze. Then, without a word, he went to the telephone in the den.

"Mr. Moriarty was at home, about to leave for City Hall," he announced on returning. "I asked him to drop by here on his way downtown." "I do hope he doesn't disappoint us," sighed Vance. "But it's worth trying."

"Are you composing a charade?" asked Markham; but there was neither humour nor good nature in the question.

"'Pon my word, old man, I'm not trying to confuse the main issue," said Vance. "Exert a little of that simple faith with which you are so gen'rously supplied—it's more desirable than Norman blood, y'know. I'll give you the guilty man before the morning's over. But, d' ye see, I must make sure that you'll accept him. These alibis are, I trust, going to prove most prof'table in paving the way for my *coup de boutoir*. . . . An alibi, as I recently confided to you, is a tricky and dang'rous thing, and open to grave suspicion. And the absence of an alibi means nothing at all. For instance, I see by these reports that Miss Hoffman has no alibi for the night of the thirteenth. She says she went to a motion picture theatre and then home. But no one saw her at any time. She was prob'bly at Benson's visiting mama until late. Looks suspicious—eh, what? And yet, even if she was there, her only crime that night was filial affection. . . . On the other hand, there are several alibis here which are, as one says, cast iron—silly metaphor: cast iron's easily broken—and I happen to know one of 'em is spurious. So be a good fellow and have patience; for it's most necess'ry that these alibis be minutely inspected."

Fifteen minutes later Mr. Moriarty arrived. He was a serious, good-looking, well-dressed youth in his late twenties—not at all my idea of an alderman—and he spoke clear and precise English with almost no trace of the Bronx accent.

Markham introduced him and briefly explained why he had been requested to call.

"One of the men from the homicide bureau," answered Moriarty, "was asking me about the matter only yesterday."

"We have the report," said Vance, "but it's a bit too general. Will you tell us exactly what you did that night after you met Colonel Ostrander?"

"The colonel had invited me to dinner and the Follies. I met him at the Marseilles at ten. We had dinner there and went to the Piccadilly a little before twelve, where we remained until about two thirty. I walked to the colonel's apartment with him, had a drink and a chat, and then took the subway home about three thirty."

"You told the detective yesterday you sat in a box at the theatre."

"That's correct."

"Did you and the colonel remain in the box throughout the performance?"

"No. After the first act a friend of mine came to the box, and the colonel excused himself and went to the washroom. After the second act the colonel and I stepped outside into the alleyway and had a smoke."

"What time, would you say, was the first act over?"

"Twelve thirty or thereabouts."

"And where is this alleyway situated?" asked Vance. "As I recall, it runs along the side of the theatre to the street."

"You're right."

"And isn't there an exit door very near the boxes, which leads into the alleyway?"

"There is. We used it that night."

"How long was the colonel gone after the first act?"

"A few minutes—I couldn't say exactly."

"Had he returned when the curtain went up on the second act?"

Moriarty reflected. "I don't believe he had. I think he came back a few minutes after the act began."

"Ten minutes?"

"I couldn't say. Certainly no more."

"Then, allowing for a ten-minute intermission, the colonel might have been away twenty minutes?"

"Yes—it's possible."

This ended the interview; and when Moriarty had gone, Vance lay back in his chair and smoked thoughtfully.

"Surprisin' luck!" he commented. "The Piccadilly Theatre, y'know, is practically round the corner from Benson's house. You grasp the possibilities of the situation, what? . . . The colonel invites an alderman to the Midnight Follies and gets box seats near an exit giving on an alley. At a little before half past twelve he leaves the box, sneaks out via the alley, goes to Benson's, taps and is admitted, shoots his man, and hurries back to the theatre. Twenty minutes would have been ample."

Markham straightened up but made no comment.

"And now," continued Vance, "let's look at the indicat'ry circumst'nces and the confirmat'ry facts. . . . Miss St. Clair told us the colonel had lost heavily in a pool of Benson's manipulation and had accused him of crookedness. He hadn't spoken to Benson for a week; so it's plain there was bad blood between 'em. He saw Miss St. Clair at the Marseilles with Benson; and, knowing she always went home at midnight, he chose half past twelve as a propitious hour; although originally he may have intended to wait until much later, say, one thirty or two, before sneaking out of the theatre. Being an army officer, he would have had a Colt forty-five, and he was probably a good shot. He was most anxious to have you arrest someone—he didn't seem to care who; and he even phoned you to inquire about it. He was one of the very few persons in the world whom Benson would have admitted, attired as he was. He'd known Benson int'mately for fifteen years, and

Mrs. Platz once saw Benson take off his toupee and show it to him. Moreover, he would have known all about the domestic arrangements of the house; he no doubt had slept there many a time when showing his old pal the wonders of New York's night life. . . . How does all that appeal to you?"

Markham had risen and was pacing the floor, his eyes almost closed.

"So that was why you were so interested in the colonel—asking people if they knew him and inviting him to lunch? . . . What gave you the idea, in the first place, that he was guilty?"

"Guilty!" exclaimed Vance. "That priceless old dunderhead guilty! Really, Markham, the notion's prepost'rous. I'm sure he went to the washroom that night to comb his eyebrows and arrange his tie. Sitting, as he was, in a box, the gels on the stage could see him, y'know."

Markham halted abruptly. An ugly colour crept into his cheeks, and his eyes blazed. But before he could speak, Vance went on, with serene indifference to his anger.

"And I played in the most astonishin' luck. Still, he's just the kind of ancient popinjay who'd go to the washroom and dandify himself—I rather counted on that, don't y'know. . . . My word! We've made amazin' progress this morning, despite your injured feelings. You now have five different people, any one of whom you can, with a little legal ingenuity, convict of the crime—in any event, you can get indictments against 'em."

He leaned his head back meditatively.

"First, there's Miss St. Clair. You were quite pos'tive she did the deed, and you told the major you were all ready to arrest her. My demonstration of the murderer's height could be thrown out on the grounds that it was intelligent and conclusive and therefore had no place in a court of law. I'm sure the judge would concur. Secondly, I give you Captain Leacock. I actu'lly had to use physical force to keep you from jailing the chap. You had a beautiful case against him—to say nothing of his delightful confession. And if you met with any diff'culties, he'd help you out; he'd adore having you convict him. Thirdly, I submit Leander the Lovely. You had a better case against him than against almost any one of the others—a perfect wealth of circumst'ntial evidence—an *embarras de richesse*, in fact. And any jury would delight in convicting him. I would, myself, if only for the way he dresses. Fourthly, I point with pride to Mrs. Platz. Another perfect circumst'ntial case, fairly bulging with clues and inf'rences and legal whatnots. Fifthly, I present the colonel. I have just rehearsed your case against him; and I could elab'rate it touchin'ly, given a little more time."

He paused and gave Markham a smile of cynical affability.

"Observe, please, that each member of this quintet meets all the demands of presumptive guilt: each one fulfils the legal requirements as to time, place, opportunity, means, motive, and conduct. The only drawback, d' ye see, is that all five are quite innocent. A most discomposin' fact, but there you are. . . . Now, if all the people against whom there's the slightest suspicion are innocent, what's to be done? . . . Annoyin', ain't it?"

He picked up the alibi reports.

"There's pos'tively nothing to be done but to go on checking up these alibis."

I could not imagine what goal he was trying to reach by these apparently irrelevant digressions; and Markham, too, was mystified. But neither of us doubted for a moment that there was method in his madness.

"Let's see," he mused. "The major's is the next in order. What do you say to tackling it? It shouldn't take long—he lives near here; and the entire alibi hinges on the evidence of the night-boy at his apartment house. Come!" He got up.

"How do you know the boy is there now?" objected Markham.

"I phoned a while ago and found out."

"But this is damned nonsense!"

Vance now had Markham by the arm, playfully urging him toward the door. "Oh, undoubtedly," he agreed. "But I've often told you, old dear, you take life much too seriously."

Markham, protesting vigorously, held back and endeavoured to disengage his arm from the other's grip. But Vance was determined; and after a somewhat heated dispute, Markham gave in.

"I'm about through with this hocus-pocus," he growled, as we got into a taxicab.

"I'm through already," said Vance.

CHAPTER 23

Checking an Alibi
Thursday, June 20; 10:30 a.m.

The Chatham Arms, where Major Benson lived, was a small exclusive bachelor apartment house in Forty-sixth Street, midway between Fifth and Sixth Avenues. The entrance, set in a simple and dignified façade, was flush with the street and only two steps above the pavement. The front door opened into a narrow hallway with a small reception room, like a cul-de-sac, on the left. At the rear could be seen the elevator; and beside it, tucked under a narrow flight of iron stairs which led round the elevator shaft, was a telephone switchboard.

When we arrived, two youths in uniform were on duty, one lounging in the door of the elevator, the other seated at the switchboard.

Vance halted Markham near the entrance.

"One of these boys, I was informed over the telephone, was on duty the night of the thirteenth. Find out which one it was and scare him into submission by your exalted title of District Attorney. Then turn him over to me."

Reluctantly Markham walked down the hallway. After a brief interrogation of the boys he led one of them into the reception room, and peremptorily explained what he wanted.*

Vance began his questioning with the confident air of one who has no doubt whatever as to another's exact knowledge.

"What time did Major Benson get home the night his brother was shot?"

The boy's eyes opened wide. "He came in about 'leven—right after show time," he answered, with only a momentary hesitation.

(I have set down the rest of the questions and answers in dramatic-dialogue form, for purposes of space economy.)

---

* The boy was Jack Prisco, of 621 Kelly Street.

201

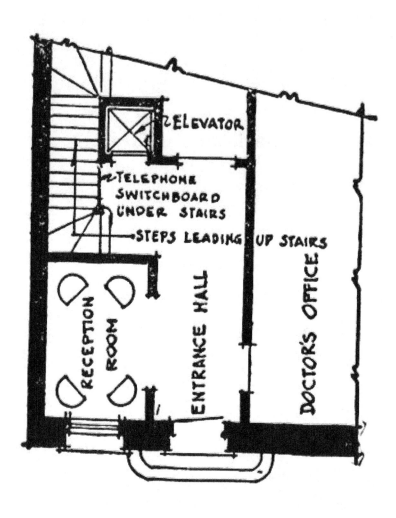

ELEVATOR

TELEPHONE
SWITCHBOARD
UNDER STAIRS

STEPS LEADING UP STAIRS

RECEPTION ROOM

ENTRANCE HALL

DOCTOR'S OFFICE

WEST 46TH. STREET

FIRST FLOOR OF CHATHAM ARMS APARTMENT IN
WEST FORTY-SIXTH STREET

Vance: He spoke to you, I suppose?

Boy: Yes, sir. He told me he'd been to the theatre, and said what a rotten show it was—and that he had an awful headache.

Vance: How do you happen to remember so well what he said a week ago?

Boy: Why, his brother was murdered that night!

Vance: And the murder caused so much excitement that you naturally recalled everything that happened at the time in connection with Major Benson?

Boy: Sure—he was the murdered guy's brother.

Vance: When he came in that night, did he say anything about the day of the month?

Boy: Nothin' except that he guessed his bad luck in pickin' a bum show was on account of it bein' the thirteenth.

Vance: Did he say anything else?

Boy (grinning): He said he'd make the thirteenth my lucky day, and he gave me all the silver he had in his pocket—nickels and dimes and quarters and one fifty-cent piece.

Vance: How much altogether?

Boy: Three dollars and forty-five cents.

Vance: And then he went to his room?

Boy: Yes, sir—I took him up. He lives on the third floor.

Vance: Did he go out again later?

Boy: No, sir.

Vance: How do you know?

Boy: I'd've seen him. I was either answerin' the switchboard or runnin' the elevator all night. He couldn't've got out without my seein' him.

Vance: Were you alone on duty?

Boy: After ten o'clock there's never but one *boy* on.

Vance: And there's no other way a person could leave the house except by the front door?

Boy: No, sir.

Vance: When did you next see Major Benson?

Boy (after thinking a moment): He rang for some cracked ice, and I took it up.

Vance: What time?

Boy: Why—I don't know exactly....Yes, I do! It was half past twelve.

Vance (smiling faintly): He asked you the time, perhaps?

Boy: Yes, sir, he did. He asked me to look at his clock in his parlour.

Vance: How did he happen to do that?

Boy: Well, I took up the ice, and he was in bed; and he asked me to put it in his pitcher in the parlour. When I was doin' it, he called me to look at the clock on the mantel and tell him what time it was. He said his watch had stopped and he wanted to set it.

Vance: What did he say then?

Boy: Nothin' much. He told me not to ring his bell, no matter who called up. He said he wanted to sleep, and didn't want to be woke up.

Vance: Was he emphatic about it?

Boy: Well—he meant it, all right.

Vance: Did he say anything else?

Boy: No. He just said good night and turned out the light, and I came on downstairs.

Vance: What light did he turn out?

Boy: The one in his bedroom.

Vance: Could you see into his bedroom from the parlour?

Boy: No. The bedroom's off the hall.

Vance: How could you tell the light was turned off then?

Boy: The bedroom door was open, and the light was shinin' into the hall.

Vance: Did you pass the bedroom door when you went out?

Boy: Sure—you have to.

Vance: And was the door still open?

Boy: Yes.

Vance: Is that the only door to the bedroom?

Boy: Yes.

Vance: Where was Major Benson when you entered the apartment?

Boy: In bed.

Vance: How do you know?

Boy (mildly indignant): I saw him.

Vance (after a pause): You're quite sure he didn't come downstairs again?

Boy: I told you I'd've seen him if he had.

Vance: Couldn't he have walked down at some time when you had the elevator upstairs, without your seeing him?

Boy: Sure, he could. But I didn't take the elevator up after I'd took the major his cracked ice until around two thirty, when Mr. Montagu came in.

Vance: You took no one up in the elevator, then, between the time you brought Major Benson the ice and when Mr. Montagu came in at two thirty?

Boy: Nobody.

Vance: And you didn't leave the hall here between those hours?

Boy: No. I was sittin' here all the time.

Vance: Then the last time you saw him was in bed at twelve thirty?

Boy: Yes—until early in the morning when some dame* phoned him and said his brother had been murdered. He came down and went out about ten minutes after.

Vance (giving the boy a dollar): That's all. But don't you open your mouth to anyone about our being here, or you may find yourself in the lockup—understand? . . . Now, get back to your job.

When the boy had left us, Vance turned a pleading gaze upon Markham.

"Now, old man, for the protection of society, and the higher demands of justice, and the greatest good for the greatest number, and *pro bono publico*, and that sort of thing, you must once more adopt a course of conduct contr'ry to your innate promptings—or whatever the phrase you used. Vulgarly put, I want to snoop through the major's apartment at once."

"What for?" Markham's tone was one of exclamatory protest. "Have you completely lost your senses? There's no getting round the boy's testimony. I may be weak minded, but I know when a witness like that is telling the truth."

"Certainly, he's telling the truth," agreed Vance serenely. "That's just why I want to go up. Come, my Markham. There's no danger of the major returning en surprise at this hour. . . . And"—he smiled cajolingly—"you promised me every assistance don't y'know."

Markham was vehement in his remonstrances, but Vance was equally vehement in his insistence; and a few minutes later we were trespassing, by means of a passkey, in Major Benson's apartment.

The only entrance was a door leading from the public hall into a narrow passageway which extended straight ahead into the living room at the rear. On the right of this passageway, near the entrance, was a door opening into the bedroom.

Vance walked directly back into the living room. On the right-hand wall was a fireplace and a mantel on which sat an old-fashioned mahogany clock. Near the mantel, in the far corner, stood a small table containing a silver ice-water service consisting of a pitcher and six goblets.

"There is our very convenient clock," said Vance. "And there is the pitcher in which the boy put the ice—imitation Sheffield plate."

Going to the window, he glanced down into the paved rear court twenty-five or thirty feet below.

---

* Obviously Mrs. Platz.

"The major certainly couldn't have escaped through the window," he remarked.

He turned and stood a moment looking into the passageway.

"The boy could easily have seen the light go out in the bedroom, if the door was open. The reflection on the glazed white wall of the passage would have been quite brilliant."

Then, retracing his steps, he entered the bedroom. It contained a small canopied bed facing the door, and beside it stood a night table on which was an electric lamp. Sitting down on the edge of the bed, he looked about him and turned the lamp on and off by the socket chain. Presently he fixed his eyes on Markham.

"You see how the major got out without the boy's knowing it— eh, what?"

"By levitation, I suppose," submitted Markham.

"It amounted to that, at any rate," replied Vance, "Deuced ingenious, too. . . . Listen, Markham:—At half past twelve the major rang for cracked ice. The boy brought it, and when he entered, he looked in through the door, which was open, and saw the major in bed. The major told him to put the ice in the pitcher in the living room. The boy walked on down the passage and across the living room to the table in the corner. The major then called to him to learn the time by the clock on the mantel. The boy looked: it was half past twelve. The major replied that he was not to be disturbed again, said good night, turned off this light on this night table, jumped out of bed—he was dressed, of course—and stepped quickly out into the public hall before the boy had time to empty the ice and return to the passage. The major ran down the stairs and was in the street before the elevator descended. The boy, when he passed the bedroom door on his way out, could not have seen whether the major was still in bed or not, even if he had looked in, for the room was then in darkness—Clever, what?"

"The thing would have been possible, of course," conceded Markham. "But your specious imaginings fail to account for his return."

"That was the simplest part of the scheme. He prob'bly waited in a doorway across the street for some other tenant to go in. The boy said a Mr. Montagu returned about two thirty. Then the major slipped in when he knew the elevator had ascended, and walked up the stairs."

Markham, smiling patiently, said nothing.

"You perceived," continued Vance, "the pains taken by the major to establish the date and the hour, and to impress them on the boy's mind. Poor show—headache—unlucky day. Why unlucky? The thirteenth, to be sure. But lucky for the boy. A handful of money—all

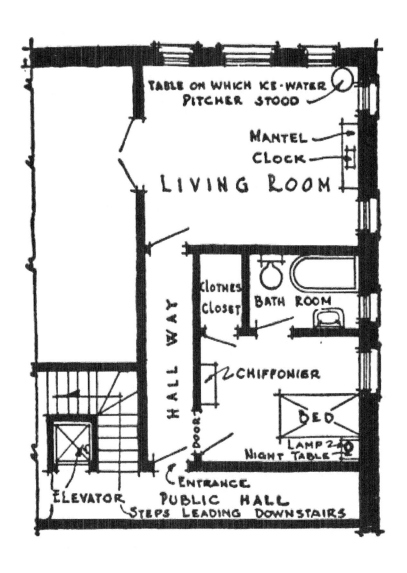

TABLE ON WHICH ICE-WATER
PITCHER STOOD

MANTEL
CLOCK

LIVING ROOM

Clothes
Closet

BATH ROOM

HALL WAY

CHIFFONIER

DOOR?

BED

LAMP 2
NIGHT TABLE

Entrance

ELEVATOR

PUBLIC HALL
Steps Leading Downstairs

THIRD FLOOR OF CHATHAM ARMS APARTMENT IN
WEST FORTY-SIXTH STREET

silver. Singular way of tipping, what? But a dollar bill might have been forgotten."

A shadow clouded Markham's face, but his voice was as indulgently impersonal as ever. "I prefer your case against Mrs. Platz."

"Ah, but I've not finished." Vance stood up. "I have hopes of finding the weapon, don't y' know."

Markham now studied him with amused incredulity. "That, of course, would be a contributory factor. . . . You really expect to find it?"

"Without the slightest diff'culty," Vance pleasantly assured him.

He went to the chiffonier and began opening the drawers. "Our absent host didn't leave the pistol at Alvin's house; and he was far too canny to throw it away. Being a major in the late war, he'd be expected to have such a weapon: in fact, several persons may actu'lly have known he possessed one. And if he is innocent—as he fully expects us to assume—why shouldn't it be in its usual place? Its absence, d' ye see, would be more incriminatin' than its presence. Also, there's a most int'restin' psychological factor involved. An innocent person who was afraid of being thought guilty, would have hidden it, or thrown it away—like Captain Leacock, for example. But a guilty man, wishing to create an appearance of innocence, would have put it back exactly where it was before the shooting."

He was still searching through the chiffonier.

"Our only problem, then, is to discover the custom'ry abiding place of the major's gun. . . . It's not here in the chiffonier," he added, closing the last drawer.

He opened a kit bag standing at the foot of the bed and rifled its contents. "Nor here," he murmured indifferently. "The clothes closet is the only other likely place."

Going across the room, he opened the closet door. Unhurriedly he switched on the light. There, on the upper shelf, in plain view, lay an army belt with a bulging holster.

Vance lifted it with extreme delicacy and placed it on the bed near the window.

"There you are, old chap," he cheerfully announced, bending over it closely. "Please take particular note that the entire belt and holster—with only the exception of the holster's flap—is thickly coated with dust. The flap is comparatively clean, showing it has been opened recently. . . . Not conclusive, of course; but you're so partial to clues, Markham."

He carefully removed the pistol from the holster.

"Note, also, that the gun itself is innocent of dust. It has been recently cleaned, I surmise."

His next act was to insert a corner of his handkerchief into the barrel. Then, withdrawing it, he held it up.

"You see—eh, what? Even the inside of the barrel is immaculate. . . . And I'll wager all my Cézannes against an LL.B. degree that there isn't a cartridge missing."

He extracted the magazine and poured the cartridges onto the night table, where they lay in a neat row before us. There were seven—the full number for that style of gun.

"Again, Markham, I present you with one of your revered clues. Cartridges that remain in a magazine for a long time become slightly tarnished, for the catch plate is not airtight. But a fresh box of cartridges is well sealed, and its contents retain their lustre much longer."

He pointed to the first cartridge that had rolled out of the magazine.

"Observe that this one cartridge—the last to be inserted into the magazine—is a bit brighter than its fellows. The inf'rence is—you're an adept at inf'rences, y'know—that it is a newer cartridge and was placed in the magazine rather recently."

He looked straight into Markham's eyes. "It was placed there to take the place of the one which Captain Hagedorn is keeping."

Markham lifted his head jerkily, as if shaking himself out of an encroaching spell of hypnosis. He smiled but with an effort.

"I still think your case against Mrs. Platz is your masterpiece."

"My picture of the major is merely blocked in," answered Vance. "The revealin' touches are to come. But first, a brief catechism:— How did the major know that brother Alvin would be home at twelve thirty on the night of the thirteenth?—He heard Alvin invite Miss St. Clair to dinner—remember Miss Hoffman's story of his eavesdropping?—and he also heard her say she'd unfailingly leave at midnight. When I said yesterday, after we had left Miss St. Clair, that something she told us would help convict the guilty person, I referred to her statement that midnight was her invariable hour of departure. The major therefore knew Alvin would be home about half past twelve, and he was pretty sure that no one else would be there. In any event, he could have waited for him, what? . . . Could he have secured an immediate audience with his brother *en déshabillé*?—Yes. He tapped on the window; his voice was recognized beyond any shadow of doubt; and he was admitted instanter. Alvin had no sartorial modesties in front of his brother and would have thought nothing of receiving him without his teeth and toupee. . . . Is the major the right height?—He is. I purposely stood beside him in your office the other day; and he is almost exactly five feet, ten and a half."

Markham sat staring silently at the disembowelled pistol. Vance had been speaking in a voice quite different from that he had used when constructing his hypothetical cases against the others; and Markham had sensed the change.

"We now come to the jewels," Vance was saying. "I once expressed the belief, you remember, that when we found the security for Pfyfe's note, we would put our hands on the murderer. I thought then the major had the jewels; and after Miss Hoffman told us of his requesting her not to mention the package, I was sure of it. Alvin took them home on the afternoon of the thirteenth, and the major undoubtedly knew it. This fact, I imagine, influenced his decision to end Alvin's life that night. He wanted those baubles, Markham."

He rose jauntily and stepped to the door.

"And now it remains only to find 'em. . . . The murderer took 'em away with him; they couldn't have left the house any other way. Therefore, they're in this apartment. If the major had taken them to the office, someone might have seen them; and if he had placed them in a safe deposit box, the clerk at the bank might have remembered the episode. Moreover, the same psychology that applied to the gun applies to the jewels. The major has acted throughout on the assumption of his innocence; and, as a matter of fact, the trinkets were safer here than elsewhere. There'd be time enough to dispose of them when the affair blew over. . . . Come with me a moment, Markham. It's painful, I know; and your heart's too weak for an anaesthetic."

Markham followed him down the passageway in a kind of daze. I felt a great sympathy for the man, for now there was no question that he knew Vance was serious in his demonstration of the major's guilt. Indeed, I have always felt that Markham suspected the true purpose of Vance's request to investigate the major's alibi, and that his opposition was due as much to his fear of the results as to his impatience with the other's irritating methods. Not that he would have balked ultimately at the truth, despite his long friendship for Major Benson; but he was struggling—as I see it now—with the inevitability of circumstances, hoping against hope that he had read Vance incorrectly and that, by vigorously contesting each step of the way, he might alter the very shape of destiny itself.

Vance led the way to the living room and stood for five minutes inspecting the various pieces of furniture, while Markham remained in the doorway watching him through narrowed lids, his hands crowded deep into his pockets.

"We could, of course, have an expert searcher rake the apartment over inch by inch," observed Vance. "But I don't think it necess'ry. The major's a bold, cunning soul. Witness his wide square forehead, the dominating stare of his globular eyes, the perpendicular spine, and the indrawn abdomen. He's forthright in all his mental operations. Like Poe's Minister D——, he would recognize the futility of painstakingly secreting the jewels in some obscure corner. And anyhow, he had no object in secreting them. He merely wished to hide 'em where there'd be no chance of their being seen. This naturally suggests a lock and key, what? There was no such cache in the bedroom—which is why I came here."

He walked to a squat rosewood desk in the corner, and tried all its drawers; but they were unlocked. He next tested the table drawer; but that, too, was unlocked. A small Spanish cabinet by the window proved equally disappointing.

"Markham, I simply must find a locked drawer," he said.

He inspected the room again and was about to return to the bedroom when his eye fell on a Circassian-walnut humidor half hidden by a pile of magazines on the undershelf of the centre table. He stopped abruptly and, going quickly to the box, endeavoured to lift the top. It was locked.

"Let's see," he mused: "what does the major smoke? *Romeo y Julieta Perfeccionados*, I believe—but they're not sufficiently valuable to keep under lock and key."

He picked up a strong bronze paper knife lying on the table and forced its point into the crevice of the humidor just above the lock.

"You can't do that!" cried Markham; and there was as much pain as reprimand in his voice.

Before he could reach Vance, however, there was a sharp click, and the lid flew open. Inside was a blue velvet jewel case.

"Ah! 'Dumb jewels more quick than words,'" said Vance, stepping back. Markham stood staring into the humidor with an expression of tragic distress. Then slowly he turned and sank heavily into a chair.

"Good God!" he murmured. "I don't know what to believe."

"In that respect," returned Vance, "you're in the same disheartenin' predic'ment as all the philosophers. But you were ready enough, don't y'know, to believe in the guilt of half a dozen innocent people. Why should you gag at the major, who actu'lly is guilty?"

His tone was contemptuous, but a curious, inscrutable look in his eyes belied his voice; and I remembered that, although these two men were welded in an indissoluble friendship, I had never heard a word of sentiment, or even sympathy, pass between them.

Markham had leaned forward in an attitude of hopelessness, elbows on knees, his head in his hands.

"But the motive!" he urged. "A man doesn't shoot his brother for a handful of jewels."

"Certainly not," agreed Vance. "The jewels were a mere addendum. There was a vital motive—rest assured. And, I fancy, when you get your report from the expert accountant, all—or at least a goodly part—will be revealed."

"So that was why you wanted his books examined?"

Markham stood up resolutely. "Come. I'm going to see this thing through."

Vance did not move at once. He was intently studying a small antique candlestick of oriental design on the mantel.

"I say!" he muttered. "That's a dev'lish fine copy!"

CHAPTER 24

The Arrest

Thursday, June 20; noon

On leaving the apartment, Markham took with him the pistol and the case of jewels. In the drug store at the corner of Sixth Avenue he telephoned Heath to meet him immediately at the office and to bring Captain Hagedorn. He also telephoned Stitt, the public accountant, to report as soon as possible.

"You observe, I trust," said Vance, when we were in the taxicab headed for the Criminal Courts Building, "the great advantage of my methods over yours. When one knows at the outset who committed a crime, one isn't misled by appearances. Without that foreknowledge, one is apt to be deceived by a clever alibi, for example.... I asked you to secure the alibis because, knowing the major was guilty, I thought he'd have prepared a good one."

"But why ask for all of them? And why waste time trying to disprove Colonel Ostrander's?"

"What chance would I have had of securing the major's alibi if I had not injected his name surreptitiously, as it were, into a list of other names? ... And had I asked you to check the major's alibi first, you'd have refused. I chose the colonel's alibi to start with because it seemed to offer a loophole—and I was lucky in the choice. I knew that if I could puncture one of the other alibis, you would be more inclined to help me test the major's."

"But if, as you say, you knew from the first that the major was guilty, why, in God's name, didn't you tell me, and save me this week of anxiety?"

"Don't be ingenuous, old man," returned Vance. "If I had accused the major at the beginning, you'd have had me arrested for *scandalum magnatum* and criminal libel. It was only by deceivin' you every minute

213

about the major's guilt, and drawing a whole school of red herrings across the trail, that I was able to get you to accept the fact even today. And yet, not once did I actu'lly lie to you. I was constantly throwing out suggestions, and pointing to significant facts, in the hope that you'd see the light for yourself; but you ignored all my intimations, or else misinterpreted them, with the most irritatin' perversity."

Markham was silent a moment. "I see what you mean. But why did you keep setting up these straw men and then knocking them over?"

"You were bound, body and soul, to circumst'ntial evidence," Vance pointed out. "It was only by letting you see that it led you nowhere that I was able to foist the major on you. There was no evidence against him—he naturally saw to that. No one even regarded him as a possibility: fratricide has been held as inconceivable—a *lusus naturae*—since the days of Cain. Even with all my finessing you fought every inch of the way, objectin' to this and that, and doing everything imag'nable to thwart my humble efforts. . . . Admit, like a good fellow, that, had it not been for my assiduousness, the major would never have been suspected."

Markham nodded slowly.

"And yet, there are some things I don't understand even now. Why, for instance, should he have objected so strenuously to my arresting the captain?"

Vance wagged his head.

"How deuced obvious you are! Never attempt a crime, my Markham, you'd be instantly apprehended. I say, can't you see how much more impregnable the major's position would be if he showed no int'rest in your arrests—if, indeed, he appeared actu'lly to protest against your incarc'ration of a victim. Could he, by any other means, have elim'nated so completely all possible suspicion against himself? Moreover, he knew very well that nothing he could say would swerve you from your course. You're so noble, don't y'know."

"But he did give me the impression once or twice that he thought Miss St. Clair was guilty."

"Ah! There you have a shrewd intelligence taking advantage of an opportunity. The major unquestionably planned the crime so as to cast suspicion on the captain. Leacock had publicly threatened his brother in connection with Miss St. Clair; and the lady was about to dine alone with Alvin. When, in the morning, Alvin was found shot with an army Colt, who but the captain would be suspected? The major knew the captain lived alone, and that he would have diff'culty in establishing an alibi. Do you now see how cunning he was in recommending Pfyfe as a source of information? He knew that if you interviewed Pfyfe, you'd hear of the threat. And don't ignore the fact that his suggestion of Pfyfe was an apparent afterthought; he wanted to make it appear casual, don't y'know.—Astute devil, what?"

Markham, sunk in gloom, was listening closely.

"Now for the opportunity of which he took advantage," continued Vance. "When you upset his calculations by telling him you knew whom Alvin dined with, and that you had almost enough evidence to ask for an indictment, the idea appealed to him. He knew no charmin' lady could ever be convicted of murder in this most chivalrous city, no matter what the evidence; and he had enough of the sporting instinct in him to prefer that no one should actu'lly be punished for the crime. Cons'quently, he was willing to switch you back to the lady. And he played his hand cleverly, making it appear that he was most reluctant to involve her."

"Was that why, when you wanted me to examine his books and to ask him to the office to discuss the confession, you told me to intimate that I had Miss St. Clair in mind?"

"Exactly!"

"And the person the major was shielding—"

"Was himself. But he wanted you to think it was Miss St. Clair."

"If you were certain he was guilty, why did you bring Colonel Ostrander into the case?"

"In the hope that he could supply us with faggots for the major's funeral pyre. I knew he was acquainted intimately with Alvin Benson and his entire camarilla; and I knew, too, that he was an egregious quidnunc who might have got wind of some enmity between the Benson boys and have suspected the truth. And I also wanted to get a line on Pfyfe, by way of elim'nating every remote counter-possibility."

"But we already had a line on Pfyfe."

"Oh, I don't mean material clues. I wanted to learn about Pfyfe's nature—his psychology, y'know—particularly his personality as a gambler. Y' see, it was the crime of a calculating, cold-blooded gambler; and no one but a man of that particular type could possibly have committed it."

Markham apparently was not interested just now in Vance's theories.

"Did you believe the major," he asked, "when he said his brother had lied to him about the presence of the jewels in the safe?"

"The wily Alvin prob'bly never mentioned 'em to Anthony," rejoined Vance. "An ear at the door during one of Pfyfe's visits was, I fancy, his source of information. . . . And speaking of the major's eaves-dropping, it was that which suggested to me a possible motive for the crime. Your man Stitt, I hope, will clarify that point."

"According to your theory, the crime was rather hastily conceived." Markham's statement was in reality a question.

"The details of its execution were hastily conceived," corrected Vance. "The major undoubtedly had been contemplating for some time elim'nating his brother. Just how or when he was to do it he hadn't decided. He may have thought out and rejected a dozen plans. Then, on the thirteenth, came the opportunity: all the conditions adjusted themselves to his purpose. He heard Miss St. Clair's promise to go to dinner; and he therefore knew that Alvin would prob'bly be home alone at twelve thirty, and that, if he were done away with at that hour, suspicion would fall on Captain Leacock. He saw Alvin take home the jewels—another prov'dential circumst'nce. The propitious moment for which he had been waiting, d' ye see, was at hand. All that remained was to establish an alibi and work out a *modus operandi*. How he did this, I've already eluc'dated."

Markham sat thinking for several minutes. At last he lifted his head.

"You've about convinced me of his guilt," he admitted. "But damn it, man! I've got to prove it; and there's not much actual legal evidence."

Vance gave a slight shrug.

"I'm not int'rested in your stupid courts and your silly rules of evidence. But, since I've convinced you, you can't charge me with not having met your challenge, don't y'know."

"I suppose not," Markham assented gloomily.

Slowly the muscles about his mouth tightened.

"You've done your share, Vance, I'll carry on."

Heath and Captain Hagedorn were waiting when we arrived at the office, and Markham greeted them in his customary reserved, matter-of-fact way. By now he had himself well in hand and he went about the task before him with the sombre forcefulness that characterized him in the discharge of all his duties.

"I think we at last have the right man, Sergeant," he said. "Sit down, and I'll go over the matter with you in a moment. There are one or two things I want to attend to first."

He handed Major Benson's pistol to the firearms expert.

"Look that gun over, Captain, and tell me if there's any way of identifying it as the weapon that killed Benson."

Hagedorn moved ponderously to the window. Laying the pistol on the sill, he took several tools from the pockets of his voluminous

216

coat and placed them beside the weapon. Then, adjusting a jeweller's magnifying glass to his eye, he began what seemed an interminable series of tinkerings. He opened the plates of the stock and, drawing back the sear, took out the firing pin. He removed the slide, unscrewed the link, and extracted the recoil spring. I thought he was going to take the weapon entirely apart, but apparently he merely wanted to let light into the barrel; for presently he held the gun to the window and placed his eye at the muzzle. He peered into the barrel for nearly five minutes, moving it slightly back and forth to catch the reflection of the sun on different points of the interior.

At last, without a word, he slowly and painstakingly went through the operation of redintegrating the weapon. Then he lumbered back to his chair and sat blinking heavily for several moments.

"I'll tell you," he said, thrusting his head forward and gazing at Markham over the tops of his steel-rimmed spectacles. "This, now, may be the right gun. I wouldn't say for sure. But when I saw the bullet the other morning, I noticed some peculiar rifling marks on it; and the rifling in this gun here looks to me as though it would match up with the marks on the bullet. I'm not certain. I'd like to look at this barrel through my *helixometer.**"

"But you believe it's the gun?" insisted Markham.

"I couldn't say, but I think so. I might be wrong."

"Very good, Captain. Take it along and call me the minute you've inspected it thoroughly."

"It's the gun, all right," asserted Heath, when Hagedorn had gone. "I know that bird. He wouldn't've said as much as he did if he hadn't been sure. . . . Whose gun is it, sir?"

"I'll answer you presently." Markham was still battling against the truth—withholding, even from himself, his pronouncement of the major's guilt until every loophole of doubt should be closed. "I want to hear from Stitt before I say anything. I sent him to look over Benson and Benson's books. He'll be here any moment."

After a wait of a quarter of an hour, during which time Markham attempted to busy himself with other matters, Stitt came in. He said a sombre good-morning to the district attorney and Heath; then, catching sight of Vance, smiled appreciatively.

"That was a good tip you gave me. You had the dope. If you'd kept Major Benson away longer, I could have done more. While he was there he was watching me every minute."

---

* A helixometer, I learned later, is an instrument that makes it possible to examine every portion of the inside of a gun's barrel through a microscope.

"I did the best I could," sighed Vance. He turned to Markham. "Y'know, I was wondering all through lunch yesterday how I could remove the major from his office during Mr. Stitt's investigation; and when we learned of Leacock's confession, it gave me just the excuse I needed. I really didn't want the major here—I simply wished to give Mr. Stitt a free hand."

"What did you find out?" Markham asked the accountant.

"Plenty!" was the laconic reply.

He took a sheet of paper from his pocket and placed it on the desk.

"There's a brief report. . . . I followed Mr. Vance's suggestion and took a look at the stock record and the cashier's collateral blotter, and traced the transfer receipts. I ignored the journal entries against the ledger, and concentrated on the activities of the firm heads. Major Benson, I found, has been consistently hypothecating securities transferred to him as collateral for marginal trading, and has been speculating steadily in mercantile curb stocks. He has lost heavily—how much, I can't say."

"And Alvin Benson?" asked Vance.

"He was up to the same tricks. But he played in luck. He made a wad on a Columbus Motors pool a few weeks back; and he has been salting the money away in his safe—or, at least, that's what the secretary told me."

"And if Major Benson has possession of the key to that safe," suggested Vance, "then it's lucky for him his brother was shot."

"Lucky?" retorted Stitt. "It'll save him from state prison."

When the accountant had gone, Markham sat like a man of stone, his eyes fixed on the wall opposite. Another straw at which he had grasped in his instinctive denial of the major's guilt had been snatched from him.

The telephone rang. Slowly he took up the receiver, and as he listened I saw a look of complete resignation come into his eyes. He leaned back in his chair, like a man exhausted.

"It was Hagedorn," he said. "That was the right gun."

Then he drew himself up and turned to Heath. "The owner of that gun, Sergeant, was Major Benson."

The detective whistled softly and his eyes opened slightly with astonishment. But gradually his face assumed its habitual stolidity of expression. "Well, it don't surprise me any," he said.

Markham rang for Swacker.

"Get Major Benson on the wire and tell him—tell him I'm about to make an arrest and would appreciate his coming here immediately."

His deputizing of the telephone call to Swacker was understood by all of us, I think.

Markham then summarized, for Heath's benefit, the case against the major. When he had finished, he rose and rearranged the chairs at the table in front of his desk.

"When Major Benson comes, Sergeant," he said, "I am going to seat him here." He indicated a chair directly facing his own. "I want you to sit at his right; and you'd better get Phelps—or one of the other men, if he isn't in—to sit at his left. But you're not to make any move until I give the signal. Then you can arrest him."

When Heath had returned with Phelps and they had taken their seats at the table, Vance said, "I'd advise you, Sergeant, to be on your guard. The minute the major knows he's in for it, he'll go bald-headed for you."

Heath smiled with heavy contempt.

"This isn't the first man I've arrested, Mr. Vance—with many thanks for your advice. And what's more, the major isn't that kind; he's too nervy."

"Have it your own way," replied Vance indifferently. "But I've warned you. The major is cool-headed; he'd take big chances and he could lose his last dollar without turning a hair. But when he is finally cornered and sees ultimate defeat, all his repressions of a lifetime, having had no safety valve, will explode physically. When a man lives without passions or emotions or enthusiasms, there's bound to be an outlet sometime. Some men explode and some commit suicide—the principle is the same: it's a matter of psychological reaction. The major isn't the self-destructive type—that's why I say he'll blow up."

Heath snorted. "We may be short on psychology down here," he rejoined, "but we know human nature pretty well."

Vance stifled a yawn and carelessly lit a cigarette. I noticed, however, that he pushed his chair back a little from the end of the table where he and I were sitting.

"Well, Chief," rasped Phelps, "I guess your troubles are about over—though I sure did think that fellow Leacock was your man. . . . Who got the dope on this Major Benson?"

"Sergeant Heath and the homicide bureau will receive entire credit for the work," said Markham; and added, "I'm sorry, Phelps, but the district attorney's office, and everyone connected with it, will be kept out of it altogether."

"Oh, well, it's all in a lifetime," observed Phelps philosophically.

We sat in strained silence until the major arrived. Markham

smoked abstractedly. He glanced several times over the sheet of notations left by Stitt and once he went to the water cooler for a drink. Vance opened at random a law book before him and perused with an amused smile a bribery case decision by a Western judge. Heath and Phelps, habituated to waiting, scarcely moved.

When Major Benson entered Markham greeted him with exaggerated casualness and busied himself with some papers in a drawer to avoid shaking hands. Heath, however, was almost jovial. He drew out the major's chair for him and uttered a ponderous banality about the weather. Vance closed the law book and sat erect with his feet drawn back.

Major Benson was cordially dignified. He gave Markham a swift glance; but if he suspected anything, he showed no outward sign of it.

"Major, I want you to answer a few questions—if you care to." Markham's voice, though low, had in it a resonant quality.

"Anything at all," returned the other easily.

"You own an army pistol, do you not?"

"Yes—a Colt automatic," he replied, with a questioning lift of the eyebrows.

"When did you last clean and refill it?"

Not a muscle of the major's face moved. "I don't exactly remember," he said. "I've cleaned it several times. But it hasn't been refilled since I returned from overseas."

"Have you lent it to anyone recently?"

"Not that I recall."

Markham took up Stitt's report and looked at it a moment. "How did you hope to satisfy your clients if suddenly called upon for their marginal securities?"

The major's upper lip lifted contemptuously, exposing his teeth.

"So! That was why, under the guise of friendship, you sent a man to look over my books!" I saw a red blotch of colour appear on the back of his neck and swell upward to his ears.

"It happens that I didn't send him there for that purpose." The accusation had cut Markham. "But I did enter your apartment this morning."

"You're a housebreaker, too, are you?" The man's face was now crimson; the veins stood out on his forehead.

"And I found Mrs. Banning's jewels. . . . How did they get there, Major?"

"It's none of your damned business how they got there," he said, his voice as cold and even as ever.

"Why did you tell Miss Hoffman not to mention them to me?"

"That's none of your damned business either."

"Is it any of my business," asked Markham quietly, "that the bullet which killed your brother was fired from your gun?"

The major looked at him steadily, his mouth a sneer.

"That's the kind of double-crossing you do!—invite me here to arrest me and then ask me questions to incriminate myself when I'm unaware of your suspicions. A fine dirty sport *you* are!"

Vance leaned forward. "You fool!" His voice was very low, but it cut like a whip. "Can't you see he's your friend and is asking you these questions in a last desp'rate hope that you're not guilty?"

The major swung round on him hotly. "Keep out of this—you damned sissy!"

"Oh, quite," murmured Vance.

"And as for *you*"—he pointed a quivering finger at Markham—"I'll make you sweat for this! . . ."

Vituperation and profanity poured from the man. His nostrils were expanded, his eyes blazing. His wrath seemed to surpass all human bounds; he was like a person in an apoplectic fit—contorted, repulsive, insensate.

Markham sat through it patiently, his head resting on his hands, his eyes closed. When, at length, the major's rage became inarticulate, he looked up and nodded to Heath. It was the signal the detective had been watching for.

But before Heath could make a move, the major sprang to his feet. With the motion of rising he swung his body swiftly about and brought his fist against Heath's face with terrific impact. The sergeant went backward in his chair and lay on the floor dazed. Phelps leaped forward, crouching; but the major's knee shot upward and caught him in the lower abdomen. He sank to the floor, where he rolled back and forth groaning.

The major then turned on Markham. His eyes were glaring like a maniac's, and his lips were drawn back. His nostrils dilated with each stertorous breath. His shoulders were hunched, and his arms hung away from his body, his fingers rigidly flexed. His attitude was the embodiment of a terrific, uncontrolled malignity.

"You're next!" The words, guttural and venomous, were like a snarl. As he spoke he sprang forward.

Vance, who had sat quietly during the melee, looking on with half-closed eyes and smoking indolently, now stepped sharply round the end of the table. His arms shot forward. With one hand he caught the major's right wrist; with the other he grasped the elbow. Then he seemed to fall back with a swift pivotal motion. The major's pinioned arm was twisted upward behind his shoulder blades. There was a cry of pain, and the man suddenly relaxed in Vance's grip.

By this time Heath had recovered. He scrambled quickly to his feet and stepped up. There was the click of handcuffs, and the major dropped heavily into a chair, where he sat moving his shoulder back and forth painfully.

"It's nothing serious," Vance told him. "The capsular ligament is torn a little. It'll be all right in a few days."

Heath came forward and, without a word, held out his hand to Vance. The action was at once an apology and a tribute. I liked Heath for it.

When he and his prisoner had gone, and Phelps had been assisted into an easy chair, Markham put his hand on Vance's arm.

"Let's get away," he said. "I'm done up."

CHAPTER 25

Vance Explains His Methods
Thursday, June 20; 9 p.m.

That same evening, after a Turkish bath and dinner, Markham, grim and weary, and Vance, bland and debonair, and myself were sitting together in the alcove of the Stuyvesant Club's lounge room. We had smoked in silence for half an hour or more, when Vance, as if giving articulation to his thoughts, remarked, "And it's stubborn, unimag'native chaps like Heath who constitute the human barrage between the criminal and society! . . . Sad, sad."

"We have no Napoleons today," Markham observed. "And if we had, they'd probably not be detectives."

"But even should they have yearnings toward that profession," said Vance, "they would be rejected on their physical measurements. As I understand it, your policemen are chosen by their height and weight; they must meet certain requirements as to heft—as though the only crimes they had to cope with were riots and gang feuds. Bulk—the great American ideal, whether in art, architecture, table d'hôte meals, or detectives. An entrancin' notion."

"At any rate, Heath has a generous nature," said Markham palliatingly. "He has completely forgiven you for everything."

Vance smiled. "The amount of credit and emulsification he received in the afternoon papers would have mellowed anyone. He should even forgive the major for hitting him. A clever blow, that, based on rotary leverage. Heath's constitution must be tough, or he wouldn't have recovered so quickly. . . . And poor Phelps! He'll have a horror of knees the rest of his life."

"You certainly guessed the major's reaction," said Markham. "I'm almost ready to grant there's something in your psychological flummery, after all. Your aesthetic deductions seemed to put you on the right track."

After a pause he turned and looked inquisitively at Vance. "Tell me exactly why, at the outset, you were convinced of the major's guilt?"

Vance settled back in his chair.

"Consider, for a moment, the characteristics—the outstanding features—of the crime. Just before the shot was fired, Benson and the murderer undoubtedly had been talking or arguing, the one seated, the other standing. Then Benson had pretended to read, he had said all he had to say. His reading was his gesture of finality; for one doesn't read when conversing with another unless for a purpose. The murderer, seeing the hopelessness of the situation and having come prepared to meet it heroically, took out a gun, aimed it at Benson's temple, and pulled the trigger. After that, he turned out the lights and went away. . . . Such are the facts indicated and actual."

He took several puffs on his cigarette.

"Now, let's analyze 'em. . . . As I pointed out to you, the murderer didn't fire at the body, where, though the chances of hitting would have been much greater, the chances of death would have been less. He chose the more diff'cult and hazardous—and, at the same time, the more certain and efficient—course. His technique, so to speak, was bold, direct, and fearless. Only a man with iron nerves and a highly developed gambler's instinct would have done it in just this forthright and audacious fashion. Therefore, all nervous, hot-headed, impulsive, or timid persons were automatically elim'nated as suspects. The neat, businesslike aspect of the crime, together with the absence of any material clues that could possibly have incriminated the culprit, indicated unmistakably that it had been premeditated and planned with coolness and precision, by a person of tremendous self-assurance, and one used to taking risks. There was nothing subtle or in the least imag'native about the crime. Every feature of it pointed to an aggressive, blunt mind—a mind at once static, determined, and intrepid, and accustomed to dealing with facts and situations in a direct, concrete, and unequivocal manner. . . . I say, Markham, surely you're a good enough judge of human nature to read the indications, what?"

"I think I get the drift of your reasoning," the other admitted a little doubtfully.

"Very well, then," Vance continued. "Having determined the exact psychological nature of the deed, it only remained to find some int'rested person whose mind and temp'rament were such that if he undertook a task of this kind in the given circumst'nces, he would inev'tably do it in precisely the manner in which it was done. As it happened, I had known the major for a long time; and so it was obvious to me, the moment I had looked over the situation that first morning, that he had done it. The crime, in every respect and feature, was a perfect psychological expression of his character and mentality. But even had I not known him personally, I would have been able—since I possessed so clear and accurate a knowledge of the murderer's personality—to pick him out from any number of suspects."

"But suppose another person of the major's type had done it?" asked Markham.

"We all differ in our natures, however similar two persons may appear at times," Vance explained. "And while, in the present case, it is barely conceivable that another man of the major's type and temp'rament might have done it, the law of probability must be taken into account. Even supposing there were two men almost identical in personality and instincts in New York, what would be the chance of their both having had a reason to kill Benson? However, despite the remoteness of the possibility, when Pfyfe came into the case and I learned he was a gambler and a hunter, I took occasion to look into his qualifications. Not knowing him personally, I appealed to Colonel Ostrander for my information; and what he told me put Pfyfe at once *hors de propos*."

"But he had nerve. He was a rash plunger; and he certainly had enough at stake," objected Markham.

"Ah! But between a rash plunger and a bold, level-headed gambler like the major there is a great difference—a psychological abyss. In fact, their animating impulses are opposites. The plunger is actuated by fear and hope and desire; the cool-headed gambler is actuated by expediency and belief and judgment. The one is emotional, the other mental. The major, unlike Pfyfe, is a born gambler and inf'nitely self-confident. This kind of self-confidence, however, is not the same as recklessness, though superficially the two bear a close resemblance. It is based on an instinctive belief in one's own infallibility and safety. It's the reverse of what the Freudians call the inferiority complex—a form of egomania, a variety of *folie de grandeur*. The major possessed it, but it was absent from Pfyfe's composition; and as the crime indicated its possession by the perpetrator, I knew Pfyfe was innocent."

"I begin to grasp the thing in a nebulous sort of way," said Markham after a pause.

"But there were other indications, psychological and otherwise," Vance went on "—the undress attire of the body, the toupee and teeth upstairs, the inferred familiarity of the murderer with the domestic arrangements, the fact that he had been admitted by Benson himself, and his knowledge that Benson would be at home alone at that time—all pointing to the major as the guilty person. Another thing—the height of the murderer corresponded to the major's height. This indication, though, was of minor importance; for had my measurements not tallied with the major, I would have known that the bullet had been deflected, despite the opinions of all the Captain Hagedorns in the universe."

"Why were you so positive a woman couldn't have done it?"

"To begin with, it wasn't a woman's crime—that is, no woman would have done it in the way it was done. The most mentalized women are emotional when it comes to a fundamental issue like taking a life. That a woman could have coldly planned such a murder and then executed it with such businesslike efficiency—aiming a single shot at her victim's temple at a distance of five or six feet—would be contr'ry, d'ye see, to everything we know of human nature. Again, women don't stand up to argue a point before a seated antagonist. Somehow they seem to feel more secure sitting down. They talk better sitting; whereas men talk better standing. And even had a woman stood before Benson, she could not have taken out a gun and aimed it without his looking up. A man's reaching in his pocket is a natural action; but a woman has no pockets and no place to hide a gun except her handbag. And a man is always on guard when an angry woman opens a handbag in front of him—the very uncertainty of women's natures has made men suspicious of their actions when aroused. . . . But—above all—it was Benson's bald pate and bedroom slippers that made the woman hypothesis untenable."

"You remarked a moment ago," said Markham, "that the murderer went there that night prepared to take heroic measures if necessary. And yet you say he planned the murder."

"True. The two statements don't conflict, y'know. The murder was planned—without doubt. But the major was willing to give his victim a last chance to save his life. My theory is this: The major, being in a tight financial hole with state prison looming before him, and knowing that his brother had sufficient funds in the safe to save him, plotted the crime and went to the house that night prepared to commit it. First, however, he told his brother of his predic'ment and asked for the money; and Alvin prob'bly told him to go to the devil. The major may even have pleaded a bit in order to avoid killing him; but when the liter'ry Alvin turned to reading, he saw the futility of appealing further, and proceeded with the dire business."

Markham smoked awhile.

"Granting all you've said," he remarked at length, "I still don't see how you could know, as you asserted this morning, that the major had planned the murder so as to throw suspicion deliberately on Captain Leacock."

"Just as a sculptor, who thoroughly understands the principles of form and composition, can accurately supply any missing integral part of a statue," Vance explained, "so can the psychologist who understands the human mind supply any missing factor in a given human action. I might add, parenthetically, that all this blather about the missing arms of the Aphrodite of Melos—the Milo Venus, y'know—is the utt'rest fiddle-faddle. Any competent artist who knew the laws of aesthetic organization could restore the arms exactly as they were originally. Such restorations are merely a matter of context—the missing factor, d' ye see, simply has to conform and harmonize with what is already known."

He made one of his rare gestures of delicate emphasis.

"Now, the problem of circumventing suspicion is an important detail in every deliberated crime. And since the general conception of this particular crime was pos'tive, conclusive, and concrete, it followed that each one of its component parts would be pos'tive, conclusive, and concrete. Therefore, for the major merely to have arranged things so that he himself should *not* be suspected would have been too negative a conception to fit consistently with the other psychological aspects of the deed. It would have been too vague, too indirect, too indef'nite. The type of literal mind which conceived this crime would logically have provided a specific and tangible object of suspicion. Cons'quently, when the material evidence began to pile up against the captain, and the major waxed vehement in defending him, I knew he had been chosen as the dupe. At first, I admit, I suspected the major of having selected Miss St. Clair as the victim; but when I learned that the presence of her gloves and handbag at Benson's was only an accident, and remembered that the major had given us Pfyfe as a source of information about the captain's threat, I realized that her projection into the role of murderer was unpremeditated."

A little later Markham rose and stretched himself.

"Well, Vance," he said, "your task is finished. Mine has just begun. And I need sleep."

Before a week had passed, Major Anthony Benson was indicted for the murder of his brother. His trial before Judge Rudolph Hansacker, as you remember, created a nationwide sensation. The Associated Press sent columns daily to its members; and for weeks the front pages of the country's newspapers were emblazoned with spectacular reports of the proceedings. How the district attorney's office won the case after a bitter struggle; how, because of the indirect character of the evidence, the verdict was for murder in the second degree; and how, after a retrial in the court of appeals, Anthony Benson finally received a sentence of from twenty years to life—all these facts are a matter of official and public record.

Markham personally did not appear as public prosecutor. Having been a lifelong friend of the defendant's, his position was an unenviable and difficult one, and no word of criticism was directed against his assignment of the case to Chief Assistant District Attorney Sullivan. Major Benson surrounded himself with an array of counsel such as is rarely seen in our criminal courts. Both Blashfield and Bauer were among the attorneys for the defence—Blashfield fulfilling the duties of the English solicitor, and Bauer acting as advocate. They fought with every legal device at their disposal, but the accumulation of evidence against their client overwhelmed them.

After Markham had been convinced of the major's guilt, he had made a thorough examination of the business affairs of the two brothers and found the situation even worse than had been indicated by Stitt's first report. The firm's securities had been systematically appropriated for private speculations; but whereas Alvin Benson had succeeded in covering himself and making a large profit, the major had been almost completely wiped out by his investments. Markham was able to show that the major's only hope of replacing the diverted securities and saving himself from criminal prosecution lay in Alvin Benson's immediate death. It was also brought out at the trial that the major, on the very day of the murder, had made emphatic promises which could have been kept only in the event of his gaining access to his brother's safe. Furthermore, these promises had involved specific amounts in the other's possession; and, in one instance, he had put up, on a forty-eight-hour note, a security already pledged—a fact which, in itself would have exposed his hand had his brother lived.

Miss Hoffman was a helpful and intelligent witness for the prosecution. Her knowledge of conditions at the Benson and Benson offices went far toward strengthening the case against the major.

Mrs. Platz also testified to overhearing acrimonious arguments between the brothers. She stated that less than a fortnight before the murder the major, after an unsuccessful attempt to borrow $50,000 from Alvin, had threatened him, saying, "If I ever have to choose between your skin and mine, it won't be mine that'll suffer."

Theodore Montagu, the man who, according to the story of the elevator boy at the Chatham Arms, had returned at half past two on the night of the murder, testified that as his taxicab turned in front of the apartment house the headlights flashed on a man standing in a tradesmen's entrance across the street, and that the man looked like Major Benson. This evidence would have had little effect had not Pfyfe come forward after the arrest and admitted seeing the major crossing Sixth Avenue at Forty-sixth Street when he had walked to Pietro's for his drink of Haig and Haig. He explained that he had attached no importance to it at the time, thinking the major was merely returning home from some Broadway restaurant. He himself had not been seen by the major.

This testimony, in connection with Mr. Montagu's, annihilated the major's carefully planned alibi; and though the defence contended stubbornly that both witnesses had been mistaken in their identification, the jury was deeply impressed by the evidence, especially when Assistant District Attorney Sullivan, under Vance's tutoring, painstakingly explained, with diagrams, how the major could have gone out and returned that night without being seen by the boy.

It was also shown that the jewels could not have been taken from the scene of the crime except by the murderer; and Vance and I were called as witnesses to the finding of them in the major's apartment. Vance's demonstration of the height of the murderer was shown in court, but, curiously, it carried little weight, as the issue was confused by a mass of elaborate scientific objections. Captain Hagedorn's identification of the pistol was the most difficult obstacle with which the defence had to contend.

The trial lasted three weeks, and much evidence of a scandalous nature was taken, although, at Markham's suggestion, Sullivan did his best to minimize the private affairs of those innocent persons whose lives unfortunately touched upon the episode. Colonel Ostrander, however, has never forgiven Markham for not having had him called as a witness.

During the last week of the trial Miss Muriel St. Clair appeared as *prima donna* in a large Broadway light opera production which ran successfully for nearly two years. She has since married her chivalrous Captain Leacock, and they appear perfectly happy.

Pfyfe is still married and as elegant as ever. He visits New York regularly, despite the absence of his "dear old Alvin"; and I have occasionally seen him and Mrs. Banning together. Somehow, I shall always like that woman. Pfyfe raised the $10,000—how, I have no idea—and reclaimed her jewels. Their ownership, by the way, was not divulged at the trial, for which I was very glad.

On the evening of the day the verdict was brought in against the major, Vance and Markham and I were sitting in the Stuyvesant Club. We had dined together, but no word of the events of the past few weeks had passed between us. Presently, however, I saw an ironic smile creep slowly to Vance's lips.

"I say, Markham," he drawled, "what a grotesque spectacle the trial was! The real evidence, y'know, wasn't even introduced. Benson was convicted entirely on suppositions, presumptions, implications and inf'rences. . . . God help the innocent Daniel who inadvertently falls into a den of legal lions!"

Markham, to my surprise, nodded gravely.

"Yes," he concurred; "but if Sullivan had tried to get a conviction on your so-called psychological theories, he'd have been adjudged insane."

"Doubtless," sighed Vance. "You *illuminati* of the law would have little to do if you went about your business intelligently."

"Theoretically," replied Markham at length, "your theories are clear enough; but I'm afraid I've dealt too long with material facts to forsake them for psychology and art. . . . However," he added lightly, "if my legal evidence should fail me in the future, may I call on you for assistance?"

"I'm always at your service, old chap, don't y'know," Vance rejoined. "I rather fancy, though, that it's when your legal evidence is leading you irresistibly to your victim that you'll need me most, what?"

And the remark, though intended merely as a good-natured sally, proved strangely prophetic.

The 'Canary'
Murder Case

Characters of the Book

Philo Vance

John F.-X. Markham *District Attorney of New York County*

Margaret Odell (The "Canary") *Famous Broadway beauty and ex-Follies girl, who was mysteriously murdered in her apartment*

Amy Gibson *Margaret Odell's maid*

Charles Cleaver *A man-about-town*

Kenneth Spotswoode *A manufacturer*

Louis Mannix *An importer*

Dr. Ambroise Lindquist *A fashionable neurologist*

Tony Skeel *A professional burglar*

William Elmer Jessup *Telephone operator*

Harry Spively *Telephone operator*

Alys La Fosse *A musical-comedy actress*

Wiley Allen *A gambler*

Potts *A street cleaner*

Amos Feathergill *Assistant District Attorney*

William M. Moran *Commanding Officer of the Detective Bureau*

Ernest Heath *Sergeant of the Homicide Bureau*

Snitkin *Detective of the Homicide Bureau*

Guilfoyle *Detective of the Homicide Bureau*

Burke *Detective of the Homicide Bureau*

Tracy *Detective assigned to District Attorney's office*

Deputy Inspector Conrad Brenner *Burglar-tools expert*

Captain Dubois Fingerprint expert

Detective Bellamy *Fingerprint expert*

Peter Quackenbush *Official photographer*

Dr. Doremus *Medical examiner*

Swacker *Secretary to the district attorney*

Currie *Vance's valet*

CHAPTER 1

The "Canary"

In the offices of the Homicide Bureau of the Detective Division of the New York Police Department, on the third floor of the police headquarters building in Centre Street, there is a large steel filing cabinet; and within it, among thousands of others of its kind, there reposes a small green index card on which is typed: "Odell, Margaret. 184 West 71st Street. Sept. 10. Murder: Strangled about 11 p.m. Apartment ransacked. Jewellery stolen. Body found by Amy Gibson, maid."

Here, in a few commonplace words, is the bleak, unadorned statement of one of the most astonishing crimes in the police annals of this country—a crime so contradictory, so baffling, so ingenious, so unique, that for many days the best minds of the police department and the district attorney's office were completely at a loss as to even a method of approach. Each line of investigation only tended to prove that Margaret Odell could not possibly have been murdered. And yet, huddled on the great silken davenport in her living room lay the girl's strangled body, giving the lie to so grotesque a conclusion.

The true story of this crime, as it eventually came to light after a disheartening period of utter darkness and confusion, revealed many strange and bizarre ramifications, many dark recesses of man's unexplored nature, and the uncanny subtlety of a human mind sharpened by desperate and tragic despair. And it also revealed a hidden page of passional melodrama which, in its essence and organisms, was no less romantic and fascinating than that vivid, theatrical section of the *Comédie Humaine* which deals with the fabulous love of Baron Nucingen for Esther van Gobseck, and with the unhappy Torpille's tragic death.

Margaret Odell was a product of the bohemian demimonde of Broadway—a scintillant figure who seemed somehow to typify the gaudy and spurious romance of transient gaiety. For nearly two years before her death she had been the most conspicuous and, in a sense, popular figure of the city's night life. In our grandparents' day she might have had conferred upon her that somewhat questionable designation "the toast of the town"; but today there are too many aspirants for this classification, too many cliques and violent schisms in the Lepidoptera of our cafe life, to permit of any one competitor being thus singled out. But, for all the darlings of both professional and lay press agents, Margaret Odell was a character of unquestioned fame in her little world.

Her notoriety was due in part to certain legendary tales of her affairs with one or two obscure potentates in the backwashes of Europe. She had spent two years abroad after her first success in *The Bretonne Maid*—a popular musical comedy in which she had been mysteriously raised from obscurity to the rank of "star"—and, one may cynically imagine, her press agent took full advantage of her absence to circulate vermilion tales of her conquests.

Her appearances went far toward sustaining her somewhat equivocal fame. There was no question that she was beautiful in a hard, slightly flamboyant way. I remember seeing her dancing one night at the Antlers Club—a famous rendezvous for post midnight pleasure-seekers, run by the notorious Red Raegan.* She impressed me then as a girl of uncommon loveliness, despite the calculating, predatory cast of her features. She was of medium height, slender, graceful in a leonine way, and, I thought, a trifle aloof and even haughty in manner—a result, perhaps, of her reputed association with European royalty. She had the traditional courtesan's full, red lips, and the wide, mongoose eyes of Rossetti's "Blessed Damozel." There was in her face that strange combination of sensual promise and spiritual renunciation with which the painters of all ages have sought to endow their conceptions of the Eternal Magdalene. Hers was the type of face, voluptuous and with a hint of mystery, which rules man's emotions and, by subjugating his mind, drives him to desperate deeds.

Margaret Odell had received the sobriquet of Canary as a result of a part she had played in an elaborate ornithological ballet of the Follies, in which each girl had been gowned to represent a variety of bird. To her had fallen the role of canary; and her costume of white and yellow satin, together with her mass of shining golden hair and

---

*The Antlers Club has since been closed by the police; and Red Raegan is now serving a long term in Sing Sing for grand larceny.

pink and white complexion, had distinguished her in the eyes of the spectators as a creature of outstanding charm. Before a fortnight had passed—so eulogistic were her press notices, and so unerringly did the audience single her out for applause—the "Bird Ballet" was changed to the "Canary Ballet," and Miss Odell was promoted to the rank of what might charitably be called premiere danseuse, at the same time having a solo waltz and a song* interpolated for the special display of her charms and talents.

She had quitted the Follies at the close of the season, and during her subsequent spectacular career in the haunts of Broadway's night life she had been popularly and familiarly called the Canary. Thus it happened that when her dead body was found, brutally strangled, in her apartment, the crime immediately became known, and was always thereafter referred to, as the Canary murder.

My own participation in the investigation of the Canary murder case—or rather my role of Boswellian spectator—constituted one of the most memorable experiences of my life. At the time of Margaret Odell's murder John F.-X. Markham was district attorney of New York, having taken office the preceding January. I need hardly remind you that during the four years of his incumbency he distinguished himself by his almost uncanny success as a criminal investigator. The praise which was constantly accorded him, however, was highly distasteful to him; for, being a man with a keen sense of honour, he instinctively shrank from accepting credit for achievements not wholly his own. The truth is that Markham played only a subsidiary part in the majority of his most famous criminal cases. The credit for their actual solution belonged to one of Markham's very close friends, who refused, at the time, to permit the facts to be made public.

This man was a young social aristocrat, whom, for purposes of anonymity, I have chosen to call Philo Vance.

Vance had many amazing gifts and capabilities. He was an art collector in a small way, a fine amateur pianist, and a profound student of aesthetics and psychology. Although an American, he had largely been educated in Europe, and still retained a slight English accent and intonation. He had a liberal independent income, and spent considerable time fulfilling the social obligations which devolved on him as a result of family connections; but he was neither an idler nor a dilettante. His manner was cynical and aloof; and those who met him only casually set him down as a snob. But knowing Vance, as I did, intimately, I was

---

* Written especially for her by B. G. De Sylva.

able to glimpse the real man beneath the surface indications; and I knew that his cynicism and aloofness, far from being a pose, sprang instinctively from a nature which was at once sensitive and solitary.

Vance was not yet thirty-five, and, in a cold, sculptural fashion, was impressively good-looking. His face was slender and mobile; but there was a stern, sardonic expression to his features, which acted as a barrier between him and his fellows. He was not emotionless, but his emotions were, in the main, intellectual. He was often criticized for his asceticism, yet I have seen him exhibit rare bursts of enthusiasm over an aesthetic or psychological problem. However, he gave the impression of remaining remote from all mundane matters; and, in truth, he looked upon life like a dispassionate and impersonal spectator at a play, secretly amused and debonairly cynical at the meaningless futility of it all. Withal, he had a mind avid for knowledge, and few details of the human comedy that came within his sphere of vision escaped him.

It was as a direct result of this intellectual inquisitiveness that he became actively, though unofficially, interested in Markham's criminal investigations.

I kept a fairly complete record of the cases in which Vance participated as a kind of *amicus curiae*, little thinking that I would ever be privileged to make them public; but Markham, after being defeated, as you remember, on a hopelessly split ticket at the next election, withdrew from politics; and last year Vance went abroad to live, declaring he would never return to America. As a result, I obtained permission from both of them to publish my notes in full. Vance stipulated only that I should not reveal his name; but otherwise no restrictions were placed upon me.

I have related elsewhere* the peculiar circumstances which led to Vance's participation in criminal research, and how, in the face of almost insuperable contradictory evidence, he solved the mysterious shooting of Alvin Benson. The present chronicle deals with his solution of Margaret Odell's murder, which took place in the early fall of the same year, and which, you will recall, created an even greater sensation than its predecessor.

The Loeb-Leopold crime, the Dorothy King case, and the Hall-Mills murder came later; but the Canary murder proved fully as conspicuous a case as the Nan Patterson "Caesar" Young affair, Durant's murder of Blanche Lamont and Minnie Williams in San Francisco, the Molineux arsenic-poisoning case, and the Carlyle Harris morphine

---

* "The Benson Murder Case"

murder. To find a parallel in point of public interest one must recall the Borden double-murder in Fall River, the Thaw case, the shooting of Elwell, and the Rosenthal murder.

A curious set of circumstances was accountable for the way in which Vance was shouldered with this new investigation. Markham for weeks had been badgered by the anti-administration newspapers for the signal failures of his office in obtaining convictions against certain underworld offenders whom the police had turned over to him for prosecution. As a result of prohibition a new and dangerous, and wholly undesirable, kind of night life had sprung up in New York. A large number of well-financed cabarets, calling themselves nightclubs, had made their appearance along Broadway and in its side streets; and already there had been an appalling number of serious crimes, both passional and monetary, which, it was said, had had their inception in these unsavoury resorts.

At last, when a case of murder accompanying a hold-up and jewel robbery in one of the family hotels uptown was traced directly to plans and preparations made in one of the nightclubs, and when two detectives of the Homicide Bureau investigating the case were found dead one morning in the neighbourhood of the club, with bullet wounds in their backs, Markham decided to pigeonhole the other affairs of his office and take a hand personally in the intolerable criminal conditions that had arisen.*

---

*The case referred to here was that of Mrs. Elinor Quiggly, a wealthy widow living at the Adlon Hotel in West 96th Street. She was found on the morning of September 5 suffocated by a gag which had been placed on her by robbers who had evidently followed her home from the Club Turque—a small but luxurious all-night cafe at 89 West 48th Street. The killing of the two detectives, McQuade and Cannison, was, the police believe, due to the fact that they were in possession of incriminating evidence against the perpetrators of the crime. Jewellery amounting to over $50,000 was stolen from the Quiggly apartment.

CHAPTER 2

Footprints in the Snow
Sunday, September 9

On the day following his decision, Markham and Vance and I were sitting in a secluded corner of the lounge room of the Stuyvesant Club. We often came together there, for we were all members of the club, and Markham frequently used it as a kind of unofficial uptown headquarters.*

"It's bad enough to have half the people in this city under the impression that the district attorney's office is a kind of high-class collection agency," he remarked that night, "without being necessitated to turn detective because I'm not given sufficient evidence, or the right kind of evidence, with which to secure convictions."

Vance looked up with a slow smile and regarded him quizzically.

"The difficulty would seem to be," he returned, with an indolent drawl, "that the police, being unversed in the exquisite abracadabra of legal procedure, labour under the notion that evidence which would convince a man of ordin'ry intelligence, would also convince a court of law. A silly notion, don't y'know. Lawyers don't really want evidence; they want erudite technicalities. And the average policeman's brain is too forthright to cope with the pedantic demands of jurisprudence."

"It's not as bad as that," Markham retorted, with an attempt at good nature, although the strain of the past few weeks had tended to upset his habitual equanimity. "If there weren't rules of evidence, grave injustice would too often be done innocent persons. And even a criminal is entitled to protection in our courts."

Vance yawned mildly.

"Markham, you should have been a pedagogue. It's positively

---

* The Stuyvesant was a large club, somewhat in the nature of a glorified hotel; and its extensive membership was drawn largely from the political, legal, and financial ranks.

amazin' how you've mastered all the standard oratorical replies to criticism. And yet, I'm unconvinced. You remember the Wisconsin case of the kidnapped man whom the courts declared presumably dead. Even when he reappeared, hale and hearty, among his former neighbours, his status of being presumably dead was not legally altered. The visible and demonstrable fact that he was actually alive was regarded by the court as an immaterial and impertinent side issue.* . . . Then there's the touchin' situation—so prevalent in this fair country—of a man being insane in one state and sane in another. . . . Really, y'know, you can't expect a mere lay intelligence, unskilled in the benign processes of legal logic, to perceive such subtle nuances. Your layman, swaddled in the darkness of ordin'ry common sense, would say that a person who is a lunatic on one bank of a river would still be a lunatic if he was on the opposite bank. And he'd also hold—erroneously, no doubt—that if a man was living, he would presumably be alive."

"Why this academic dissertation?" asked Markham, this time a bit irritably.

"It seems to touch rather vitally on the source of your present predicament," Vance explained equably. "The police, not being lawyers, have apparently got you into hot water, what? . . . Why not start an agitation to send all detectives to law school?"

"You're a great help," retorted Markham.

Vance raised his eyebrows slightly.

"Why disparage my suggestion? Surely you must perceive that it has merit. A man without legal training, when he knows a thing to be true, ignores all incompetent testimony to the contr'ry, and clings to the facts. A court of law listens solemnly to a mass of worthless testimony, and renders a decision not on the facts but according to a complicated set of rules. The result, d'ye see, is that a court often acquits a prisoner, realizing full well that he is guilty. Many a judge has said, in effect, to a culprit, 'I know, and the jury knows, that you committed the crime, but in view of the legally admissible evidence, I declare you innocent. Go and sin again.'"

Markham grunted. "I'd hardly endear myself to the people of this country if I answered the current strictures against me by recommending law courses for the police department."

"Permit me, then, to suggest the alternative of Shakespeare's butcher: 'Let's kill all the lawyers.'"

---

* The case to which Vance referred, I ascertained later, was Shatterham v. Shatterham, 417 Mich., 79—a testamentary case.

"Unfortunately, it's a situation, not a utopian theory, that has to be met."

"And just how," asked Vance lazily, "do you propose to reconcile the sensible conclusions of the police with what you touchingly call correctness of legal procedure?"

"To begin with," Markham informed him, "I've decided henceforth to do my own investigating of all important nightclub criminal cases. I called a conference of the heads of my departments yesterday, and from now on there's going to be some real activity radiating direct from my office. I intend to produce the kind of evidence I need for convictions."

Vance slowly took a cigarette from his case and tapped it on the arm of his chair. "Ah! So you are going to substitute the conviction of the innocent for the acquittal of the guilty?"

Markham was nettled; turning in his chair, he frowned at Vance. "I won't pretend not to understand your remark," he said acidulously. "You're back again on your favourite theme of the inadequacy of circumstantial evidence as compared with your psychological theories and aesthetic hypotheses."

"Quite so," agreed Vance carelessly. "Y'know, Markham, your sweet and charmin' faith in circumstantial evidence is positively disarming. Before it, the ordin'ry powers of ratiocination are benumbed. I tremble for the innocent victims you are about to gather into your legal net. You'll eventually make the mere attendance at any cabaret a frightful hazard."

Markham smoked awhile in silence. Despite the seeming bitterness at times in the discussions of these two men, there was at bottom no animosity in their attitude toward each other. Their friendship was of long standing, and, despite the dissimilarity of their temperaments and the marked difference in their points of view, a profound mutual respect formed the basis of their intimate relationship.

At length Markham spoke. "Why this sweeping deprecation of circumstantial evidence? I admit that at times it may be misleading; but it often forms powerful presumptive proof of guilt. Indeed, Vance, one of our greatest legal authorities has demonstrated that it is the most powerful actual evidence in existence. Direct evidence, in the very nature of crime, is almost always unavailable. If the courts had to depend on it, the great majority of criminals would still be at large."

"I was under the impression that this precious majority had always enjoyed its untrammelled freedom."

Markham ignored the interruption. "Take this example: A dozen adults see an animal running across the snow, and testify that it was a chicken; whereas a child sees the same animal, and declares it was a duck. They thereupon examine the animal's footprints and find them to be the web-footed tracks made by a duck. Is it not conclusive, then, that the animal was a duck and not a chicken, despite the preponderance of direct evidence?"

"I'll grant you your duck," acceded Vance indifferently.

"And having gratefully accepted the gift," pursued Markham, "I propound a corollary: A dozen adults see a human figure crossing the snow, and take oath it was a woman; whereas a child asserts that the figure was a man. Now, will you not also grant that the circumstantial evidence of a man's footprints in the snow would supply incontrovertible proof that it was, in fact, a man, and not a woman?"

"Not at all, my dear Justinian," replied Vance, stretching his legs languidly in front of him; "unless, of course, you could show that a human being possesses no higher order of brain than a duck."

"What have brains to do with it?" Markham asked impatiently. "Brains don't affect one's footprints."

"Not those of a duck, certainly. But brains might very well—and, no doubt, often do—affect the footprints of a human being."

"Am I having a lesson in anthropology, Darwinian adaptability, or merely metaphysical speculation?"

"In none of those abstruse subjects," Vance assured him. "I'm merely stating a simple fact culled from observation."

"Well, according to your highly and peculiarly developed processes of reasoning, would the circumstantial evidence of those masculine footprints indicate a man or a woman?"

"Not necessarily either," Vance answered, "or, rather, a possibility of each. Such evidence, when applied to a human being—to a creature, that is, with a reasoning mind—would merely mean to me that the figure crossing the snow was either a man in his own shoes or a woman in man's shoes; or perhaps, even, a long-legged child. In short, it would convey to my purely unlegal intelligence only that the tracks were made by some descendant of the Pithecanthropus erectus wearing men's shoes on his nether limbs—sex and age unknown. A duck's spoors, on the other hand, I might be tempted to take at their face value."

"I'm delighted to observe," said Markham, "that at least you repudiate the possibility of a duck dressing itself up in the gardener's boots."

Vance was silent for a moment; then he said, "The trouble with you modern Solons, d'ye see, is that you attempt to reduce human nature to a formula; whereas the truth is that man, like life, is infinitely complex. He's shrewd and tricky—skilled for centuries in all the most diabolical chicaneries. He is a creature of low cunning, who, even in the normal course of his vain and idiotic struggle for existence, instinctively and deliberately tells ninety-nine lies to one truth. A duck, not having had the heaven-kissing advantages of human civilization, is a straightforward and eminently honest bird."

"How," asked Markham, "since you jettison all the ordinary means of arriving at a conclusion, would you decide the sex or species of this person who left the masculine footprints in the snow?"

Vance blew a spiral of smoke toward the ceiling.

"First, I'd repudiate all the evidence of the twelve astigmatic adults and the one bright-eyed child. Next, I'd ignore the footprints in the snow. Then, with a mind unprejudiced by dubious testimony and uncluttered with material clues, I'd determine the exact nature of the crime which this fleeing person had committed. After having analyzed its various factors, I could infallibly tell you not only whether the culprit was a man or a woman, but I could describe his habits, character, and personality. And I could do all this whether the fleeing figure left male or female or kangaroo tracks, or used stilts, or rode off on a velocipede, or levitated without leaving tracks at all."

Markham smiled broadly. "You'd be worse than the police in the matter of supplying me legal evidence, I fear."

"I, at least, wouldn't procure evidence against some unsuspecting person whose boots had been appropriated by the real culprit," retorted Vance. "And, y'know, Markham, as long as you pin your faith to footprints, you'll inevitably arrest just those persons whom the actual criminals want you to—namely, persons who have had nothing to do with the criminal conditions you're about to investigate."

He became suddenly serious.

"See here, old man; there are some shrewd intelligences at present allied with what the theologians call the powers of darkness. The surface appearances of many of these crimes that are worrying you are palpably deceptive. Personally, I don't put much stock in the theory that a malevolent gang of cutthroats have organized an American camorra and made the silly nightclubs their headquarters. The idea is too melodramatic. It smacks too much of the gaudy journalistic imagination; it's too Eugène Sue-ish. Crime isn't a mass instinct except during wartime, and then it's merely an obscene sport. Crime, d'ye see, is a personal and individual business. One doesn't make up a *partie carée* for a murder as one does for a bridge game. . . . Markham, old dear, don't let this romantic criminological idea lead you astray. And don't scrutinize the figurative footprints in the snow too closely. They'll confuse you most horribly—you're far too trustin' and literal for this wicked world. I warn you that no clever criminal is going to leave his own footprints for your tape measure and callipers."

He sighed deeply and gave Markham a look of bantering commiseration. "And have you paused to consider that your first case may even be devoid of footprints? . . . Alas! What, then, will you do?"

"I could overcome that difficulty by taking you along with me," suggested Markham, with a touch of irony. "How would you like to accompany me on the next important case that breaks?"

"I am ravished by the idea," said Vance.

Two days later the front pages of our metropolitan press carried glaring headlines telling of the murder of Margaret Odell.

CHAPTER 3

The Murder

Tuesday, September 11; 8:30 a.m.

It was barely half past eight on that momentous morning of September the 11th when Markham brought word to us of the event.

I was living temporarily with Vance at his home in East 38th Street—a large remodelled apartment occupying the two top floors of a beautiful mansion. For several years I had been Vance's personal legal representative and adviser, having resigned from my father's law firm of Van Dine, Davis, and Van Dine to devote myself to his needs and interests. His affairs were by no means voluminous, but his personal finances, together with his numerous purchases of paintings and *objets d'art*, occupied my full time without burdening me. This monetary and legal stewardship was eminently congenial to my tastes; and my friendship with Vance, which had dated from our undergraduate days at Harvard, supplied the social and human element in an arrangement which otherwise might easily have degenerated into one of mere drab routine.

On this particular morning I had risen early and was working in the library when Currie, Vance's valet and major-domo, announced Markham's presence in the living room. I was considerably astonished at this early morning visit, for Markham well knew that Vance, who rarely rose before noon, resented any intrusion upon his matutinal slumbers. And in that moment I received the curious impression that something unusual and portentous was toward.

I found Markham pacing restlessly up and down, his hat and gloves thrown carelessly on the centre table. As I entered he halted and looked at me with harassed eyes. He was a moderately tall man, clean-shaven, grey-haired, and firmly set up. His appearance was distinguished, and his manner courteous and kindly. But beneath his gracious exterior there was an aggressive sternness, an indomitable, grim strength, that gave one the sense of dogged efficiency and untiring capability.

"Good morning, Van," he greeted me, with impatient perfunctoriness. "There's been another half-world murder—the worst and ugliest thus far. . . ." He hesitated and regarded me searchingly. "You recall my chat with Vance at the club the other night? There was something damned prophetic in his remarks. And you remember I half promised to take him along on the next important case. Well, the case has broken—with a vengeance. Margaret Odell, whom they called the Canary, has been strangled in her apartment; and from what I just got over the phone, it looks like another nightclub affair. I'm headed for the Odell apartment now. . . . What about rousing out the sybarite?"

"By all means," I agreed, with an alacrity which, I fear, was in large measure prompted by purely selfish motives. The Canary! If one had sought the city over for a victim whose murder would stir up excitement, there could have been but few selections better calculated to produce this result.

Hastening to the door, I summoned Currie and told him to call Vance at once.

"I'm afraid, sir—" began Currie, politely hesitant.

"Calm your fears," cut in Markham. "I'll take all responsibility for waking him at this indecent hour."

Currie sensed an emergency and departed.

A minute or two later Vance, in an elaborately embroidered silk kimono and sandals, appeared at the living room door.

"My word!" he greeted us, in mild astonishment, glancing at the clock. "Haven't you chaps gone to bed yet?"

He strolled to the mantel and selected a gold-tipped Régie cigarette from a small Florentine humidor.

Markham's eyes narrowed; he was in no mood for levity.

"The Canary has been murdered," I blurted out.

Vance held his wax vesta poised and gave me a look of indolent inquisitiveness. "Whose canary?"

"Margaret Odell was found strangled this morning," amended Markham brusquely. "Even *you*, wrapped in your scented cotton-wool, have heard of her. And you can realize the significance of the crime. I'm personally going to look for those footprints in the snow; and if you want to come along, as you intimated the other night, you'll have to get a move on."

Vance crushed out his cigarette.

"Margaret Odell, eh?—Broadway's blond Aspasia—or was it

Phryne who had the *coiffure d'or*? . . . Most distressin'!" Despite his off-hand manner, I could see he was deeply interested. "The base enemies of law and order are determined to chivvy you most horribly, aren't they, old dear? Deuced inconsiderate of 'em! . . . Excuse me while I seek habiliments suitable to the occasion."

He disappeared into his bedroom, while Markham took out a large cigar and resolutely prepared it for smoking, and I returned to the library to put away the papers on which I had been working.

In less than ten minutes Vance reappeared, dressed for the street. *"Bien, mon vieux,"* he announced gaily, as Currie handed him his hat and gloves and a malacca cane. *"Allons-y!"*

We rode uptown along Madison Avenue, turned into Central Park, and came out by the West 72d Street entrance. Margaret Odell's apartment was at 184 West 71st Street, near Broadway; and as we drew up to the curb, it was necessary for the patrolman on duty to make a passage for us through the crowd that had already gathered as a result of the arrival of the police.

Feathergill, an assistant district attorney, was waiting in the main hall for his chief's arrival.

"It's too bad, sir," he lamented. "A rotten show all round. And just at this time! . . ." He shrugged his shoulders discouragingly.

"It may collapse quickly," said Markham, shaking the other's hand. "How are things going? Sergeant Heath phoned me right after you called, and said that, at first glance, the case looked a bit stubborn."

"Stubborn?" repeated Feathergill lugubriously. "It's downright impervious. Heath is spinning round like a turbine. He was called off the Boyle case, by the way, to devote his talents to this new shocker. Inspector Moran arrived ten minutes ago and gave him the official imprimatur."

"Well, Heath's a good man," declared Markham. "We'll work it out. . . . Which is the apartment?"

Feathergill led the way to a door at the rear of the main hall. "Here you are, sir," he announced. "I'll be running along now. I need sleep. Good luck!" And he was gone.

It will be necessary to give a brief description of the house and its interior arrangement, for the somewhat peculiar structure of the building played a vital part in the seemingly insoluble problem posed by the murder.

The house, which was a four-story stone structure originally built as a residence, had been remodelled, both inside and outside, to meet the requirements of an exclusive individual apartment dwelling. There

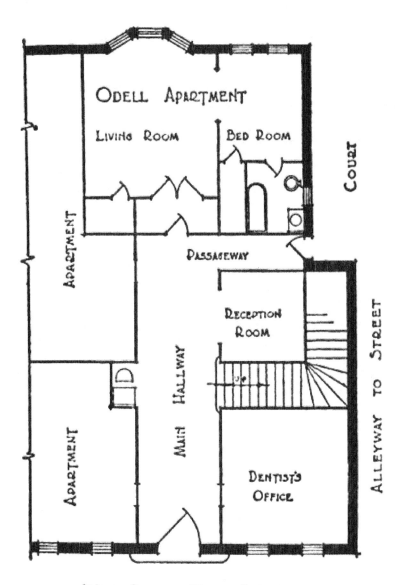

ODELL APARTMENT

LIVING ROOM

BED ROOM

COURT

APARTMENT

PASSAGEWAY

RECEPTION ROOM

MAIN HALLWAY

ALLEYWAY TO STREET

APARTMENT

DENTIST'S OFFICE

WEST SEVENTY-FIRST STREET

were, I believe, three or four separate suites on each floor; but the quarters upstairs need not concern us. The main floor was the scene of the crime, and here there were three apartments and a dentist's office.

The main entrance to the building was directly on the street, and extending straight back from the front door was a wide hallway. Directly at the rear of this hallway, and facing the entrance, was the door to the Odell apartment, which bore the numeral "3." About halfway down the front hall, on the right-hand side, was the stairway leading to the floors above; and directly beyond the stairway, also on the right, was a small reception room with a wide archway instead of a door. Directly opposite to the stairway, in a small recess, stood the telephone switchboard. There was no elevator in the house.

Another important feature of this ground-floor plan was a small passageway at the rear of the main hall and at right angles to it, which led past the front walls of the Odell apartment to a door opening on a court at the west side of the building. This court was connected with the street by an alley four feet wide.

In the accompanying diagram this arrangement of the ground floor can be easily visualized, and I suggest that the reader fix it in his mind; for I doubt if ever before so simple and obvious an architectural design played such an important part in a criminal mystery. By its very simplicity and almost conventional familiarity—indeed, by its total lack of any puzzling complications—it proved so baffling to the investigators that the case threatened, for many days, to remain forever insoluble.

As Markham entered the Odell apartment that morning Sergeant Ernest Heath came forward at once and extended his hand. A look of relief passed over his broad, pugnacious features and it was obvious that the animosity and rivalry which always exist between the detective division and the district attorney's office during the investigation of any criminal case had no place in his attitude on this occasion.

"I'm glad you've come, sir," he said, and meant it.

He then turned to Vance with a cordial smile, and held out his hand.*

"So the amachoor sleuth is with us again!" His tone held a friendly banter.

"Oh, quite," murmured Vance. "How's your induction coil working this beautiful September morning, Sergeant?"

---

* Heath had become acquainted with Vance during the investigation of the Benson murder case two months previously.

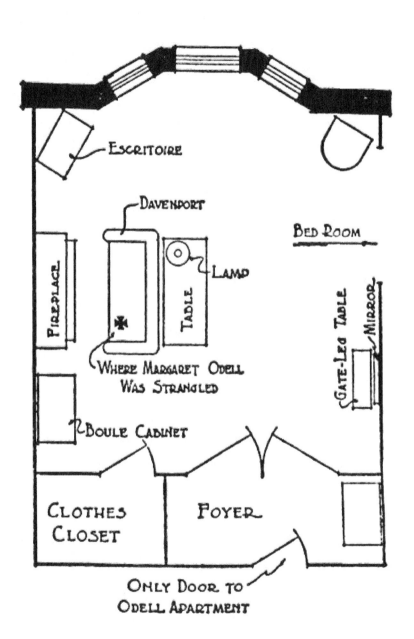

ESCRITOIRE

DAVENPORT

BED ROOM

FIREPLACE

LAMP

TABLE

GATE-LEG TABLE

MIRROR

WHERE MARGARET ODELL
WAS STRANGLED

BOULE CABINET

CLOTHES
CLOSET

FOYER

ONLY DOOR TO
ODELL APARTMENT

"I'd hate to tell you!" Then Heath's face grew suddenly grave, and he turned to Markham. "It's a raw deal, sir. Why in hell couldn't they have picked someone besides the Canary for their dirty work? There's plenty of Janes on Broadway who coulda faded from the picture without causing a second alarm; but they gotta go and bump off the Queen of Sheba!"

As he spoke, William M. Moran, the commanding officer of the detective bureau, came into the little foyer and performed the usual handshaking ceremony. Though he had met Vance and me but once before, and then casually, he remembered us both and addressed us courteously by name.

"Your arrival," he said to Markham, in a well-bred, modulated voice, "is very welcome. Sergeant Heath will give you what preliminary information you want. I'm still pretty much in the dark myself—only just arrived."

"A lot of information *I've* got to give," grumbled Heath, as he led the way into the living room.

Margaret Odell's apartment was a suite of two fairly large rooms connected by a wide archway draped with heavy damask portieres. The entrance door from the main hall of the building led into a small rectangular foyer about eight feet long and four feet deep, with double Venetian-glass doors opening into the main room beyond. There was no other entrance to the apartment, and the bedroom could be reached only through the archway from the living room.

There was a large davenport, covered with brocaded silk, in front of the fireplace in the left-hand wall of the living room, with a long narrow library table of inlaid rosewood extending along its back. On the opposite wall, between the foyer and the archway into the bedroom, hung a triplicate Marie Antoinette mirror, beneath which stood a mahogany gate-legged table. On the far side of the archway, near the large oriel window, was a baby grand Steinway piano with a beautifully designed and decorated case of Louis-Seize ornamentation. In the corner to the right of the fireplace was a spindle-legged escritoire and a square hand-painted wastepaper basket of vellum. To the left of the fireplace stood one of the loveliest Boule cabinets I have ever seen. Several excellent reproductions of Boucher, Fragonard, and Watteau hung about the walls. The bedroom contained a chest of drawers, a dressing table, and several gold-leaf chairs. The whole apartment seemed eminently in keeping with the Canary's fragile and evanescent personality.

As we stepped from the little foyer into the living room and stood for a moment looking about, a scene bordering on wreckage met our eyes. The rooms had apparently been ransacked by someone in a frenzy of haste, and the disorder of the place was appalling.

"They didn't exactly do the job in dainty fashion," remarked Inspector Moran.

"I suppose we oughta be grateful they didn't blow the joint up with dynamite," returned Heath acridly.

But it was not the general disorder that most attracted us. Our gaze was almost immediately drawn and held by the body of the dead girl, which rested in an unnatural, semi-recumbent attitude in the corner of the davenport nearest to where we stood. Her head was turned backward, as if by force, over the silken tufted upholstery; and her hair had come unfastened and lay beneath her head and over her bare shoulder like a frozen cataract of liquid gold. Her face, in violent death, was distorted and unlovely. Her skin was discoloured; her eyes were staring; her mouth was open, and her lips were drawn back. Her neck, on either side of the thyroid cartilage, showed ugly dark bruises. She was dressed in a flimsy evening gown of black Chantilly lace over cream-colored chiffon, and across the arm of the davenport had been thrown an evening cape of cloth-of-gold trimmed with ermine.

There were evidences of her ineffectual struggle with the person who had strangled her. Besides the dishevelled condition of her hair, one of the shoulder straps of her gown had been severed, and there was a long rent in the fine lace across her breast. A small corsage of artificial orchids had been torn from her bodice, and lay crumpled in her lap. One satin slipper had fallen off, and her right knee was twisted inward on the seat of the davenport, as if she had sought to lift herself out of the suffocating clutches of her antagonist. Her fingers were still flexed, no doubt as they had been at the moment of her capitulation to death, when she had relinquished her grip upon the murderer's wrists.

The spell of horror cast over us by the sight of the tortured body was broken by the matter-of-fact tones of Heath.

"You see, Mr. Markham, she was evidently sitting in the corner of this settee when she was grabbed suddenly from behind."

Markham nodded. "It must have taken a pretty strong man to strangle her so easily."

"I'll say!" agreed Heath. He bent over and pointed to the girl's fingers, on which showed several abrasions. "They stripped her rings off, too; and they didn't go about it gentle, either." Then he indicated a segment of fine platinum chain, set with tiny pearls, which hung over one of her shoulders. "And they grabbed whatever it was hanging around her neck, and broke the chain doing it. They weren't overlooking anything, or losing any time. . . . A swell, gentlemanly job. Nice and refined."

"Where's the medical examiner?" asked Markham.

"He's coming," Heath told him. "You can't get Doc Doremus to go anywheres without his breakfast."

"He may find something else—something that doesn't show."

"There's plenty showing for me," declared Heath. "Look at this apartment. It wouldn't be much worse if a Kansas cyclone had struck it."

We turned from the depressing spectacle of the dead girl and moved toward the centre of the room.

"Be careful not to touch anything, Mr. Markham," warned Heath. "I've sent for the fingerprint experts—they'll be here any minute now."

Vance looked up in mock astonishment.

"Fingerprints? You don't say—really! How delightful!—Imagine a johnnie in this enlightened day leaving his fingerprints for you to find."

"All crooks aren't clever, Mr. Vance," declared Heath combatively.

"Oh, dear, no! They'd never be apprehended if they were. But, after all, Sergeant, even an authentic fingerprint merely means that the person who made it was dallying around at some time or other. It doesn't indicate guilt."

"Maybe so," conceded Heath doggedly. "But I'm here to tell you that if I get any good honest-to-God fingerprints outa this devastated area, it's not going so easy with the bird that made 'em."

Vance appeared to be shocked. "You positively terrify me, Sergeant. Henceforth I shall adopt mittens as a permanent addition to my attire. I'm always handling the furniture and the teacups and the various knickknacks in the houses where I call, don't y'know."

Markham interposed himself at this point and suggested they make a tour of inspection while waiting for the medical examiner.

"They didn't add anything much to the usual methods," Heath pointed out. "Killed the girl, and then ripped things wide open."

The two rooms had apparently been thoroughly ransacked. Clothes and various articles were strewn about the floor. The doors of both clothes closets (there was one in each room) were open, and to judge from the chaos in the bedroom closet, it had been hurriedly searched; although the closet off the living room, which was given over to the storage of infrequently used items, appeared to have been ignored. The drawers of the dressing table and chest had been partly emptied on to the floor, and the bedclothes had been snatched away and the mattress turned back. Two chairs and a small occasional table were upset; several vases were broken, as if they had been searched and then thrown down in the wrath of disappointment; and the Marie Antoinette mirror had been broken. The escritoire was open, and its pigeonholes had been emptied in a jumbled pile upon the blotter. The doors of the Boule cabinet swung wide, and inside there was the same confusion of contents that marked the interior of the escritoire. The bronze-and-porcelain lamp on the end of the library table was lying on its side, its satin shade torn where it had struck the sharp corner of a silver *bonbonnière*.

Two objects in the general disarray particularly attracted my attention—a black metal document box of the kind purchasable at any stationery store, and a large jewel case of sheet steel with a circular inset lock. The latter of these objects was destined to play a curious and sinister part in the investigation to follow.

The document box, which was now empty, had been placed on the library table, next to the overturned lamp. Its lid was thrown back, and the key was still in the lock. In all the litter and disorganization of the room, this box seemed to be the one outstanding indication of calm and orderly activity on the part of the wrecker.

The jewel case, on the other hand, had been violently wrenched open. It sat on the dressing table in the bedroom, dented and twisted out of shape by the terrific leverage that had been necessary to force it, and beside it lay a brass-handled, cast iron poker which had evidently been brought from the living room and used as a makeshift chisel with which to prize open the lock.

Vance had glanced but casually at the different objects in the rooms as we made our rounds, but when he came to the dressing table, he paused abruptly. Taking out his monocle, he adjusted it carefully, and leaned over the broken jewel case.

"Most extr'ordin'ry!" he murmured, tapping the edge of the lid with his gold pencil. "What do you make of that, Sergeant?"

Heath had been eyeing Vance with narrowed lids as the latter bent over the dressing table.

"What's in your mind, Mr. Vance?" he, in turn, asked.

"Oh, more than you could ever guess," Vance answered lightly. "But just at the moment I was toying with the idea that this steel case was never torn open by that wholly inadequate iron poker, what?"

Heath nodded his head approvingly. "So you, too, noticed that, did you? . . . And you're dead right. That poker might've twisted the box a little, but it never snapped that lock."

He turned to Inspector Moran.

"That's the puzzler I've sent for 'Prof' Brenner to clean up—IF he can. The jimmying of that jewel case looks to me like a high-class professional job. No Sunday school superintendent did it."

Vance continued for a while to study the box, but at length he turned away with a perplexed frown.

"I say!" he commented. "Something devilish queer took place here last night."

"Oh, not so queer," Heath amended. "It was a thorough job, all right, but there's nothing mysterious about it."

Vance polished his monocle and put it away.

"If you go to work on that basis, Sergeant," he returned carelessly, "I greatly fear you'll run aground on a reef. And may kind Heaven bring you safe to shore!"

CHAPTER 4

The Print of a Hand
Tuesday, September 11, 9:30 a.m.

A few minutes after we had returned to the living room Doctor Doremus, the chief medical examiner, arrived, jaunty and energetic. Immediately in his train came three other men, one of whom carried a bulky camera and a folded tripod. These were Captain Dubois and Detective Bellamy, fingerprint experts, and Peter Quackenbush, the official photographer.

"Well, well, well!" exclaimed Doctor Doremus. "Quite a gathering of the clans. More trouble, eh? . . . I wish your friends, Inspector, would choose a more respectable hour for their little differences. This early rising upsets my liver."

He shook hands with everybody in a brisk, businesslike manner.

"Where's the body?" he demanded breezily, looking about the room. He caught sight of the girl on the davenport. "Ah! A lady."

Stepping quickly forward, he made a rapid examination of the dead girl, scrutinizing her neck and fingers, moving her arms and head to determine the condition of rigor mortis, and finally unflexing her stiffened limbs and laying her out straight on the long cushions, preparatory to a more detailed necropsy.

The rest of us moved toward the bedroom, and Heath motioned to the fingerprint men to follow.

"Go over everything," he told them. "But take a special look at this jewel case and the handle of this poker, and give that document box in the other room a close up—and—down."

"Right," assented Captain Dubois. "We'll begin in here while the doc's busy in the other room." And he and Bellamy set to work.

Our interest naturally centred on the captain's labours. For fully five minutes we watched him inspecting the twisted steel sides of the jewel case and the smooth, polished handle of the poker. He held the objects gingerly by their edges, and, placing a jeweller's glass in his eye, flashed his pocket light on every square inch of them. At length he put them down, scowling.

"No fingerprints here," he announced. "Wiped clean."

"I mighta known it," grumbled Heath. "It was a professional job, all right." He turned to the other expert. "Found anything, Bellamy?"

"Nothing to help," was the grumpy reply. "A few old smears with dust over 'em."

"Looks like a washout," Heath commented irritably; "though I'm hoping for something in the other room."

At this moment Doctor Doremus came into the bedroom and, taking a sheet from the bed, returned to the davenport and covered the body of the murdered girl. Then he snapped shut his case and, putting on his hat at a rakish angle, stepped forward with the air of a man in great haste to be on his way.

"Simple case of strangulation from behind," he said, his words running together. "Digital bruises about the front of the throat; thumb bruises in the sub-occipital region. Attack must have been unexpected. A quick, competent job though deceased evidently battled a little."

"How do you suppose her dress became torn, Doctor?" asked Vance.

"Oh, that? Can't tell. She may have done it herself—instinctive motions of clutching for air."

"Not likely though, what?"

"Why not? The dress was torn and the bouquet was ripped off, and the fellow who was choking her had both hands on her throat. Who else could've done it?"

Vance shrugged his shoulders and began lighting a cigarette.

Heath, annoyed by his apparently inconsequential interruption, put the next question.

"Don't those marks on the fingers mean that her rings were stripped off?"

"Possibly. They're fresh abrasions. Also, there's a couple of lacerations on the left wrist and slight contusions on the *thenar* eminence, indicating that a bracelet may have been forcibly pulled over her hand."

"That fits O.K.," pronounced Heath, with satisfaction. "And it looks like they snatched a pendant of some kind off her neck."

"Probably," indifferently agreed Doctor Doremus. "The piece of chain had cut into her flesh a little behind the right shoulder."

"And the time?"

"Nine or ten hours ago. Say, about eleven thirty—maybe a little before. Not after midnight, anyway." He had been teetering restlessly on his toes. "Anything else?"

Heath pondered.

"I guess that's all, doc," he decided. "I'll get the body to the mortuary right away. Let's have the post-mortem as soon as you can."

"You'll get a report in the morning." And despite his apparent eagerness to be off, Doctor Doremus stepped into the bedroom and shook hands with Heath and Markham and Inspector Moran before he hurried out.

Heath followed him to the door, and I heard him direct the officer outside to telephone the Department of Public Welfare to send an ambulance at once for the girl's body.

"I positively adore that official *archiater* of yours," Vance said to Markham. "Such detachment! Here are you stewing most distressingly over the passing of one damsel fair and frail, and that blithe *medicus* is worrying only over a sluggish liver brought on by early rising."

"What has he to be upset over?" complained Markham. "The newspapers are not riding him with spurs. . . . And by the way, what was the point of your questions about the torn dress?"

Vance lazily inspected the tip of his cigarette. "Consider," he said. "The lady was evidently taken by surprise; for, had there been a struggle beforehand, she would not have been strangled from behind while sitting down. Therefore, her gown and corsage were undoubtedly intact at the time she was seized. But, despite the conclusion of your dashing Paracelsus, the damage to her toilet was not of a nature that could have been self-inflicted in her struggle for air. If she had felt the constriction of the gown across her breast, she would have snatched the bodice itself by putting her fingers inside the band. But, if you noticed, her bodice was intact; the only thing that had been torn was the deep lace flounce on the outside; and it had been torn, or rather ripped, by a strong lateral pull; whereas, in the circumstances, any wrench on her part would have been downward or outward."

Inspector Moran was listening intently, but Heath seemed restless and impatient; apparently he regarded the torn gown as irrelevant to the simple main issue.

"Moreover," Vance went on, "there is the corsage. If she herself had torn it off while being strangled, it would doubtless have fallen to the floor; for, remember, she offered considerable resistance. Her body was twisted sidewise; her knee was drawn up, and one slipper had been kicked off. Now, no bunch of silken posies is going to remain in a lady's lap during such a commotion. Even when ladies sit still, their gloves and handbags and handkerchiefs and programs and serviettes are forever sliding off of their laps onto the floor, don't y'know."

"But if your argument's correct," protested Markham, "then, the tearing of the lace and the snatching off of the corsage could have been done only after she was dead. And I can't see any object in such senseless vandalism."

"Neither can I," sighed Vance. "It's all devilish queer."

Heath looked up at him sharply. "That's the second time you've said that. But there's nothing what you'd call queer about this mess. It is a straightaway case." He spoke with an overtone of insistence, like a man arguing against his own insecurity of opinion. "The dress might've been torn almost anytime," he went on stubbornly. "And the flower might've got caught in the lace of her skirt so it couldn't roll off."

"And how would you explain the jewel case, Sergeant?" asked Vance.

"Well, the fellow might've tried the poker and then, finding it wouldn't work, used his jimmy."

"If he had the efficient jimmy," countered Vance, "why did he go to the trouble of bringing the silly poker from the living room?"

The sergeant shook his head perplexedly.

"You never can tell why some of these crooks act the way they do."

"Tut, tut!" Vance chided him. "There should be no such word as *never* in the bright lexicon of detecting."

Heath regarded him sharply. "Was there anything else that struck you as queer?" His subtle doubts were welling up again.

"Well, there's the lamp on the table in the other room."

We were standing near the archway between the two rooms, and Heath turned quickly and looked blankly at the fallen lamp.

"I don t see anything queer about that."

"It has been upset—eh, what?" suggested Vance.

"What if it has?" Health was frankly puzzled. "Damn near everything in this apartment has been knocked crooked."

"Ah! But there's a reason for most of the other things having been disturbed—like the drawers and pigeonholes and closets and vases. They all indicate a search; they're consistent with a raid for loot. But that lamp, now, d'ye see, doesn't fit into the picture. It's a false note. It was standing on the opposite end of the table to where the murder was committed, at least five feet away; and it couldn't possibly have been knocked over in the struggle.... No, it won't do. It's got no business being upset, any more than that pretty mirror over the gate-legged table has any business being broken. That's why it's queer."

"What about those chairs and the little table?" asked Heath, pointing to two small gilded chairs which had been overturned, and a fragile tip-table that lay on its side near the piano.

"Oh, they fit into the ensemble," returned Vance. "They're all light pieces of furniture which could easily have been knocked over, or thrown aside, by the hasty gentleman who rifled these rooms."

"The lamp might've been knocked over in the same way," argued Heath. Vance shook his head. "Not tenable, Sergeant. It has a solid bronze base and isn't at all top-heavy; and, being set well back on the table, it wasn't in anyone's way. . . . That lamp was upset deliberately."

The sergeant was silent for a while. Experience had taught him not to underestimate Vance's observations; and, I must confess, as I looked at the lamp lying on its side on the end of the library table, well removed from any of the other disordered objects in the room, Vance's argument seemed to possess considerable force. I tried hard to fit it into a hasty reconstruction of the crime but was utterly unable to do so.

"Anything else that don't seem to fit into the picture?" Heath at length asked.

Vance pointed with his cigarette toward the clothes closet in the living room. This closet was alongside of the foyer, in the corner near the Boule cabinet, directly opposite to the end of the davenport.

"You might let your mind dally a moment with the condition of that clothes press," suggested Vance carelessly. "You will note that, though the door's ajar, the contents have not been touched. And it's about the only area in the apartment that hasn't been disturbed."

Heath walked over and looked into the closet.

"Well, anyway, I'll admit that's queer," he finally conceded.

Vance had followed him indolently and stood gazing over his shoulder.

"And my word!" he exclaimed suddenly. "The key's on the inside of the lock. Fancy that, now! One can't lock a closet door with the key on the inside—can one, Sergeant?"

"The key may not mean anything," Heath observed hopefully. "Maybe the door was never locked. Anyhow, we'll find out about that pretty soon. I'm holding the maid outside, and I'm going to have her on the carpet as soon as the captain finishes his job here."

He turned to Dubois, who, having completed his search for fingerprints in the bedroom, was now inspecting the piano.

"Any luck yet?"

The captain shook his head.

"Gloves," he answered succinctly.

"Same here," supplemented Bellamy gruffly, on his knees before the escritoire.

Vance, with a sardonic smile, turned and walked to the window, where he stood looking out and smoking placidly, as if his entire interest in the case had evaporated.

At this moment the door from the main hall opened, and a short, thin little man, with grey hair and a scraggly grey beard, stepped inside and stood blinking against the vivid sunlight.

"Good morning, Professor," Heath greeted the newcomer. "Glad to see you. I've got something nifty, right in your line."

Deputy Inspector Conrad Brenner was one of that small army of obscure, but highly capable, experts who are connected with the New York Police Department, and who are constantly being consulted on abstruse technical problems, but whose names and achievements rarely get into the public prints. His specialty was locks and burglars' tools; and I doubt if, even among those exhaustively painstaking criminologists of the University of Lausanne, there was a more accurate reader of the evidential signs left by the implements of housebreakers. In appearance and bearing he was like a withered little college professor.* His black, unpressed suit was old-fashioned in cut; and he wore a very high stiff collar, like a *fin-de-siècle* clergyman, with a narrow black string tie. His gold-rimmed spectacles were so thick-lensed that the pupils of his eyes gave the impression of acute belladonna poisoning.

When Heath had spoken to him, he merely stood staring with a sort of detached expectancy; he seemed utterly unaware that there was anyone else in the room. The sergeant, evidently familiar with the little man's idiosyncrasies of manner, did not wait for a response, but started at once for the bedroom.

"This way, please, Professor," he directed cajolingly, going to the dressing table and picking up the jewel case. "Take a squint at this and tell me what you see."

Inspector Brenner followed Heath, without looking to right or left, and, taking the jewel case, went silently to the window and began to examine it. Vance, whose interest seemed suddenly to be reawakened, came forward and stood watching him.

---

* It is an interesting fact that for the nineteen years he had been connected with the New York Police Department, he had been referred to, by his superiors and subordinates alike, as "the Professor."

262

For fully five minutes the little expert inspected the case, holding it within a few inches of his myopic eyes. Then he lifted his glance to Heath and winked several times rapidly.

"Two instruments were used in opening this case." His voice was small and high-pitched, but there was in it an undeniable quality of authority. "One bent the lid and made several fractures on the baked enamel. The other was, I should say, a steel chisel of some kind, and was used to break the lock. The first instrument, which was blunt, was employed amateurishly, at the wrong angle of leverage; and the effort resulted only in twisting the overhang of the lid. But the steel chisel was inserted with a knowledge of the correct point of oscillation, where a minimum of leverage would produce the counteracting stress necessary to displace the lock bolts."

"A professional job?" suggested Heath.

"Highly so," answered the inspector, again blinking. "That is to say, the forcing of the lock was professional. And I would even go so far as to advance the opinion that the instrument used was one especially constructed for such illegal purposes."

"Could this have done the job?" Heath held out the poker.

The other looked at it closely and turned it over several times. "It might have been the instrument that bent the cover, but it was not the one used for prying open the lock. This poker is cast iron and would have snapped under any great pressure; whereas this box is of cold rolled eighteen-gauge steel plate, with an inset cylinder pin-tumbler lock taking a paracentric key. The leverage force necessary to distort the flange sufficiently to lift the lid could have been made only by a steel chisel."

"Well, that's that." Heath seemed well satisfied with Inspector Brenner's conclusion. "I'll send the box down to you, Professor, and you can let me know what else you find out."

"I'll take it along, if you have no objection." And the little man tucked it under his arm and shuffled out without another word.

Heath grinned at Markham. "Queer bird. He ain't happy unless he's measuring jimmy marks on doors and windows and things. He couldn't wait till I sent him the box. He'll hold it lovingly on his lap all the way down in the subway, like a mother with a baby."

Vance was still standing near the dressing table, gazing perplexedly into space. "Markham," he said, "the condition of that jewel case is positively astounding. It's unreasonable, illogical—insane. It complicates the situation most damnably. That steel box simply couldn't have been chiselled open by a professional burglar . . . and yet, don't y'know, it actually was."

263

Before Markham could reply, a satisfied grunt from Captain Dubois attracted our attention. "I've got something for you, Sergeant," he announced.

We moved expectantly into the living room. Dubois was bending over the end of the library table almost directly behind the place where Margaret Odell's body had been found. He took out an insufflator, which was like a very small hand bellows, and blew a fine light yellow powder evenly over about a square foot of the polished rosewood surface of the table top. Then he gently blew away the surplus powder, and there appeared the impression of a human hand distinctly registered in saffron. The bulb of the thumb and each fleshy hummock between the joints of the fingers and around the palm stood out like tiny circular islands. All the papillary ridges were clearly discernible. The photographer then hooked his camera to a peculiar adjustable tripod and, carefully focusing his lens, took two flashlight pictures of the hand mark.

"This ought to do." Dubois was pleased with his find. "It's the right hand—a clear print—and the guy who made it was standing right behind the dame. . . . And it's the newest print in the place."

"What about this box?" Heath pointed to the black document box on the table near the overturned lamp.

"Not a mark—wiped clean."

Dubois began putting away his paraphernalia.

"I say, Captain Dubois," interposed Vance, "did you take a good look at the inside doorknob of that clothes press?"

The man swung about abruptly and gave Vance a glowering look. "People ain't in the habit of handling the inside knobs of closet doors. They open and shut closets from the outside."

Vance raised his eyebrows in simulated astonishment.

"Do they, now, really?—Fancy that! . . . Still, don't y'know, if one were inside the closet, one couldn't reach the outside knob."

"The people *I* know don't shut themselves in clothes closets." Dubois' tone was ponderously sarcastic.

"You positively amaze me!" declared Vance. "All the people I know are addicted to the habit—a sort of daily pastime, don't y'know."

Markham, always diplomatic, intervened. "What idea have you about that closet, Vance?"

"Alas! I wish I had one," was the dolorous answer. "It's because I can't, for the life of me, make sense of its neat and orderly appearance that I'm so interested in it. Really, y'know, it should have been artistically looted."

264

Heath was not entirely free from the same vague misgivings that were disturbing Vance, for he turned to Dubois and said, "You might go over the knob, Captain. As this gentleman says, there's something funny about the condition of that closet."

Dubois, silent and surly, went to the closet door and sprayed his yellow powder over the inside knob. When he had blown the loose particles away, he bent over it with his magnifying glass. At length he straightened up and gave Vance a look of ill-natured appraisal.

"There's fresh prints on it, all right," he grudgingly admitted; "and, unless I'm mistaken, they were made by the same hand as those on the table. Both thumb marks are *ulnar* loops, and the index fingers are both *whorl* patterns. . . . Here, Pete," he ordered the photographer, "make some shots of that knob."

When this had been done, Dubois, Bellamy, and the photographer left us. A few minutes later, after an interchange of pleasantries, Inspector Moran also departed. At the door he passed two men in the white uniforms of interns, who had come to take away the girl's body.

CHAPTER 5

The Bolted Door
Tuesday, September 11; 10:30 a.m.

Markham and Heath and Vance and I were now alone in the apartment. Dark, low-hanging clouds had drifted across the sun, and the grey spectral light intensified the tragic atmosphere of the rooms. Markham had lighted a cigar, and stood leaning against the piano, looking about him with a disconsolate but determined air. Vance had moved over to one of the pictures on the side wall of the living room—Boucher's "La Bergère Endormie" I think it was—and stood looking at it with cynical contempt.

"Dimpled nudities, gambolling Cupids and woolly clouds for royal cocottes," he commented. His distaste for all the painting of the French decadence under Louis XV was profound. "One wonders what pictures courtesans hung in their boudoirs before the invention of these amorous eclogues, with their blue verdure and beribboned sheep."

"I'm more interested at present in what took place in this particular boudoir last night," retorted Markham impatiently.

"There's not much doubt about that, sir," said Heath encouragingly. "And I've an idea that when Dubois checks up those fingerprints with our files, we'll about know who did it."

Vance turned toward him with a rueful smile. "You're so trusting, Sergeant. I, in turn, have an idea that, long before this touchin' case is clarified, you'll wish the irascible captain with the insect powder had never found those fingerprints." He made a playful gesture of emphasis. "Permit me to whisper into your ear that the person who left his sign manuals on yonder rosewood table and cutlass doorknob had nothing whatever to do with the precipitate demise of the fair Mademoiselle Odell."

"What is it you suspect?" demanded Markham sharply.

"Not a thing, old dear," blandly declared Vance. "I'm wandering about in a mental murk as empty of signposts as interplanetary space. The jaws of darkness do devour me up; I'm in the dead vast and middle of the night. My mental darkness is Egyptian, Stygian, Cimmerian—I'm in a perfect Erebus of tenebrosity."

Markham's jaw tightened in exasperation; he was familiar with this evasive loquacity of Vance's. Dismissing the subject, he addressed himself to Heath.

"Have you done any questioning of the people in the house here?"

"I talked to Odell's maid and to the janitor and the switchboard operators, but I didn't go much into details—I was waiting for you. I'll say this, though: what they did tell me made my head swim. If they don't back down on some of their statements, we're up against it."

"Let's have them in now, then," suggested Markham; "the maid first." He sat down on the piano bench with his back to the keyboard.

Heath rose but, instead of going to the door, walked to the oriel window. "There's one thing I want to call your attention to, sir, before you interview these people, and that's the matter of entrances and exits in this apartment."

He drew aside the gold-gauze curtain. "Look at that iron grating. All the windows in this place, including the ones in the bathroom, are equipped with iron bars just like these. It's only eight or ten feet to the ground here, and whoever built this house wasn't taking any chances of burglars getting in through the windows."

He released the curtain and strode into the foyer. "Now, there's only one entrance to this apartment, and that's this door here opening off the main hall. There isn't a transom or an airshaft or a dumbwaiter in the place, and that means that the only way—*the only way*—that anybody can get in or out of this apartment is through this door. Just keep that fact in your mind, sir, while you're listening to the stories of these people. . . . Now, I'll have the maid brought in."

In response to Heath's order a detective led in a mulatto woman about thirty years old. She was neatly dressed and gave one the impression of capability. When she spoke, it was with a quiet, clear enunciation which attested to a greater degree of education than is ordinarily found in members of her class.

Her name, we learned, was Amy Gibson; and the information elicited by Markham's preliminary questioning consisted of the following facts:

She had arrived at the apartment that morning a few minutes after seven, and, as was her custom, had let herself in with her own key, as her mistress generally slept till late.

Once or twice a week she came early to do sewing and mending for Miss Odell before the latter arose. On this particular morning she had come early to make an alteration in a gown.

As soon as she had opened the door, she had been confronted by the disorder of the apartment, for the Venetian-glass doors of the foyer were wide open; and almost simultaneously she had noticed the body of her mistress on the davenport.

She had called at once to Jessup, the night telephone operator then on duty, who, after one glance into the living room, had notified the police. She had then sat down in the public reception room and waited for the arrival of the officers.

Her testimony had been simple and direct and intelligently stated. If she was nervous or excited, she managed to keep her feelings well under control.

"Now," continued Markham, after a short pause, "let us go back to last night. At what time did you leave Miss Odell?"

"A few minutes before seven, sir," the woman answered, in a colourless, even tone which seemed to be characteristic of her speech.

"Is that your usual hour for leaving?"

"No; I generally go about six. But last night Miss Odell wanted me to help her dress for dinner."

"Don't you always help her dress for dinner?"

"No, sir. But last night she was going with some gentleman to dinner and the theatre, and wanted to look specially nice."

"Ah!" Markham leaned forward. "And who was this gentleman?"

"I don't know, sir—Miss Odell didn't say."

"And you couldn't suggest who it might have been?"

"I couldn't say, sir."

"And when did Miss Odell tell you that she wanted you to come early this morning?"

"When I was leaving last night."

"So she evidently didn't anticipate any danger, or have any fear of her companion."

"It doesn't look that way." The woman paused, as if considering. "No, I know she didn't. She was in good spirits."

Markham turned to Heath.

"Any other questions you want to ask, Sergeant?"

Heath removed an unlighted cigar from his mouth, and bent forward, resting his hands on his knees.

"What jewellery did this Odell woman have on last night?" he demanded gruffly.

The maid's manner became cool and a bit haughty.

"Miss Odell"—she emphasized the "Miss," by way of reproaching him for the disrespect implied in his omission—"wore all her rings, five or six of them, and three bracelets—one of square diamonds, one of rubies, and one of diamonds and emeralds. She also had on a sun-burst of pear-shaped diamonds on a chain round her neck, and she carried a platinum lorgnette set with diamonds and pearls."

"Did she own any other jewellery?"

"A few small pieces, maybe, but I'm not sure."

"And did she keep 'em in the steel jewel case in the room?"

"Yes—when she wasn't wearing them." There was more than a suggestion of sarcasm in the reply.

"Oh, I thought maybe she kept 'em locked up when she had 'em on." Heath's antagonism had been aroused by the maid's attitude; he could not have failed to note that she had consistently omitted the punctilious "sir" when answering him. He now stood up and pointed loweringly to the black document box on the rosewood table.

"Ever see that before?"

The woman nodded indifferently. "Many times."

"Where was it generally kept?"

"In that thing." She indicated the Boule cabinet with a motion of the head.

"What was in the box?"

"How should I know?"

"You don't know—huh?" Heath thrust out his jaw, but his bully-ing attitude had no effect upon the impassive maid.

"I've got no idea," she replied calmly. "It was always kept locked, and I never saw Miss Odell open it."

The sergeant walked over to the door of the living room closet.

"See that key?" he asked angrily.

Again the woman nodded; but this time I detected a look of mild astonishment in her eyes.

"Was that key always kept on the inside of the door?"

"No, it was always on the outside."

Heath shot Vance a curious look. Then, after a moment's frowning contemplation of the knob, he waved his hand to the detective who had brought the maid in.

"Take her back to the reception room, Snitkin, and get a detailed description from her of all the Odell jewellery. . . . And keep her out-side; I'll want her again."

When Snitkin and the maid had gone out, Vance lay back lazily on the davenport, where he had sat during the interview, and sent a spiral of cigarette smoke toward the ceiling.

"Rather illuminatin', what?" he remarked. "The dusky *demoiselle* got us considerably forrader. Now we know that the closet key is on the wrong side of the door, and that our *fille de joie* went to the theatre with one of her favourite *inamorati*, who presumably brought her home shortly before she took her departure from this wicked world."

"You think that's helpful, do you?" Heath's tone was contemptuously triumphant. "Wait till you hear the crazy story the telephone operator's got to tell."

"All right, Sergeant," put in Markham impatiently. "Suppose we get on with the ordeal."

"I'm going to suggest, Mr. Markham, that we question the janitor first. And I'll show you why." Heath went to the entrance door of the apartment, and opened it. "Look here for just a minute, sir."

He stepped out into the main hall and pointed down the little passageway on the left. It was about ten feet in length and ran between the Odell apartment and the blank rear wall of the reception room. At the end of it was a solid oak door which gave on the court at the side of the house.

"That door," explained Heath, "is the only side or rear entrance to this building; and when that door is bolted, nobody can get into the house except by the front entrance. You can't even get into the building through the other apartments, for every window on this floor is barred. I checked up on that point as soon as I got here."

He led the way back into the living room.

"Now, after I'd looked over the situation this morning," he went on, "I figured that our man had entered through that side door at the end of the passageway, and had slipped into this apartment without the night operator seeing him. So I tried the side door to see if it was open. But it was bolted on the inside—not locked, mind you, but bolted. And it wasn't a slip bolt, either, that could have been jimmied or worked open from the outside, but a tough old-fashioned turn bolt of solid brass. . . . And now I want you to hear what the janitor's got to say about it."

Markham nodded acquiescence, and Heath called an order to one of the officers in the hall. A moment later a stolid, middle-aged German, with sullen features and high cheekbones, stood before us. His jaw was clamped tight, and he shifted his eyes from one to the other of us suspiciously.

Heath straightway assumed the role of inquisitor. "What time do you leave here at night?" He had, for some reason, assumed a belligerent manner.

"Six o'clock—sometimes earlier, sometimes later." The man spoke in a surly monotone. He was obviously resentful at this unexpected intrusion upon his orderly routine.

"And what time do you get here in the morning?"

"Eight o'clock, regular."

"What time did you go home last night?"

"About six—maybe quarter past."

Heath paused and finally lighted the cigar on which he had been chewing at intervals during the past hour.

"Now, tell me about that side door," he went on, with undiminished aggressiveness. "You told me you lock it every night before you leave—is that right?"

"*Ja*—that's right." The man nodded his head affirmatively several times. "Only I don't lock it—I bolt it."

"All right, you bolt it, then." As Heath talked his cigar bobbed up and down between his lips; smoke and words came simultaneously from his mouth. "And last night you bolted it as usual about six o'clock?"

"Maybe a quarter past," the janitor amended, with Germanic precision.

"You're sure you bolted it last night?" The question was almost ferocious.

"*Ja, ja.* Sure, I am. I do it every night. I never miss."

The man's earnestness left no doubt that the door in question had indeed been bolted on the inside at about six o'clock of the previous evening. Heath, however, belaboured the point for several minutes, only to be reassured doggedly that the door had been bolted. At last the janitor was dismissed.

"Really, y' know, Sergeant," remarked Vance with an amused smile, "that honest Rheinlander bolted the door."

"Sure, he did," spluttered Heath, "and I found it still bolted this morning at quarter of eight. That's just what messes things up so nice and pretty. If that door was bolted from six o'clock last evening until eight o'clock this morning, I'd appreciate having someone drive up in a hearse and tell me how the Canary's little playmate got in here last night. And I'd also like to know how he got out."

"Why not through the main entrance?" asked Markham. "It seems the only logical way left, according to your own findings."

"That's how I had it figured out, sir," returned Heath. "But wait till you hear what the phone operator has to say."

"And the phone operator's post," mused Vance, "is in the main hall halfway between the front door and this apartment. Therefore, the gentleman who caused all the disturbance hereabouts last night would have had to pass within a few feet of the operator both on arriving and departing—eh, what?"

"That's it!" snapped Heath. "And, according to the operator, no such person came or went."

Markham seemed to have absorbed some of Heath's irritability. "Get the fellow in here, and let me question him," he ordered.

Heath obeyed with a kind of malicious alacrity.

Chapter 6

A Call For Help
Tuesday, September 11; 11 a.m.

Jessup made a good impression from the moment he entered the room. He was a serious, determined-looking man in his early thirties, rugged and well built; and there was a squareness to his shoulders that carried a suggestion of military training. He walked with a decided limp—his right foot dragged perceptibly—and I noted that his left arm had been stiffened into a permanent arc, as if by an unreduced fracture of the elbow. He was quiet and reserved, and his eyes were steady and intelligent. Markham at once motioned him to a wicker chair beside the closet door, but he declined it, and stood before the district attorney in a soldierly attitude of respectful attention. Markham opened the interrogation with several personal questions. It transpired that Jessup had been a sergeant in the World War,* had twice been seriously wounded, and had been invalided home shortly before the armistice. He had held his present post of telephone operator for over a year.

"Now, Jessup," continued Markham, "there are things connected with last night's tragedy that you can tell us."

"Yes, sir." There was no doubt that this ex-soldier would tell us accurately anything he knew, and also that, if he had any doubt as to the correctness of his information, he would frankly say so. He possessed all the qualities of a careful and well-trained witness.

"First of all, what time did you come on duty last night?"

"At ten o'clock, sir." There was no qualification to this blunt statement; one felt that Jessup would arrive punctually at whatever hour he was due. "It was my short shift. The day man and myself alternate in long and short shifts."

---

* His full name was William Elmer Jessup, and he had been attached to the 308th Infantry of the 77th Division of the Overseas Forces.

"And did you see Miss Odell come in last night after the theatre?"

"Yes, sir. Everyone who comes in has to pass the switchboard."

"What time did she arrive?"

"It couldn't have been more than a few minutes after eleven."

"Was she alone?"

"No, sir. There was a gentleman with her."

"Do you know who he was?"

"I don't know his name, sir. But I have seen him several times before when he has called on Miss Odell."

"You could describe him, I suppose."

"Yes, sir. He's tall and clean-shaven except for a very short grey moustache, and is about forty-five, I should say. He looks—if you understand me, sir—like a man of wealth and position."

Markham nodded. "And now, tell me: did he accompany Miss Odell into her apartment or did he go immediately away?"

"He went in with Miss Odell and stayed about half an hour."

Markham's eyes brightened, and there was a suppressed eagerness in his next words. "Then he arrived about eleven, and was alone with Miss Odell in her apartment until about half past eleven. You're sure of these facts?"

"Yes, sir, that's correct," the man affirmed.

Markham paused and leaned forward.

"Now, Jessup, think carefully before answering: did any one else call on Miss Odell at any time last night?"

"No one, sir," was the unhesitating reply.

"How can you be so sure?"

"I would have seen them, sir. They would have had to pass the switchboard in order to reach this apartment."

"And don't you ever leave the switchboard?" asked Markham.

"No, sir," the man assured him vigorously, as if protesting against the implication that he would desert a post of duty. "When I want a drink of water, or go to the toilet, I use the little lavatory in the reception room; but I always hold the door open and keep my eye on the switchboard in case the pilot light should show up for a telephone call. Nobody could walk down the hall, even if I was in the lavatory, without my seeing them."

One could well believe that the conscientious Jessup kept his eye at all times on the switchboard lest a call should flash and go unanswered. The man's earnestness and reliability were obvious; and there was no doubt in any of our minds, I think, that if Miss Odell had had another visitor that night, Jessup would have known of it.

But Heath, with the thoroughness of his nature, rose quickly and stepped out into the main hall. In a moment he returned, looking troubled but satisfied.

"Right!" He nodded to Markham. "The lavatory door's on a direct unobstructed line with the switchboard."

Jessup took no notice of this verification of his statement, and stood, his eyes attentively on the district attorney, awaiting any further questions that might be asked him. There was something both admirable and confidence-inspiring in his unruffled demeanour.

"What about last night?" resumed Markham. "Did you leave the switchboard often, or for long?"

"Just once, sir; and then only to go to the lavatory for a minute or two. But I watched the board the whole time."

"And you'd be willing to state on oath that no one else called on Miss Odell from ten o'clock on, and that no one, except her escort, left her apartment after that hour?"

"Yes, sir, I would."

He was plainly telling the truth, and Markham pondered several moments before proceeding.

"What about the side door?"

"That's kept locked all night, sir. The janitor bolts it when he leaves and unbolts it in the morning. I never touch it."

Markham leaned back and turned to Heath.

"The testimony of the janitor and Jessup here," he said, "seems to limit the situation pretty narrowly to Miss Odell's escort. If, as seems reasonable to assume, the side door was bolted all night, and if no other caller came or went through the front door, it looks as if the man we wanted to find was the one who brought her home."

Heath gave a short, mirthless laugh. "That would be fine, sir, if something else hadn't happened around here last night." Then to Jessup: "Tell the district attorney the rest of the story about this man."

Markham looked toward the operator with expectant interest; and Vance, lifting himself on one elbow, listened attentively.

Jessup spoke in a level voice, with the alert and careful manner of a soldier reporting to his superior officer.

"It was just this, sir. When the gentleman came out of Miss Odell's apartment at about half past eleven, he stopped at the switchboard and asked me to get him a Yellow Taxicab. I put the call through, and while he was waiting for the car, Miss Odell screamed and called for help. The gentleman turned and rushed to the apartment door, and I followed quickly behind him. He knocked; but at first there was no answer. Then he knocked again, and at the same time called out to Miss Odell and asked her what was the matter. This time she answered. She said everything was all right, and told him to go home and not to worry. Then he walked back with me to the switchboard, remarking that he guessed Miss Odell must have fallen asleep and had a nightmare. We talked for a few minutes about the war, and then the taxicab came. He said good night and went out, and I heard the car drive away."

It was plain to see that this epilogue of the departure of Miss Odell's anonymous escort completely upset Markham's theory of the case. He looked down at the floor with a baffled expression and smoked vigorously for several moments. At last he said:

"How long was it after this man came out of the apartment that you heard Miss Odell scream?"

"About five minutes. I had put my connection through to the taxicab company, and it was a minute or so later that she screamed."

"Was the man near the switchboard?"

"Yes, sir. In fact, he had one arm resting on it."

"How many times did Miss Odell scream? And just what did she say when she called for help?"

"She screamed twice and then cried, 'Help! Help!'"

"And when the man knocked on the door the second time, what did he say?"

"As near as I can recollect, sir, he said, 'Open the door, Margaret! What's the trouble?'"

"And can you remember her exact words when she answered him?"

Jessup hesitated and frowned reflectively. "As I recall, she said, 'There's nothing the matter. I'm sorry I screamed. Everything's all right, so please go home, and don't worry.' . . . Of course, that may not be exactly what she said, but it was something very close to it."

"You could hear her plainly through the door, then?"

"Oh, yes. These doors are not very thick."

Markham rose and began pacing meditatively. At length, halting in front of the operator, he asked another question:

"Did you hear any other suspicious sounds in this apartment after the man left?"

"Not a sound of any kind, sir," Jessup declared. "Someone from outside the building, however, telephoned Miss Odell about ten minutes later, and a man's voice answered from her apartment."

"What's this!" Markham spun round, and Heath sat up at attention, his eyes wide. "Tell me every detail of that call."

276

Jessup complied unemotionally.

"About twenty minutes to twelve a trunk light flashed on the board, and when I answered it, a man asked for Miss Odell. I plugged the connection through, and after a short wait the receiver was lifted from her phone—you can tell when a receiver's taken off the hook, because the guide light on the board goes out—and a man's voice answered 'Hello.' I pulled the listening-in key over, and, of course, didn't hear any more."

There was silence in the apartment for several minutes. Then Vance, who had been watching Jessup closely during the interview, spoke.

"By the bye, Mr. Jessup," he asked carelessly, "were you yourself, by any chance, a bit fascinated—let us say—by the charming Miss Odell?"

For the first time since entering the room the man appeared ill at ease. A dull flush overspread his cheeks. "I thought she was a very beautiful lady," he answered resolutely.

Markham gave Vance a look of disapproval, and then addressed himself abruptly to the operator. "That will be all for the moment, Jessup."

The man bowed stiffly and limped out.

"This case is becoming positively fascinatin'," murmured Vance, relaxing once more upon the davenport.

"It's comforting to know that someone's enjoying it." Markham's tone was irritable. "And what, may I ask, was the object of your question concerning Jessup's sentiments toward the dead woman?"

"Oh, just a vagrant notion struggling in my brain," returned Vance. "And then, y'know, a bit of *boudoir racontage* always enlivens a situation, what?"

Heath, rousing himself from gloomy abstraction, spoke up.

"We've still got the fingerprints, Mr. Markham. And I'm thinking that they're going to locate our man for us."

"But even if Dubois does identify those prints," said Markham, "we'll have to show how the owner of them got into this place last night. He'll claim, of course, they were made prior to the crime."

"Well, it's a sure thing," declared Heath stubbornly, "that there was some man in here last night when Odell got back from the theatre, and that he was still here until after the other man left at half past eleven. The woman's screams and the answering of that phone call at twenty minutes to twelve prove it. And since Doc Doremus said that the murder took place before midnight, there's no getting away from the fact that the guy who was hiding in here did the job."

"That appears incontrovertible," agreed Markham. "And I'm inclined to think it was someone she knew. She probably screamed when he first revealed himself, and then, recognizing him, calmed down and told the other man out in the hall that nothing was the matter. . . . Later on he strangled her."

"And, I might suggest," added Vance, "that his place of hiding was that clothes press."

"Sure," the sergeant concurred. "But what's bothering me is how he got in here. The day operator who was at the switchboard until ten last night told me that the man who called and took Odell out to dinner was the only visitor she had."

Markham gave a grunt of exasperation.

"Bring the day man in here," he ordered. "We've got to straighten this thing out. *Somebody* got in here last night, and before I leave, I'm going to find out how it was done."

Vance gave him a look of patronizing amusement.

"Y'know, Markham," he said, "I'm not blessed with the gift of psychic inspiration, but I have one of those strange, indescribable feelings, as the minor poets say, that if you really contemplate remaining in this bestrewn boudoir till you've discovered how the mysterious visitor gained admittance here last night, you'd do jolly well to send for your toilet access'ries and several changes of fresh linen—not to mention your pyjamas. The chap who engineered this little soiree planned his entrance and exit most carefully and perspicaciously."

Markham regarded Vance dubiously but made no reply.

CHAPTER 7

A Nameless Visitor

Tuesday, September 11; 11:15 a.m.

Heath had stepped out into the hall, and now returned with the day telephone operator, a sallow, thin young man who, we learned, was named Spively. His almost black hair, which accentuated the pallor of his face, was sleeked back from his forehead with pomade; and he wore a very shallow moustache which barely extended beyond the *alae* of his nostrils. He was dressed in an exaggeratedly dapper fashion, in a dazzling chocolate-coloured suit cut very close to his figure, a pair of cloth-topped buttoned shoes, and a pink shirt with a stiff turn-over collar to match. He appeared nervous, and immediately sat down in the wicker chair by the door, fingering the sharp creases of his trousers, and running the tip of his tongue over his lips.

Markham went straight to the point.

"I understand you were at the switchboard yesterday afternoon and last night until ten o'clock. Is that correct?"

Spively swallowed hard and nodded his head. "Yes, sir."

"What time did Miss Odell go out to dinner?"

"About seven o'clock. I'd just sent to the restaurant next door for some sandwiches—"

"Did she go alone?" Markham interrupted his explanation.

"No. A fella called for her."

"Did you know this 'fella'?"

"I'd seen him a couple of times calling on Miss Odell, but I didn't know who he was."

"What did he look like?" Markham's question was uttered with hurried impatience.

Spively's description of the girl's escort tallied with Jessup's description of the man who had accompanied her home, though Spively was

279

more voluble and less precise than Jessup had been. Patently, Miss Odell had gone out at seven and returned at eleven with the same man.

"Now," resumed Markham, putting an added stress on his words, "I want to know who else called on Miss Odell between the time she went out to dinner and ten o'clock when you left the switchboard."

Spively was puzzled by the question, and his thin arched eyebrows lifted and contracted. "I—don't understand," he stammered. "How could any one call on Miss Odell when she was out?"

"Someone evidently did," said Markham. "And he got into her apartment and was there when she returned at eleven."

The youth's eyes opened wide, and his lips fell apart. "My God, sir!" he exclaimed. "So that's how they murdered her!—laid in wait for her! . . ." He stopped abruptly, suddenly realizing his own proximity to the mysterious chain of events that had led up to the crime. "But nobody got into her apartment while I was on duty," he blurted, with frightened emphasis. "Nobody! I never left the board from the time she went out until quitting time."

"Couldn't anyone have come in the side door?"

"What! Was it unlocked?" Spively's tone was startled. "It never is unlocked at night. The janitor bolts it when he leaves at six."

"And you didn't unbolt it last night for any purpose? Think!"

"No, sir, I didn't!" He shook his head earnestly.

"And you are positive that no one got into the apartment through the front door after Miss Odell left?"

"Positive! I tell you I didn't leave the board the whole time, and nobody could've got by me without my knowing it. There was only one person that called and asked for her—"

"Oh! So someone did call!" snapped Markham. "When was it? And what happened?—Jog your memory before you answer."

"It wasn't anything important," the youth assured him, genuinely frightened. "Just a fella who came in and rang her bell and went right out again."

"Never mind whether it was important or not." Markham's tone was cold and peremptory. "What time did he call?"

"About half past nine."

"And who was he?"

"A young fella I've seen come here several times to see Miss Odell. I don't know his name."

"Tell me exactly what took place," pursued Markham.

Again Spively swallowed hard and wetted his lips.

"It was like this," he began, with effort. "The fella came in and started walking down the hall and I said to him, 'Miss Odell isn't in.' But he kept on going and said, 'Oh, well, I'll ring the bell anyway to make sure.' A telephone call came through just then, and I let him go on. He rang the bell and knocked on the door, but of course there wasn't any answer; and pretty soon he came on back and said, 'I guess you were right.' Then he tossed me half a dollar and went out."

"You actually saw him go out?" There was a note of disappointment in Markham's voice.

"Sure, I saw him go out. He stopped just inside the front door and lit a cigarette. Then he opened the door and turned toward Broadway."

"'One by one the rosy petals fall,'" came Vance's indolent voice. "A most amusin' situation!"

Markham was loath to relinquish his hope in the criminal possibilities of this one caller who had come and gone at half past nine.

"What was this man like?" he asked. "Can you describe him?"

Spively sat up straight, and when he answered, it was with an enthusiasm that showed he had taken special note of the visitor.

"He was good-looking, not so old—maybe thirty. And he had on a full-dress suit and patent-leather pumps, and a pleated silk shirt—"

"What, what?" demanded Vance, in simulated unbelief, leaning over the back of the davenport. "A silk shirt with evening dress! Most extr'ordin'ry!"

"Oh, a lot of the best dressers are wearing them," Spively explained, with condescending pride. "It's all the fashion for dancing."

"You don't say—really!" Vance appeared dumbfounded. "I must look into this. . . . And, by the bye, when this Beau Brummel of the silk shirt paused by the front door, did he take his cigarette from a long flat silver case carried in his lower waistcoat pocket?"

The youth looked at Vance in admiring astonishment.

"How did you know?" he exclaimed.

"Simple deduction," Vance explained, resuming his recumbent posture. "Large metal cigarette cases carried in the waistcoat pocket somehow go with silk shirts for evening wear."

Markham, clearly annoyed at the interruption, cut in sharply with a demand for the operator to proceed with his description.

"He wore his hair smoothed down," Spively continued, "and you could see it was kind of long; but it was cut in the latest style. And he had a small waxed moustache; and there was a big carnation in the lapel of his coat, and he had on chamois gloves. . . ."

"My word!" murmured Vance. "A *gigolo!*"

Markham, with the incubus of the nightclubs riding him heavily, frowned and took a deep breath. Vance's observation evidently had launched him on an unpleasant train of thought.

"Was this man short or tall?" he asked next.

"He wasn't so tall—about my height," Spively explained. "And he was sort of thin."

There was an easily recognizable undercurrent of admiration in his tone, and I felt that this youthful telephone operator had seen in Miss Odell's caller a certain physical and sartorial ideal. This palpable admiration, coupled with the somewhat outré clothes affected by the youth, permitted us to read between the lines of his remarks a fairly accurate description of the man who had unsuccessfully rung the dead girl's bell at half past nine the night before.

When Spively had been dismissed, Markham rose and strode about the room, his head enveloped in a cloud of cigar smoke, while Heath sat stolidly watching him, his brows knit.

Vance stood up and stretched himself.

"The absorbin' problem, it would seem, remains in *status quo*," he remarked airily. "How, oh, how, did the fair Margaret's executioner get in?"

"You know, Mr. Markham," rumbled Heath sententiously, "I've been thinking that the fellow may have come here earlier in the afternoon—say, before that side door was locked. Odell herself may have let him in and hidden him when the other man came to take her to dinner."

"It looks that way," Markham admitted. "Bring the maid in here again, and we'll see what we can find out."

When the woman had been brought in, Markham questioned her as to her actions during the afternoon, and learned that she had gone out at about four to do some shopping and had returned about half past five.

"Did Miss Odell have any visitor with her when you got back?"

"No, sir," was the prompt answer. "She was alone."

"Did she mention that anyone had called?"

"No, sir."

"Now," continued Markham, "could anyone have been hidden in this apartment when you went home at seven?"

The maid was frankly astonished and even a little horrified. "Where could anyone hide?" she asked, looking round the apartment.

"There are several possible places," Markham suggested: "in the bathroom, in one of the clothes closets, under the bed, behind the window draperies. . . ."

The woman shook her head decisively. "No one could have been hidden," she declared. "I was in the bathroom half a dozen times, and I got Miss Odell's gown out of the clothes closet in the bedroom. As soon as it began to get dark, I drew all the window shades myself. And as for the bed, it's built almost down to the floor; no one could squeeze under it."

I glanced closely at the bed and realized that this statement was quite true.

"What about the clothes closet in this room?" Markham put the question hopefully, but again the maid shook her head.

"Nobody was in there. That's where I keep my own hat and coat, and I took them out myself when I was getting ready to go. I even put away one of Miss Odell's old dresses in that closet before I left."

"And you are absolutely certain," reiterated Markham, "that no one could have been hidden anywhere in these rooms at the time you went home?"

"Absolutely, sir."

"Do you happen to remember if the key of this clothes closet was on the inside or the outside of the lock when you opened the door to get your hat?"

The woman paused and looked thoughtfully at the closet door. "It was on the outside, where it always was," she announced, after several moments' reflection. "I remember because it caught in the chiffon of the old dress I put away."

Markham frowned and then resumed his questioning. "You say you don't know the name of Miss Odell's dinner companion last night. Can you tell us the names of any men she was in the habit of going out with?"

"Miss Odell never mentioned any names to me," the woman said. "She was very careful about it, too—secretive, you might say. You see, I'm only here in the daytime, and the gentlemen she knew generally came in the evening."

"And you never heard her speak of anyone of whom she was frightened—anyone she had reason to fear?"

"No, sir—although there was one man she was trying to get rid of. He was a bad character—I wouldn't have trusted him anywhere—and I told Miss Odell she'd better look out for him. But she'd known him a long time, I guess, and had been pretty soft on him once."

"How do you happen to know this?"

"One day, about a week ago," the maid explained, "I came in after lunch, and he was with her in the other room. They didn't hear me, because the portieres were drawn. He was demanding money, and when she tried to put him off, he began threatening her. And she said something that showed she'd given him money before. I made a noise, and then they stopped arguing; and pretty soon he went out."

"What did this man look like?" Markham's interest was reviving.

"He was kind of thin—not very tall—and I'd say he was around thirty. He had a hard face—good-looking, some would say—and pale blue eyes that gave you the shivers. He always wore his hair greased back, and he had a little yellow moustache pointed at the ends."

"Ah!" said Vance. "Our *gigolo!*"

"Has this man been here since?" asked Markham.

"I don't know, sir—not when I was here."

"That will be all," said Markham; and the woman went out.

"She didn't help us much," complained Heath.

"What!" exclaimed Vance. "I think she did remarkably well. She cleared up several moot points."

"And just what portions of her information do you consider particularly illuminating?" asked Markham, with ill-concealed annoyance.

"We now know, do we not," rejoined Vance serenely, "that no one was lying *perdu* in here when the *bonne* departed yester evening."

"Instead of that fact being helpful," retorted Markham, "I'd say it added materially to the complications of the situation."

"It would appear that way, wouldn't it, now? But, then—who knows?—it may prove to be your brightest and most comfortin' clue. . . . Furthermore, we learned that someone evidently locked himself in that clothes press, as witness the shifting of the key, and that, moreover, this occulation did not occur until the abigail had gone, or, let us say, after seven o'clock."

"Sure," said Heath with sour facetiousness; "when the side door was bolted and an operator was sitting in the front hall, who swears nobody came in that way."

"It is a bit mystifyin'," Vance conceded sadly.

"Mystifying? It's impossible!" grumbled Markham.

Heath, who was now staring with meditative pugnacity into the closet, shook his head helplessly.

"What I don't understand," he ruminated, "is why, if the fellow was hiding in the closet, he didn't ransack it when he came out, like he did all the rest of the apartment."

"Sergeant," said Vance, "you've put your finger on the crux of the matter. . . . Y'know, the neat, undisturbed aspect of that closet rather suggests that the crude person who rifled these charming rooms omitted to give it his attention because it was locked on the inside and he couldn't open it."

"Come, come!" protested Markham. "That theory implies that there were two unknown persons in here last night."

Vance sighed. "Harrow and alas! I know it. And we can't introduce even one into this apartment logically. . . . Distressin', ain't it?"

Heath sought consolation in a new line of thought.

"Anyway," he submitted, "we know that the fancy fellow with the patent-leather pumps who called here last night at half past nine was probably Odell's lover, and was grafting on her."

"And in just what recondite way does that obvious fact help to roll the clouds away?" asked Vance. "Nearly every modern Delilah has an avaricious *amoroso*. It would be rather singular if there wasn't such a chap in the offing, what?"

"That's all right, too," returned Heath. "But I'll tell you something, Mr. Vance, that maybe you don't know. The men that these girls lose their heads over are generally crooks of some kind—professional criminals, you understand. That's why, knowing that this job was the work of a professional, it don't leave me cold, as you might say, to learn that this fellow who was threatening Odell and grafting on her was the same one who was prowling round here last night. . . . And I'll say this, too: the description of him sounds a whole lot like the kind of high-class burglars that hang out at these swell all-night cafes."

"You're convinced, then," asked Vance mildly, "that this job, as you call it, was done by a professional criminal?"

Heath was almost contemptuous in his reply. "Didn't the guy wear gloves and use a jimmy? It was a yeggman's job, all right."

Chapter 8

The Invisible Murderer

Tuesday, September 11; 11:45 a.m.

Markham went to the window and stood, his hands behind him, looking down into the little paved rear yard. After several minutes he turned slowly.

"The situation, as I see it," he said, "boils down to this:—The Odell girl has an engagement for dinner and the theatre with a man of some distinction. He calls for her a little after seven, and they go out together. At eleven o'clock they return. He goes with her into her apartment and remains half an hour. He leaves at half past eleven and asks the phone operator to call him a taxi. While he is waiting the girl screams and calls for help, and, in response to his inquiries, she tells him nothing is wrong and bids him go away. The taxi arrives, and he departs in it. Ten minutes later someone telephones her, and a man answers from her apartment. This morning she is found murdered, and the apartment ransacked."

He took a long draw on his cigar.

"Now, it is obvious that when she and her escort returned last night, there was another man in this place somewhere; and it is also obvious that the girl was alive after her escort had departed. Therefore, we must conclude that the man who was already in the apartment was the person who murdered her. This conclusion is further corroborated by Doctor Doremus's report that the crime occurred between eleven and twelve. But since her escort did not leave till half past eleven, and spoke with her after that time, we can put the actual hour of the murder as between half past eleven and midnight. . . . These are the inferable facts from the evidence thus far adduced."

"There's not much getting away from 'em," agreed Heath.

"At any rate, they're interestin'," murmured Vance.

Markham, walking up and down earnestly, continued: "The features of the situation revolving round these inferable facts are as follows:—There was no one hiding in the apartment at seven o'clock—the hour the maid went home. Therefore, the murderer entered the apartment later. First, then, let us consider the side door. At six o'clock, an hour before the maid's departure, the janitor bolted it on the inside, and both operators disavow emphatically that they went near it. Moreover, you, Sergeant, found it bolted this morning. Hence, we may assume that the door was bolted on the inside all night, and that nobody could have entered that way. Consequently, we are driven to the inevitable alternative that the murderer entered by the front door. Now, let us consider this other means of entry. The phone operator who was on duty until ten o'clock last night asserts positively that the only person who entered the front door and passed down the main hall to this apartment was a man who rang the bell and, getting no answer, immediately walked out again. The other operator, who was on duty from ten o'clock until this morning, asserts with equal positiveness that no one entered the front door and passed the switchboard coming to this apartment. Add to all this the fact that every window on this floor is barred, and that no one from upstairs can descend into the main hall without coming face to face with the operator, and we are, for the moment, confronted with an impasse."

Heath scratched his head and laughed mirthlessly. "It don't make sense, does it, sir?"

"What about the next apartment?" asked Vance, "the one with the door facing the rear passageway—No. 2, I think?"

Heath turned to him patronizingly. "I looked into that the first thing this morning. Apartment No. 2 is occupied by a single woman; and I woke her up at eight o'clock and searched the place. Nothing there. Anyway, you have to walk past the switchboard to reach her apartment the same as you do to reach this one; and nobody called on her or left her apartment last night. What's more, Jessup, who's a shrewd sound lad, told me this woman is a quiet, ladylike sort, and that she and Odell didn't even know each other."

"You're so thorough, Sergeant!" murmured Vance.

"Of course," put in Markham, "it would have been possible for someone from the other apartment to have slipped in here behind the operator's back between seven and eleven, and then to have slipped back after the murder. But as Sergeant Heath's search this morning failed to uncover anyone, we can eliminate the possibility of our man having operated from that quarter."

"I dare say you're right," Vance indifferently admitted. "But it strikes me, Markham old dear, that your own affectin' recapitulation of the situation jolly well eliminates the possibility of your man's having operated from any quarter. . . . And yet he came in, garrotted the unfortunate damsel, and departed—eh, what? . . . It's a charmin' little problem. I wouldn't have missed it for worlds."

"It's uncanny," pronounced Markham gloomily.

"It's positively spiritualistic," amended Vance. "It has the caressin' odor of a séance. Really, y'know, I'm beginning to suspect that some medium was hovering in the vicinage last night doing some rather tip-top materializations. . . . I say, Markham, could you get an indictment against an ectoplasmic emanation?"

"It wasn't no spook that made those fingerprints," growled Heath, with surly truculence.

Markham halted his nervous pacing and regarded Vance irritably. "Damn it! This is rank nonsense. The man got in some way, and he got out, too. There's something wrong somewhere. Either the maid is mistaken about someone being here when she left, or else one of those phone operators went to sleep and won't admit it."

"Or else one of 'em's lying," supplemented Heath.

Vance shook his head. "The dusky *fille de chambre*, I'd say, is eminently trustworthy. And if there was any doubt about anyone's having come in the front door unnoticed, the lads on the switchboard would, in the present circumstances, be only too eager to admit it. . . . No, Markham, you'll simply have to approach this affair from the astral plane, so to speak."

Markham grunted his distaste of Vance's jocularity. "That line of investigation I leave to you with your metaphysical theories and esoteric hypotheses."

"But, consider," protested Vance banteringly. "You've proved conclusively—or, rather, you've demonstrated legally—that no one could have entered or departed from this apartment last night; and, as you've often told me, a court of law must decide all matters, not in accord with the known or suspected facts, but according to the evidence; and the evidence in this case would prove a sound alibi for every corporeal being extant. And yet, it's not exactly tenable, d'ye see, that the lady strangled herself. If only it had been poison, what an exquisite and satisfyin' suicide case you'd have! . . . Most inconsiderate of her homicidal visitor not to have used arsenic instead of his hands!"

"Well, he strangled her," pronounced Heath. "Furthermore, I'll lay my money on the fellow who called here last night at half past nine and couldn't get in. He's the bird I want to talk to."

"Indeed?" Vance produced another cigarette. "I shouldn't say, to judge from our description of him, that his conversation would prove particularly fascinatin'."

An ugly light came into Heath's eyes. "We've got ways," he said through his teeth, "of getting damn interesting conversation outta people who haven't no great reputation for repartee."

Vance sighed. "How the Four Hundred needs you, my Sergeant!"

Markham looked at his watch.

"I've got pressing work at the office," he said, "and all this talk isn't getting us anywhere." He put his hand on Heath's shoulder. "I leave you to go ahead. This afternoon I'll have these people brought down to my office for another questioning—maybe I can jog their memories a bit. . . . You've got some line of investigation planned?"

"The usual routine," replied Heath drearily. "I'll go through Odell's papers, and I'll have three or four of my men check up on her."

"You'd better get after the Yellow Taxicab Company right away," Markham suggested. "Find out, if you can, who the man was who left here at half past eleven last night, and where he went."

"Do you imagine for one moment," asked Vance, "that if this man knew anything about the murder, he would have stopped in the hall and asked the operator to call a taxi for him?"

"Oh, I don't look for much in that direction." Markham's tone was almost listless. "But the girl may have said something to him that'll give us a lead."

Vance shook his head facetiously. "O welcome pure-ey'd Faith, white-handed Hope, thou hovering angel, girt with golden wings!"

Markham was in no mood for chaffing. He turned to Heath, and spoke with forced cheeriness. "Call me up later this afternoon. I may get some new evidence out of the outfit we've just interviewed. . . . And," he added, "be sure to put a man on guard here. I want this apartment kept just as it is until we see a little more light."

"I'll attend to that," Heath assured him.

Markham and Vance and I went out and entered the car. A few minutes later we were winding rapidly across town through Central Park.

"Recall our recent conversazione about footprints in the snow?" asked Vance, as we emerged into Fifth Avenue and headed south.

Markham nodded abstractedly.

"As I remember," mused Vance, "in the hypothetical case you presented there were not only footprints but a dozen or more witnesses—including a youthful prodigy—who saw a figure of some kind cross the hibernal landscape. . . . *Grau, teurer Freund, ist alle Theorie!*

Here you are in a most beastly bother because of the disheartenin' fact that there are neither footprints in the snow nor witnesses who saw a fleeing figure. In short, you are bereft of both direct and circumstantial evidence. . . . Sad, sad."

He wagged his head dolefully.

"Y'know, Markham, it appears to me that the testimony in this case constitutes conclusive legal proof that no one could have been with the deceased at the hour of her passing, and that, ergo, she is presumably alive. The strangled body of the lady is, I take it, simply an irrelevant circumstance from the standpoint of legal procedure. I know that you learned lawyers won't admit a murder without a body; but how, in sweet Heaven's name, do you get around a *corpus delicti* without a murder?"

"You're talking nonsense," Markham rebuked him, with a show of anger.

"Oh, quite," agreed Vance. "And yet, it's a distressin' thing for a lawyer not to have footprints of some kind, isn't it, old dear? It leaves one so up in the air."

Suddenly Markham swung round. "*You*, of course, don't need footprints, or any other kind of material clues," he flung at Vance tauntingly. "*You* have powers of divination such as are denied ordinary mortals. If I remember correctly, you informed me, somewhat grandiloquently, that, knowing the nature and conditions of a crime, you could lead me infallibly to the culprit, whether he left footprints or not. You recall that boast? . . . Well, here's a crime, and the perpetrator left no footprints coming or going. Be so kind as to end my suspense by confiding in me who killed the Odell girl."

Vance's serenity was not ruffled by Markham's ill-humoured challenge. He sat smoking lazily for several minutes; then he leaned over and flicked his cigarette ash out of the window.

"'Pon my word, Markham," he rejoined evenly, "I'm half inclined to look into this silly murder. I think I'll wait, though, and see whom the nonplussed Heath turns up with his inquiries."

Markham grunted scoffingly and sank back on the cushions. "Your generosity wrings me," he said.

CHAPTER 9

The Pack in Full Cry
Tuesday, September 11; afternoon

On our way downtown that morning we were delayed for a considerable time in the traffic congestion just north of Madison Square, and Markham anxiously looked at his watch.

"It's past noon," he said. "I think I'll stop at the club and have a bite of lunch. . . . I presume that eating at this early hour would be too plebeian for so exquisite a hothouse flower as you."

Vance considered the invitation.

"Since you deprived me of my breakfast," he decided, "I'll permit you to buy me some eggs Benedictine."

A few minutes later we entered the almost empty grill of the Stuyvesant Club and took a table near one of the windows looking southward over the treetops of Madison Square.

Shortly after we had given our order a uniformed attendant entered and, bowing deferentially at the district attorney's elbow, held out an unaddressed communication sealed in one of the club's envelopes. Markham read it with an expression of growing curiosity, and as he studied the signature a look of mild surprise came into his eyes. At length he looked up and nodded to the waiting attendant. Then, excusing himself, he left us abruptly. It was fully twenty minutes before he returned.

"Funny thing," he said. "That note was from the man who took the Odell woman to dinner and the theatre last night. . . . A small world," he mused. "He's staying here at the club—he's a non-resident member and makes it his headquarters when he's in town."

"You know him?" Vance put the question disinterestedly.

"I've met him several times—chap named Spotswoode." Markham seemed perplexed. "He's a man of family, lives in a country house on

Long Island, and is regarded generally as a highly respectable member of society—one of the last persons I'd suspect of being mixed up with the Odell girl. But, according to his own confession, he played around a good deal with her during his visits to New York—'sowing a few belated wild oats,' as he expressed it—and last night took her to Francelle's for dinner and to the Winter Garden afterwards."

"Not my idea of an intellectual, or even edifyin', evening," commented Vance. "And he selected a deuced unlucky day for it I say, imagine opening the morning paper and learning that your petite dame of the preceding evening had been strangled! Disconcertin', what?"

"He's certainly disconcerted," said Markham. "The early afternoon papers were out about an hour ago, and he'd been phoning my office every ten minutes, when I suddenly walked in here. He's afraid his connection with the girl will leak out and disgrace him."

"And won't it?"

"I hardly see the necessity. No one knows who her escort was last evening; and since he obviously had nothing to do with the crime, what's to be gained by dragging him into it? He told me the whole story, and offered to stay in the city as long as I wanted him to."

"I infer, from the cloud of disappointment that enveloped you when you returned just now, that his story held nothing hopeful for you in the way of clues."

"No," Markham admitted. "The girl apparently never spoke to him of her intimate affairs; and he couldn't give me a single helpful suggestion. His account of what happened last night agreed perfectly with Jessup's. He called for the girl at seven, brought her home at about eleven, stayed with her half an hour or so, and then left her. When he heard her call for help, he was frightened, but on being assured by her there was nothing wrong, he concluded she had dozed off into a nightmare, and thought no more of it. He drove direct to the club here, arriving about ten minutes to twelve. Judge Redfern, who saw him descend from the taxi, insisted on his coming upstairs and playing poker with some men who were waiting in the judge's rooms for him. They played until three o'clock this morning."

"Your Long Island Don Juan has certainly not supplied you with any footprints in the snow."

"Anyway, his coming forward at this time closes one line of inquiry over which we might have wasted considerable time."

"If many more lines of inquiry are closed," remarked Vance dryly, "you'll be in a distressin' dilemma, don't y'know."

"There are enough still open to keep me busy," said Markham, pushing back his plate and calling for the check. He rose; then pausing, regarded Vance meditatingly. "Are you sufficiently interested to want to come along?"

"Eh, what? My word! . . . Charmed, I'm sure. But, I say, sit down just a moment—there's a good fellow!—till I finish my coffee."

I was considerably astonished at Vance's ready acceptance, careless and bantering though it was, for there was an exhibition of old Chinese prints at the Montross Galleries that afternoon, which he had planned to attend. A Riokai and a Moyeki, said to be very fine examples of Sung painting, were to be shown; and Vance was particularly eager to acquire them for his collection.

We rode with Markham to the Criminal Courts building and, entering by the Franklin Street door, took the private elevator to the district attorney's spacious but dingy private office, which overlooked the grey-stone ramparts of the Tombs. Vance seated himself in one of the heavy leather-upholstered chairs near the carved oak table on the right of the desk and lighted a cigarette with an air of cynical amusement.

"I await with anticipat'ry delight the grinding of the wheels of justice," he confided, leaning back lazily.

"You are doomed not to hear the first turn of those wheels," retorted Markham. "The initial revolution will take place outside of this office." And he disappeared through a swinging door which led to the judge's chambers.

Five minutes later he returned and sat down in the high-backed swivel chair at his desk, with his back to the four tall narrow windows in the south wall of the office.

"I just saw Judge Redfern," he explained—"it happened to be the midday recess—and he verified Spotswoode's statement in regard to the poker game. The judge met him outside of the club at ten minutes before midnight, and was with him until three in the morning. He noted the time because he had promised his guests to be back at half past eleven and was twenty minutes late."

"Why all this substantiation of an obviously unimportant fact?" asked Vance.

"A matter of routine," Markham told him, slightly impatient. "In a case of this kind every factor, however seemingly remote to the main issue, must be checked."

"Really, y'know, Markham"—Vance laid his head back on the chair and gazed dreamily at the ceiling—"one would think that this eternal routine, which you lawyer chaps worship so devoutly, actually got one somewhere occasionally; whereas it never gets one anywhere. Remember the Red Queen in 'Through the Looking-Glass—'"

"I'm too busy at present to debate the question of routine versus inspiration," Markham answered brusquely, pressing a button beneath the edge of his desk.

Swacker, his youthful and energetic secretary, appeared at the door which communicated with a narrow inner chamber between the district attorney's office and the main waiting room.

"Yes, Chief?" The secretary's eyes gleamed expectantly behind his enormous horn-rimmed glasses.

"Tell Ben to send me in a man at once."*

Swacker went out through the corridor door, and a minute or two later a suave, rotund man, dressed immaculately and wearing a pince-nez, entered, and stood before Markham with an ingratiating smile.

"Morning, Tracy." Markham's tone was pleasant but curt. "Here's a list of four witnesses in connection with the Odell case that I want brought down here at once—the two phone operators, the maid, and the janitor. You'll find them at 184 West 71st Street. Sergeant Heath is holding them there."

"Right, sir." Tracy took the memorandum, and with a priggish, but by no means inelegant, bow went out.

During the next hour Markham plunged into the general work that had accumulated during the forenoon, and I was amazed at the man's tremendous vitality and efficiency. He disposed of as many important matters as would have occupied the ordinary businessman for an entire day. Swacker bobbed in and out with electric energy, and various clerks appeared at the touch of a buzzer, took their orders, and were gone with breathless rapidity. Vance, who had sought diversion in a tome of famous arson trials, looked up admiringly from time to time and shook his head in mild reproach at such spirited activity.

It was just half past two when Swacker announced the return of Tracy with the four witnesses; and for two hours Markham questioned and cross-questioned them with a thoroughness and an insight that even I, as a lawyer, had rarely seen equalled. His interrogation of the two phone operators was quite different from his casual questioning of them earlier in the day; and if there had been a single relevant omission in their former testimony, it would certainly have

---

* "Ben" was Colonel Benjamin Hanlon, the commanding officer of the Detective Division attached to the district attorney's office.

been caught now by Markham's gruelling catechism. But when, at last, they were told they could go, no new information had been brought to light. Their stories now stood firmly grounded: no one—with the exception of the girl herself and her escort, and the disappointed visitor at half past nine—had entered the front door and passed down the hall to the Odell apartment from seven o'clock on; and no one had passed out that way. The janitor reiterated stubbornly that he had bolted the side door a little after six, and no amount of wheedling or aggression could shake his dogged certainty on that point. Amy Gibson, the maid, could add nothing to her former testimony. Markham's intensive examination of her produced only repetitions of what she had already told him.

Not one new possibility—not one new suggestion—was brought out. In fact, the two hours' interlocutory proceedings resulted only in closing up every loophole in a seemingly incredible situation. When, at half past four, Markham sat back in his chair with a weary sigh, the chance of unearthing a promising means of approach to the astonishing problem seemed more remote than ever.

Vance closed his treatise on arson and threw away his cigarette.

"I tell you, Markham old chap"—he grinned—"this case requires umbilicular contemplation, not routine. Why not call in an Egyptian seeress with a flair for crystal-gazing?"

"If this sort of thing goes on much longer," returned Markham dispiritedly, "I'll be tempted to take your advice."

Just then Swacker looked in through the door to say that Inspector Brenner was on the wire. Markham picked up the telephone receiver, and as he listened he jotted down some notes on a pad. When the call had ended, he turned to Vance.

"You seemed disturbed over the condition of the steel jewel case we found in the bedroom. Well, the expert on burglar tools just called up; and he verifies his opinion of this morning. The case was pried open with a specially-made cold chisel such as only a professional burglar would carry or would know how to use. It had an inch-and-three-eighths bevelled bit and a one-inch flat handle. It was an old instrument—there was a peculiar nick in the blade—and is the same one that was used in a successful housebreak on upper Park Avenue early last summer. . . . Does that highly exciting information ameliorate your anxiety?"

"Can't say that it does." Vance had again become serious and perplexed. "In fact, it makes the situation still more fantastic. . . . I could see a glimmer of light—eerie and unearthly, perhaps, but still a perceptible illumination—in all this murkiness if it wasn't for that jewel case and the steel chisel."

Markham was about to answer when Swacker again looked in and informed him that Sergeant Heath had arrived and wanted to see him.

Heath's manner was far less depressed than when we had taken leave of him that morning. He accepted the cigar Markham offered him, and seating himself at the conference table in front of the district attorney's desk, drew out a battered notebook.

"We've had a little good luck," he began. "Burke and Emery—two of the men I put on the case—got a line on Odell at the first place they made inquiries. From what they learned, she didn't run around with many men—limited herself to a few live wires, and played the game with what you'd call finesse. . . . The principal one—the man who's been seen most with her—is Charles Cleaver."

Markham sat up. "I know Cleaver—if it's the same one."

"It's him, all right," declared Heath. "Former Brooklyn Tax Commissioner; been interested in a poolroom for pony-betting over in Jersey City ever since. Hangs out at the Stuyvesant Club, where he can hobnob with his old Tammany Hall cronies."

"That's the one," nodded Markham. "He's a kind of professional gay dog—known as Pop, I believe."

Vance gazed into space.

"Well, well," he murmured. "So old Pop Cleaver was also entangled with our subtle and sanguine Dolores. She certainly couldn't have loved him for his *beaux yeux*."

"I thought, sir," went on Heath, "that, seeing as how Cleaver is always in and out of the Stuyvesant Club, you might ask him some questions about Odell. He ought to know something."

"Glad to, Sergeant." Markham made a note on his pad. "I'll try to get in touch with him tonight. . . . Anyone else on your list?"

"There's a fellow named Mannix—Louis Mannix—who met Odell when she was in the 'Follies'; but she chucked him over a year ago, and they haven't been seen together since. He's got another girl now. He's the head of the firm of Mannix and Levine, fur importers, and is one of your nightclub rounders—a heavy spender. But I don't see much use of barking up that tree—his affair with Odell went cold too long ago."

"Yes," agreed Markham; "I think we can eliminate him."

"I say, if you keep up this elimination much longer," observed Vance, "you won't have anything left but the lady's corpse."

"And then, there's the man who took her out last night," pursued Heath. "Nobody seems to know his name—he must've been one of those discreet, careful old boys. I thought at first he might have been Cleaver, but the descriptions don't tally. . . . And by the way, sir, here's a funny thing: when he left Odell last night he took the taxi down to the Stuyvesant Club and got out there."

Markham nodded. "I know all about that, Sergeant. And I know who the man was; and it wasn't Cleaver."

Vance was chuckling. "The Stuyvesant Club seems to be well in the forefront of this case," he said. "I do hope it doesn't suffer the sad fate of the Knickerbocker Athletic."*

Heath was intent on the main issue.

"Who was the man, Mr. Markham?"

Markham hesitated, as if pondering the advisability of taking the other into his confidence. Then he said: "I'll tell you his name, but in strict confidence. The man was Kenneth Spotswoode."

He then recounted the story of his being called away from lunch, and of his failure to elicit any helpful suggestions from Spotswoode. He also informed Heath of his verification of the man's statements regarding his movements after meeting Judge Redfern at the club.

"And," added Markham, "since he obviously left the girl before she was murdered, there's no necessity to bother him. In fact, I gave him my word I'd keep him out of it for his family's sake."

"If you're satisfied, sir, I am." Heath closed his notebook and put it away. "There's just one other little thing. Odell used to live on 110th Street, and Emery dug up her former landlady and learned that this fancy guy the maid told us about used to call on her regularly."

"That reminds me, Sergeant." Markham picked up the memorandum he had made during Inspector Brenner's phone call. "Here's some data the Professor gave me about the forcing of the jewel case."

Heath studied the paper with considerable eagerness. "Just as I thought!" He nodded his head with satisfaction. "Clear-cut professional job, by somebody who's been in the line of work before."

Vance roused himself. "Still, if such is the case," he said, "why did this experienced burglar first use the insufficient poker? And why did he overlook the living room clothes press?"

---

* Vance was here referring to the famous Molineux case, which, in 1898, sounded the death knell of the old Knickerbocker Athletic Club at Madison Avenue and 45th Street. But it was commercialism that ended the Stuyvesant's career. This club, which stood on the north side of Madison Square, was razed a few years later to make room for a skyscraper.

"I'll find all that out, Mr. Vance, when I get my hands on him," asserted Heath, with a hard look in his eyes. "And the guy I want to have a nice quiet little chat with is the one with the pleated silk shirt and the chamois gloves."

"*Chacun à son goût,*" sighed Vance. "For myself, I have no yearning whatever to hold converse with him. Somehow, I can't just picture a professional looter trying to rend a steel box with a cast iron poker."

"Forget the poker," Heath advised gruffly. "He jimmied the box with a steel chisel; and that same chisel was used last summer in another burglary on Park Avenue. What about *that?*"

"Ah! That's what torments me, Sergeant. If it wasn't for that disturbin' fact, d'ye see, I'd be lightsome and *sans souci* this afternoon, inviting my soul over a dish of tea at Claremont."

Detective Bellamy was announced, and Heath sprang to his feet. "That'll mean news about those fingerprints," he prophesied hopefully.

Bellamy entered unemotionally and walked up to the district attorney's desk.

"Cap'n Dubois sent me over," he said. "He thought you'd want the report on those Odell prints." He reached into his pocket and drew out a small flat folder which, at a sign from Markham, he handed to Heath. "We identified 'em. Both made by the same hand, like Cap'n Dubois said: and that hand belonged to Tony Skeel."

"'Dude' Skeel, eh?" The sergeant's tone was vibrant with suppressed excitement. "Say, Mr. Markham, that gets us somewhere. Skeel's an exconvict and an artist in his line."

He opened the folder and took out an oblong card and a sheet of blue paper containing eight or ten lines of typewriting. He studied the card, gave a satisfied grunt, and handed it to Markham. Vance and I stepped up and looked at it. At the top was the familiar rogues' gallery photograph showing the full face and profile of a regular-featured youth with thick hair and a square chin. His eyes were wideset and pale, and he wore a small, evenly trimmed moustache with waxed, needlepoint ends. Below the double photograph was a brief tabulated description of its sitter, giving his name, aliases, residence, and Bertillon measurements, and designating the character of his illegal profession. Underneath were ten little squares arranged in two rows, each containing a fingerprint impress made in black ink—the upper row being the impressions of the right hand, the lower row those of the left.

"So that's the *arbiter elegantiarum* who introduced the silk shirt for full-dress wear! My word!" Vance regarded the identification card satirically. "I wish he'd start a craze for gaiters with dinner jackets—these New York theatres are frightfully draughty in winter."

Heath put the card back in the folder and glanced over the type-written paper that had accompanied it.

"He's our man, and no mistake, Mr. Markham. Listen to this: 'Tony (Dude) Skeel. Two years Elmira Reformatory, 1902 to 1904. One year in the Baltimore County jail for petit larceny, 1906. Three years in San Quentin for assault and robbery, 1908 to 1911. Arrested Chicago for housebreaking, 1912; case dismissed. Arrested and tried for burglary in Albany, 1913; no conviction. Served two years and eight months in Sing-Sing for housebreaking and burglary, 1914 to 1916.'" He folded the paper and put it, with the card, into his breast pocket. "Sweet little record."

"That dope what you wanted?" asked the imperturbable Bellamy.

"I'll say!" Heath was almost jovial.

Bellamy lingered expectantly with one eye on the district attorney; and Markham, as if suddenly remembering something, took out a box of cigars and held it out.

"Much obliged, sir," said Bellamy, helping himself to two Mi Favoritas; and putting them into his waistcoat pocket with great care, he went out.

"I'll use your phone now, if you don't mind, Mr. Markham," said Heath.

He called the Homicide Bureau.

"Look up Tony Skeel—Dude Skeel—pronto, and bring him in as soon as you find him," were his orders to Snitkin. "Get his address from the files and take Burke and Emery with you. If he's hopped it, send out a general alarm and have him picked up—some of the boys'll have a line on him. Lock him up without booking him, see? . . . And, listen. Search his room for burglar tools: he probably won't have any laying around, but I specially want a one-and-three-eighths-inch chisel with a nick in the blade. . . . I'll be at headquarters in half an hour."

He hung up the receiver and rubbed his hands together.

"Now we're sailing," he rejoiced.

Vance had gone to the window and stood staring down on the "Bridge of Sighs," his hands thrust deep into his pockets. Slowly he turned, and fixed Heath with a contemplative eye.

"It simply won't do, don't y'know," he asserted. "Your friend, the Dude may have ripped open that bally box, but his head isn't the right shape for the rest of last evening's performance."

Heath was contemptuous. "Not being a phrenologist, I'm going by the shape of his fingerprints."

"A woeful error in the technic of criminal approach, *sergente mio*," replied Vance dulcetly. "The question of culpability in this case isn't so simple as you imagine. It's deuced complicated. And this glass of fashion and mould of form whose portrait you're carryin' next to your heart has merely added to its intricacy."

CHAPTER 10

A Forced Interview

Tuesday, September 11; 8 p.m.

Markham dined at the Stuyvesant Club, as was his custom, and at his invitation Vance and I remained with him. He no doubt figured that our presence at the dinner table would act as a bulwark against the intrusion of casual acquaintances; for he was in no mood for the pleasantries of the curious. Rain had begun to fall late in the afternoon, and when dinner was over, it had turned into a steady downpour which threatened to last well into the night. Dinner over, the three of us sought a secluded corner of the lounge room, and settled ourselves for a protracted smoke.

We had been there less than a quarter of an hour when a slightly rotund man, with a heavy, florid face and thin grey hair, strolled up to us with a stealthy, self-assured gait, and wished Markham a jovial good evening. Though I had not met the newcomer I knew him to be Charles Cleaver.

"Got your note at the desk saying you wanted to see me." He spoke with a voice curiously gentle for a man of his size; but, for all its gentleness, there was in it a timbre of calculation and coldness.

Markham rose and, after shaking hands, introduced him to Vance and me—though, it seemed, Vance had known him slightly for some time. He took the chair Markham indicated, and, producing a Corona Corona, he carefully cut the end with a gold clipper attached to his heavy watch chain, rolled the cigar between his lips to dampen it and lighted it in closely cupped hands. "I'm sorry to trouble you, Mr. Cleaver," began Markham, "but, as you probably have read, a young woman by the name of Margaret Odell was murdered last night in her apartment in 71st Street. . . ."

He paused. He seemed to be considering just how he could best

301

broach a subject so obviously delicate; and perhaps he hoped that Cleaver would volunteer the fact of his acquaintance with the girl. But not a muscle of the man's face moved; and, after a moment, Markham continued.

"In making inquiries into the young woman's life I learned that you, among others, were fairly well acquainted with her."

Again he paused. Cleaver lifted his eyebrows almost imperceptibly but said nothing.

"The fact is," went on Markham, a trifle annoyed by the other's deliberately circumspect attitude, "my report states that you were seen with her on many occasions during a period of nearly two years. Indeed, the only inference to be drawn from what I've learned is that you were more than casually interested in Miss Odell."

"Yes?" The query was as noncommittal as it was gentle.

"Yes," repeated Markham. "And I may add, Mr. Cleaver, that this is not the time for pretences or suppressions. I am talking to you tonight, in large measure *ex officio*, because it occurred to me that you could give me some assistance in clearing the matter up. I think it only fair to say that a certain man is now under grave suspicion, and we hope to arrest him very soon. But, in any event, we will need help, and that is why I requested this little chat with you at the club."

"And how can I assist you?" Cleaver's face remained blank; only his lips moved as he put the question.

"Knowing this young woman as well as you did," explained Markham patiently, "you are no doubt in possession of some information—certain facts or confidences, let us say—which would throw light on her brutal, and apparently unexpected, murder."

Cleaver was silent for some time. His eyes had shifted to the wall before him, but otherwise his features remained set.

"I'm afraid I can't accommodate you," he said at length.

"Your attitude is not quite what might be expected in one whose conscience is entirely clear," returned Markham, with a show of resentment.

The man turned a mildly inquisitive gaze upon the district attorney.

"What has my knowing the girl to do with her being murdered? She didn't confide in me who her murderer was to be. She didn't even tell me that she knew anyone who intended to strangle her. If she'd known, she most likely could have avoided being murdered."

Vance was sitting close to me, a little removed from the others, and, leaning over, murmured in my ear *sotto voce*: "Markham's up against another lawyer—poor dear! . . . A crumplin' situation."

But however inauspiciously this interlocutory skirmish may have begun, it soon developed into a grim combat which ended in Cleaver's complete surrender. Markham, despite his suavity and graciousness, was an unrelenting and resourceful antagonist; and it was not long before he had forced from Cleaver some highly significant information.

In response to the man's ironically evasive rejoinder, he turned quickly and leaned forward.

"You're not on the witness stand in your own defence, Mr. Cleaver," he said sharply, "however much you appear to regard yourself as eligible for that position."

Cleaver glared back fixedly without replying; and Markham, his eyelids level, studied the man opposite, determined to decipher all he could from the other's phlegmatic countenance. But Cleaver was apparently just as determined that his *vis-à-vis* should decipher absolutely nothing; and the features that met Markham's scrutiny were as arid as a desert. At length Markham sank back in his chair.

"It doesn't matter particularly," he remarked indifferently, "whether you discuss the matter or not here in the club tonight. If you prefer to be brought to my office in the morning by a sheriff with a subpoena, I'll be only too glad to accommodate you."

"That's up to you," Cleaver told him hostilely.

"And what's printed in the newspapers about it will be up to the reporters," rejoined Markham. "I'll explain the situation to them and give them a verbatim report of the interview."

"But I've nothing to tell you." The other's tone was suddenly conciliatory; the idea of publicity was evidently highly distasteful to him.

"So you informed me before," said Markham coldly. "Therefore I wish you good evening."

He turned to Vance and me with the air of a man who had terminated an unpleasant episode.

Cleaver, however, made no move to go. He smoked thoughtfully for a minute or two; then he gave a short, hard laugh which did not even disturb the contours of his face.

"Oh, hell!" he grumbled, with forced good nature. "As you said, I'm not on the witness stand. . . . What do you want to know?"

"I've told you the situation." Markham's voice betrayed a curious irritation. "You know the sort of thing I want. How did this Odell girl live? Who were her intimates? Who would have been likely to want her out of the way? What enemies had she?—Anything that might lead us to an explanation of her death. . . . And incidentally," he added with tartness, "anything that'll eliminate yourself from any suspected participation, direct or indirect, in the affair."

Cleaver stiffened at these last words and started to protest indignantly. But immediately he changed his tactics. Smiling contemptuously, he took out a leather pocket case and, extracting a small folded paper, handed it to Markham.

"I can eliminate myself easily enough," he proclaimed, with easy confidence. "There's a speeding summons from Boonton, New Jersey. Note the date and the time: September the tenth—last night—at half past eleven. Was driving down to Hopatcong, and was ticketed by a motorcycle cop just as I had passed Boonton and was heading for Mountain Lakes. Got to appear in court there tomorrow morning. Damn nuisance, these country constables." He gave Markham a long, calculating look. "You couldn't square it for me, could you? It's a rotten ride to Jersey, and I've got a lot to do tomorrow."

Markham, who had inspected the summons casually, put it in his pocket.

"I'll attend to it for you," he promised, smiling amiably. "Now tell me what you know."

Cleaver puffed meditatively on his cigar. Then, leaning back and crossing his knees, he spoke with apparent candour.

"I doubt if I know much that'll help you. . . . I liked the Canary, as she was called—in fact, was pretty much attached to her at one time. Did a number of foolish things; wrote her a lot of damn-fool letters when I went to Cuba last year. Even had my picture taken with her down at Atlantic City." He made a self-condemnatory grimace. "Then she began to get cool and distant; broke several appointments with me. I raised the devil with her, but the only answer I got was a demand for money. . . ."

He stopped and looked down at his cigar ash. A venomous hatred gleamed from his narrowed eyes, and the muscles of his jowls hardened.

"No use lying about it. She had those letters and things, and she touched me for a neat little sum before I got 'em back. . . ."

"When was this?"

There was a momentary hesitation. "Last June," Cleaver replied. Then he hurried on: "Mr. Markham"—his voice was bitter—"I don't want to throw mud on a dead person; but that woman was the shrewdest, coldest-blooded blackmailer it's ever been my misfortune to meet. And I'll say this, too: I wasn't the only easy mark she squeezed. She had others on her string. . . . I happen to know she once dug into old Louey Mannix for a plenty—he told me about it."

"Could you give me the names of any of these other men?" asked Markham, attempting to dissemble his eagerness. "I've already heard of the Mannix episode."

"No, I couldn't." Cleaver spoke regretfully. "I've seen the Canary here and there with different men; and there's one in particular I've noticed lately. But they were all strangers to me."

"I suppose the Mannix affair is dead and buried by this time?"

"Yes—ancient history. You won't get any line on the situation from that angle. But there are others—more recent than Mannix—who might bear looking into, if you could find them. I'm easygoing myself; take things as they come. But there's a lot of men who'd go redheaded if she did the things to them that she did to me."

Cleaver, despite his confession, did not strike me as easygoing, but rather as a cold, self-contained, nerveless person whose immobility was at all times dictated by policy and expediency.

Markham studied him closely.

"You think, then, her death may have been due to vengeance on the part of some disillusioned admirer?"

Cleaver carefully considered his answer. "Seems reasonable," he said finally. "She was riding for a fall."

There was a short silence; then Markham asked: "Do you happen to know of a young man she was interested in—good-looking, small, blond moustache, light blue eyes—named Skeel?"

Cleaver snorted derisively. "That wasn't the Canary's specialty—she let the young ones alone, as far as I know."

At this moment a pageboy approached Cleaver and bowed. "Sorry to disturb you, sir, but there's a phone call for your brother. Party said it was important and, as your brother isn't in the club now, the operator thought you might know where he'd gone."

"How would I know?" fumed Cleaver. "Don't ever bother me with his calls."

"Your brother in the city?" asked Markham casually. "I met him years ago. He's a San Franciscan, isn't he?"

"Yes—rabid Californian. He's visiting New York for a couple of weeks so he'll appreciate Frisco more when he gets back."

It seemed to me that this information was given reluctantly; and I got the impression that Cleaver, for some reason, was annoyed. But Markham, apparently, was too absorbed in the problem before him to take notice of the other's disgruntled air, for he reverted at once to the subject of the murder. "I happen to know one man who has been interested in the Odell woman recently; he may be the same one you've seen her with—tall, about forty-five, and wears a grey, closed-cropped moustache." (He was, I knew, describing Spotswoode.)

"That's the man," averred Cleaver. "Saw them together only last week at Mouquin's."

Markham was disappointed. "Unfortunately, he's checked off the list. . . . But there must be somebody who was in the girl's confidence. You're sure you couldn't cudgel your brains to my advantage?"

Cleaver appeared to think.

"If it's merely a question of someone who had her confidence," he said, "I might suggest Doctor Lindquist—first name's Ambroise, I think; and he lives somewhere in the Forties near Lexington Avenue. But I don't know that he'd be of any value to you. Still, he was pretty close to her at one time."

"You mean that this Doctor Lindquist might have been interested in her otherwise than professionally?"

"I wouldn't like to say." Cleaver smoked for a while as if inwardly debating the situation. "Anyway, here are the facts: Lindquist is one of these exclusive society specialists—a neurologist he calls himself—and I believe he's the head of a private sanatorium of some kind for nervous women. He must have money, and, of course, his social standing is a vital asset to him—just the sort of man the Canary might have selected as a source of income. And I know this: he came to see her a good deal oftener than a doctor of his type would be apt to. I ran into him one night at her apartment, and when she introduced us, he wasn't even civil."

"It will at least bear looking into," replied Markham unenthusiastically. "You've no one else in mind who might know something helpful?"

Cleaver shook his head.

"No—no one."

"And she never mentioned anything to you that indicated she was in fear of anyone, or anticipated trouble?"

"Not a word. Fact is, I was bowled over by the news. I never read any paper but the morning Herald—except, of course, The Daily Racing Form at night. And as there was no account of the murder in this morning's paper, I didn't hear about it until just before dinner. The boys in the billiard room were talking about it, and I went out and looked at an afternoon paper. If it hadn't been for that, I might not have known of it till tomorrow morning."

Markham discussed the case with him until half past eight but could elicit no further suggestions. Finally Cleaver rose to go.

"Sorry I couldn't give you more help," he said. His rubicund face was beaming now, and he shook hands with Markham in the friendliest fashion.

"You wangled that viscid old sport rather cleverly, don't y'know," remarked Vance, when Cleaver had gone. "But there's something deuced queer about him. The transition from his gambler's glassy stare to his garrulous confidences was too sudden—suspiciously sudden, in fact. I may be evil-minded, but he didn't impress me as a luminous pillar of truth. Maybe it's because I don't like those cold, boiled eyes of his—somehow they didn't harmonize with his gushing imitation of openhearted frankness."

"We can allow him something for his embarrassing position," suggested Markham charitably. "It isn't exactly pleasant to admit having been taken in and blackmailed by a charmer."

"Still, if he got his letters back in June, why did he continue paying court to the lady? Heath reported he was active in that sector right up to the end."

"He may be the complete amorist," smiled Markham.

"Some like Abra, what?—'Abra was ready ere I call'd her name; And, though I call'd another, Abra came.' Maybe—yes. He might qualify as a modern Cayley Drummle."

"At any rate, he gave us, in Doctor Lindquist, a possible source of information."

"Quite so," agreed Vance. "And that's about the only point of his whole passionate unfoldment that I particularly put any stock in, because it was the only point he indicated with any decent reticence. . . . My advice is that you interview this Aesculapius of the fair sex without further delay."

"I'm dog-tired," objected Markham. "Let it wait till tomorrow."

Vance glanced at the great clock over the stone mantel.

"It's latish, I'll admit, but why not, as Pittacus advised, seize time by the forelock?

'Who lets slip fortune, her shall never find: Occasion once past by, is a bald behind.'

But the elder Cato anticipated Cowley. In his *Disticha de Moribus* he wrote: *Fronte capillata*—"

"Come!" pleaded Markham, rising. "Anything to dam this flow of erudition."

CHAPTER 11

Seeking Information
Tuesday September 11; 9 p.m.

Ten minutes later we were ringing the bell of a stately old brownstone house in East 44th Street.

A resplendently caparisoned butler opened the door, and Markham presented his card.

"Take this to the doctor at once and say that it's urgent."

"The doctor is just finishing dinner," the stately seneschal informed him, and conducted us into a richly furnished reception room, with deep, comfortable chairs, silken draperies, and subdued lights.

"A typical gynaecologist's *seraglio*," observed Vance, looking around. "I'm sure the *pasha* himself is a majestic and elegant personage."

The prediction proved true. Doctor Lindquist entered the room a moment later inspecting the district attorney's card as if it had been a cuneiform inscription whose import he could not quite decipher. He was a tall man in his late forties, with bushy hair and eyebrows, and a complexion abnormally pale. His face was long, and, despite the asymmetry of his features, he might easily have been called handsome. He was in dinner clothes, and he carried himself with the self-conscious precision of a man unduly impressed with his own importance. He seated himself at a kidney-shaped desk of carved mahogany and lifted his eyes with polite inquiry to Markham.

"To what am I indebted for the honour of this call?" he asked in a studiously melodious voice, lingering over each word caressingly. "You are most fortunate to have found me in," he added, before Markham could speak. "I confer with patients only by appointment." One felt that he experienced a certain humiliation at having received us without elaborate ceremonial preliminaries.

Markham, whose nature was opposed to all circumlocution and pretence, came direct to the point.

"This isn't a professional consultation, Doctor; but it happens that I want to speak to you about one of your former patients—a Miss Margaret Odell."

Doctor Lindquist regarded the gold paperweight before him with vacantly reminiscent eyes.

"Ah, yes. Miss Odell. I was just reading of her violent end. A most unfortunate and tragic affair. . . . In just what way can I be of service to you?—You understand, of course, that the relationship between a physician and his patient is one of sacred confidence—"

"I understand that thoroughly," Markham assured him abruptly. "On the other hand, it is the sacred duty of every citizen to assist the authorities in bringing a murderer to justice. And if there is anything you can tell me which will help toward that end, I shall certainly expect you to tell me."

The doctor raised his hand slightly in polite protestation. "I shall, of course, do all I can to assist you, if you will but indicate your desires."

"There's no need to beat about the bush, Doctor," said Markham. "I know that Miss Odell was a patient of yours for a long time; and I realize that it is highly possible, not to say probable, that she told you certain personal things which may have direct bearing on her death."

"But, my dear Mr.—," Doctor Lindquist glanced ostentatiously at the card, "ah—Markham, my relations with Miss Odell were of a purely professional character."

"I had understood, however," ventured Markham, "that, while what you say may be technically true, nevertheless there was an informality, let me say, in that relationship. Perhaps I may state it better by saying that your professional attitude transcended a merely scientific interest in her case."

I heard Vance chuckle softly; and I myself could hardly suppress a smile at Markham's verbose and orbicular accusation. But Doctor Lindquist, it seemed, was in no wise disconcerted. Assuming an air of beguiling pensiveness, he said: "I will confess, in the interests of strict accuracy, that during my somewhat protracted treatment of her case, I came to regard the young woman with a certain—shall I say, fatherly liking? But I doubt if she was even aware of this mild sentiment on my part."

The corners of Vance's mouth twitched slightly. He was sitting with drowsy eyes, watching the doctor with a look of studious amusement.

"And she never at any time told you of any private or personal affairs that were causing her anxiety?" persisted Markham.

Doctor Lindquist pyramided his fingers, and appeared to give the question his undivided thought.

"No, I can't recall a single statement of that nature." His words were measured and urbane. "I know, naturally, in a general way, her manner of living; but the details, you will readily perceive, were wholly outside my province as a medical consultant. The disorganization of her nerves was due—so my diagnosis led me to conclude—to late hours, excitement, irregular and rich eating—what, I believe, is referred to vulgarly as going the pace. The modern woman, in this febrile age, sir—"

"When did you see her last, may I ask?" Markham interrupted impatiently.

The doctor made a pantomime of eloquent surprise.

"When did I see her last? . . . Let me see." He could, apparently, recall the occasion only with considerable difficulty. "A fortnight ago, perhaps—though it may have been longer. I really can't recall. . . . Shall I refer to my files?"

"That won't be necessary," said Markham. He paused and regarded the doctor with a look of disarming affability. "And was this last visit a paternal or merely a professional one?"

"Professional, of course." Doctor Lindquist's eyes were impassive and only mildly interested; but his face, I felt, was by no means the unedited reflection of his thoughts.

"Did the meeting take place here or at her apartment?"

"I believe I called on her at her home."

"You called on her a great deal, Doctor—so I am informed—and at rather unconventional hours. . . . Is this entirely in accord with your practice of seeing patients only by appointment?"

Markham's tone was pleasant; but from the nature of his question I knew that he was decidedly irritated by the man's bland hypocrisy, and felt that he was deliberately withholding relevant information.

Before Doctor Lindquist could reply, however, the butler appeared at the door and silently indicated an extension telephone on a *taboret* beside the desk. With an unctuously murmured apology, the doctor turned and lifted the receiver.

Vance took advantage of this opportunity to scribble something on a piece of paper and pass it surreptitiously to Markham.

His call completed, Doctor Lindquist drew himself up haughtily and faced Markham with chilling scorn.

"Is it the function of the district attorney," he asked distantly, "to harass respectable physicians with insulting questions? I did not know that it was illegal—or even original, for that matter—for a doctor to visit his patients."

"I am not discussing *now*"—Markham emphasized the adverb—"your infractions of the law; but since you suggest a possibility which, I assure you, was not in my mind, would you be good enough to tell me—merely as a matter of form—where you were last night between eleven and twelve?"

The question produced a startling effect. Doctor Lindquist became suddenly like a tautly drawn rope, and rising slowly and stiffly, he glared, with cold intense venom, at the district attorney. His velvety mask had fallen off; and I detected another emotion beneath his repressed anger: his expression cloaked a fear, and his wrath but partly veiled a passionate uncertainty.

"My whereabouts last night is no concern of yours." He spoke with great effort, his breath coming and going noisily.

Markham waited, apparently unmoved, his eyes riveted on the trembling man before him. This calm scrutiny completely broke down the other's self-control.

"What do you mean by forcing yourself in here with your contemptible insinuations?" he shouted. His face, now livid and mottled, was hideously contorted; his hands made spasmodic movements; and his whole body shook as with a tremor. "Get out of here—you and your two myrmidons! Get out, before I have you thrown out!"

Markham, himself enraged now, was about to reply, when Vance took him by the arm.

"The doctor is gently hinting that we go," he said. And with amazing swiftness he spun Markham round and led him firmly out of the room.

When we were again in the taxicab on our way back to the club, Vance sniggered gaily. "A sweet specimen, that! Paranoia. Or, more likely, manic-depressive insanity—the *folie circulaire* type: recurring periods of maniacal excitement alternating with periods of the clearest sanity, don't y'know. Anyway, the doctor's disorder belongs in the category of psychoses—associated with the maturation or waning of the sexual instinct. He's just the right age, too. Neurotic degenerate—that's what this oily Hippocrates is. In another minute he would have attacked you. . . . My word! It's a good thing I came to the rescue. Such chaps are about as safe as rattlesnakes."

He shook his head in a mock discouragement.

"Really, y'know, Markham, old thing," he added, "you should

study the cranial indications of your fellow man more carefully—*vultus est index animi*. Did you, by any chance, note the gentleman's wide rectangular forehead, his irregular eyebrows, and pale luminous eyes, and his outstanding ears with their thin upper rims, their pointed *tragi* and split lobes? . . . A clever devil, this Ambroise—but a moral imbecile. Beware of those *pseudo-pyriform* faces, Markham; leave their Apollonian Greek suggestiveness to misunderstood women."

"I wonder what he really knows?" grumbled Markham irritably.

"Oh, he knows something—rest assured of that! And if only we knew it, too, we'd be considerably further along in the investigation. Furthermore, the information he is hiding is somewhat unpleasantly connected with himself. His euphoria is a bit shaken. He frightfully overdid the grand manner; his valedict'ry fulmination was the true expression of his feeling toward us."

"Yes," agreed Markham. "That question about last night acted like a petard. What prompted you to suggest my asking it?"

"A number of things—his gratuitous and obviously mendacious statement that he had just read of the murder; his wholly insincere homily on the sacredness of professional confidences; the cautious and Pecksniffian confession of his fatherly regard for the girl; his elaborate struggle to remember when he had last seen her—this particularly, I think, made me suspicious; and then, the psychopathic indicants of his physiognomy."

"Well," admitted Markham, "the question had its effect. . . . I feel that I shall see this fashionable M.D. again."

"You will," iterated Vance. "We took him unawares. But when he has had time to ponder the matter and concoct an appealin' tale, he'll become downright garrulous. . . . Anyhow, the evening is over, and you can meditate on buttercups till the morrow."

But the evening was not quite over as far as the Odell case was concerned. We had been back in the lounge room of the club but a short time when a man walked by the corner in which we sat, and bowed with formal courtesy to Markham. Markham, to my surprise, rose and greeted him, at the same time indicating a chair.

"There's something further I wanted to ask you, Mr. Spotswoode," he said, "if you can spare a moment."

At the mention of the name I regarded the man closely, for, I confess, I was not a little curious about the anonymous escort who had taken the girl to dinner and the theatre the night before. Spotswoode was a typical New England aristocrat, inflexible, slow in his move-

ments, reserved, and quietly but modishly dressed. His hair and moustache were slightly grey—which, no doubt, enhanced the pinkness of
his complexion. He was just under six feet tall and well proportioned,
but a trifle angular.

Markham introduced him to Vance and me, and briefly explained
that we were working with him on the case and that he had thought
it best to take us fully into his confidence.

Spotswoode gave him a dubious look but immediately bowed his
acceptance of the decision.

"I'm in your hands, Mr. Markham," he replied, in a well-bred but
somewhat high-pitched voice, "and I concur, of course, with whatever
you think advisable." He turned to Vance with an apologetic smile.
"I'm in a rather unpleasant position and naturally feel a little sensitive
about it."

"I'm something of an antinomian," Vance pleasantly informed him.
"At any rate, I'm not a moralist; so my attitude in the matter is quite
academic."

Spotswoode laughed softly. "I wish my family held a similar point
of view; but I'm afraid they would not be so tolerant of my foibles."

"It's only fair to tell you, Mr. Spotswoode," interposed Markham,
"that there is a bare possibility I may have to call you as a witness."

The man looked up quickly, his face clouding over, but he made
no comment.

"The fact is," continued Markham, "we are about to make an arrest, and your testimony may be needed to establish the time of Miss
Odell's return to her apartment, and also to substantiate the fact that
there was presumably someone in her room after you had left. Her
screams and calls for help, which you heard, may prove vital evidence
in obtaining a conviction."

Spotswoode seemed rather appalled at the thought of his relations
with the girl becoming public, and for several minutes he sat with
averted eyes.

"I see your point," he acknowledged at length. "But it would be a
terrible thing for me if the fact of my delinquencies became known."

"That contingency may be entirely avoided," Markham encouraged him. "I promise you that you will not be called upon unless it is
absolutely necessary. . . . And now, what I especially wanted to ask you
is this: do you happen to know a Doctor Lindquist, who, I understand,
was Miss Odell's personal physician?"

Spotswoode was frankly puzzled. "I never heard the name," he answered. "In fact, Miss Odell never mentioned any doctor to me."

"And did you ever hear her mention the name of Skeel . . . or refer to any one as Tony?"

"Never." His answer was emphatic.

Markham lapsed into a disappointed silence. Spotswoode, too, was silent; he sat as if in a reverie.

"You know, Mr. Markham," he said, after several minutes, "I ought to be ashamed to admit it, but the truth is I cared a good deal for the girl. I suppose you've kept her apartment intact. . . ." He hesitated, and a look almost of appeal came into his eyes. "I'd like to see it again if I could."

Markham regarded him sympathetically but finally shook his head.

"It wouldn't do. You'd be sure to be recognized by the operator— or there might be a reporter about—and then I'd be unable to keep you out of the case."

The man appeared disappointed but did not protest; and for several minutes no one spoke. Then Vance raised himself slightly in his chair.

"I say, Mr. Spotswoode, do you happen to remember anything unusual occurring last night during the half hour you remained with Miss Odell after the theatre?"

"Unusual?" the man's manner was eloquent of his astonishment. "To the contrary. We chatted awhile, and then, as she seemed tired, I said good night and came away, making a luncheon appointment with her for today."

"And yet, it now seems fairly certain that some other man was hiding in the apartment when you were there."

"There's little doubt on that point," agreed Spotswoode, with the suggestion of a shudder. "And her screams would seem to indicate that he came forth from hiding a few minutes after I went."

"And you had no suspicion of the fact when you heard her call for help?"

"I did at first—naturally. But when she assured me that nothing was the matter, and told me to go home, I attributed her screams to a nightmare. I knew she had been tired, and I had left her in the wicker chair near the door, from where her screams seemed to come; so I naturally concluded she had dozed off and called out in her sleep. . . . If only I hadn't taken so much for granted!"

"It's a harrowin' situation." Vance was silent for a while; then he asked: "Did you, by any chance, notice the door of the living room closet? Was it open or closed?"

Spotswoode frowned, as if attempting to visualize the picture; but the result was a failure.

"I suppose it was closed. I probably would have noticed it if it had been open."

"Then, you couldn't say if the key was in the lock or not?"

"Good Lord, no! I don't even know if it ever had a key."

The case was discussed for another half hour; then Spotswoode excused himself and left us.

"Funny thing," ruminated Markham, "how a man of his upbringing could be so attracted by the empty-headed, butterfly type."

"I'd say it was quite natural," returned Vance. . . . "You're such an incorrigible moralist, Markham."

CHAPTER 12

Circumstantial Evidence

Wednesday, September 12; 9 a.m.

The following day, which was Wednesday, not only brought forth an important and, as it appeared, conclusive development in the Odell case but marked the beginning of Vance's active cooperation in the proceedings. The psychological elements in the case had appealed to him irresistibly, and he felt, even at this stage of the investigation, that a final answer could never be obtained along the usual police lines. At his request Markham had called for him at a little before nine o'clock, and we had driven direct to the district attorney's office.

Heath was waiting impatiently when we arrived. His eager and covertly triumphant expression plainly indicated good news.

"Things are breaking fine and dandy," he announced, when we had sat down. He himself was too elated to relax, and stood between Markham's desk rolling a large black cigar between his fingers. "We got the Dude—six o'clock yesterday evening—and we got him right. One of the C. O. boys, named Riley, who was patrolling Sixth Avenue in the Thirties, saw him swing off a surface car and head for McAnerny's Pawn Shop. Right away Riley wigwags the traffic officer on the corner and follows the Dude into McAnerny's. Pretty soon the traffic officer comes in with a patrolman, who he's picked up; and the three of 'em nab our stylish friend in the act of pawning this ring."

He tossed a square solitaire diamond in a filigreed platinum setting on the district attorney's desk.

"I was at the office when they brought him in, and I sent Snitkin with the ring up to Harlem to see what the maid had to say about it, and she identified it as belonging to Odell."

"But, I say, it wasn't a part of the *bijouterie* the lady was wearing that night, was it, Sergeant?" Vance put the question casually.

316

Heath jerked about and eyed him with sullen calculation.

"What if it wasn't? It came out of that jimmied jewel case—or I'm Ben Hur."

"Of course it did," murmured Vance, lapsing into lethargy.

"And that's where we're in luck," declared Heath, turning back to Markham. "It connects Skeel directly with the murder and the robbery."

"What has Skeel to say about it?" Markham was leaning forward intently. "I suppose you questioned him."

"I'll say we did," replied the sergeant; but his tone was troubled. "We had him up all night giving him the works. And the story he tells is this: he says the girl gave him the ring a week ago, and that he didn't see her again until the afternoon of the day before yesterday. He came to her apartment between four and five—you remember the maid said she was out then—and entered and left the house by the side door, which was unlocked at that time. He admits he called again at half past nine that night, but he says that when he found she was out, he went straight home and stayed there. His alibi is that he sat up with his landlady till after midnight playing Khun Khan and drinking beer. I hopped up to his place this morning, and the old girl verified it. But that don't mean anything. The house he lives in is a pretty tough hangout, and this landlady, besides being a heavy boozer, has been up the river a coupla times for shoplifting."

"What does Skeel say about the fingerprints?"

"He says, of course, he made 'em when he was there in the afternoon."

"And the one on the closet doorknob?"

Heath gave a derisive grunt.

"He's got an answer for that, too—says he thought he heard someone coming in, and locked himself in the clothes closet. Didn't want to be seen and spoil any game Odell mighta been playing."

"Most considerate of him to keep out of the way of the *belles poires*," drawled Vance. "Touchin' loyalty, what?"

"You don't believe the rat, do you, Mr. Vance?" asked Heath, with indignant surprise.

"Can't say that I do. But our Antonio at least spins a consistent yarn."

"Too damn consistent to suit me," growled the sergeant.

"That's all you could get out of him?" It was plain that Markham was not pleased with the results of Heath's third degree of Skeel.

"That's about all, sir. He stuck to his story like a leech."

"You found no chisel in his room?"

317

Heath admitted that he hadn't. "But you couldn't expect him to keep it around," he added.

Markham pondered the facts for several minutes. "I can't see that we've got a very good case, however much we may be convinced of Skeel's guilt. His alibi may be thin, but taken in connection with the phone operator's testimony, I'm inclined to think it would hold tight in court."

"What about the ring, sir?" Heath was desperately disappointed. "And what about his threats, and his fingerprints, and his record of similar burglaries?"

"Contributory factors only," Markham explained. "What we need for a murder is more than a *prima facie* case. A good criminal lawyer could have him discharged in twenty minutes, even if I could secure an indictment. It's not impossible, you know, that the woman gave him the ring a week ago—you recall that the maid said he was demanding money from her about that time. And there's nothing to show that the fingerprints were not actually made late Monday afternoon. Moreover, we can't connect him in any way with the chisel, for we don't know who did the Park Avenue job last summer. His whole story fits the facts perfectly; and we haven't anything contradictory to offer." Heath shrugged helplessly; all the wind had been taken out of his sails.

"What do you want done with him?" he asked desolately.

Markham considered—he, too, was discomfited.

"Before I answer, I think I'll have a go at him myself."

He pressed a buzzer and ordered a clerk to fill out the necessary requisition. When it had been signed in duplicate, he sent Swacker with it to Ben Hanlon.

"Do ask him about those silk shirts," suggested Vance. "And find out, if you can, if he considers a white waistcoat *de rigueur* with a dinner jacket."

"This office isn't a male millinery shop," snapped Markham.

"But, Markham dear, you won't learn anything else from this Petronius."

Ten minutes later a deputy sheriff from the Tombs entered with his handcuffed prisoner.

Skeel's appearance that morning belied his sobriquet of "Dude." He was haggard and pale; his ordeal of the previous night had left its imprint upon him. He was unshaven; his hair was uncombed; the ends of his moustache drooped; and his cravat was awry. But despite his bedraggled condition, his manner was jaunty and contemptuous. He gave Heath a defiant leer and faced the district attorney with swaggering indifference.

To Markham's questions he doggedly repeated the same story he had told Heath. He clung tenaciously to every detail of it with the ready accuracy of a man who had painstakingly memorized a lesson and was thoroughly familiar with it. Markham coaxed, threatened, bullied. All hint of his usual affability was gone; he was like an inexorable dynamic machine. But Skeel, whose nerves seemed to be made of iron, withstood the vicious fire of his cross-questioning without wincing; and, I confess, his resistance somewhat aroused my admiration despite my revulsion toward him and all he stood for.

After half an hour Markham gave up, completely baffled in his efforts to elicit any damaging admissions from the man. He was about to dismiss him when Vance rose languidly and strolled to the district attorney's desk. Seating himself on the edge of it, he regarded Skeel with impersonal curiosity.

"So you're a devotee of Khun Khan, eh?" he remarked indifferently. "Silly game, what? More interestin' than Conquain or Rum, though. Used to be played in the London clubs. Of East Indian origin, I believe. . . . You still play it with two decks, I suppose, and permit round-the-corner mating?"

An involuntary frown gathered on Skeel's forehead. He was used to violent district attorneys and familiar with the bludgeoning methods of the police, but here was a type of inquisitor entirely new to him; and it was plain that he was both puzzled and apprehensive. He decided to meet this novel antagonist with a smirk of arrogant amusement.

"By the bye," continued Vance, with no change in tone, "can anyone hidden in the clothes press of the Odell living room see the davenport through the keyhole?"

Suddenly all trace of a smile was erased from the man's features.

"And I say," Vance hurried on, his eyes fixed steadily on the other, "why didn't you give the alarm?"

I was watching Skeel closely, and though his set expression did not alter, I saw the pupils of his eyes dilate. Markham, also, I think, noted this phenomenon.

"Don't bother to answer," pursued Vance, as the man opened his lips to speak. "But tell me: didn't the sight shake you up a bit?"

"I don't know what you're talking about," Skeel retorted with sullen impertinence. But, for all his sangfroid, one sensed an uneasiness in his manner. There was an overtone of effort in his desire to appear indifferent, which robbed his words of complete conviction.

"Not a pleasant situation, that." Vance ignored his retort. "How did you feel, crouching there in the dark, when the closet doorknob was turned and someone tried to get in?" His eyes were boring into the man, though his voice retained its casual intonation.

The muscles of Skeel's face tightened, but he did not speak.

"Lucky thing you took the precaution of locking yourself in—eh, what?"Vance went on. "Suppose he'd got the door open—my word! Then what? . . ."

He paused and smiled with a kind of silky sweetness which was more impressive than any glowering aggression.

"I say, did you have your steel chisel ready for him? Maybe he'd have been too quick and strong for you—maybe there would have been thumbs pressing against your larynx, too, before you could have struck him—eh? . . . Did you think of that, there in the dark? . . . No, not precisely a pleasant situation. A bit gruesome, in fact."

"What are you raving about?" Skeel spat out insolently. "You're balmy." But his swagger had been forgotten, and a look akin to horror had passed across his face. This slackening of pose was momentary, however; almost at once his smirk returned, and his head swayed in contempt.

Vance sauntered back to his chair and stretched himself in it listlessly, as if all his interest in the case had again evaporated.

Markham had watched the little drama attentively, but Heath had sat smoking with ill-concealed annoyance. The silence that followed was broken by Skeel.

"Well, I suppose I'm to be railroaded. Got it all planned, have you? . . . Try and railroad me!" He laughed harshly. "My lawyer's Abe Rubin, and you might phone him that I'd like to see him."*

Markham, with a gesture of annoyance, waved to the deputy sheriff to take Skeel back to the Tombs.

"What were you trying to get at?" he asked Vance when the man was gone.

"Just an elusive notion in the depths of my being struggling for the light."Vance smoked placidly a moment. "I thought Mr. Skeel might be persuaded to pour out his heart to us. So I wooed him with words."

"That's just bully," gibed Heath. "I was expecting you any minute to ask him if he played mumbly-peg or if his grandmother was a hoot owl."

"Sergeant, dear Sergeant," pleaded Vance, "don't be unkind. I sim-

---

* Abe Rubin was at that time the most resourceful and unscrupulous criminal lawyer in New York. Since his disbarment two years ago, little has been heard from him.

ply couldn't endure it. . . . And really, now, didn't my chat with Mr. Skeel suggest a possibility to you?"

"Sure," said Heath, "that he was hiding in the closet when Odell was killed. But where does that get us? It lets Skeel out, although the job was a professional one, and he was caught red-handed with some of the swag."

He turned disgustedly to the district attorney.

"And now what, sir?"

"I don't like the look of things," Markham complained. "If Skeel has Abe Rubin to defend him, we won't stand a chance with the case we've got. I feel convinced he was mixed up in it; but no judge will accept my personal feelings as evidence."

"We could turn the Dude loose and have him tailed," suggested Heath grudgingly. "We might catch him doing something that'll give the game away."

Markham considered.

"That might be a good plan," he acceded. "We'll certainly get no more evidence on him as long as he's locked up."

"It looks like our only chance, sir."

"Very well," agreed Markham. "Let him think we're through with him; he may get careless. I'll leave the whole thing to you, Sergeant. Keep a couple of good men on him day and night. Something may happen."

Heath rose, an unhappy man. "Right, sir. I'll attend to it."

"And I'd like to have more data on Charles Cleaver," added Markham. "Find out what you can of his relations with the Odell girl. Also, get me a line on Doctor Ambroise Lindquist. What's his history? What are his habits? You know the kind of thing. He treated the girl for some mysterious or imaginary ailment; and I think he has something up his sleeve. But don't go near him personally—yet."

Heath jotted the name down in his notebook, without enthusiasm.

"And before you set your stylish captive free," put in Vance, yawning, "you might, don't y'know, see if he carries a key that fits the Odell apartment."

Heath jerked up short and grinned. "Now, that idea's got some sense to it. . . . Funny I didn't think of it myself." And, shaking hands with all of us, he went out.

CHAPTER 13

An Erstwhile Gallant
Wednesday, September 12; 10:30 a.m.

Swacker was evidently waiting for an opportunity to interrupt, for, when Sergeant Heath had passed through the door, he at once stepped into the room.

"The reporters are here, sir," he announced, with a wry face. "You said you'd see them at ten thirty."

In response to a nod from his chief, he held open the door, and a dozen or more newspaper men came trooping in.

"No questions, please, this morning," Markham begged pleasantly. "It's too early in the game. But I'll tell you all I know. . . . I agree with Sergeant Heath that the Odell murder was the work of a professional criminal—the same who broke into Arnheim's house on Park Avenue last summer."

Briefly he told of Inspector Brenner's findings in connection with the chisel. "We've made no arrest, but one may be expected in the very near future. In fact, the police have the case well in hand but are going carefully in order to avoid any chance of an acquittal. We've already recovered some of the missing jewellery. . . ."

He talked to the reporters for five minutes or so, but he made no mention of the testimony of the maid or the phone operators, and carefully avoided the mention of any names.

When we were again alone, Vance chuckled admiringly.

"A masterly evasion, my dear Markham! Legal training has its advantages—decidedly it has its advantages. . . . 'We've recovered some of the missing jewellery!' Sweet winged words! Not an untruth—oh, no!—but how deceivin'! Really, y'know, I must devote more time to the caressin' art of *suggestio falsi* and *suppressio veri*. You should be crowned with an *anadem* of myrtle."

"Leaving all that to one side," Markham rejoined impatiently, "suppose you tell me, now that Heath's gone, what was in your mind when you applied your verbal voodooism to Skeel. What was all the conjurer-talk about dark closets, and alarums, and pressing thumbs, and peering through keyholes?"

"Well, now, I didn't think my little chit-chat was so cryptic," answered Vance. "The *recherché* Tony was undoubtedly ambuscaded *à la sourdine* in the clothes press at some time during the fatal evening; and I was merely striving, in my amateurish way, to ascertain the exact hour of his concealment."

"And did you?"

"Not conclusively." Vance shook his head sadly. "Y'know, Markham, I'm the proud possessor of a theory—it's vague and obscure and unsubstantial; and it's downright unintelligible. And even if it were verified, I can't see how it would help us any, for it would leave the situation even more incomprehensible than it already is. . . . I almost wish I hadn't questioned Heath's Beau Nash. He upset my ideas frightfully."

"From what I could gather, you seem to think it possible that Skeel witnessed the murder. That couldn't, by any stretch of the imagination, be your precious theory?"

"That's part of it, anyway."

"My dear Vance, you do astonish me!" Markham laughed outright. "Skeel, then, according to you, is innocent; but he keeps his knowledge to himself, invents an alibi, and doesn't even tattle when he's arrested. . . . It won't hold water."

"I know," sighed Vance. "It's a veritable sieve. And yet, the notion haunts me—it rides me like a hag—it eats into my vitals."

"Do you realize that this mad theory of yours presupposes that, when Spotswoode and Miss Odell returned from the theatre, there were *two* men hidden in the apartment—two men *unknown to each other*—namely Skeel and your hypothetical murderer?"

"Of course I realize it; and the thought of it is breaking down my reason."

"Furthermore, they must have entered the apartment separately and hidden separately. . . . How, may I ask, did they get in? And how did they get out? And which one caused the girl to scream after Spotswoode had left? And what was the other one doing in the meantime? And if Skeel was a passive spectator, horrified and mute, how do you account for his breaking open the jewel case and securing the ring—?"

"Stop! Stop! Don't torture me so," Vance pleaded. "I know I'm insane. Been given to hallucinations since birth; but—Merciful Heaven!—I've never before had one as crazy as this."

"On that point at least, my dear Vance, we are in complete and harmonious agreement," smiled Markham.

Just then Swacker came in and handed Markham a letter.

"Brought by messenger, and marked 'immediate,'" he explained.

The letter, written on heavy engraved stationery, was from Doctor Lindquist, and explained that between the hours of 11 p.m. and 1 a.m. on Monday night he had been in attendance on a patient at his sanatorium. It also apologized for his actions when asked regarding his whereabouts, and offered a wordy, but not particularly convincing, explanation of his conduct. He had had an unusually trying day, it seemed—neurotic cases were trying, at best—and the suddenness of our visit, together with the apparently hostile nature of Markham's questions, had completely upset him. He was more than sorry for his outburst, he said, and stood ready to assist in any way he could. It was unfortunate for all concerned, he added, that he had lost his temper, for it would have been a simple matter for him to explain about Monday night.

"He has thought the situation over calmly," said Vance, "and hereby offers you a neat little alibi which, I think, you will have difficulty in shaking. . . . An artful beggar—like all these unbalanced pseudo-psychiatrists. Observe: he was with a patient. To be sure! What patient? Why, one too ill to be questioned. . . . There you are. A cul-de-sac masquerading as an alibi. Not bad, what?"

"It doesn't interest me overmuch." Markham put the letter away. "That pompous professional ass could never have got into the Odell apartment without having been seen; and I can't picture him sneaking in by devious means." He reached for some papers. . . . "And now, if you don't object, I'll make an effort to earn my $15,000 salary."

But Vance, instead of making a move to go, sauntered to the table and opened a telephone directory.

"Permit me a suggestion, Markham," he said, after a moment's search. "Put off your daily grind for a bit, and let's hold polite converse with Mr. Louis Mannix. Y'know, he's the only presumptive swain of the inconstant Margaret, so far mentioned, who hasn't been given an audience. I hanker to gaze upon him and hearken to his rune. He'd make the family circle complete, so to speak. . . . He still holds forth in Maiden Lane, I see; and it wouldn't take long to fetch him here."

Markham had swung half round in his chair at the mention of

Mannix's name. He started to protest, but he knew from experience that Vance's suggestions were not the results of idle whims; and he was silent for several moments weighing the matter. With practically every other avenue of inquiry closed for the moment, I think the idea of questioning Mannix rather appealed to him.

"All right," he consented, ringing for Swacker; "though I don't see how he can help. According to Heath, the Odell girl gave him his *congé* a year ago."

"He may still have hay on his horns, or, like Hotspur, be drunk with choler. You can't tell." Vance resumed his chair. "With such a name, he'd bear investigation *ipso facto*."

Markham sent Swacker for Tracy; and when the latter arrived, suave and beaming, he was given instructions to take the district attorney's car and bring Mannix to the office.

"Get a subpoena," said Markham; "and use it if necessary."

Half an hour or so later Tracy returned.

"Mr. Mannix made no difficulty about coming," he reported. "Was quite agreeable, in fact. He's in the waiting room now."

Tracy was dismissed, and Mannix was ushered in.

He was a large man, and he walked with the forced elasticity of gait which epitomizes the silent struggle of incipiently corpulent middle age to deny the onrush of the years and cling to the semblance of youth. He carried a slender *wanghee* cane; and his chequered suit, brocaded waistcoat, pearl-gray gaiters, and gaily beribboned Homburg hat gave him an almost foppish appearance. But these various indications of sportiveness were at once forgotten when one inspected his features. His small eyes were bright and crafty; his nose was *bibative*, and appeared disproportionately small above his thick, sensual lips and *prognathous* jaw. There was an oiliness and shrewdness in the man's manner which were at once repulsive and arresting.

At a gesture from Markham he sat down on the edge of a chair, placing a podgy hand on each knee. His attitude was one of alert suspicion.

"Mr. Mannix," said Markham, an engaging note of apology in his voice, "I am sorry to have discommoded you; but the matter in hand is both serious and urgent. . . . A Miss Margaret Odell was murdered night before last, and in the course of inquiries we learned that you had at one time known her quite well. It occurred to me that you might be in possession of some facts about her that would assist us in our investigation."

A saponaceous smile, meant to be genial, parted the man's heavy lips.

"Sure, I knew the Canary—a long time ago, y' understand." He permitted himself a sigh. "A fine, high-class girl, if I do say so. A good looker and a good dresser. Too damn bad she didn't go on with the show business. But"—he made a repudiative motion with his hand—"I haven't seen the lady, y' understand, for over a year—not to speak to, if you know what I mean."

Mannix clearly was on his guard, and his beady little eyes did not once leave the district attorney's face.

"You had a quarrel with her perhaps?" Markham asked the question incuriously.

"Well, now, I wouldn't go so far as to say we quarrelled. No." Mannix paused, seeking the correct word. "You might say we disagreed—got tired of the arrangement and decided to separate; kind of drifted apart. Last thing I told her was, if she ever needed a friend, she'd know where to find me."

"Very generous of you," murmured Markham. "And you never renewed your little affair?"

"Never—never. Don't remember ever speaking to her from that day to this."

"In view of certain things I've learned, Mr. Mannix"—Markham's tone was regretful—"I must ask you a somewhat personal question. Did she ever make an attempt to blackmail you?"

Mannix hesitated, and his eyes seemed to grow even smaller, like those of a man thinking rapidly.

"Certainly not!" he replied, with belated emphasis. "Not at all. Nothing of the kind." He raised both hands in protest against the thought. Then he asked furtively: "What gave you such an idea?"

"I have been told," explained Markham, "that she had extorted money from one or two of her admirers."

Mannix made a wholly unconvincing grimace of astonishment. "Well well! You don't tell me! Can it be possible?" He peered shrewdly at the district attorney. "Maybe it was Charlie Cleaver she blackmailed—yes?"

Markham picked him up quickly.

"Why do you say Cleaver?"

Again Mannix waved his thick hand, this time deprecatingly.

"No special reason, y' understand. Just thought it might be him. . . . No special reason."

"Did Cleaver ever tell you he'd been blackmailed?"

"Cleaver tell me? . . . Now, I ask you, Mr. Markham: why should Cleaver tell me such a story—why should he?"

"And you never told Cleaver that the Odell girl had blackmailed you?"

"Positively not!" Mannix gave a scornful laugh which was far too theatrical to have been genuine. "Me tell Cleaver I'd been black-mailed? Now, that's funny, that is."

"Then, why did you mention Cleaver a moment ago?"

"No reason at all—like I told you. . . . He knew the Canary; but that ain't no secret."

Markham dropped the subject. "What do you know about Miss Odell's relations with a Doctor Ambroise Lindquist?"

Mannix was now obviously perplexed. "Never heard of him—no, never. She didn't know him when I was taking her around."

"Whom else besides Cleaver did she know well?"

Mannix shook his head ponderously.

"Now, that I couldn't say—positively I couldn't say. Seen her with this man and that, same as everybody saw her; but who they were I don't know—absolutely."

"Ever hear of Tony Skeel?" Markham quickly leaned over and met the other's gaze inquiringly.

Once more Mannix hesitated, and his eyes glittered calculatingly. "Well, now that you ask me, I believe I did hear of the fellow. But I couldn't swear to it, y' understand. . . . What makes you think I heard of this Skeel fellow?"

Markham ignored the question.

"Can you think of no one who might have borne Miss Odell a grudge, or had cause to fear her?" Mannix was volubly emphatic on the subject of his complete ignorance of any such person; and after a few more questions, which elicited only denials, Markham let him go.

"Not bad at all, Markham old thing—eh, what?" Vance seemed pleased with the conference. "Wonder why he's so coy? Not a nice person, this Mannix. And he's so fearful lest he be informative. Again, I wonder why. He was so careful—oh, so careful."

"He was sufficiently careful, at any rate, not to tell us anything," declared Markham gloomily.

"I shouldn't say that, don't y'know." Vance lay back and smoked placidly. "A ray of light filtered through here and there. Our fur-im-porting philogynist denied he'd been blackmailed—which was obvi-ously untrue—and tried to make us believe that he and the lovely Margaret cooed like turtledoves at parting—Tosh! . . . And then, that mention of Cleaver. That wasn't spontaneous—dear me, no. Brother Mannix and spontaneity are as the poles apart. He had a reason for

327

bringing Cleaver in; and I fancy that if you knew what that reason was, you'd feel like flinging roses riotously, and that sort of thing. Why Cleaver? That *secret-de-Polichinelle* explanation was a bit weak. The orbits of these two paramours cross somewhere. On that point, at least, Mannix inadvertently enlightened us. . . . Moreover, it's plain that he doesn't know our fashionable healer with the satyr ears. But, on the other hand, he's aware of the existence of Mr. Skeel, and would rather like to deny the acquaintance. . . . So—*voilà l'affaire*. Plenty of information; but—my word!—what to do with it?"

"I give it up," acknowledged Markham hopelessly.

"I know; it's a sad sad world," Vance commiserated him. "But you must face the *olla podrida* with a bright eye. It's time for lunch, and a fillet of sole Marguéry will cheer you no end."

Markham glanced at the clock and permitted himself to be led to the Lawyers Club.

CHAPTER 14

Vance Outlines a Theory
Wednesday, September 12; evening

Vance and I did not return to the district attorney's office after lunch, for Markham had a busy afternoon before him, and nothing further was likely to transpire in connection with the Odell case until Sergeant Heath had completed his investigations of Cleaver and Doctor Lindquist. Vance had seats for Giordano's Madame Sans-Gêne, and two o'clock found us at the Metropolitan. Though the performance was excellent, Vance was too distrait to enjoy it; and it was significant that, after the opera, he directed the chauffeur to the Stuyvesant Club. I knew he had a tea appointment, and that he had planned to motor to Longue Vue for dinner; and the fact that he should have dismissed these social engagements from his mind in order to be with Markham showed how intensely the problem of the murder had absorbed his interest.

It was after six o'clock when Markham came in, looking harassed and tired. No mention of the case was made during dinner, with the exception of Markham's casual remark that Heath had turned in his reports on Cleaver and doctor Lindquist and Mannix. (It seemed that, immediately after lunch, he had telephoned to the sergeant to add Mannix's name to the two others as a subject for inquiry.) It was not until we had retired to our favourite corner of the lounge room that the topic of the murder was brought up for discussion.

And that discussion, brief and one-sided, was the beginning of an entirely new line of investigation—a line which, in the end, led to the guilty person.

Markham sank wearily into his chair. He had begun to show the strain of the last two days of fruitless worry. His eyes were a trifle heavy, and there was a grim tenacity in the lines of his mouth. Slowly and deliberately he lighted a cigar, and took several deep inhalations.

"Damn the newspapers!" he grumbled. "Why can't they let the district attorney's office handle its business in its own way? . . . Have you seen the afternoon papers? They're all clamouring for the murderer. You'd think I had him up my sleeve."

"You forget, my dear chap," grinned Vance, "that we are living under the benign and upliftin' reign of Democritus, which confers upon every ignoramus the privilege of promiscuously criticising his betters."

Markham snorted. "I don't complain about criticism; it's the lurid imagination of these bright young reporters that galls me. They're trying to turn this sordid crime into a spectacular Borgia melo-drama, with passion running rampant, and mysterious influences at work, and all the pomp and trappings of a medieval romance. . . . You'd think even a schoolboy could see that it was only an ordi-nary robbery and murder of the kind that's taking place regularly throughout the country."

Vance paused in the act of lighting a cigarette, and his eyebrows lifted. Turning, he regarded Markham with a look of mild incredulity. "I say! Do you really mean to tell me that your statement for the press was given out in good faith?"

Markham looked up in surprise. "Certainly it was. . . . What do you mean by 'good faith'?"

Vance smiled indolently. "I rather thought, don't y'know, that your oration to the reporters was a bit of strategy to lull the real culprit into a state of false security, and to give you a clear field for investigation."

Markham contemplated him a moment.

"See here, Vance," he demanded irritably, "what are you driving at?"

"Nothing at all—really, old fellow," the other assured him affably. "I knew that Heath was deadly sincere about his belief in Skeel's guilt, but it never occurred to me, d'ye see, that you yourself actually regarded the crime as one committed by a professional burglar. I foolishly thought that you let Skeel go this morning in the hope that he would lead you somehow to the guilty person. I rather imagined you were spoofing the trusting sergeant by pretending to fall in with his silly notion."

"Ah, I see! Still clinging to your weird theory that a brace of vil-lains were present, hiding in separate clothes closets, or something of the kind." Markham made no attempt to temper his sarcasm. "A sapi-ent idea—so much more intelligent that Heath's!"

"I know it's weird. But it happens not to be any weirder than your theory of a lone yeggman."

"And for what reason, pray," persisted Markham, with considerable warmth, "do you consider the yeggman theory weird?"

"For the simple reason that it was not the crime of a professional thief at all, but the wilfully deceptive act of a particularly clever man who doubtless spent weeks in its preparation."

Markham sank back in his chair and laughed heartily. "Vance, you have contributed the one ray of sunshine to an otherwise gloomy and depressing case."

Vance bowed with mock humility.

"It gives me great pleasure," was his dulcet rejoinder, "to be able to bring even a wisp of light into so clouded a mental atmosphere."

A brief silence followed. Then Markham asked, "Is this fascinating and picturesque conclusion of yours regarding the highly intellectual character of the Odell woman's murderer based on your new and original psychological methods of deduction?" There was no mistaking the ridicule in his voice.

"I arrived at it," explained Vance sweetly, "by the same process of logic I used in determining the guilt of Alvin Benson's murderer."

Markham smiled. "*Touché!* . . . Don't think I'm so ungrateful as to belittle the work you did in that case. But this time, I fear, you've permitted your theories to lead you hopelessly astray. The present case is what the police call an open-and-shut affair."

"Particularly shut," amended Vance dryly. "And both you and the police are in the distressin' situation of waiting inactively for your suspected victim to give the game away."

"I'll admit the situation is not all one could desire." Markham spoke morosely. "But even so, I can't see that there's any opportunity in this affair for your recondite psychological methods. The thing's too obvious—that's the trouble. What we need now is evidence, not theories. If it wasn't for the spacious and romantic imaginings of the newspaper men, public interest in the case would already have died out."

"Markham," said Vance quietly, but with unwonted seriousness, "if that's what you really believe, then you may as well drop the case now; for you're foredoomed to failure. You think it's an obvious crime. But let me tell you, it's a subtle crime, if ever there was one. And it's as clever as it is subtle. No common criminal committed it—believe me. It was done by a man of very superior intellect and astoundin' ingenuity."

Vance's assured, matter-of-fact tone had a curiously convincing quality; and Markham, restraining his impulse to scoff, assumed an air of indulgent irony.

"Tell me," he said, "by what cryptic mental process you arrived at so fantastic a conclusion."

"With pleasure." Vance took a few puffs on his cigarette and lazily watched the smoke curl upward.*

"Y'know, Markham," he began, in his emotionless drawl, "every genuine work of art has a quality which the critics call élan—namely, enthusiasm and spontaneity. A copy, or imitation, lacks that distinguishing characteristic; it's too perfect, too carefully done, too exact. Even enlightened scions of the law, I fancy, are aware that there is bad drawing in Botticelli and disproportions in Rubens, what? In an original, d'ye see, such flaws don't matter. But an imitator never puts 'em in: he doesn't dare—he's too intent on getting all the details correct. The imitator works with a self-consciousness and a meticulous care which the artist, in the throes of creative labour, never exhibits. And here's the point: there's no way of imitating that enthusiasm and spontaneity—that élan—which an original painting possesses. However closely a copy may resemble an original, there's a vast psychological difference between them. The copy breathes an air of insincerity, of ultra-perfection, of conscious effort. . . . You follow me, eh?"

"Most instructive, my dear Ruskin."

Vance meekly bowed his appreciation, and proceeded pleasantly. "Now, let us consider the Odell murder. You and Heath are agreed that it is a commonplace, brutal, sordid, unimaginative crime. But, unlike you two bloodhounds on the trail, I have ignored its mere appearances and have analyzed its various factors—I have looked at it psychologically, so to speak. And I have discovered that it is not a genuine and sincere crime—that is to say, an original—but only a sophisticated, self-conscious and clever imitation, done by a skilled copyist. I grant you it is correct and typical in every detail. But just there is where it fails, don't y'know. Its technic is too good, its craftsmanship too perfect. The ensemble, as it were, is not convincing—it lacks élan. Aesthetically speaking, it has all the earmarks of a *tour de force*. Vulgarly speaking, it's a fake." He paused and gave Markham an engaging smile. "I trust this somewhat oracular peroration has not bored you."

"Pray continue," urged Markham, with exaggerated politeness. His manner was jocular, but something in his tone led me to believe that he was seriously interested.

"What is true of art is true of life," Vance resumed placidly. "Every human action, d'ye see, conveys unconsciously an impression either of

---

* I sent a proof of the following paragraphs to Vance, and he edited and corrected them; so that, as they now stand, they represent his theories in practically his own words.

genuineness or of spuriousness—of sincerity or calculation. For example, two men at table eat in a similar way, handle their knives and forks in the same fashion, and apparently do the identical things. Although the sensitive spectator cannot put his finger on the points of difference, he nonetheless senses at once which man's breeding is genuine and instinctive and which man's is imitative and self-conscious."

He blew a wreath of smoke toward the ceiling and settled more deeply into his chair.

"Now, Markham, just what are the universally recognized features of a sordid crime of robbery and murder? . . . Brutality, disorder, haste, ransacked drawers, cluttered desks, broken jewel cases, rings stripped from the victim's fingers, severed pendant chains, torn clothing, tipped-over chairs, upset lamps, broken vases, twisted draperies, strewn floors, and so forth. Such are the accepted immemorial indications—eh, what? But—consider a moment, old chap. Outside of fiction and the drama, in how many crimes do they *all* appear—all in perfect ordination, and without a single element to contradict the general effect? That is to say, how many actual crimes are technically perfect in their settings? . . . None! And why? Simply because nothing actual in this life—nothing that is spontaneous and genuine—runs to accepted form in every detail. The law of chance and fallibility invariably steps in."

He made a slight indicative gesture.

"But regard this particular crime: look at it closely. What do you find? You will perceive that its *mise en scène* has been staged, and its drama enacted, down to every minute detail—like a Zola novel. It is almost mathematically perfect. And therein, d'ye see, lies the irresistible inference of its having been carefully premeditated and planned. To use an art term, it is a tickled-up crime. Therefore, its conception was not spontaneous. . . . And yet, don't y'know, I can't point out any specific flaw; for its great flaw lies in its being flawless. And nothing flawless, my dear fellow, is natural or genuine."

Markham was silent for a while.

"You deny even the remote possibility of a common thief having murdered the girl?" he asked at length; and now there was no hint of sarcasm in his voice.

"If a common thief did it," contended Vance, "then there's no science of psychology, there are no philosophic truths, and there are no laws of art. If it was a genuine crime of robbery, then, by the same token, there is no difference whatever between an old master and a clever technician's copy."

"You'd entirely eliminate robbery as the motive, I take it."

"The robbery," Vance affirmed, "was only a manufactured detail. The fact that the crime was committed by a highly astute person indicates unquestionably that there was a far more potent motive behind it. Any man capable of so ingenious and clever a piece of deception is obviously a person of education and imagination; and he most certainly would not have run the stupendous risk of killing a woman unless he had feared some overwhelming disaster—unless, indeed, her continuing to live would have caused him greater mental anguish, and would have put him in greater jeopardy, even than the crime itself. Between two colossal dangers, he chose the murder as the lesser."

Markham did not speak at once; he seemed lost in reflection. But presently he turned and, fixing Vance with a dubious stare, said, "What about that chiselled jewel box? A professional burglar's jimmy wielded by an experienced hand doesn't fit into your aesthetic hypothesis—it is, in fact, diametrically opposed to such a theory."

"I know it only too well." Vance nodded slowly. "And I've been harried and hectored by that steel chisel ever since I beheld the evidence of its work that first morning. . . . Markham, that chisel is the one genuine note in an otherwise spurious performance. It's as if the real artist had come along at the moment the copyist had finished his faked picture, and painted in a single small object with the hand of a master."

"But doesn't that bring us back inevitably to Skeel?"

"Skeel—ah, yes. That's the explanation, no doubt; but not the way you conceive it. Skeel ripped the box open—I don't question that; but—deuce take it!—it's the only thing he did do; it's the only thing that was left for him to do. That's why he got only a ring which La Belle Marguerite was not wearing that night. All her other baubles—to wit, those that adorned her—had been stripped from her and were gone."

"Why are you so positive on this point?"

"The poker, man—the poker! . . . Don't you see? That amateurish assault upon the jewel case with a cast iron coal prodder couldn't have been made *after* the case had been prized open—it would have had to be made *before*. And that seemingly insane attempt to break steel with cast iron was part of the stage setting. The real culprit didn't care if he got the case open or not. He merely wanted it to look as if he had *tried* to get it open; so he used the poker and then left it lying beside the dented box."

"I see what you mean." This point, I think, impressed Markham more strongly than any other Vance had raised; for the presence of the poker on the dressing table had not been explained away either by Heath or Inspector Brenner. . . . "Is that the reason you questioned Skeel as if he might have been present when your other visitor was there?"

"Exactly. By the evidence of the jewel case I knew he either was in the apartment when the bogus crime of robbery was being staged, or else had come upon the scene when it was over and the stage director had cleared out. . . . From his reactions to my questions I rather fancy he was present."

"Hiding in the closet?"

"Yes. That would account for the closet not having been disturbed. As I see it, it wasn't ransacked, for the simple and rather grotesque reason that the elegant Skeel was locked within. How else could that one clothes press have escaped the rifling activities of the pseudo-burglar? He wouldn't have omitted it deliberately, and he was far too thoroughgoing to have overlooked it accidentally. Then there are the fingerprints on the knob. . . ."

Vance lightly tapped on the arm of his chair.

"I tell you, Markham old dear, you simply must build your conception of the crime on this hypothesis and proceed accordingly. If you don't, each edifice you rear will come toppling about your ears."

CHAPTER 15

Four Possibilities

Wednesday, September 12; evening

When Vance finished speaking, there was a long silence. Markham, impressed by the other's earnestness, sat in a brown study. His ideas had been shaken. The theory of Skeel's guilt, to which he had clung from the moment of the identification of the fingerprints, had, it must be admitted, not entirely satisfied him, although he had been able to suggest no alternative. Now Vance had categorically repudiated this theory and at the same time had advanced another which, despite its indefiniteness, had nevertheless taken into account all the physical points of the case; and Markham, at first antagonistic, had found himself, almost against his will, becoming more and more sympathetic to this new point of view.

"Damn it, Vance!" he said. "I'm not in the least convinced by your theatrical theory. And yet, I feel a curious undercurrent of plausibility in your analyses. . . . I wonder—"

He turned sharply, and scrutinized the other steadfastly for a moment.

"Look here! Have you anyone in mind as the protagonist of the drama you've outlined?"

"'Pon my word, I haven't the slightest notion as to who killed the lady," Vance assured him. "But if you are ever to find the murderer, you must look for a shrewd, superior man with nerves of iron, who was in imminent danger of being irremediably ruined by the girl—a man of inherent cruelty and vindictiveness; a supreme egoist; a fatalist more or less; and, I'm inclined to believe, something of a madman."

"Mad!"

"Oh, not a lunatic, just a madman, a perfectly normal, logical, calculating madman—same as you and I and Van here. Only, our hobbies are harmless, d'ye see. This chap's mania is outside your preposterously revered law. That's why you're after him. If his aberration were stamp collecting or golf, you wouldn't give him a second thought. But his perfectly rational penchant for eliminating *déclassées* ladies who bothered him fills you with horror; it's not *your* hobby. Consequently, you have a hot yearning to flay him alive."

"I'll admit," said Markham coolly, "that a homicidal mania is my idea of madness."

"But he didn't have a homicidal mania, Markham old thing. You miss all the fine distinctions in psychology. This man was annoyed by a certain person, and set to work, masterfully and reasonably, to do away with the source of his annoyance. And he did it with surpassin' cleverness. To be sure, his act was a bit grisly. But when, if ever, you get your hands on him, you'll be amazed to find how normal he is. And able, too—oh, able no end."

Again Markham lapsed into a long, thoughtful silence. At last he spoke.

"The only trouble with your ingenious deductions is that they don't accord with the known circumstances of the case. And facts, my dear Vance, are still regarded by a few of us old-fashioned lawyers as more or less conclusive."

"Why this needless confession of your shortcomings?" inquired Vance whimsically. Then, after a moment: "Let me have the facts which appear to you antagonistic to my deductions."

"Well, there are only four men of the type you describe who could have had any remote reason for murdering the Odell woman. Heath's scouts went into her history pretty thoroughly, and for over two years—that is, since her appearance in the 'Follies'—the only *personae gratae* at her apartment have been Mannix, Doctor Lindquist, Pop Cleaver, and, of course, Spotswoode. The Canary was a bit exclusive, it seems; and no other man got near enough to her even to be considered as a possible murderer."

"It appears, then, that you have a complete quartet to draw on." Vance's tone was apathetic. "What do you crave—a regiment?"

"No," answered Markham patiently. "I crave only one logical possibility. But Mannix was through with the girl over a year ago; Cleaver and Spotswoode both have watertight alibis; and that leaves only Doctor Lindquist, whom I can't exactly picture as a strangler and meretricious burglar, despite his irascibility. Moreover, he, too, has an alibi; and it may be a genuine one."

Vance wagged his head. "There's something positively pathetic about the childlike faith of the legal mind."

"It does cling to rationality at times, doesn't it?" observed Markham.

"My dear fellow!" Vance rebuked him. "The presumption implied in that remark is most immodest. If you could distinguish between rationality and irrationality you wouldn't be a lawyer—you'd be a god. . . . No; you're going at this thing the wrong way. The real factors in the case are not what you call the known circumstances, but the unknown quantities—the human X's, so to speak—the personalities, or natures, of your quartet."

He lit a fresh cigarette, and lay back, closing his eyes.

"Tell me what you know of these four *cavalieri serventi*—you say Heath has turned in his report. Who were their mamas? What do they eat for breakfast? Are they susceptible to poison ivy? . . . Let's have Spotswoode's dossier first. Do you know anything about him?"

"In a general way," returned Markham. "Old Puritan stock, I believe—governors, burgomasters, a few successful traders. All Yankee forebears—no intermixture. As a matter of fact, Spotswoode represents the oldest and hardiest of the New England aristocracy—although I imagine the so-called wine of the Puritans has become pretty well diluted by now. His affair with the Odell girl is hardly consonant with the older Puritans' mortification of the flesh."

"It's wholly consonant, though, with the psychological reactions which are apt to follow the inhibitions produced by such mortification," submitted Vance. "But what does he do? Whence cometh his lucre?"

"His father manufactured automobile accessories, made a fortune at it, and left the business to him. He tinkers at it, but not seriously, though I believe he has designed a few appurtenances."

"I do hope the hideous cut-glass olla for holding paper bouquets is not one of them. The man who invented that tonneau decoration is capable of any fiendish crime."

"It couldn't have been Spotswoode, then," said Markham tolerantly, "for he certainly can't qualify as your potential strangler. We know the girl was alive after he left her, and that, during the time she was murdered, he was with Judge Redfern. . . . Even you, friend Vance, couldn't manipulate those facts to the gentleman's disadvantage."

"On that, at least, we agree," conceded Vance. "And that's all you know of the gentleman?"

"I think that's all, except that he married a well-to-do woman—a daughter of a Southern senator, I believe."

"Doesn't help any. . . . And now, let's have Mannix's history."

Markham referred to a typewritten sheet of paper.

"Both parents immigrants—came over in the steerage. Original

338

name Mannikiewicz, or something like that. Born on the East Side; learned the fur business in his father's retail shop in Hester Street; worked for the Sanfrasco Cloak Company and got to be factory foreman. Saved his money and sweetened the pot by manipulating real estate; then went into the fur business for himself and steadily worked up to his present opulent state. Public school and night commercial college. Married in 1900 and divorced a year later. Lives a gay life—helps support the nightclubs, but never gets drunk. I suppose he comes under the head of a spender and wine opener. Has invested some money in musical comedies and always has a stage beauty in tow. Runs to blondes."

"Not very revealin'," sighed Vance. "The city is full of Mannixes. . . . What did you garner in connection with our *bon-ton* medico?"

"The city has its quota of Doctor Lindquists, too, I fear. He was brought up in a small Middle-West bailiwick—French and Magyar extraction; took his M.D. from the Ohio State Medical, practiced in Chicago—some shady business there, but never convicted; came to Albany and got in on the X-ray-machine craze; invented a breast pump and formed a stock company—made a small fortune out of it; went to Vienna for two years—"

"Ah, the Freudian motif!"

"—returned to New York and opened a private sanatorium; charged outrageous prices and thereby endeared himself to the nouveau riche. Has been at the endearing process ever since. Was defendant in a breach-of-promise suite some years ago, but the case was settled out of court. He's not married."

"He wouldn't be," commented Vance. "Such gentry never are. . . . Interestin' summary, though—yes, decidedly interestin'. I'm tempted to develop a psychoneurosis and let Ambroise treat me. I do so want to know him better. And where—oh, where—was this egregious healer at the moment of our erring sister's demise? Ah, who can tell, my Markham; who knows—who knows?"

"In any event, I don't think he was murdering anyone."

"You're so prejudicial!" said Vance. "But let us move reluctantly on. What's your *portrait parlé* of Cleaver? The fact that he's familiarly called Pop is helpful as a starter. You simply couldn't imagine Beethoven being called Shorty, or Bismarck being referred to as Snookums."

"Cleaver has been a politician all of his life—a Tammany Hall 'regular.' Was a ward boss at twenty-five; ran a Democratic club of some kind in Brooklyn for a time; was an alderman for two terms and practiced general law. Was appointed Tax Commissioner; left politics and raised a small racing stable. Later secured an illegal gambling concession at Saratoga; and now operates a poolroom in Jersey City. He's what you might call a professional sport. Loves his liquor."

"No marriages?"

"None on the records. But see here: Cleaver's out of it. He was ticketed in Boonton that night at half past eleven."

"Is that, by any chance, the watertight alibi you mentioned a moment ago?"

"In any primitive legal way I considered it as such." Markham resented Vance's question. "The summons was handed him at half past eleven; it's so marked and dated. And Boonton is fifty miles from here—a good two hours' motor ride. Therefore, Cleaver unquestionably left New York about half past nine; and even if he'd driven directly back, he couldn't have reached here until long after the time the medical examiner declared the girl was dead. As a matter of routine, I investigated the summons and even spoke by phone to the officer who issued it. It was genuine enough—I ought to know: I had it quashed."

"Did this Boonton Dogberry know Cleaver by sight?"

"No, but he gave me an accurate description of him. And naturally he took the car's number."

Vance looked at Markham with open-eyed sorrow.

"My dear Markham—my very dear Markham—can't you see that all you've actually proved is that a bucolic traffic Nemesis handed a speed-violation summons to a smooth-faced, middle-aged, stout man who was driving Cleaver's car near Boonton at half past eleven on the night of the murder? . . . And, my word! Isn't that exactly the sort of alibi the old boy would arrange if he intended taking the lady's life at midnight or thereabouts?"

"Come, come!" laughed Markham. "That's a bit too far-fetched. You'd give every lawbreaker credit for concocting schemes of the most diabolical cunning."

"So I would," admitted Vance apathetically. "And—d'ye know?—rather fancy that's just the kind of schemes a lawbreaker would concoct, if he was planning a murder, and his own life was at stake. What really amazes me is the naïve assumption of you investigators that a murderer gives no intelligent thought whatever to his future safety. It's rather touchin', y'know."

Markham grunted. "Well, you can take it from me, it was Cleaver himself who got the summons."

"I dare say you're right," Vance conceded. "I merely suggested the possibility of deception, don't y'know. The only point I really insist on is that the fascinatin' Miss Odell was killed by a man of subtle and superior mentality."

"And I, in turn," irritably rejoined Markham, "insist that the only men of that type who touched her life intimately enough to have had any reason to do it are Mannix, Cleaver, Lindquist, and Spotswoode. And I further insist that not one of them can be regarded as a promising possibility."

"I fear I must contradict you, old dear," said Vance serenely. "They're all possibilities—and one of them is guilty."

Markham glared at him derisively.

"Well, well! So the case is settled! Now, if you'll but indicate which is the guilty one, I'll arrest him at once and return to my other duties."

"You're always in such haste," Vance lamented. "Why leap and run? The wisdom of the world's philosophers is against it. *Festina lente*, says Caesar; or, as Rufus has it, *Festinatio tarda est*. And the Koran says quite frankly that haste is of the Devil. Shakespeare was constantly belittling speed: 'He tires betimes that spurs too fast betimes'; and, 'Wisely, and slow; they stumble that run fast.' Then there was Molière—remember Sganarelle?—: *'Le trop de promptitude à l'erreur nous expose.'* Chaucer also held similar views. 'He hasteth wel,' said he, 'that wysely can abyde.' Even God's common people have embalmed the idea in numberless proverbs: 'Good and quickly seldom meet'; and 'Hasty men never want woe—'"

Markham rose with a gesture of impatience.

"Hell! I'm going home before you start a bedtime story," he growled.

The ironical aftermath of this remark was that Vance did tell a "bedtime story" that night; but he told it to me in the seclusion of his own library; and the gist of it was this:

"Heath is committed, body and soul, to a belief in Skeel's guilt; and Markham is as effectively strangled with legal red tape as the poor Canary was strangled with powerful hands. *Eheu*, Van! There's nothing left for me but to set forth tomorrow a cappella, like Gaboriau's Monsieur Lecoq, and see what can be done in the noble cause of justice. I shall ignore both Heath and Markham, and become as a pelican of the wilderness, an owl of the desert, a sparrow alone upon the housetop. . . . Really, y'know, I'm no avenger of society, but I do detest an unsolved problem."

Significant Disclosures

Thursday, September 13; forenoon

Greatly to Currie's astonishment Vance gave instructions to be called at nine o'clock the following morning; and at ten o'clock we were sitting on his little roof garden having breakfast in the mellow mid-September sunshine.

"Van," he said to me, when Currie had brought us our second cup of coffee, "however secretive a woman may be, there's always someone to whom she unburdens her soul. A confidant is an essential to the feminine temperament. It may be a mother, or a lover, or a priest, or a doctor, or, more generally, a girl chum. In the Canary's case we haven't a mother or a priest. Her lover, the elegant Skeel, was a potential enemy; and we're pretty safe in ruling out her doctor—she was too shrewd to confide in such a creature as Lindquist. The girl chum, then, remains. And today we seek her." He lit a cigarette and rose. "But, first, we must visit Mr. Benjamin Browne of Seventh Avenue."

Benjamin Browne was a well-known photographer of stage celebrities, with galleries in the heart of the city's theatrical district; and as we entered the reception room of his luxurious studio later that morning my curiosity as to the object of our visit was at the breaking point. Vance went straight to the desk, behind which sat a young woman with flaming red hair and mascara-shaded eyes, and bowed in his most dignified manner. Then, taking a small unmounted photograph from his pocket, he laid it before her.

"I am producing a musical comedy, *mademoiselle*," he said, "and I wish to communicate with the young lady who left this picture of herself with me. Unfortunately I've misplaced her card; but as her photograph bore the imprint of Browne's, I thought you might be good enough to look in your files and tell me who she is and where I may find her."

He slipped a five-dollar bill under the edge of the blotter, and waited with an air of innocent expectancy.

The young woman looked at him quizzically, and I thought I detected the hint of a smile at the corners of her artfully rouged lips. But after a moment she took the photograph without a word and disappeared through a rear door. Ten minutes later she returned and handed Vance the picture. On the back of it she had written a name and address.

"The young lady is Miss Alys La Fosse, and she lives at the Belafield Hotel." There was now no doubt as to her smile. "You really shouldn't be so careless with the addresses of your applicants—some poor girl might lose an engagement." And her smile suddenly turned into soft laughter.

"*Mademoiselle*," replied Vance, with mock seriousness, "in the future I shall be guided by your warning." And with another dignified bow, he went out.

"Good Lord!" he said, as we emerged into Seventh Avenue. "Really, y'know, I should have disguised myself as an impresario, with a gold-headed cane, a derby, and a purple shirt. That young woman is thoroughly convinced that I'm contemplating an intrigue. . . . A jolly smart *tête-rouge*, that."

He turned into a florist's shop at the corner, and selecting a dozen American Beauties, addressed them to "Benjamin Browne's Receptionist."

"And now," he said, "let us stroll to the Belafield, and seek an audience with Alys."

As we walked across town Vance explained.

"That first morning, when we were inspecting the Canary's rooms, I was convinced that the murder would never be solved by the usual elephantine police methods. It was a subtle and well-planned crime, despite its obvious appearances. No routine investigation would suffice. Intimate information was needed. Therefore, when I saw this photograph of the xanthous Alys half hidden under the litter of papers on the escritoire, I reflected: 'Ah! A girl friend of the departed Margaret's. She may know just the things that are needed.' So, when the Sergeant's broad back was turned, I put the picture in my pocket. There was no other photograph about the place, and this one bore the usual sentimental inscription. 'Ever thine,' and was signed 'Alys.' I concluded, therefore, that Alys had played Anactoria to the Canary's Sappho. Of course I erased the inscription before presenting the picture to the penetrating sibyl at Browne's. . . . And here we are at the Belafield, hopin' for a bit of enlightenment."

The Belafield was a small, expensive apartment-hotel in the East Thirties, which, to judge from the guests to be seen in the Americanized Queen Anne lobby, catered to the well-off sporting set. Vance sent his card up to Miss La Fosse, and received the message that she would see him in a few minutes. The few minutes, however, developed into three-quarters of an hour, and it was nearly noon when a resplendent bellboy came to escort us to the lady's apartment.

Nature had endowed Miss La Fosse with many of its arts, and those that Nature had omitted, Miss La Fosse herself had supplied. She was slender and blond. Her large blue eyes were heavily lashed, but though she looked at one with a wide-eyed stare, she was unable to disguise their sophistication. Her toilet had been made with elaborate care; and as I looked at her, I could not help thinking what an excellent model she would have been for Chéret's pastel posters.

"So you are Mr. Vance," she cooed. "I've often seen your name in Town Topics."

Vance gave a shudder.

"And this is Mr. Van Dine," he said sweetly, "—a mere attorney, who, thus far, has been denied the pages of that fashionable weekly."

"Won't you sit down?" (I am sure Miss La Fosse had spoken the line in a play; she made of the invitation an impressive ceremonial.) "I really don't know why I should have received you. But I suppose you called on business. Perhaps you wish me to appear at a society bazaar, or something of the kind. But I'm so busy, Mr. Vance. You simply can't imagine how occupied I am with my work. . . . I just love my work," she added, with an ecstatic sigh.

"And I'm sure there are many thousands of others who love it, too," returned Vance, in his best drawing-room manner. "But unfortunately I have no bazaar to be graced by your charming presence. I have come on a much more serious matter. . . . You were a very close friend of Miss Margaret Odell's—"

The mention of the Canary's name brought Miss La Fosse suddenly to her feet. Her ingratiating air of affected elegance had quickly disappeared. Her eyes flashed, and their lids drooped harshly. A sneer distorted the lines of her cupid's-bow mouth, and she tossed her head angrily.

"Say, listen! Who do you think you are? I don't know nothing, and I got nothing to say. So run along—you and your lawyer."

But Vance made no move to obey. He took out his cigarette case and carefully selected a Régie.

"Do you mind if I smoke? And won't you have one? I import them direct from my agent in Constantinople. They're exquisitely blended."

The girl snorted, and gave him a look of cold disdain. The doll-baby had become a virago.

"Get yourself outa my apartment, or I'll call the house detective." She turned to the telephone on the wall at her side.

Vance waited until she had lifted the receiver.

"If you do that, Miss La Fosse, I'll order you taken to the district attorney's office for questioning," he told her indifferently, lighting his cigarette and leaning back in his chair.

Slowly she replaced the receiver and turned. "What's your game, anyway? . . . Suppose I did know Margy—then what? And where do you fit into the picture?"

"Alas! I don't fit in at all." Vance smiled pleasantly. "But, for that matter, nobody seems to fit in. The truth is, they're about to arrest a poor blighter for killing your friend, who wasn't in the tableau, either. I happen to be a friend of the district attorney's; and I know exactly what's being done. The police are scouting round in a perfect frenzy of activity, and it's hard to say what trail they'll strike next. I thought, don't y'know, I might save you a lot of unpleasantness by a friendly little chat. . . . Of course," he added, "if you prefer to have me give your name to the police, I'll do so, and let them hold the audience in their own inimitable but crude fashion. I might say, however, that, as yet, they are blissfully unaware of your relationship with Miss Odell, and that, if you are reasonable, I see no reason why they should be informed of it."

The girl had stood, one hand on the telephone, studying Vance intently. He had spoken carelessly and with a genial inflection; and she at length resumed her seat.

"Now, won't you have one of my cigarettes?" he asked, in a tone of gracious reconciliation.

Mechanically she accepted his offer, keeping her eyes on him all the time, as if attempting to determine how far he was to be trusted.

"Who are they thinking of arresting?" She asked the question with scarcely a movement of her features.

"A johnny named Skeel. Silly idea, isn't it?"

"Him!" Her tone was one of mingled contempt and disgust. "That cheap crook? He hasn't got nerve enough to strangle a cat."

"Precisely. But that's no reason for sending him to the electric chair, what?" Vance leaned forward and smiled engagingly. "Miss La Fosse, if you will talk to me for five minutes, and forget I'm a stranger, I'll give you my word of honour not to let the police or the district attorney know anything about you. I'm not connected with the authorities, but somehow I dislike the idea of seeing the wrong man punished. And I'll promise to forget the source of any information you will be kind enough to give me. If you will trust me, it will be infinitely easier for you in the end."

The girl made no answer for several minutes. She was, I could see, trying to estimate Vance; and evidently she decided that, in any case, she had nothing to lose—now that her friendship with the Canary had been discovered—by talking to this man who had promised her immunity from further annoyance.

"I guess you're all right," she said, with a reservation of dubiety; "but I don't know why I should think so." She paused. "But, look here: I was told to keep out of this. And if I don't keep out of it, I'm apt to be back hoofing it in the chorus again. And that's no life for a sweet young thing like me with extravagant tastes—believe me, my friend!"

"That calamity will never befall you through any lack of discretion on my part," Vance assured her, with good-natured earnestness. . . . "Who told you to keep out of it?"

"My—fiancé" She spoke somewhat coquettishly. "He's very well known and he's afraid there might be scandal if I got mixed up in the case as a witness, or anything like that."

"I can readily understand his feelings." Vance nodded sympathetically. "And who, by the bye, is this luckiest of men?"

"Say! You're good." She complimented him with a coy moue. "But I'm not announcing my engagement yet."

"Don't be horrid," begged Vance. "You know perfectly well that I could find out his name by making a few inquiries. And if you drove me to learn the facts elsewhere, then my promise to keep your name a secret would no longer bind me."

Miss La Fosse considered this point.

"I guess you could find out all right . . . so I might as well tell you—only I'm trusting to your word to protect me." She opened her eyes wide and gave Vance a melting look. "I know you wouldn't let me down."

"My dear Miss La Fosse!" His tone was one of pained surprise.

"Well, my fiancé is Mr. Mannix, and he's the head of a big fur-importing house. . . . You see"—she became clingingly confidential—"Louey—that is, Mr. Mannix—used to go round with Margy. That's why he didn't want me to get mixed up in the affair. He said the police might bother him with questions, and his name might get into the papers. And that would hurt his commercial standing."

"I quite understand," murmured Vance. "And do you happen to know where Mr. Mannix was Monday night?"

The girl looked startled.

"Of course I know. He was right here with me from half past ten until two in the morning. We were discussing a new musical show he was interested in; and he wanted me to take the leading role."

"I'm sure it will be a success." Vance spoke with disarming friendliness. "Were you home alone all Monday evening?"

"Hardly." The idea seemed to amuse her. "I went to the Scandals—but I came home early. I knew Louey—Mr. Mannix—was coming."

"I trust he appreciated your sacrifice." Vance, I believe, was disappointed by this unexpected alibi of Mannix's. It was, indeed, so final that further interrogation concerning it seemed futile. After a momentary pause; he changed the subject.

"Tell me; what do you know about a Mr. Charles Cleaver? He was a friend of Miss Odell's."

"Oh, Pop's all right." The girl was plainly relieved by this turn in the conversation. "A good scout. He was certainly gone on Margy. Even after she threw him over for Mr. Spotswoode, he was faithful, as you might say—always running after her, sending her flowers and presents. Some men are like that. Poor old Pop! He even phoned me Monday night to call up Margy for him and try to arrange a party. Maybe if I'd done it, she wouldn't be dead now. . . . It's a funny world, isn't it?"

"Oh, no end funny." Vance smoked calmly for a minute; I could not help admiring his self-control. "What time did Mr. Cleaver phone you Monday night—do you recall?" From his voice one would have thought the question of no importance.

"Let me see. . . ." She pursed her lips prettily. "It was just ten minutes to twelve. I remember that the little chime clock on the mantel over there was striking midnight, and at first I couldn't hear Pop very well. You see, I always keep my clock ten minutes fast so I'll never be late for an appointment."

Vance compared the clock with his watch.

"Yes, it's ten minutes fast. And what about the party?"

"Oh, I was too busy talking about the new show, and I had to refuse. Anyway, Mr. Mannix didn't want to have a party that night. . . . It wasn't my fault was it?"

"Not a bit of it," Vance assured her. "Work comes before pleasure—especially work as important as yours. . . . And now, there is one other man I want to ask you about, and then I won't bother you any more.—What was the situation between Miss Odell and Doctor Lindquist?"

Miss La Fosse became genuinely perturbed.

"I was afraid you were going to ask me about him." There was apprehension in her eyes. "I don't know just what to say. He was wildly in love with Margy; and she led him on, too. But she was sorry for it afterward, because he got jealous—like a crazy person. He used to pester the life out of her. And once—do you know!—he threatened to shoot her and then shoot himself. I told Margy to look out for him. But she didn't seem to be afraid. Anyway, I think she was taking awful chances. . . . Oh! Do you think it could have been—do you really think—?"

"And wasn't there anyone else," Vance interrupted, "who might have felt the same way? Anyone Miss Odell had reason to fear?"

"No." Miss La Fosse shook her head. "Margy didn't know many men intimately. She didn't change often, if you know what I mean. There wasn't anybody else outside of those you've mentioned, except, of course, Mr. Spotswoode. He cut Pop out several months ago. She went to dinner with him Monday night, too. I wanted her to go to the Scandals with me—that's how I know."

Vance rose and held out his hand.

"You've been very kind. And you have nothing whatever to fear. No one shall ever know of our little visit this morning."

"Who do you think killed Margy?" There was genuine emotion in the girl's voice. "Louey says it was probably some burglar who wanted her jewels."

"I'm too wise to sow discord in this happy ménage by even questioning Mr. Mannix's opinion," said Vance half banteringly. "No one *knows* who's guilty; but the police agree with Mr. Mannix."

For a moment the girl's doubts returned, and she gave Vance a searching look. "Why are you so interested? You didn't know Margy, did you? She never mentioned you."

Vance laughed. "My dear child! I only wish I knew why I am so deuced concerned in this affair. 'Pon my word, I can't give you even the sketchiest explanation. . . . No, I never met Miss Odell. But it would offend my sense of proportion if Mr. Skeel were punished and the real culprit went free. Maybe I'm getting sentimental. A sad fate, what?"

"I guess I'm getting soft, too." She nodded her head, still looking Vance square in the eyes. "I risked my happy home to tell you what I did, because somehow I believed you. . . . Say, you weren't stringing me, by any chance?"

Vance put his hand to his heart, and became serious.

"My dear Miss La Fosse, when I leave here it will be as though I had never entered. Dismiss me and Mr. Van Dine here from your mind."

Something in his manner banished her misgivings, and she bade us a kittenish farewell.

CHAPTER 17

Checking an Alibi

Thursday, September 13; afternoon

"My sleuthing goes better," exulted Vance, when we were again in the street. "Fair Alys was a veritable mine of information—eh, what? Only, you should have controlled yourself better when she mentioned her beloved's name—really, you should, Van old thing. I saw you jump and heard you heave. Such emotion is unbecoming in a lawyer."

From a booth in a drugstore near the hotel he telephoned Markham: "I am taking you to lunch. I have numerous confidences I would pour into your ear." A debate ensued, but in the end Vance emerged triumphant; and a moment later a taxicab was driving us downtown.

"Alys is clever—there are brains in that fluffy head," he ruminated. "She's much smarter than Heath; she knew at once that Skeel wasn't guilty. Her characterization of the immaculate Tony was inelegant but how accurate—oh, how accurate! And you noticed, of course, how she trusted me. Touchin', wasn't it? . . . It's a knotty problem, Van. Something's amiss somewhere."

He was silent, smoking, for several blocks.

"Mannix. . . . Curious he should crop up again. And he issued orders to Alys to keep mum. Now, why? Maybe the reason he gave her was the real one. Who knows? On the other hand, was he with his *chère amie* from half past ten till early morning? Well, well. Again, who knows? Something queer about that business discussion. . . . Then Cleaver. He called up just ten minutes before midnight—oh, yes, he called up. That wasn't a fairytale. But how could he telephone from a speeding car? He couldn't. Maybe he really wanted to have a party with his recalcitrant Canary, don't y'know. But, then, why the brummagem alibi? Funk? Maybe. But why the circuitousness? Why didn't he call his lost love direct? Ah, perhaps he did! Someone certainly called her by phone at twenty minutes to twelve. We must look into that, Van. . . . Yes, he may have called her, and then when a man answered—who the deuce was that man, anyway?—he may have appealed to Alys. Quite natural, y'know. Anyway, he wasn't in Boonton. Poor Markham! How upset he'll be when he finds out! . . . But what really worries me is that story of the doctor. Jealous mania: it squares with Ambroise's character perfectly. He's the kind that does go off his head. I knew his confession of paternalism was a red herring. My word! So the doctor was making threats and flourishing pistols, eh? Bad, bad. I don't like it. With those ears of his, he wouldn't hesitate to pull the trigger. Paranoia—that's it. Delusions of persecution. Probably thought the girl and Pop—or maybe the girl and Spotswoode—were plotting his misery and laughing at him. You can't tell about those chaps. They're deep and they're dangerous. The canny Alys had him sized up—warned the Canary against him. . . . Taken by and large, it's a devilish tangle. Anyway, I feel rather bucked. We're moving—oh, undoubtedly we're moving—though in what direction I can't even guess. It's beastly annoyin'."

Markham was waiting for us at the Bankers' Club. He greeted Vance irritably. "What have you got to tell me that's so damned important?"

"Now, don't get ratty." Vance was beaming. "How's your lodestar, Skeel, behaving?"

"So far he's done everything that's pure and refined except join the Christian Endeavour Society."

"Sunday's coming. Give him time. . . . So you're not happy, Markham dear?"

"Was I dragged away from another engagement to report on my state of mind?"

"No need. Your state of mind's execrable. . . . Cheerio! I've brought you something to think about."

"Damn it! I've got too much to think about now."

"Here, have some *brioche*." Vance gave the order for lunch without consulting either of us. "And now for my revelations. *Imprimis*: Pop Cleaver wasn't in Boonton last Monday night. He was very much in the midst of our modern Gomorrah, trying to arrange a midnight party."

"Wonderful!" snorted Markham. "I lave in the font of your wisdom. His alter ego, I take it, was on the road to Hopatcong. The supernatural leaves me cold."

"You may be as pan-cosmic as you choose. Cleaver was in New York at midnight Monday, craving excitement."

"What about the summons for speeding?"

"That's for you to explain. But if you'll take my advice, you'll send for this Boonton catchpole and let him have a look at Pop. If he says Cleaver is the man he ticketed, I'll humbly do away with myself."

"Well! That makes it worth trying. I'll have the officer at the Stuyvesant Club this afternoon and I'll point out Cleaver to him.... What other staggering revelations have you in store?"

"Mannix will bear looking into."

Markham put down his knife and fork and leaned back. "I'm overcome! Such Himalayan sagacity! With that evidence against him, he should be arrested at once.... Vance, my dear old friend, are you feeling quite normal? No dizzy spells lately? No shooting pains in the head? Knee jerks all right?"

"Furthermore, Doctor Lindquist was wildly infatuated with the Canary, and insanely jealous. Recently threatened to take a pistol and hold a little pogrom of his own."

"That's better." Markham sat up. "Where did you get this information?"

"Ah! That's my secret."

Markham was annoyed.

"Why so mysterious?"

"Needs must, old chap. Gave my word and all that sort of thing. And I'm a bit quixotic, don't y'know—too much Cervantes in my youth." He spoke lightly, but Markham knew him too well to push the question.

In less than five minutes after we had returned to the district attorney's office, Heath came in.

"I got something else on Mannix, sir; thought you might want to add it to the report I turned in yesterday. Burke secured a picture of him and showed it to the phone operators at Odell's house. Both of 'em recognized it. He's been there several times, but it wasn't the Canary he called on. It was the woman in Apartment 2. She's named Frisbee and used to be one of Mannix's fur models. He's been to see her several times during the past six months and has taken her out once or twice; but he hasn't called on her for a month or more.... Any good?"

"Can't tell." Markham shot Vance an inquisitive look. "But thanks for the information, Sergeant."

"By the bye," said Vance dulcetly, when Heath had left us, "I'm feeling tophole. No pains in the head; no dizzy spells. Knee jerks perfect."

"Delighted. Still, I can't charge a man with murder because he calls on his fur model."

"You're so hasty! Why should you charge him with murder?" Vance rose and yawned. "Come, Van. I'd rather like to gaze on Perneb's tomb at the Metropolitan this afternoon. Could you bear it?" At the door he paused. "I say, Markham, what about the Boonton bailiff?" Markham rang for Swacker. "I'll see to it at once. Drop in at the club around five, if you feel like it. I'll have the officer there then, as Cleaver is sure to come in before dinner."

When Vance and I returned to the club late that afternoon, Markham was stationed in the lounge room facing the main door of the rotunda; and beside him sat a tall, heavyset, bronzed man of about forty, alert but ill at ease.

"Traffic Officer Phipps arrived from Boonton a little while ago," said Markham, by way of introduction. "Cleaver is expected at any moment now. He has an appointment here at half past five."

Vance drew up a chair.

"I do hope he's a punctual beggar."

"So do I," returned Markham viciously. "I'm looking forward to your *felo-de-se*."

"'Our hap is loss, our hope but sad despair,'" murmured Vance.

Less than ten minutes later Cleaver entered the rotunda from the street, paused at the desk, and sauntered into the lounge room. There was no escaping the observation point Markham had chosen; and as he walked by us he paused and exchanged greetings. Markham detained him a moment with a few casual questions; and then Cleaver passed on.

"That the man you ticketed, Officer?" asked Markham, turning to Phipps.

Phipps was scowling perplexedly. "It looks something like him, sir; there's a kind of resemblance. But it ain't him." He shook his head. "No, sir; it ain't him. The fellow I hung a summons on was stouter than this gent and wasn't as tall."

"You're positive?"

"Yes, sir—no mistake. The guy I tagged tried to argue with me and then he tried to slip me a flyer to forget it. I had my headlight on him full."

Phipps was dismissed with a substantial pourboire.

"*Vae misero mihi!*" sighed Vance. "My worthless existence is to be prolonged. Sad. But you must try to bear it. . . . I say, Markham, what does Pop Cleaver's brother look like?"

"That's it," nodded Markham. "I've met his brother; he's shorter and stouter. . . . This thing is getting beyond me. I think I'll have it out with Cleaver now."

He started to rise, but Vance forced him back into his seat.

"Don't be impetuous. Cultivate patience. Cleaver's not going to do a bunk; and there are one or two prelimin'ry steps strongly indicated. Mannix and Lindquist still seduce my curiosity."

Markham clung to his point. "Neither Mannix nor Lindquist is here now, and Cleaver is. And I want to know why he lied to me about that summons."

"I can tell you that," said Vance. "He wanted you to think he was in the wilds of New Jersey at midnight Monday. Simple, what?"

"The inference is a credit to your intelligence! But I hope you don't seriously think that Cleaver is guilty. It's possible he knows something; but I certainly cannot picture him as a strangler."

"And why?"

"He's not the type. It's inconceivable—even if there were evidence against him."

"Ah! The psychological judgment! You eliminate Cleaver because you don't think his nature harmonizes with the situation. I say, doesn't that come perilously near being an esoteric hypothesis?—or a metaphysical deduction? . . . However, I don't entirely agree with you in your application of the theory to Cleaver. That fish-eyed gambler has unsuspected potentialities for evil. But with the theory itself I am wholly in accord. And behold, my dear Markham: you yourself apply psychology in its abecedarian implications, yet ridicule my application of it in its higher developments. Consistency may be the hobgoblin of little minds, y'know, but it's nonetheless a priceless jewel. . . . How about a cup of tea?"

We sought the Palm Room and sat down at a table near the entrance. Vance ordered oolong tea, but Markham and I took black coffee. A very capable four-piece orchestra was playing Tchaikovsky's *Casse-Noisette Suite*, and we sat restfully in the comfortable chairs without speaking. Markham was tired and dispirited, and Vance was busy with the problem that had absorbed him continuously since Tuesday morning. Never before had I seen him so preoccupied.

We had been there perhaps half an hour when Spotswoode strolled in. He stopped and spoke, and Markham asked him to join us. He, too, appeared depressed, and his eyes showed signs of worry.

"I hardly dare ask you, Mr. Markham," he said diffidently, after he had ordered a ginger ale, "but how do my chances stand now of being called as a witness?"

"That fate is certainly no nearer than when I last saw you," Markham replied. "In fact, nothing has happened to change the situation materially."

"And the man you had under suspicion?"

"He's still under suspicion, but no arrest has been made. We're hoping, however, that something will break before long."

"And I suppose you still want me to remain in the city?"

"If you can arrange it—yes."

Spotswoode was silent for a time; then he said, "I don't want to appear to shirk any responsibility—and perhaps it may seem wholly selfish for me even to suggest it—but, in any event, wouldn't the testimony of the telephone operator as to the hour of Miss Odell's return and her calls for help be sufficient to establish the facts, without my corroboration?"

"I have thought of that, of course; and if it is at all possible to prepare the case for the prosecution without summoning you to appear, I assure you it will be done. At the moment, I can see no necessity of your being called as a witness. But one never knows what may turn up. If the defence hinges on a question of exact time, and the operator's testimony is questioned or disqualified for any reason, you may be required to come forward. Otherwise not."

Spotswoode sipped his ginger ale. A little of his depression seemed to have departed.

"You're very generous, Mr. Markham. I wish there was some adequate way of thanking you." He looked up hesitantly. "I presume you are still opposed to my visiting the apartment. . . . I know you think me unreasonable and perhaps sentimental; but the girl represented something in my life that I find very difficult to tear out. I don't expect you to understand it—I hardly understand it myself."

"I think it's easily understandable, don't y'know," remarked Vance, with a sympathy I had rarely seen him manifest. "Your attitude needs no apology. History and fable are filled with the same situation, and the protagonists have always exhibited sentiments similar to yours. Your most famous prototype, of course, was Odysseus on the citron-scented isle of Ogygia with the fascinatin' Calypso. The soft arms of sirens have gone snaking round men's necks ever since the red-haired Lilith worked her devastatin' wiles on the impressionable Adam. We're all sons of that racy old boy."

Spotswoode smiled. "You at least give me an historic background," he said. Then he turned to Markham. "What will become of Miss Odell's possessions—her furniture and so forth?"

"Sergeant Heath heard from an aunt of hers in Seattle," Markham told him. "She's on her way to New York, I believe, to take over what there is of the estate."

"And everything will be kept intact until then?"

"Probably longer, unless something unexpected happens. Anyway, until then."

"There are one or two little trinkets I'd like to keep," Spotswoode confessed, a bit shamefacedly, I thought.

After a few more minutes of desultory talk he rose and, pleading an engagement, bade us good afternoon.

"I hope I can keep his name clear of the case," said Markham, when he had gone.

"Yes; his situation is not an enviable one," concurred Vance. "It's always sad to be found out. The moralist would set it down to retribution."

"In this instance chance was certainly on the side of righteousness. If he hadn't chosen Monday night for the Winter Garden, he might now be in the bosom of his family, with nothing more troublesome to bother him than a guilty conscience."

"It certainly looks that way." Vance glanced at his watch. "And your mention of the Winter Garden reminds me. Do you mind if we dine early? Frivolity beckons me tonight. I'm going to the Scandals."

We both looked at him as though he had taken leave of his senses.

"Don't be so horrified, my Markham. Why should I not indulge an impulse? . . . And, incidentally, I hope to have glad tidings for you by lunchtime tomorrow."

CHAPTER 18

The Trap

Friday, September 14; noon

Vance slept late the following day. I had accompanied him to the Scandals the night before, utterly at a loss to understand his strange desire to attend a type of entertainment which I knew he detested. At noon he ordered his car, and instructed the chauffeur to drive to the Belafield Hotel.

"We are about to call again on the allurin' Alys," he said. "I'd bring posies to lay at her shrine, but I fear dear Mannix might question her unduly about them."

Miss La Fosse received us with an air of crestfallen resentment.

"I might've known it!" She nodded her head with sneering perception. "I suppose you've come to tell me the cops found out about me without the slightest assistance from you." Her disdain was almost magnificent. "Did you bring 'em with you? . . . A swell guy *you* are!— But it's my own fault for being a damn fool."

Vance waited unmoved until she had finished her contemptuous tirade. Then he bowed pleasantly.

"Really, y'know, I merely dropped in to pay my respects, and to tell you that the police have turned in their report of Miss Odell's acquaintances, and that your name was not mentioned on it. You seemed a little worried yesterday on that score, and it occurred to me I could set your mind wholly at ease."

The vigilance of her attitude relaxed. "Is that straight? . . . My God! I don't know what would happen if Louey'd find out I'd been blabbing."

"I'm sure he won't find out, unless you choose to tell him. . . . Won't you be generous and ask me to sit down a moment?"

"Of course—I'm so sorry. I'm just having my coffee. Please join me." She rang for two extra services.

Vance had drunk two cups of coffee less than half an hour before, and I marvelled at his enthusiasm for this atrocious hotel beverage.

"I was a belated spectator of the Scandals last night," he remarked in a negligent, conversational tone. "I missed the revue earlier in the season. How is it you yourself were so late in seeing it?"

"I've been so busy," she confided. "I was rehearsing for 'A Pair of Queens'; but the production's been postponed. Louey couldn't get the theatre he wanted."

"Do you like revues?" asked Vance. "I should think they'd be more difficult for the principals than the ordin'ry musical comedy."

"They are." Miss La Fosse adopted a professional air. "And they're unsatisfactory. The individual is lost in them. There's no real scope for one's talent. They're breathless if you know what I mean."

"I should imagine so." Vance bravely sipped his coffee. "And yet, there were several numbers in the Scandals that you could have done charmingly; they seemed particularly designed for you. I thought of you doing them, and—d'ye know?—the thought rather spoiled my enjoyment of the young lady who appeared in them."

"You flatter me, Mr. Vance. But, really, I have a good voice. I've studied very hard. And I learned dancing with Professor Markoff."

"Indeed!" (I'm sure Vance had never heard the name before, but his exclamation seemed to imply that he regarded Professor Markoff as one of the world's most renowned ballet masters.) "Then, you certainly should have been starred in the Scandals. The young lady I have in mind sang rather indifferently, and her dancing was most inadequate. Moreover, she was many degrees your inferior in personality and attractiveness. . . . Confess: didn't you have just a little desire Monday night to be singing the 'Chinese Lullaby' song?"

"Oh, I don't know." Miss La Fosse carefully considered the suggestion. "They kept the lights awfully low; and I don't look so well in cerise. But the costumes were adorable, weren't they?"

"On you they certainly would have been adorable. . . . What colour are you partial to?"

"I love the orchid shades," she told him enthusiastically; "though I don't look at all bad in turquoise blue. But an artist once told me I should always wear white. He wanted to paint my portrait, but the gentleman I was engaged to then didn't like him."

Vance regarded her appraisingly.

"I think your artist friend was right. And, y'know, the St. Moritz scene in the Scandals would have suited you perfectly. The little brunette who sang the snow song, all in white, was delightful; but really, now, she should have had golden hair. Dusky beauties belong to the southern climes. And she impressed me as lacking the sparkle and vitality of a Swiss resort in midwinter. You could have supplied those qualities admirably."

"Yes; I'd have liked that better than the Chinese number, I think. White fox is my favourite fur, too. But, even so, in a revue you're on in one number and off in another. When it's all over, you're forgotten." She sighed unhappily.

Vance set down his cup and looked at her with whimsically reproachful eyes. After a moment he said, "My dear, why did you fib to me about the time Mr. Mannix returned to you last Monday night? It wasn't a bit nice of you."

"What do you mean?" Miss La Fosse exclaimed in frightened indignation, drawing herself up into an attitude of withering hauteur.

"You see," explained Vance, "the St. Moritz scene of the Scandals doesn't go on until nearly eleven, and it closes the bill. So you couldn't possible have seen it and also received Mr. Mannix here at half past ten. Come. What time did he arrive here Monday night?"

The girl flushed angrily. "You're pretty slick, aren't you? You shoulda been a cop. . . . Well, what if I didn't get home till after the show? Any crime in that?"

"None whatever," answered Vance mildly. "Only a little breach of good faith in telling me you came home early." He bent forward earnestly. "I'm not here to make you trouble. On the contr'ry, I'd like to protect you from any distress or bother. You see, if the police go nosing round, they may run on to you. But if I'm able to give the district attorney accurate information about certain things connected with Monday night, there'll be no danger of the police being sent to look for you."

Miss La Fosse's eyes grew suddenly hard, and her brow crinkled with determination. "Listen! I haven't got anything to hide, and neither has Louey. But if Louey asks me to say he's somewhere at half past ten, I'm going to say it—see? That's my idea of friendship. Louey had some good reason to ask it, too, or he wouldn't have done it. However, since you're so smart, and have accused me of playing unfair, I'm going to tell you that he didn't get in till after midnight. But if anybody else asks me about it, I'll see 'em in hell before I tell 'em anything but the half-past-ten story. Get that?"

Vance bowed. "I get it; and I like you for it."

"But don't go away with the wrong idea," she hurried on, her eyes sparkling with fervour. "Louey may not have got here till after midnight, but if you think he knows anything about Margy's death, you're crazy. He was through with Margy a year ago. Why, he hardly knew she was on earth. And if any fool cop gets the notion in his head that Louey was mixed up in the affair, I'll alibi him—so help me God!—if it's the last thing I do in this world."

"I like you more and more," said Vance; and when she gave him her hand at parting he lifted it to his lips.

As we rode downtown Vance was thoughtful. We were nearly to the Criminal Courts Building before he spoke.

"The primitive Alys rather appeals to me," he said. "She's much too good for the oleaginous Mannix. . . . Women are so shrewd—and so gullible. A woman can read a man with almost magical insight; but, on the other hand, she is inexpressibly blind when it comes to *her* man. Witness sweet Alys's faith in Mannix. He probably told her he was slaving at the office Monday night. Naturally, she doesn't believe it; but she knows—*knows*, mind you—that her Louey just couldn't have been concerned in the Canary's death. Ah, well, let us hope she's right and that Mannix is not apprehended—at least not until her new show is financed. . . . My word! If this being a detective involves many more revues, I shall have to resign. Thank Heaven, though, the lady didn't attend the cinema Monday night!" When we arrived at the District Attorney's office we found Heath and Markham in consultation. Markham had a pad before him, several pages of which were covered with tabulated and annotated entries. A cloud of cigar smoke enveloped him. Heath sat facing him, his elbows on the table, his chin resting in his hands. He looked pugnacious but disconsolate.

"I'm going over the case with the sergeant," Markham explained, with a brief glance in our direction. "We're trying to get all the salient points down in some kind of order, to see if there are any connecting links we've overlooked. I've told the sergeant about the doctor's infatuation and his threats, and of the failure of Traffic Officer Phipps to identify Cleaver. But the more we learn, the worse, apparently, the jumble grows."

He picked up the sheets of paper and fastened them together with a clip. "The truth is, we haven't any real evidence against anybody. There are suspicious circumstances connected with Skeel and Doctor Lindquist and Cleaver; and our interview with Mannix didn't precisely allay suspicions in his direction, either. But when we come right down to it, what's the situation! We've got some fingerprints of Skeel, which might have been made late Monday afternoon. Doctor Lindquist goes berserk when we ask him where he was Monday night, and then offers us a weak alibi. He admits a fatherly interest in the girl, whereas he's really in love with her—a perfectly natural bit of mendacity. Cleaver lent his car to his brother and lied about it, so that I'd think he was in Boonton Monday at midnight. And Mannix gives us a number of shifty answers to our questions concerning his relations with the girl. . . . Not an embarrassment of riches."

"I wouldn't say your information was exactly negligent," observed Vance, taking a chair beside the sergeant. "It may all prove devilish valuable if only it could be put together properly. The difficulty, it appears to me, is that certain parts of the puzzle are missing. Find 'em, and I'll warrant everything will fit beautifully—like a mosaic."

"Easy enough to say 'find 'em,'" grumbled Markham. "The trouble is to know where to look."

Heath relighted his dead cigar and made an impatient gesture.

"You can't get away from Skeel. He's the boy that did it, and, if it wasn't for Abe Rubin, I'd sweat the truth outa him. And by the way, Mr. Vance, he had his own private key to the Odell apartment, all right." He glanced at Markham hesitantly. "I don't want to look as if I was criticising, sir, but I got a feeling we're wasting time chasing after these gentlemen friends of Odell—Cleaver and Mannix and this here doctor."

"You may be right." Markham seemed inclined to agree with him. "However, I'd like to know why Lindquist acted the way he did."

"Well, that might help some," Heath compromised. "If the doc was so far gone on Odell as to threaten to shoot her, and if he went off his head when you asked him to alibi himself, maybe he could tell us something. Why not throw a little scare into him? His record ain't any too good, anyway."

"An excellent idea," chimed in Vance.

Markham looked up sharply. Then he consulted his appointment book. "I'm fairly free this afternoon, so suppose you bring him down here, Sergeant. Get a subpoena if you have to—only see that he comes. And make it as soon after lunch as you can." He tapped on the desk irritably. "If I don't do anything else, I'm going to eliminate some of this human flotsam that's cluttering up the case. And Lindquist is as good as any to start with. I'll either develop these various suspicious circumstances into something workable or I'll root them up. Then we'll see where we stand."

Heath shook hands pessimistically and went out.

"Poor hapless man!" sighed Vance, looking after him. "He giveth way to all the pangs and fury of despair."

"And so would you," snapped Markham, "if the newspapers were butchering you for a political holiday. By the way, weren't you to be a harbinger of glad tidings this noon, or something of the sort?"

"I believe I did hold out some such hope." Vance sat looking meditatively out of the window for several minutes. "Markham, this fellow Mannix lures me like a magnet. He irks and whirrets me. He infests my slumbers. He's the raven on my bust of Pallas. He plagues me like a banshee."

"Does this jeremiad come under the head of tidings?"

"I sha'n't rest peacefully," pursued Vance, "until I know where Louey the furrier was between eleven o'clock and midnight Monday. He was somewhere he shouldn't have been. And you, Markham, must find out. Please make Mannix the second offensive in your assault upon the flotsam. He'll parley, with the right amount of pressure. Be brutal, old dear; let him think you suspect him of the throttling. Ask him about the fur model—what's her name?—Frisbee—" He stopped short and knit his brows. "My eye—oh, my eye! I wonder. . . . Yes, yes, Markham; you must question him about the fur model. Ask him when he saw her last, and try to look wise and mysterious when you're doing it."

"See here, Vance"—Markham was exasperated—"you've been harping on Mannix for three days. What's keeping your nose to that scent?"

"Intuition—sheer intuition. My psychic temperament, don't y'know."

"I'd believe that if I hadn't known you for fifteen years." Markham inspected him shrewdly, then shrugged his shoulders. "I'll have Mannix on the *tapis* when I'm through with Lindquist."

CHAPTER 19

The Doctor Explains

Friday, September 14; 2 p.m.

We lunched in the district attorney's private sanctum; and at two o'clock Doctor Lindquist was announced. Heath accompanied him, and, from the expression on the sergeant's face, it was plain he did not at all like his companion.

The doctor, at Markham's request, seated himself facing the district attorney's desk.

"What is the meaning of this new outrage?" he demanded coldly. "Is it your prerogative to force a citizen to leave his private affairs in order to be bullied?"

"It's my duty to bring murderers to justice," replied Markham, with equal coldness. "And if any citizen considers that giving aid to the authorities is an outrage, that's *his* prerogative. If you have anything to fear by answering my questions, Doctor, you are entitled to have your attorney present. Would you care to phone him to come here now and give you legal protection?"

Doctor Lindquist hesitated. "I need no legal protection, sir. Will you be good enough to tell me at once why I was brought here?"

"Certainly; to explain a few points which have been discovered regarding your relationship with Miss Odell, and to elucidate—if you care to—your reasons for deceiving me, at our last conference, in regard to that relationship."

"You have, I infer, been prying unwarrantably into my private affairs. I had heard that such practices were once common in Russia. . . ."

"If the prying was unwarranted, you can, Doctor Lindquist, easily convince me on that point; and whatever we may have learned concerning you will be instantly forgotten. It is true, is it not, that your interest in Miss Odell went somewhat beyond mere paternal affection?"

"Are not even a man's sacred sentiments respected by the police of this country?" There was insolent scorn in the doctor's tone.

"Under some conditions, yes; under others, no." Markham controlled his fury admirably. "You need not answer me, of course; but, if you choose to be frank, you may possibly save yourself the humiliation of being questioned publicly by the people's attorney in a court of law."

Doctor Lindquist winced and considered the matter at some length. "And if I admit that my affection for Miss Odell was other than paternal—what then?"

Markham accepted the question as an affirmation.

"You were intensely jealous of her, were you not, Doctor?"

"Jealousy," Doctor Lindquist remarked, with an air of ironic professionalism, "is not an unusual accompaniment to an infatuation. Authorities such as Kraft-Ebing, Moll, Freud, Ferenczi, and Adler, I believe, regard it as an intimate psychological corollary of amatory attraction."

"Most instructive." Markham nodded his head appreciatively. "I am to assume, then, that you were infatuated with—or, let us say, amatorily attracted by—Miss Odell, and that on occasions you exhibited the intimate psychological corollary of jealousy?"

"You may assume what you please. But I fail to understand why my emotions are any of your affair."

"Had your emotions not led you to highly questionable and suspicious acts, I would not be interested in them. But I have it on unimpeachable authority that your emotions so reacted on your better judgment that you threatened to take Miss Odell's life and also your own. And, in view of the fact that the young woman has since been murdered, the law naturally—and reasonably—is curious."

The doctor's normally pale face seemed to turn yellow, and his long splay fingers tightened over the arms of his chair; but otherwise he sat immobile and rigidly dignified, his eyes fixed intently on the district attorney.

"I trust," added Markham, "you will not augment my suspicions by any attempt at denial."

Vance was watching the man closely. Presently he leaned forward.

"I say, Doctor, what method of extermination did you threaten Miss Odell with?"

Doctor Lindquist jerked round, thrusting his head toward Vance. He drew in a long rasping breath, and his whole frame became tense. Blood suffused his cheeks; and there was a twitching of the muscles about his mouth and throat. For a moment I was afraid he was going to lose his self-control. But after a moment's effort he steadied himself.

"You think perhaps I threatened to strangle her?" His words were vibrant with the intensity of his passionate anger. "And you would like to turn my threat into a noose to hang me?—Paugh!" He paused, and when he spoke again, his voice had become calmer. "It is quite true I once unadvisedly attempted to frighten Miss Odell with a threat to kill her and to commit suicide. But if your information is as accurate as you would have me believe, you are aware that I threatened her with a revolver. It is the weapon, I believe, that is conventionally mentioned when making empty threats. I certainly would not have threatened her with *thuggee*, even had I contemplated so abominable an act."

"True," nodded Vance. "And it's a rather good point, don't y'know."

The doctor was evidently encouraged by Vance's attitude. He again faced Markham and elaborated his confession. "A threat, I presume you know, is rarely the forerunner of a violent deed. Even a brief study of the human mind would teach you that a threat is prima facie evidence of one's innocence. A threat, generally, is made in anger, and acts as its own safety valve." He shifted his eyes. "I am not a married man; my emotional life has not been stabilized, as it were; and I am constantly coming in close contact with hypersensitive and overwrought people. During a period of abnormal susceptibility I conceived an infatuation for the young woman, an infatuation which she did not reciprocate—certainly not with an ardour commensurate with my own. I suffered deeply; and she made no effort to mitigate my sufferings. Indeed, I suspected her, more than once, of deliberately and perversely torturing me with other men. At any rate, she took no pains to hide her infidelities from me. I confess that once or twice I was almost distracted. And it was in the hope of frightening her into a more amenable and considerate attitude that I threatened her. I trust that you are a sufficiently discerning judge of human nature to believe me."

"Leaving that point for a moment," answered Markham noncommittally, "will you give me more specific information as to your whereabouts Monday night?"

Again I noted a yellow tinge creep over the man's features, and his body stiffened perceptibly. But when he spoke, it was with his habitual suavity.

"I considered that my note to you covered that question satisfactorily. What did I omit?"

"What was the name of the patient on whom you were calling that night?"

"Mrs. Anna Breedon. She is the widow of the late Amos H. Breedon of the Breedon National Bank of Long Branch."

"And you were with her, I believe you stated, from eleven until one?"

"That is correct."

"And was Mrs. Breedon the only witness to your presence at the sanatorium between those hours?"

"I am afraid that is so. You see, after ten o'clock at night I never ring the bell. I let myself in with my own key."

"And I suppose that I may be permitted to question Mrs. Breedon?"

Doctor Lindquist was profoundly regretful. "Mrs. Breedon is a very ill woman. She suffered a tremendous shock at the time of her husband's death last summer, and has been practically in a semiconscious condition ever since. There are times when I even fear for her reason. The slightest disturbance of excitement might produce very serious results."

He took a newspaper cutting from a gold-edged letter case and handed it to Markham.

"You will observe that this obituary notice mentions her prostration and confinement in a private sanatorium. I have been her physician for years."

Markham, after glancing at the cutting, handed it back. There was a short silence broken by a question from Vance.

"By the bye, Doctor, what is the name of the night nurse at your sanatorium?"

Doctor Lindquist looked up quickly.

"My night nurse? Why—what has she to do with it? She was very busy Monday night. I can't understand. . . . Well, if you want her name I have no objection. It's Finckle—Miss Amelia Finckle."

Vance wrote down the name and, rising, carried the slip of paper to Heath.

"Sergeant, bring Miss Finckle here tomorrow morning at eleven," he said, with a slight lowering of one eyelid.

"I sure will, sir. Good idea." His manner boded no good for Miss Finckle.

A cloud of apprehension spread over Doctor Lindquist's face.

"Forgive me if I say that I am insensible to the sanity of your cavalier methods." His tone betrayed only contempt. "May I hope that for the present your inquisition is ended?"

"I think that will be all, Doctor," returned Markham politely. "May I have a taxicab called for you?"

"Your consideration overwhelms me. But my car is below." And Doctor Lindquist haughtily withdrew.

Markham immediately summoned Swacker and sent him for Tracy. The detective came at once, polishing his pince-nez and bowing affably. One would have taken him for an actor rather than a detective, but his ability in matters requiring delicate handling was a byword in the department.

"I want you to fetch Mr. Louis Mannix again," Markham told him. "Bring him here at once; I'm waiting to see him."

Tracy bowed genially and, adjusting his glasses, departed on his errand.

"And now," said Markham, fixing Vance with a reproachful look, "I want to know what your idea was in putting Lindquist on his guard about the night nurse. Your brain isn't at par this afternoon. Do you think I didn't have the nurse in mind? And now you've warned him. He'll have until eleven tomorrow morning to coach her in her answers. Really, Vance, I can't conceive of anything better calculated to defeat us in our attempt to substantiate the man's alibi."

"I did put a little fright into him, didn't I?" Vance grinned complacently. "Whenever your antagonist begins talking exaggeratedly about the insanity of your notions, he's already deuced hot under the collar. But, Markham old thing, don't burst into tears over my mental shortcomings. If you and I both thought of the nurse, don't you suppose the wily doctor also thought of her? If this Miss Finckle were the type that could be suborned, he would have enlisted her perjurious service two days ago, and she would have been mentioned, along with the comatose Mrs. Breedon, as a witness to his presence at the sanatorium Monday night. The fact that he avoided all reference to the nurse shows that she's not to be wheedled into swearing falsely. . . . No, Markham. I deliberately put him on his guard. Now he'll have to do something before we question Miss Finckle. And I'm vain enough to think I know what it'll be."

"Let me get this right," put in Heath. "Am I, or am I not, to round up the Finckle woman tomorrow morning?"

"There'll be no need," said Vance. "We are doomed, I fear, not to gaze upon this Florence Nightingale. A meeting between us is about the last thing the doctor would desire."

"That may be true," admitted Markham. "But don't forget that he may have been up to something Monday night wholly unconnected with the murder, that he simply doesn't want known."

"Quite—quite. And yet, nearly everyone who knew the Canary

seems to have selected Monday night for the indulgence of *sub rosa* peccadilloes. It's a bit thick, what? Skeel tries to make us believe he was immersed in Khun Khan. Cleaver was—if you take his word for it—touring the countryside in Jersey's lake district. Lindquist wants us to picture him as comforting the afflicted. And Mannix, I happen to know, has gone to some trouble to build up an alibi in case we get nosey. All of 'em, in fact, were doing something they don't want us to know about. Now, what was it? And why did they, of one accord, select the night of the murder for mysterious affairs which they don't dare mention, even to clear themselves of suspicion? Was there an invasion of efreets in the city that night? Was there a curse on the world, driving men to dark bawdy deeds? Was there Black Magic abroad? I think not."

"I'm laying my money on Skeel," declared Heath stubbornly. "I know a professional job when I see it. And you can't get away from those fingerprints and the Professor's report on the chisel."

Markham was sorely perplexed. His belief in Skeel's guilt had, I knew, been undermined in some measure by Vance's theory that the crime was the carefully premeditated act of a shrewd and educated man. But now he seemed to swing irresolutely back to Heath's point of view.

"I'll admit," he said, "that Lindquist and Cleaver and Mannix don't inspire one with a belief in their innocence. But since they're all tarred with the same stick, the force of suspicion against them is somewhat dispersed. After all, Skeel is the only logical aspirant for the role of strangler. He's the only one with a visible motive; and he's the only one against whom there's any evidence."

Vance sighed wearily. "Yes, yes. Fingerprints—chisel marks. You're such a trustin' soul, Markham. Skeel's fingerprints are found in the apartment; therefore, Skeel strangled the lady. So beastly simple. Why bother further? *A chose jugée*—an adjudicated case. Send Skeel to the chair, and that's that! . . . It's effective, y'know, but is it art?"

"In your critical enthusiasm you understate our case against Skeel," Markham reminded him testily.

"Oh, I'll grant that your case against him is ingenious. It's so deuced ingenious I just haven't the heart to reject it. But most popular truth is mere ingenuity—that's why it's so wrong-headed. Your theory would appeal strongly to the popular mind. And yet, y'know, Markham, it isn't true."

The practical Heath was unmoved. He sat stolidly, scowling at the table. I doubt if he had even heard the exchange of opinions between Markham and Vance.

"You know, Mr. Markham," he said, like one unconsciously voicing an obscure line of thought, "if we could show how Skeel got in and out of Odell's apartment, we'd have a better case against him. I can't figure it out—it's got me stopped. So, I've been thinking we oughta get an architect to go over those rooms. The house is an old-timer—God knows when it was originally built—and there may be some way of getting into it that we haven't discovered yet."

"'Pon my soul!" Vance stared at him in satirical wonderment. "You're becoming downright romantic! Secret passageways, hidden doors, stairways between the walls. So that's it, is it? Oh, my word! . . . Sergeant, beware of the cinema. It has ruined many a good man. Try grand opera for a while—it's more borin' but less corruptin'."

"That's all right, Mr. Vance." Apparently Heath himself did not relish the architectural idea particularly. "But as long as we don't know how Skeel got in, it's just as well to make sure of a few ways he didn't get in."

"I agree with you, Sergeant," said Markham. "I'll get an architect on the job at once." He rang for Swacker and gave the necessary instructions.

Vance extended his legs and yawned.

"All we need now is a Favourite of the Harem, a few blackamoors with palm-leaf fans, and some *pizzicato* music."

"You will joke, Mr. Vance." Heath lit a fresh cigar. "But even if the architect don't find anything wrong with the apartment, Skeel's liable to give his hand away 'most any time."

"I'm pinnin' my childish faith on Mannix," said Vance. "I don't know why I should; but he's not a nice man, and he's suppressing something. Markham, don't you dare let him go until he tells you where he was Monday night. And don't forget to hint mysteriously about the fur model."

CHAPTER 20

A Midnight Witness
Friday, September 14; 3:30 p.m.

In less than half an hour Mannix arrived. Heath relinquished his seat to the newcomer and moved to a large chair beneath the windows. Vance had taken a place at the small table on Markham's right where he was able to face Mannix obliquely.

It was patent that Mannix did not relish the idea of another interview. His little eyes shifted quickly about the office, lingered suspiciously for a moment on Heath, and at last came to rest on the district attorney. He was more vigilant even than during his first visit; and his greeting to Markham, while fulsome, had in it a note of trepidation. Nor was Markham's air calculated to put him at ease. It was an ominous, indomitable Public Prosecutor who motioned him to be seated. Mannix laid his hat and cane on the table and sat down on the edge of his chair, his back as perpendicular as a flagpole.

"I'm not at all satisfied with what you told me Wednesday, Mr. Mannix," Markham began, "and I trust you won't necessitate me to take drastic steps to find out what you know about Miss Odell's death."

"What I know!" Mannix forced a smile intended to be disarming. "Mr. Markham—Mr. Markham!" He seemed oilier than usual as he spread his hands in hopeless appeal. "If I knew anything, believe me, I would tell you—positively I would tell you."

"I'm delighted to hear it. Your willingness makes my task easier. First, then, please tell me where you were at midnight Monday."

Mannix's eyes slowly contracted until they looked like two tiny shining disks, but otherwise the man did not move. After what seemed an interminable pause, he spoke.

"I should tell you where I was Monday? Why should I have to do that? . . . Maybe I'm suspected of the murder—yes?"

"You're not suspected now. But your apparent unwillingness to answer my question is certainly suspicious. Why don't you care to have me know where you were?"

"I got no reason to keep it from you, y' understand." Mannix shrugged. "I got nothing to be ashamed of—absolutely! ... I had a lot of accounts to go over at the office—winter-season stocks. I was down at the office until ten o'clock—maybe later. Then at half past ten—"

"That'll do!" Vance's voice cut in tartly. "No need to drag anyone else into this thing."

He spoke with a curious significance of emphasis, and Mannix studied him craftily, trying to read what knowledge, if any, lay behind his words. But he received no enlightenment from Vance's features. The warning, however, had been enough to halt him.

"You don't want to know where I was at half past ten?"

"Not particularly," said Vance. "We want to know where you were at midnight. And it won't be necess'ry to mention anyone who saw you at that time. When you tell us the truth, we'll know it." He himself had assumed the air of wisdom and mystery that he had deputed to Markham earlier in the afternoon. Without breaking faith with Alys La Fosse, he had sowed the seeds of doubt in Mannix's mind.

Before the man could frame an answer, Vance stood up and leaned impressively over the district attorney's desk.

"You know a Miss Frisbee. Lives in 71st Street; accurately speaking—at number 184; to be more exact—in the house where Miss Odell lived; to put it precisely—in Apartment Number 2. Miss Frisbee was a former model of yours. Sociable girl: still charitable to the advances of her erstwhile employer—meanin' yourself. When did you see her last, Mr. Mannix? ... Take your time about answering. You may want to think it over."

Mannix took his time. It was a full minute before he spoke, and then it was to put another question.

"Haven't I got a right to call on a lady—-haven't I?"

"Certainly. Therefore, why should a question about so obviously correct and irreproachable an episode make you uneasy?"

"Me uneasy?" Mannix, with considerable effort, produced a grin. "I'm just wondering what you got in your mind, asking me about my private affairs."

"I'll tell you. Miss Odell was murdered at about midnight Monday. No one came or went through the front door of the house, and the side door was locked. The only way any one could have entered her apartment was by way of Apartment 2; and nobody who knew Miss Odell ever visited Apartment 2 except yourself."

At these words Mannix leaned over the table, grasping the edge of it with both hands for support. His eyes were wide and his sensual lips hung open. But it was not fear that one read in his attitude; it was sheer amazement. He sat for a moment staring at Vance, stunned and incredulous.

"That's what you think, is it? No one could've got in or out except by Apartment 2, because the side door was locked?" He gave a short, vicious laugh. "If that side door didn't happen to be locked Monday night, where'd I stand then—huh? Where'd I stand?"

"I rather think you'd stand with us—with the district attorney." Vance was watching him like a cat.

"Sure I would!" spat Mannix. "And let me tell you something, my friend: that's just where I stand—absolutely!" He swung heavily about and faced Markham. "I'm a good fellow, y' understand, but I've kept my mouth shut long enough. . . . That side door wasn't locked Monday night. And I know who sneaked out of it at five minutes to twelve!"

"*Ça marche!*" murmured Vance, reseating himself and calmly lighting a cigarette.

Markham was too astonished to speak at once; and Heath sat stock-still, his cigar halfway to his mouth.

At length Markham leaned back and folded his arms.

"I think you'd better tell us the whole story, Mr. Mannix." His voice held a quality which made the request an imperative.

Mannix, too, settled back in his chair.

"Oh, I'm going to tell it—believe me, I'm going to tell it. You had the right idea. I spent the evening with Miss Frisbee. No harm in that, though."

"What time did you go there?"

"After office hours—half past five, quarter to six. Came up in the subway, got off at 72nd, and walked over."

"And you entered the house through the front door?"

"No. I walked down the alleyway and went in the side door—like I generally do. It's nobody's business who I call on, and what the telephone operator in the front hall don't know don't hurt him."

"That's all right so far," observed Heath. "The janitor didn't bolt the side door until after six."

"And did you stay the entire evening, Mr. Mannix?" asked Markham.

"Sure—till just before midnight. Miss Frisbee cooked the dinner, and I'd brought along a bottle of wine. Social little party—just the two of us. And I didn't go outside the apartment, understand, until five minutes to twelve. You can get the lady down here and ask her. I'll call

371

her up now and tell her to explain the exact situation about Monday night. I'm not asking you to take my word for it—positively not."

Markham made a gesture dismissing the suggestion.

"What took place at five minutes to twelve?"

Mannix hesitated, as if loath to come to the point.

"I'm a good fellow, y' understand. And a friend's a friend. But—I ask you—is that any reason why I should get in wrong for something I didn't have absolutely nothing to do with?"

He waited for an answer, but receiving none, continued.

"Sure, I'm right. Anyway, here's what happened. As I said, I was calling on the lady. But I had another date for later that night; so a few minutes before midnight I said good-bye and started to go. Just as I opened the door I saw someone sneaking away from the Canary's apartment down the little back hall to the side door. There was a light in the hall, and the door of Apartment 2 faces that side door. I saw the fellow as plain as I see you—positively as plain."

"Who was it?"

"Well, if you got to know, it was Pop Cleaver."

Markham's head jerked slightly.

"What did you do then?"

"Nothing, Mr. Markham—nothing at all. I didn't think much about it, y' understand. I knew Pop was chasing after the Canary, and I just supposed he'd been calling on her. But I didn't want Pop to see me—none of his business where I spend my time. So I waited quietly till he went out—"

"By the side door?"

"Sure. Then I went out the same way. I was going to leave by the front door, because I knew the side door was always locked at night. But when I saw Pop go out that way, I said to myself I'd do the same. No sense giving your business away to a telephone operator if you haven't got to—no sense at all. So I went out the same way I came in. Picked up a taxi on Broadway, and went—"

"That's enough!" Again Vance's command cut him short.

"Oh, all right—all right." Mannix seemed content to end his statement at this point. "Only, y' understand, I don't want you to think—"

"We don't."

Markham was puzzled at these interruptions, but made no comment.

"When you read of Miss Odell's death," he said, "why didn't you come to the police with this highly important information?"

"I should get mixed up in it!" exclaimed Mannix in surprise. "I got enough trouble without looking for it—plenty."

"An exigent course," commented Markham with open disgust. "But you nevertheless suggested to me, after you knew of the murder, that Cleaver was being blackmailed by Miss Odell."

"Sure I did. Don't that go to show I wanted to do the right thing by you—giving you a valuable tip?"

"Did you see anyone else that night in the halls or alleyway?"

"Nobody—absolutely nobody."

"Did you hear anyone in the Odell apartment—anyone speaking or moving about, perhaps?"

"Didn't hear a thing." Mannix shook his head emphatically.

"And you're certain of the time you saw Cleaver go out—five minutes to twelve?"

"Positively. I looked at my watch, and I said to the lady: 'I'm leaving the same day I came; it won't be tomorrow for five minutes yet.'"

Markham went over his story point by point, attempting by various means to make him admit more than he had already told. But Mannix neither added to his statement nor modified it in any detail; and after half an hour's cross-examination he was permitted to go.

"We've found one missing piece of the puzzle, at any rate," commented Vance. "I don't see now just how it fits into the complete pattern, but it's helpful and suggestive. And, I say, how beautifully my intuition about Mannix was verified, don't y'know!"

"Yes, of course—your precious intuition." Markham looked at him sceptically. "Why did you shut him up twice when he was trying to tell me something?"

"*O, tu ne sauras jamais,*" recited Vance. "I simply can't tell you, old dear. Awfully sorry, and all that."

His manner was whimsical, but Markham knew that at such times Vance was at heart most serious, and he did not press the question. I could not help wondering if Miss La Fosse realized just how secure she had been in putting her faith in Vance's integrity.

Heath had been considerably shaken by Mannix's story.

"I don't savvy that side door being unlocked," he complained. "How the hell did it get bolted again on the inside after Mannix went out? And who unbolted it after six o'clock?"

"In God's good time, my sergeant, all things will be revealed," said Vance.

"Maybe—and maybe not. But if we do find out, you can take it from me that the answer'll be Skeel. He's the bird we gotta get the goods on. Cleaver is no expert jimmy artist; and neither is Mannix."

"Just the same, there was a very capable technician on hand that night, and it wasn't your friend the Dude, though he was probably the Donatello who sculptured open the jewel case."

"A pair of 'em, was there? That's your theory, is it, Mr. Vance? You said that once before; and I'm not saying you're wrong. But if we can hang any part of it on Skeel, we'll make him come across as to who his pal was."

"It wasn't a pal, Sergeant. It was more likely a stranger."

Markham sat glowering into space.

"I don't at all like the Cleaver end of this affair," he said. "There's been something damned wrong about him ever since Monday."

"And I say," put in Vance, "doesn't the gentleman's false alibi take on a certain shady significance now, what? You apprehend, I trust, why I restrained you from questioning him about it at the club yesterday. I rather fancied that if you could get Mannix to pour out his heart to you, you'd be in a stronger position to draw a few admissions from Cleaver. And behold? Again the triumph of intuition! With what you now know about him, you can chivvy him most unconscionably—eh, what?"

"And that's precisely what I'm going to do." Markham rang for Swacker. "Get hold of Charles Cleaver," he ordered irritably. "Phone him at the Stuyvesant Club and also his home—he lives round the corner from the club in West 27th Street. And tell him I want him to be here in half an hour, or I'll send a couple of detectives to bring him in handcuffs."

For five minutes Markham stood before the window, smoking agitatedly, while Vance, with a smile of amusement, busied himself with The Wall Street Journal. Heath got himself a drink of water, and took a turn up and down the room. Presently Swacker re-entered.

"Sorry, Chief, but there's nothing doing. Cleaver's gone into the country somewhere. Won't be back till late tonight."

"Hell! . . . All right—that'll do." Markham turned to Heath. "You have Cleaver rounded up tonight, Sergeant, and bring him in here tomorrow morning at nine."

"He'll be here, sir!" Heath paused in his pacing and faced Markham. "I've been thinking, sir; and there's one thing that keeps coming up in my mind, so to speak. You remember that black document box that was setting on the living room table? It was empty; and what a woman generally keeps in that kind of a box is letters and things like that. Well, now, here's what's been bothering me: that box wasn't jimmied open—it was unlocked with a key. And, anyway, a professional crook don't take letters and documents. . . . You see what I mean, sir?"

"Sergeant of mine!" exclaimed Vance. "I abase myself before you! I sit at your feet! . . . The document box—the tidily opened, empty document box! Of course. Skeel didn't open it—never in this world! That was the other chap's handiwork."

"What was in your mind about that box, Sergeant?" asked Markham.

"Just this, sir. As Mr. Vance has insisted right along, there mighta been someone besides Skeel in that apartment during the night. And you told me that Cleaver admitted to you he'd paid Odell a lot of money last June to get back his letters. But suppose he never paid that money; suppose he went there Monday night and took those letters. Wouldn't he have told you just the story he did about buying 'em back? Maybe that's how Mannix happened to see him there."

"That's not unreasonable," Markham acknowledged. "But where does it lead us?"

"Well, sir, if Cleaver did take 'em Monday night, he mighta held on to 'em. And if any of those letters were dated later than last June, when he says he bought 'em back, then we'd have the goods on him."

"Well?"

"As I say, sir, I've been thinking. . . . Now, Cleaver is outa town today; and if we could get hold of those letters. . . ."

"It might prove helpful, of course," said Markham coolly, looking the sergeant straight in the eye. "But such a thing is quite out of the question."

"Still and all," mumbled Heath. "Cleaver's been pulling a lot of raw stuff on you, sir."

CHAPTER 21

A Contradiction in Dates
Saturday, September 15; 9 a.m.

The next morning Markham and Vance and I breakfasted together at the Prince George, and arrived at the district attorney's office a few minutes past nine. Heath, with Cleaver in tow, was waiting in the reception room.

To judge by Cleaver's manner as he entered, the sergeant had been none too considerate of him. He strode belligerently to the district attorney's desk and fixed a cold, resentful eye on Markham.

"Am I, by any chance, under arrest?" he demanded softly, but it was the rasping, suppressed softness of wrathful indignation.

"Not yet," said Markham curtly. "But if you were, you'd have only yourself to blame. Sit down."

Cleaver hesitated, and took the nearest chair.

"Why was I routed out of bed at seven thirty by this detective of yours"—he jerked his thumb toward Heath—"and threatened with patrol wagons and warrants because I objected to such high-handed and illegal methods?"

"You were merely threatened with legal procedure if you refused to accept my invitation voluntarily. This is my short day at the office; and there was some explaining I wanted from you without delay."

"I'm damned if I'll explain anything to you under these conditions!" For all his nerveless poise, Cleaver was finding it difficult to control himself. "I'm no pickpocket that you can drag in here when it suits your convenience and put through a third degree."

"That's eminently satisfactory to me." Markham spoke ominously. "But since you refuse to do your explaining as a free citizen, I have no other course than to alter your present status." He turned to

Heath. "Sergeant, go across the hall and have Ben swear out a warrant for Charles Cleaver. Then lock this gentleman up."

Cleaver gave a start and caught his breath sibilantly. "On what charge?" he demanded.

"The murder of Margaret Odell."

The man sprang to his feet. The colour had gone from his face, and the muscles of his jowls worked spasmodically. "Wait! You're giving me a raw deal. And you'll lose out, too. You couldn't make that charge stick in a thousand years."

"Maybe not. But if you don't want to talk here, I'll make you talk in court."

"I'll talk here," Cleaver sat down again. "What do you want to know?"

Markham took out a cigar and lit it with deliberation. "First: why did you tell me you were in Boonton Monday night?"

Cleaver apparently had expected the question. "When I read of the Canary's death, I wanted an alibi; and my brother had just given me the summons he'd been handed in Boonton. It was a ready-made alibi right in my hand. So I used it."

"Why did you need an alibi?"

"I didn't need it; but I thought it might save me trouble. People knew I'd been running round with the Odell girl; and some of them knew she'd been blackmailing me—I'd told 'em, like a damn fool. I told Mannix, for instance. We'd both been stung."

"Is that your only reason for concocting this alibi?" Markham was watching him sharply.

"Wasn't it reason enough? Blackmail would have constituted a motive, wouldn't it?"

"It takes more than a motive to arouse unpleasant suspicion."

"Maybe so. Only I didn't want to be drawn into it. You can't blame me for trying to keep clear of it."

Markham leaned over with a threatening smile. "The fact that Miss Odell had blackmailed you wasn't your only reason for lying about the summons. It wasn't even your main reason."

Cleaver's eyes narrowed, but otherwise he was like a graven image. "You evidently know more about it than I do." He managed to make his words sound casual.

"Not more, Mr. Cleaver," Markham corrected him, "but nearly as much. Where were you between eleven o'clock and midnight Monday?"

"Perhaps that's one of the things you know."

"You're right. You were in Miss Odell's apartment."

Cleaver sneered, but he did not succeed in disguising the shock that Markham's accusation caused him.

"If that's what you think, then it happens you don't know, after all. I haven't put foot in her apartment for two weeks."

"I have the testimony of reliable witnesses to the contrary."

"Witnesses!" The word seemed to force itself from Cleaver's compressed lips.

Markham nodded. "You were seen coming out of Miss Odell's apartment and leaving the house by the side door at five minutes to twelve on Monday night."

Cleaver's jaw sagged slightly, and his laboured breathing was quite audible.

"And between half past eleven and twelve o'clock," pursued Markham's relentless voice, "Miss Odell was strangled and robbed. What do you say to that?"

For a long time there was tense silence. Then Cleaver spoke.

"I've got to think this thing out."

Markham waited patiently. After several minutes Cleaver drew himself together and squared his shoulders.

"I'm going to tell you what I did that night, and you can take it or leave it." Again he was the cold, self-contained gambler. "I don't care how many witnesses you've got; it's the only story you'll ever get out of me. I should have told you in the first place, but I didn't see any sense of stepping into hot water if I wasn't pushed in. You might have believed me last Tuesday, but now you've got something in your head, and you want to make an arrest to shut up the newspapers—"

"Tell your story," ordered Markham. "If it's straight, you needn't worry about the newspapers."

Cleaver knew in his heart that this was true. No one, not even his bitterest political enemies, had ever accused Markham of buying kudos with any act of injustice, however small.

"There's not much to tell, as a matter of fact," the man began. "I went to Miss Odell's house a little before midnight, but I didn't enter her apartment; I didn't even ring her bell."

"Is that your customary way of paying visits?"

"Sounds fishy, doesn't it? But it's the truth, nevertheless. I intended to see her—that is, I wanted to—but when I reached her door, something made me change my mind—"

"Just a moment. How did you enter the house?"

"By the side door, the one off the alleyway. I always used it when it was open. Miss Odell requested me to, so that the telephone operator wouldn't see me coming in so often."

"And the door was unlocked at that time Monday night?"

"How else could I have got in by it? A key wouldn't have done me any good, even if I'd had one, for the door locks by a bolt on the inside. I'll say this, though: that's the first time I ever remember finding the door unlocked at night."

"All right. You went in the side entrance. Then what?"

"I walked down the rear hall and listened at the door of Miss Odell's apartment for a minute. I thought there might be someone else with her, and I didn't want to ring unless she was alone. . . ."

"Pardon my interrupting, Mr. Cleaver," interposed Vance. "But what made you think someone else was there?"

The man hesitated.

"Was it," prompted Vance, "because you had telephoned to Miss Odell a little while before, and had been answered by a man's voice?"

Cleaver nodded slowly. "I can't see any particular point in denying it. . . . Yes, that's the reason."

"What did this man say to you?"

"Damn little. He said 'Hello,' and when I asked to speak to Miss Odell, he informed me she wasn't in, and hung up."

Vance addressed himself to Markham. "That, I think, explains Jessup's report of the brief phone call to the Odell apartment at twenty minutes to twelve."

"Probably." Markham spoke without interest. He was intent on Cleaver's account of what happened later and he took up the interrogation at the point where Vance had interrupted.

"You say you listened at the apartment door. What caused you to refrain from ringing?"

"I heard a man's voice inside."

Markham straightened up.

"A man's voice? You're sure?"

"That's what I said." Cleaver was matter of fact about it. "A man's voice. Otherwise I'd have rung the bell."

"Could you identify the voice?"

"Hardly. It was very indistinct; and it sounded a little hoarse. It wasn't anyone's voice I was familiar with; but I'd be inclined to say it was the same one that answered me over the phone."

"Could you make out anything that was said?"

Cleaver frowned and looked past Markham through the open window. "I know what the words sounded like," he said slowly. "I didn't think anything of them at the time. But after reading the papers the next day, those words came back to me——"

"What were the words?" Markham cut in impatiently.

"Well, as near as I could make out, they were: 'Oh, my God! Oh, my God!'—repeated two or three times."

This statement seemed to bring a sense of horror into the dreary old office—a horror all the more potent because of the casual, phlegmatic way in which Cleaver repeated that cry of anguish. After a brief pause Markham asked, "When you heard this man's voice, what did you do?"

"I walked softly back down the rear hall and went out again through the side door. Then I went home."

A short silence ensued. Cleaver's testimony had been in the nature of a surprise; but it fitted perfectly with Mannix's statement.

Presently Vance lifted himself out of the depths of his chair. "I say, Mr. Cleaver, what were you doing between twenty minutes to twelve, when you phoned Miss Odell, and five minutes to twelve, when you entered the side door of her apartment house?"

"I was riding uptown in the subway from 23d Street," came the answer after a short pause.

"Strange—very strange." Vance inspected the tip of his cigarette. "Then you couldn't possibly have phoned to anyone during that fifteen minutes—eh, what?"

I suddenly remembered Alys La Fosse's statement that Cleaver had telephoned to her on Monday night at ten minutes to twelve. Vance, by his question, had, without revealing his own knowledge, created a state of uncertainty in the other's mind. Afraid to commit himself too emphatically, Cleaver resorted to an evasion.

"It's possible, is it not, that I could have phoned someone after leaving the subway at 72nd Street and before I walked the block to Miss Odell's house?"

"Oh, quite," murmured Vance. "Still, looking at it mathematically, if you phoned Miss Odell at twenty minutes to twelve, and then entered the subway, rode to 72nd Street, walked a block to 71st, went into the building, listened at her door, and departed at five minutes to twelve—making the total time consumed only fifteen minutes—you'd scarcely have sufficient leeway to stop en route and phone to anyone. However, I sha'n't press the point. But I'd really like to know what you did between eleven o'clock and twenty minutes to twelve, when you phoned to Miss Odell."

Cleaver studied Vance intently for a moment. "To tell you the truth,

I was upset that night. I knew Miss Odell was out with another man—she'd broken an appointment with me—and I walked the streets for an hour or more, fuming and fretting."

"Walked the streets?" Vance frowned.

"That's what I said." Cleaver spoke with animus. Then, turning, he gave Markham a long, calculating look. "You remember I once suggested to you that you might learn something from a Doctor Lindquist. . . . Did you ever get after him?"

Before Markham could answer, Vance broke in. "Ah! That's it!—Doctor Lindquist! Well, well—of course! . . . So, Mr. Cleaver, you were walking the streets? The *streets*, mind you! Precisely! You state the fact, and I echo the word *streets*. And you—apparently out of a clear sky—ask about Doctor Lindquist. Why Doctor Lindquist? No one has mentioned him. But that word *streets*—that's the connection. The streets and Doctor Lindquist are one—same as Paris and springtime are one. Neat, very neat. . . . And now I've got another piece to the puzzle."

Markham and Heath looked at him as if he had suddenly gone mad. He calmly selected a Régie from his case and proceeded to light it. Then he smiled beguilingly at Cleaver.

"The time has come, my dear sir, for you to tell us when and where you met Doctor Lindquist while roaming the streets Monday night. If you don't, 'pon my word, I'll come pretty close to doing it for you."

A full minute passed before Cleaver spoke; and during that time his cold, staring eyes never moved from the district attorney's face.

"I've already told most of the story; so here's the rest." He gave a soft mirthless laugh. "I went to Miss Odell's house a little before half past eleven—thought she might be home by that time. There I ran into Doctor Lindquist standing in the entrance to the alleyway. He spoke to me and told me someone was with Miss Odell in her apartment. Then I walked round the corner to the Ansonia Hotel. After ten minutes or so I telephoned Miss Odell, and, as I said, a man answered. I waited another ten minutes and phoned a friend of Miss Odell's, hoping to arrange a party; but, failing, I walked back to the house. The doctor had disappeared, and I went down the alleyway and in the side door. After listening a minute, as I told you, and hearing a man's voice, I came away and went home. . . . That's everything."

At that moment Swacker came in and whispered something to Heath. The sergeant rose with alacrity and followed the secretary out of the room. Almost at once he returned, bearing a bulging manila folder. Handing it to Markham, he said something in a low voice inaudible to the rest of us. Markham appeared both astonished and displeased. Waving the sergeant back to his seat, he turned to Cleaver.

"I'll have to ask you to wait in the reception room for a few minutes. Another urgent matter has just arisen."

Cleaver went out without a word, and Markham opened the folder. "I don't like this sort of thing, Sergeant. I told you so yesterday when you suggested it."

"I understand, sir." Heath, I felt, was not as contrite as his tone indicated. "But if those letters and things are all right, and Cleaver hasn't been lying to us about 'em, I'll have my man put 'em back so's no one'll ever know they were taken. And if they do make Cleaver out a liar, then we've got a good excuse for grabbing 'em."

Markham did not argue the point. With a gesture of distaste he began running through the letters, looking particularly at the dates. Two photographs he put back after a cursory glance; and one piece of paper, which appeared to contain a pen-and-ink sketch of some kind, he tore up with disgust and threw into the wastebasket. Three letters, I noticed, he placed to one side. After five minutes' inspection of the others, he returned them to the folder. Then he nodded to Heath.

"Bring Cleaver back." He rose and, turning, gazed out of the window.

As soon as Cleaver was again seated before the desk, Markham said, without looking round, "You told me it was last June that you bought your letters back from Miss Odell. Do you recall the date?"

"Not exactly," said Cleaver easily. "It was early in the month, though—during the first week, I think."

Markham now spun about and pointed to the three letters he had segregated.

"How, then, do you happen to have in your possession compromising letters which you wrote to Miss Odell from the Adirondacks late in July?"

Cleaver's self-control was perfect. After a moment's stoical silence, he merely said in a mild, quiet voice, "You of course came by those letters legally."

Markham was stung, but he was also exasperated by the other's persistent deceptions.

"I regret to confess," he said, "that they were taken from your apartment—though, I assure you, it was against my instructions. But since they have come unexpectedly into my possession, the wisest thing you can do is to explain them. There was an empty document box in Miss Odell's apartment the morning her body was found, and, from all appearances, it had been opened Monday night."

"I see." Cleaver laughed harshly. "Very well. The fact is—though I frankly don't expect you to believe me—I didn't pay my blackmail to Miss Odell until the middle of August, about three weeks ago. That's when all my letters were returned. I told you it was June in order to set back the date as far as possible. The older the affair was, I figured, the less likelihood there'd be of your suspecting me."

Markham stood fingering the letters undecidedly. It was Vance who put an end to his irresolution.

"I rather think, don't y'know," he said, "that you'd be safe in accepting Mr. Cleaver's explanation and returning his billets-doux."

Markham, after a momentary hesitation, picked up the manila folder and, replacing the three letters, handed it to Cleaver.

"I wish you to understand that I did not sanction the appropriating of this correspondence. You'd better take it home and destroy it—I won't detain you any longer now. But please arrange to remain where I can reach you if necessary."

"I'm not going to run away," said Cleaver; and Heath directed him to the elevator.

CHAPTER 22

A Telephone Call

Saturday, September 15; 10 a.m.

Heath returned to the office, shaking his head hopelessly. "There musta been a regular wake at Odell's Monday night."

"Quite," agreed Vance. "A midnight conclave of the lady's admirers. Mannix was there, unquestionably; and he saw Cleaver; and Cleaver saw Lindquist; and Lindquist saw Spotswoode—"

"Humph! But nobody saw Skeel."

"The trouble is," said Markham, "we don't know how much of Cleaver's story is true. And, by the way, Vance, do you believe he really bought his letters back in August?"

"If only we knew! Dashed confusin', ain't it?"

"Anyway," argued Heath, "Cleaver's statement about phoning Odell at twenty minutes to twelve, and a man answering, is verified by Jessup's testimony. And I guess Cleaver saw Lindquist all right that night, for it was him who first tipped us off about the doc. He took a chance doing it, because the doc was liable to tell us he saw Cleaver."

"But if Cleaver had an allurin' alibi," said Vance, "he could simply have said the doctor was lying. However, whether you accept Cleaver's absorbin' legend or not, you can take my word for it there was a visitor, other than Skeel, in the Odell apartment that night."

"That's all right, too," conceded Heath reluctantly. "But, even so, this other fellow is only valuable to us as a possible source of evidence against Skeel."

"That may be true, Sergeant." Markham frowned perplexedly. "Only, I'd like to know how that side door was unbolted and then re-bolted on the inside. We know now that it was open around midnight, and that Mannix and Cleaver both used it."

384

"You worry so over trifles," said Vance negligently. "The door problem will solve itself once we discover who was keeping company with Skeel in the Canary's gilded cage."

"I should say it boils down to Mannix, Cleaver, and Lindquist. They were the only three at all likely to be present; and if we accept Cleaver's story in its essentials, each of them had an opportunity of getting into the apartment between half past eleven and midnight."

"True. But you have only Cleaver's word that Lindquist was in the neighbourhood. And that evidence, uncorroborated, can't be accepted as the lily-white truth."

Heath stirred suddenly and looked at the clock. "Say, what about that nurse you wanted at eleven o'clock?"

"I've been worrying horribly about her for an hour." Vance appeared actually troubled. "Really, y'know, I haven't the slightest desire to meet the lady. I'm hoping for a revelation, don't y'know. Let's wait for the doctor until half past ten, Sergeant."

He had scarcely finished speaking when Swacker informed Markham that Doctor Lindquist had arrived on a mission of great urgency. It was an amusing situation. Markham laughed outright, while Heath stared at Vance with uncomprehending astonishment.

"It's not necromancy, Sergeant," smiled Vance. "The doctor realized yesterday that we were about to catch him in a falsehood; so he decided to forestall us by explaining personally. Simple, what?"

"Sure." Heath's look of wonderment disappeared.

As Doctor Lindquist entered the room I noted that his habitual urbanity had deserted him. His air was at once apologetic and apprehensive. That he was labouring under some great strain was evident.

"I've come, sir," he announced, taking the chair Markham indicated, "to tell you the truth about Monday night."

"The truth is always welcome, Doctor," said Markham encouragingly.

Doctor Lindquist bowed agreement.

"I deeply regret that I did not follow that course at our first interview. But at that time I had not weighed the matter sufficiently; and, having once committed myself to a false statement, I felt I had no option but to abide by it. However, after more mature consideration, I have come to the conclusion that frankness is the wiser course. The fact is, sir, I was not with Mrs. Breedon Monday night between the hours I mentioned. I remained at home until about half past ten. Then I went to Miss Odell's house, arriving a little before eleven. I stood outside in the street until half past eleven; then I returned home."

"Such a bare statement needs considerable amplification."

"I realize it, sir; and I am prepared to amplify it." Doctor Lindquist hesitated, and a strained look came into his white face. His hands were tightly clenched. "I had learned that Miss Odell was going to dinner and the theatre with a man named Spotswoode; and the thought of it began to prey on my mind. It was Spotswoode to whom I owed the alienation of Miss Odell's affections; and it was his interference that had driven me to my threat against the young woman. As I sat at home that night, letting my mind dwell morbidly on the situation, I was seized by the impulse to carry out that threat. Why not, I asked myself, end the intolerable situation at once? And why not include Spotswoode in the debacle? . . ."

As he talked he became more and more agitated. The nerves about his eyes had begun to twitch, and his shoulders jerked like those of a man attempting vainly to control a chill.

"Remember, sir, I was suffering agonies, and my hatred of Spotswoode seemed to cloud my reason. Scarcely realizing what I was doing, and yet operating under an irresistible determination, I put my automatic in my pocket and hurried out of the house. I thought Miss Odell and Spotswoode would be returning from the theatre soon, and I intended to force my way into the apartment and perform the act I had planned. . . . From across the street I saw them enter the house—it was about eleven then—but, when I came face to face with the actuality, I hesitated. I delayed my revenge; I—I played with the idea, getting a kind of insane satisfaction out of it—knowing they were now at my mercy. . . ."

His hands were shaking as with a coarse tremor; and the twitching about his eyes had increased.

"For half an hour I waited, gloating. Then, as I was about to go in and have it over with, a man named Cleaver came along and saw me. He stopped and spoke. I thought he might be going to call on Miss Odell, so I told him she already had a visitor. He then went on toward Broadway, and while I was waiting for him to turn the corner, Spotswoode came out of the house and jumped into a taxicab that had just driven up. . . . My plan had been thwarted—I had waited too long. Suddenly I seemed to awake as from some terrible nightmare. I was almost in a state of collapse, but I managed to get home. . . . That's what happened—so help me God!"

He sank back weakly in his chair. The suppressed nervous excitement that had fired him while he spoke had died out, and he appeared listless and indifferent. He sat several minutes breathing stertorously, and twice he passed his hand vaguely across his forehead. He was in no condition to be questioned, and finally Markham sent for Tracy and gave orders that he was to be taken to his home.

"Temporary exhaustion from hysteria," commented Vance indifferently. "All these paranoia lads are hyper-neurasthenic. He'll be in a psychopathic ward in another year."

"That's as may be, Mr. Vance," said Heath, with an impatience that repudiated all enthusiasm for the subject of abnormal psychology. "What interests me just now is the way all these fellows' stories hang together."

"Yes," nodded Markham. "There is undeniably a groundwork of truth in their statements."

"But please observe," Vance pointed out, "that their stories do not eliminate any one of them as a possible culprit. Their tales, as you say, synchronize perfectly; and yet, despite all that neat coordination, any one of the three could have got into the Odell apartment that night. For instance: Mannix could have entered from Apartment 2 before Cleaver came along and listened; and he could have seen Cleaver going away when he himself was leaving the Odell apartment. Cleaver could have spoken to the doctor at half past eleven, walked to the Ansonia, returned a little before twelve, gone into the lady's apartment, and come out just as Mannix opened Miss Frisbee's door. Again, the excitable doctor may have gone in after Spotswoode came out at half past eleven, stayed twenty minutes or so, and departed before Cleaver returned from the Ansonia. . . . No; the fact that their stories dovetail doesn't in the least tend to exculpate any one of them."

"And," supplemented Markham, "that cry of 'Oh, my God!' might have been made by either Mannix or Lindquist—provided Cleaver really heard it."

"He heard it unquestionably," said Vance. "Someone in the apartment was invoking the Deity around midnight. Cleaver hasn't sufficient sense of the dramatic to fabricate such a thrillin' *bonne-bouche*."

"But if Cleaver actually heard that voice," protested Markham, "then, he is automatically eliminated as a suspect."

"Not at all, old dear. He may have heard it after he had come out of the apartment, and realized then, for the first time, that someone had been hidden in the place during his visit."

"Your man in the clothes closet, I presume you mean."

"Yes—of course. . . . You know, Markham, it might have been the horrified Skeel, emerging from his hiding place upon a scene of tragic wreckage, who let out that evangelical invocation."

"Except," commented Markham, with sarcasm, "Skeel doesn't impress me as particularly religious."

"Oh, that?" Vance shrugged. "A point in substantiation. Irreligious persons call on God much more than Christians. The only true and consistent theologians, don't y'know, are the atheists."

Heath, who had been sitting in gloomy meditation, took his cigar from his mouth and heaved a heavy sigh.

"Yes," he rumbled, "I'm willing to admit somebody besides Skeel got into Odell's apartment, and that the Dude hid in the clothes closet. But, if that's so, then, this other fellow didn't see Skeel; and it's not going to do us a whole lot of good even if we identify him."

"Don't fret on that point, Sergeant," Vance counselled him cheerfully. "When you've identified this other mysterious visitor, you'll be positively amazed how black care will desert you. You'll rubricate the hour you find him. You'll leap gladsomely in the air. You'll sing a roundelay."

"The hell I will!" said Heath.

Swacker came in with a typewritten memorandum and put it on the district attorney's desk. "The architect just phoned in this report."

Markham glanced it over; it was very brief. "No help here," he said. "Walls solid. No waste space. No hidden entrances."

"Too bad, Sergeant," sighed Vance. "You'll have to drop the cinema idea. . . . Sad."

Heath grunted and looked disconsolate. "Even without no other way of getting in or out except that side door," he said to Markham, "couldn't we get an indictment against Skeel, now that we know the door was unlocked Monday night?"

"We might, Sergeant. But our chief snag would be to show how it was originally unlocked and then rebolted after Skeel left. And Abe Rubin would concentrate on that point. No, we'd better wait awhile and see what develops."

Something "developed" at once. Swacker entered and informed the sergeant that Snitkin wanted to see him immediately.

Snitkin came in, visibly agitated, accompanied by a wizened, shabbily dressed little man of about sixty, who appeared awed and terrified. In the detective's hand was a small parcel wrapped in newspaper, which he laid on the district attorney's desk with an air of triumph.

"The Canary's jewellery," he announced. "I've checked it up from the list the maid gave me, and it's all there."

Heath sprang forward, but Markham was already untying the package with nervous fingers. When the paper had been opened, there lay before us a small heap of dazzling trinkets—several rings of exquisite workmanship, three magnificent bracelets, a sparkling sunburst, and a delicately wrought lorgnette. The stones were all large and of unconventional cut.

Markham looked up from them inquisitively, and Snitkin, not waiting for the inevitable question, explained.

"This man Potts found 'em. He's a street cleaner, and he says they were in one of the D. S. C. cans at 23d Street near the Flatiron Building. He found 'em yesterday afternoon, so he says, and took 'em home. Then he got scared and brought 'em to Police Headquarters this morning."

Mr. Potts, the "white-wing," was trembling visibly.

"Thass right, sir—thass right," he assured Markham, with frightened eagerness. "I allus look into any bundles I find. I didn't mean no harm takin' 'em home, sir. I wasn't gonna keep 'em. I laid awake worryin' all night, an' this mornin', as soon as I got a chance, I took 'em to the p'lice." He shook so violently I was afraid he was going to break down completely.

"That's all right, Potts," Markham told him in a kindly voice. Then to Snitkin: "Let the man go—only get his full name and address."

Vance had been studying the newspaper in which the jewels had been wrapped.

"I say, my man," he asked, "is this the original paper you found them in?"

"Yes, sir—the same. I ain't touched nothin'."

"Right-o."

Mr. Potts, greatly relieved, shambled out, followed by Snitkin.

"The Flatiron Building is directly across Madison Square from the Stuyvesant Club," observed Markham, frowning.

"So it is." Vance then pointed to the left-hand margin of the newspaper that held the jewels. "And you'll notice that this Herald of yesterday has three punctures evidently made by the pins of a wooden holder such as is generally used in a club's reading room."

"You got a good eye, Mr. Vance." Heath nodded, inspecting the newspaper.

"I'll see about this." Markham viciously pressed a button. "They keep their papers on file for a week at the Stuyvesant Club."

When Swacker appeared, he asked that the club's steward be got immediately on the telephone. After a short delay, the connection was made. At the end of five minutes' conversation Markham hung up the receiver and gave Heath a baffled look.

"The club takes two Heralds. Both of yesterday's copies are there, on the rack."

389

"Didn't Cleaver once tell us he read nothing but *The Herald*—that and some racing sheet at night?" Vance put the question offhandedly.

"I believe he did." Markham considered the suggestion. "Still, both the club Heralds are accounted for." He turned to Heath. "When you were checking up on Mannix, did you find out what clubs he belonged to?"

"Sure." The sergeant took out his notebook and riffled the pages for a minute or two. "He's a member of the Furriers' and the Cosmopolis."

Markham pushed the telephone toward him.

"See what you can find out."

Heath was fifteen minutes at the task. "A blank," he announced finally. "The Furriers' don't use holders, and the Cosmopolis don't keep any back numbers."

"What about Mr. Skeel's clubs, Sergeant?" asked Vance, smiling.

"Oh, I know the finding of that jewellery gums up my theory about Skeel," said Heath, with surly ill nature. "But what's the good of rubbing it in? Still, if you think I'm going to give that bird a clean bill of health just because the Odell swag was found in a trashcan, you're mighty mistaken. Don't forget we're watching the Dude pretty close. He may have got leery, and tipped off some pal he'd cached the jewels with."

"I rather fancy the experienced Skeel would have turned his booty over to a professional receiver. But even had he passed it on to a friend, would this friend have been likely to throw it away because Skeel was worried?"

"Maybe not. But there's some explanation for those jewels being found, and when we get hold of it, it won't eliminate Skeel."

"No; the explanation won't eliminate Skeel," said Vance; "but—my word!—how it'll change his *locus standi*."

Heath contemplated him with shrewdly appraising eyes. Something in Vance's tone had apparently piqued his curiosity and set him to wondering. Vance had too often been right in his diagnoses of persons and things for the sergeant to ignore his opinions wholly.

But before he could answer, Swacker stepped alertly into the room, his eyes animated.

"Tony Skeel's on the wire, Chief, and wants to speak to you."

Markham, despite his habitual reserve, gave a start. "Here, Sergeant," he said quickly. "Take that extension phone on the table and listen in." He nodded curtly to Swacker, who disappeared to make the connection. Then he took up the receiver of his own telephone and spoke to Skeel.

For a minute or so he listened. Then, after a brief argument, he concurred with some suggestion that had evidently been made; and the conversation ended.

"Skeel craves an audience, I gather," said Vance. "I've rather been expecting it, y'know."

"Yes. He's coming here tomorrow at ten."

"And he hinted that he knew who slew the Canary—eh, what?"

"That's just what he did say. He promised to tell me the whole story tomorrow morning."

"He's the lad that's in a position to do it," murmured Vance.

"But, Mr. Markham," said Heath, who still sat with his hand on the telephone, gazing at the instrument with dazed incredulity, "I don't see why you don't have him brought here today."

"As you heard, Sergeant, Skeel insisted on tomorrow and threatened to say nothing if I forced the issue. It's just as well not to antagonize him. We might spoil a good chance of getting some light on this case if I ordered him brought here and used pressure. And tomorrow suits me. It'll be quiet around here then. Moreover, your man's watching Skeel, and he won't get away."

"I guess you're right, sir. The Dude's touchy and he can give a swell imitation of an oyster when he feels like it." The sergeant spoke with feeling.

"I'll have Swacker here tomorrow to take down his statement," Markham went on; "and you'd better put one of your men on the elevator. The regular operator is off Sundays. Also, plant a man in the hall outside and put another one in Swacker's office."

Vance stretched himself luxuriously and rose.

"Most considerate of the gentleman to call up at this time, don't y'know. I had a longing to see the Monets at Durand-Ruel's this afternoon, and I was afraid I wasn't going to be able to drag myself away from this fascinatin' case. Now that the apocalypse has been definitely scheduled for tomorrow, I'll indulge my taste for Impressionism.... À demain, Markham. Bye-bye, Sergeant."

CHAPTER 23

The Ten-O'clock Appointment
Sunday, September 16; 10 a.m.

A fine drizzle was falling the next morning when we rose; and a chill—the first forerunner of winter—was in the air. We had breakfast in the library at half past eight, and at nine o'clock Vance's car, which had been ordered the night before, called for us. We rode down Fifth Avenue, now almost deserted in its thick blanket of yellow fog, and called for Markham at his apartment in West 12th Street. He was waiting for us in front of the house and stepped quickly into the car with scarcely a word of greeting. From his anxious, preoccupied look I knew that he was depending a good deal on what Skeel had to tell him.

We had turned into West Broadway beneath the Elevated tracks before any of us spoke. Then Markham voiced a doubt which was plainly an articulation of his troubled ruminations.

"I'm wondering if, after all, this fellow Skeel can have any important information to give us. His phone call was very strange. Yet he spoke confidently enough regarding his knowledge. No dramatics, no request for immunity—just a plain, assured statement that he knew who murdered the Odell girl, and had decided to come clean."

"It's certain he himself didn't strangle the lady," pronounced Vance. "My theory, as you know, is that he was hiding in the clothes press when the shady business was being enacted; and all along I've clung lovingly to the idea that he was au secret to the entire proceedings. The keyhole of that closet door is on a direct line with the end of the davenport where the lady was strangled; and if a rival was operating at the time of his concealment, it's not unreasonable to assume that he peered forth—eh, what? I questioned him on this point, you remember; and he didn't like it a bit."

"But, in that case—"

"Oh, I know. There are all kinds of erudite objections to my wild dream. Why didn't he give the alarm? Why didn't he tell us about it before? Why this? and why that? . . . I make no claim to omniscience, y'know; I don't even pretend to have a logical explanation for the various *traits d'union* of my vagary. My theory is only sketched in, as it were. But I'm convinced, nevertheless, that the modish Tony knows who killed his *bona roba* and looted her apartment."

"But of the three persons who possibly could have got into the Odell apartment that night—namely, Mannix, Cleaver, and Lindquist—Skeel evidently knows only one—Mannix."

"Yes, to be sure. And Mannix, it would seem, is the only one of the trio who knows Skeel. . . . An interestin' point."

Heath met us at the Franklin Street entrance to the Criminal Courts Building. He, too, was anxious and subdued and he shook hands with us in a detached manner devoid of his usual heartiness.

"I've got Snitkin running the elevator," he said, after the briefest of salutations. "Burke's in the hall upstairs, and Emery is with him, waiting to be let into Swacker's office."

We entered the deserted and almost silent building and rode up to the fourth floor. Markham unlocked his office door and we passed in.

"Guilfoyle, the man who's tailing Skeel," Heath explained, when we were seated, "is to report by phone to the Homicide Bureau as soon as the Dude leaves his rooms."

It was now twenty minutes to ten. Five minutes later Swacker arrived. Taking his stenographic notebook, he stationed himself just inside of the swinging door of Markham's private sanctum, where he could hear all that was said without being seen. Markham lit a cigar, and Heath followed suit. Vance was already smoking placidly. He was the calmest person in the room, and lay back languorously in one of the great leather chairs as though immune to all cares and vicissitudes. But I could tell by the over-deliberate way he flicked his ashes into the receiver that he, too, was uneasy.

Five or six minutes passed in complete silence. Then the sergeant gave a grunt of annoyance. "No, sir," he said, as if completing some unspoken thought, "I can't get a slant on this business. The finding of that jewellery, now, all nicely wrapped up . . . and then the Dude offering to squeal. . . . There's no sense to it."

"It's tryin', I know, Sergeant; but it's not altogether senseless." Vance was gazing lazily at the ceiling. "The chap who confiscated those baubles didn't have any use for them. He didn't want them, in fact—they worried him abominably."

The point was too complex for Heath. The previous day's developments had shaken the foundation of all his arguments; and he lapsed again into brooding silence.

At ten o'clock he rose impatiently and, going to the hall door, looked out. Returning, he compared his watch with the office clock and began pacing restlessly. Markham was attempting to sort some papers on his desk, but presently he pushed them aside with an impatient gesture.

"He ought to be coming along now," he remarked, with an effort at cheerfulness.

"He'll come," growled Heath, "or he'll get a free ride." And he continued his pacing.

A few minutes later he turned abruptly and went out into the hall. We could hear him calling to Snitkin down the elevator shaft, but when he came back into the office, his expression told us that as yet there was no news of Skeel.

"I'll call up the bureau," he decided, "and see what Guilfoyle had to report. At least we'll know then when the Dude left his house."

But when the sergeant had been connected with police headquarters, he was informed that Guilfoyle had as yet made no report.

"That's damn funny," he commented, hanging up the receiver.

It was now twenty minutes past ten. Markham was growing restive. The tenacity with which the Canary murder case had resisted all his efforts toward a solution had filled him with discouragement; and he had hoped, almost desperately, that this morning's interview with Skeel would clear up the mystery, or at least supply him with information on which definite action could be taken. Now, with Skeel late for this all-important appointment, the strain was becoming tense.

He pushed back his chair nervously and, going to the window, gazed out into the dark haze of fine rain. When he returned to his desk his face was set.

"I'll give our friend until half past ten," he said grimly. "If he isn't here then, Sergeant, you'd better call up the local station house and have them send a patrol wagon for him."

There was another few minutes of silence. Vance lolled in his chair with half-closed eyes, but I noticed that, though he still held his cigarette, he was not smoking. His forehead was puckered by a frown, and he was very quiet. I knew that some unusual problem was occupying him. His lethargy had in it a quality of intentness and concentration.

As I watched him he suddenly sat up straight, his eyes open and alert. He tossed his dead cigarette into the receiver with a jerky movement that attested to some inner excitement.

"Oh, my word!" he exclaimed. "It really can't be, y'know! And yet"—his face darkened—"and yet, by Jove, that's it! . . . What an ass I've been—what an unutterable ass! . . . Oh!"

He sprang to his feet, then stood looking down at the floor like a man dazed, afraid of his own thoughts.

"Markham, I don't like it—I don't like it at all." He spoke almost as if he were frightened. "I tell you, there's something terrible going on—something uncanny. The thought of it makes my flesh creep. . . . I must be getting old and sentimental," he added, with an effort at lightness; but the look in his eyes belied his tone. "Why didn't I see this thing yesterday? . . . But I let it go on. . . ."

We were all staring at him in amazement. I had never seen him affected in this way before, and the fact that he was habitually so cynical and aloof, so adamant to emotion and impervious to outside influences, gave his words and actions an impelling and impressive quality.

After a moment he shook himself slightly, as if to throw off the pall of horror that had descended upon him, and, stepping to Markham's desk, he leaned over, resting on both hands.

"Don't you see?" he asked. "Skeel's not coming. No use to wait—no use of our having come here in the first place. We have to go to him. He's waiting for us. . . . Come! Get your hat."

Markham had risen, and Vance took him firmly by the arm.

"You needn't argue," he persisted. "You'll have to go to him sooner or later. You might as well go now, don't y'know. My word! What a situation!"

He had led Markham, astonished and but mildly protesting, into the middle of the room, and he now beckoned to Heath with his free hand.

"You, too, Sergeant. Sorry you had all this trouble. My fault. I should have foreseen this thing. A devilish shame; but my mind was on Monets all yesterday afternoon. . . . You know where Skeel lives?"

Heath nodded mechanically. He had fallen under the spell of Vance's strange and dynamic importunities.

"Then, don't wait. And, Sergeant! You'd better bring Burke or Snitkin along. They won't be needed here—nobody'll be needed here any more today."

Heath looked inquiringly to Markham for counsel; his bewilderment had thrown him into a state of mute indecision. Markham nodded his approval of Vance's suggestions, and, without a word, slipped into his raincoat. A few minutes later the four of us, accompanied by Snitkin, had entered Vance's car and were lurching uptown. Swacker had been sent home; the office had been locked up; and Burke and Emery had departed for the Homicide Bureau to await further instructions.

Skeel lived in 35th Street, near the East River, in a dingy, but once pretentious, house which formerly had been the residence of some old family of the better class. It now had an air of dilapidation and decay; there was rubbish in the areaway; and a large sign announcing rooms for rent was posted in one of the ground-floor windows.

As we drew up before it Heath sprang to the street and looked sharply about him. Presently he espied an unkempt man slouching in the doorway of a grocery store diagonally opposite, and beckoned to him. The man shambled over furtively.

"It's all right, Guilfoyle," the sergeant told him. "We're paying the Dude a social visit. What's the trouble? Why didn't you report?"

Guilfoyle looked surprised. "I was told to phone in when he left the house, sir. But he ain't left yet. Mallory tailed him home last night round ten o'clock, and I relieved Mallory at nine this morning. The Dude's still inside."

"Of course he's still inside, Sergeant," said Vance, a bit impatiently.

"Where's his room situated, Guilfoyle?" asked Heath.

"Second floor, at the back."

"Right. We're going in. Stand by."

"Look out for him," admonished Guilfoyle. "He's got a gat."

Heath took the lead up the worn steps which led from the pavement to the little vestibule. Without ringing, he roughly grasped the doorknob and shook it. The door was unlocked, and we stepped into the stuffy lower hallway.

A bedraggled woman of about forty, in a disreputable dressing gown, and with hair hanging in strings over her shoulders, emerged suddenly from a rear door and came toward us unsteadily, her bleary eyes focused on us with menacing resentment.

"Say!" she burst out, in a rasping voice. "What do youse mean by bustin' in like this on a respectable lady?" And she launched forth upon a stream of profane epithets.

Heath, who was nearest her, placed his large hand over her face, and gave her a gentle but firm shove backward.

"You keep outa this, Cleopatra!" he advised her, and began to ascend the stairs.

The second-floor hallway was dimly lighted by a small flickering gas jet, and at the rear we could distinguish the outlines of a single door set in the middle of the wall.

"That'll be Mr. Skeel's abode," observed Heath.

He walked up to it and, dropping one hand in his right coat pocket, turned the knob. But the door was locked. He then knocked violently upon it and, placing his ear to the jamb, listened. Snitkin stood directly behind him, his hand also in his pocket. The rest of us remained a little in the rear.

Heath had knocked a second time when Vance's voice spoke up from the semidarkness. "I say, Sergeant, you're wasting time with all that formality."

"I guess you're right," came the answer after a moment of what seemed unbearable silence.

Heath bent down and looked at the lock. Then he took some instrument from his pocket and inserted it into the keyhole.

"You're right," he repeated. "The key's gone."

He stepped back and, balancing on his toes like a sprinter, sent his shoulders crashing against the panel directly over the knob. But the lock held.

"Come on, Snitkin," he ordered.

The two detectives hurled themselves against the door. At the third onslaught there was a splintering of wood and a tearing of the lock's bolt through the moulding. The door swung drunkenly inward.

The room was in almost complete darkness. We all hesitated on the threshold, while Snitkin crossed warily to one of the windows and sent the shade clattering up. The yellow-grey light filtered in, and the objects of the room at once took definable form. A large, old-fashioned bed projected from the wall on the right.

"Look!" cried Snitkin, pointing; and something in his voice sent a shiver over me.

We pressed forward. On the foot of the bed, at the side toward the door, sprawled the crumpled body of Skeel. Like the Canary, he had been strangled. His head hung back over the footboard, his face a hideous distortion. His arms were outstretched, and one leg trailed over the edge of the mattress, resting on the floor.

"*Thuggee,*" murmured Vance. "Lindquist mentioned it. Curious!"

Heath stood staring fixedly at the body, his shoulders hunched. His normal ruddiness of complexion was gone, and he seemed like a man hypnotized.

"Mother o' God!" he breathed, awestricken. And, with an involuntary motion, he crossed himself.

Markham was shaken also. He set his jaw rigidly.

"You're right, Vance." His voice was strained and unnatural.

"Something sinister and terrible has been going on here. . . . There's a fiend loose in this town—a werewolf."

"I wouldn't say that, old man." Vance regarded the murdered Skeel critically. "No, I wouldn't say that. Not a werewolf. Just a desperate human being. A man of extremes, perhaps, but quite rational, and logical—oh, how deuced logical!"

CHAPTER 24

An Arrest

Sunday, p.m., Monday, a.m.; September 16-17

The investigation into Skeel's death was pushed with great vigour by the authorities. Doctor Doremus, the medical examiner, arrived promptly and declared that the crime had taken place between ten o'clock and midnight. Immediately Vance insisted that all the men who were known to have been intimately acquainted with the Odell girl—Mannix, Lindquist, Cleaver, and Spotswoode—be interviewed at once and made to explain where they were during these two hours. Markham agreed without hesitation and gave the order to Heath, who at once put four of his men on the task.

Mallory, the detective who had shadowed Skeel the previous night, was questioned regarding possible visitors; but inasmuch as the house where Skeel lived accommodated over twenty roomers, who were constantly coming and going at all hours, no information could be gained through that channel. All that Mallory could say definitely was that Skeel had returned home at about ten o'clock, and had not come out again. The landlady, sobered and subdued by the tragedy, repudiated all knowledge of the affair. She explained that she had been "ill" in her room from dinnertime until we had disturbed her recuperation the next morning. The front door, it seemed, was never locked, since her tenants objected to such an unnecessary inconvenience. The tenants themselves were questioned, but without result; they were not of a class likely to give information to the police, even had they possessed any.

The fingerprint experts made a careful examination of the room but failed to find any marks except Skeel's own. A thorough search through the murdered man's effects occupied several hours; but nothing was discovered that gave any hint of the murderer's identity. A .38 Colt automatic, fully loaded, was found under one of the pillows on the bed; and eleven hundred dollars, in bills of large denomination, was taken from a hollow brass curtain rod. Also, under a loose board in the hall, the missing steel chisel, with the fissure in the blade, was found. But these items were of no value in solving the mystery of Skeel's death; and at four o'clock in the afternoon the room was closed with an emergency padlock and put under guard.

Markham and Vance and I had remained several hours after our discovery of the body. Markham had taken immediate charge of the case and had conducted the interrogation of the tenants. Vance had watched the routine activities of the police with unwonted intentness, and had even taken part in the search. He had seemed particularly interested in Skeel's evening clothes, and had examined them garment by garment. Heath had looked at him from time to time, but there had been neither contempt nor amusement in the sergeant's glances.

At half past two Markham departed, after informing Heath that he would be at the Stuyvesant Club during the remainder of the day; and Vance and I went with him. We had a belated luncheon in the empty grill.

"This Skeel episode rather knocks the foundation from under everything," Markham said dispiritedly, as our coffee was served.

"Oh, no—not that," Vance answered. "Rather, let us say that it has added a new column to the edifice of my giddy theory."

"Your theory—yes. It's about all that's left to go on." Markham sighed. "It has certainly received substantiation this morning. . . . Remarkable how you called the turn when Skeel failed to show up."

Again Vance contradicted him.

"You overestimate my little flutter in forensics, Markham dear. You see, I assumed that the lady's strangler knew of Skeel's offer to you. That offer was probably a threat of some kind on Skeel's part; otherwise he wouldn't have set the appointment a day ahead. He no doubt hoped the victim of his threat would become amenable in the meantime. And that money hidden in the curtain rod leads me to think he was blackmailing the Canary's murderer and had been refused a further donation just before he phoned you yesterday. That would account, too, for his having kept his guilty knowledge to himself all this time."

"You may be right. But now we're worse off than ever, for we haven't even Skeel to guide us."

"At least we've forced our elusive culprit to commit a second crime to cover up his first, don't y'know. And when we have learned what the Canary's various amorists were doing last night between ten and twelve, we may have something suggestive on which to work. By the bye, when may we expect this thrillin' information?"

"It depends upon what luck Heath's men have. Tonight sometime, if everything goes well."

It was, in fact, about half past eight when Heath telephoned the reports. But here again Markham seemed to have drawn a blank. A less satisfactory account could scarcely be imagined. Doctor Lindquist had suffered a "nervous stroke" the preceding afternoon, and had been taken to the Episcopal Hospital. He was still there under the care of two eminent physicians whose word it was impossible to doubt; and it would be a week at least before he would be able to resume his work. This report was the only definite one of the four, and it completely exonerated the doctor from any participation in the previous night's crime.

By a curious coincidence neither Mannix, nor Cleaver, nor Spotswoode could furnish a satisfactory alibi. All three of them, according to their statements, had remained at home the night before. The weather had been inclement; and though Mannix and Spotswoode admitted to having been out earlier in the evening, they stated that they had returned home before ten o'clock. Mannix lived in an apartment hotel, and, as it was Saturday night, the lobby was crowded, so that no one would have been likely to see him come in. Cleaver lived in a small private apartment house without a doorman or hall-boys to observe his movements. Spotswoode was staying at the Stuyvesant Club, and since his rooms were on the third floor, he rarely used the elevator. Moreover, there had been a political reception and dance at the club the previous night, and he might have walked in and out at random a dozen times without being noticed.

"Not what you'd call illuminatin'," said Vance, when Markham had given him this information.

"It eliminates Lindquist, at any rate."

"Quite. And, automatically, it eliminates him as an object of suspicion in the Canary's death also; for these two crimes are part of a whole—integers of the same problem. They complement each other. The latter was conceived in relation to the first—was, in fact, a logical outgrowth of it."

Markham nodded.

"That's reasonable enough. Anyway, I've passed the combative stage. I think I'll drift for a while on the stream of your theory and see what happens."

"What irks me is the disquietin' feeling that positively nothing will happen unless we force the issue. The lad who manoeuvred those two obits had real bean in him."

As he spoke Spotswoode entered the room and looked about as if searching for someone. Catching sight of Markham, he came briskly forward, with a look of inquisitive perplexity.

"Forgive me for intruding, sir," he apologized, nodding pleasantly to Vance and me, "but a police officer was here this afternoon inquiring as to my whereabouts last night. It struck me as strange, but I thought little of it until I happened to see the name of Tony Skeel in the headlines of a 'special' tonight and read he had been strangled. I remember you asked me regarding such a man in connection with Miss Odell, and I wondered if, by any chance, there could be any connection between the two murders, and if I was, after all, to be drawn into the affair."

"No, I think not," said Markham. "There seemed a possibility that the two crimes were related; and, as a matter of routine, the police questioned all the close friends of Miss Odell in the hope of turning up something suggestive. You may dismiss the matter from your mind. I trust," he added, "the officer was not unpleasantly importunate."

"Not at all." Spotswoode's look of anxiety disappeared. "He was extremely courteous but a bit mysterious. Who was this man Skeel?"

"A half-world character and ex-burglar. He had some hold on Miss Odell, and, I believe, extorted money from her."

A cloud of angry disgust passed over Spotswoode's face. "A creature like that deserves the fate that overtook him."

We chatted on various matters until ten o'clock, when Vance rose and gave Markham a reproachful look.

"I'm going to try to recover some lost sleep. I'm temperamentally unfitted for a policeman's life."

Despite this complaint, however, nine o'clock the next morning found him at the district attorney's office. He had brought several newspapers with him, and was reading, with much amusement, the first complete accounts of Skeel's murder. Monday was generally a busy day for Markham and he arrived at the office before half past eight in an effort to clean up some pressing routine matters before proceeding with his investigation of the Odell case. Heath, I knew, was to come for a conference at ten o'clock. In the meantime there was nothing for Vance to do but read the newspapers; and I occupied myself in like manner.

Punctually at ten Heath arrived, and from his manner it was plain that something had happened to cheer him immeasurably. He was almost jaunty, and his formal, self-satisfied salutation to Vance was like that of a conqueror to a vanquished adversary. He shook hands with Markham with more than his customary punctility.

"Our troubles are over, sir," he said, and paused to light his cigar. "I've arrested Jessup."

It was Vance who broke the dramatic silence following this astounding announcement.

"In the name of Heaven—what for?"

Heath turned deliberately, in no wise abashed by the other's tone.

"For the murder of Margaret Odell and Tony Skeel."

"Oh, my aunt! Oh, my precious aunt!" Vance sat up and stared at him in amazement. "Sweet angels of Heaven, come down and solace me!"

Heath's complacency was unshaken. "You won't need no angels, or aunts either, when you hear what I've found out about this fellow. I've got him tied up in a sack, ready to hand to the jury."

The first wave of Markham's astonishment had subsided. "Let's have the story, Sergeant."

Heath settled himself in a chair. He took a few moments to arrange his thoughts.

"It's like this, sir. Yesterday afternoon I got to thinking. Here was Skeel murdered, same like Odell, after he'd promised to squeal; and it certainly looked as though the same guy had strangled both of 'em. Therefore, I concluded that there musta been two guys in the apartment Monday night—the Dude and the murderer—just like Mr. Vance has been saying all along. Then I figured that they knew each other pretty well, because not only did the other fellow know where the Dude lived, but he musta been wise to the fact that the Dude was going to squeal yesterday. It looked to me, sir, like they had pulled the Odell job together—which is why the Dude didn't squeal in the first place. But after the other fellow lost his nerve and threw the jewellery away, Skeel thought he'd play safe by turning state's evidence, so he phoned you."

The sergeant smoked a moment.

"I never put much stock in Mannix and Cleaver and the doc. They weren't the kind to do a job like that, and they certainly weren't the kind that would be mixed up with a jailbird like Skeel. So I stood all three of 'em to one side and began looking around for a bad egg—somebody who'd have been likely to be Skeel's accomplice. But first I tried to figure out what you might call the physical obstacles in the case—that is, the snags we were up against in our reconstruction of the crime."

Again he paused.

"Now, the thing that's been bothering us most is that side door. How did it get unbolted after six o'clock? And who bolted it again after the crime? Skeel musta come in by it before eleven, because he was in the apartment when Spotswoode and Odell returned from the theatre; and he probably went out by it after Cleaver had come to the apartment at about midnight. But that wasn't explaining how it got bolted again on the inside. Well, sir, I studied over this for a long time yesterday and then I went up to the house and took another look at the door. Young Spively was running the switchboard, and I asked him where Jessup was, for I wanted to ask him some questions. And Spively told me he'd quit his job the day before—Saturday afternoon!"

Heath waited to let this fact sink in.

"I was on my way downtown before the idea came to me. Then it hit me sudden-like; and the whole case broke wide open. Mr. Markham, nobody but Jessup coulda opened that side door and locked it again—nobody. Figure it out for yourself, sir—though I guess you've pretty well done it already. Skeel couldn't've done it. And there wasn't nobody else to do it."

Markham had become interested and leaned forward.

"After this idea had hit me," Heath continued, "I decided to take a chance; so I got outa the subway at the Penn Station and phoned Spively for Jessup's address. Then I got my first good news: Jessup lived on Second Avenue, right around the corner from Skeel! I picked up a coupla men from the local station and went to his house. We found him packing up his things, getting ready to go to Detroit. We locked him up, and I took his fingerprints and sent 'em to Dubois. I thought I might get a line on him that way, because crooks don't generally begin with a job as big as the Canary prowl."

Heath permitted himself a grin of satisfaction.

"Well, sir, Dubois nailed him up! His name ain't Jessup at all. The William part is all right, but his real moniker is Benton. He was convicted of assault and battery in Oakland in 1909 and served a year in San Quentin when Skeel was a prisoner there. He was also grabbed as a lookout in a bank robbery in Brooklyn in 1914, but didn't come to trial—that's how we happen to have his fingerprints at Headquarters. When we put him on the grill last night, he said he changed his name after the Brooklyn racket and enlisted in the army. That's all we could get outa him; but we didn't need any more. Now, here are the facts: Jessup has served time for assault and battery. He was mixed up in a bank robbery. Skeel was a fellow prisoner of his. He's got no alibi for

Saturday night when Skeel was killed and he lives round the corner. He quit his job suddenly Saturday afternoon. He's husky and strong and could easily have done the business. He was planning his getaway when we nabbed him. *And*—he's the only person who could've unbolted and rebolted that side door Monday night. . . . Is that a case, or ain't it, Mr. Markham?"

Markham sat several minutes in thought.

"It's a good case as far as it goes," he said slowly. "But what was his motive in strangling the girl?"

"That's easy. Mr. Vance here suggested it the first day. You remember he asked Jessup about his feelings for Odell; and Jessup turned red and got nervous."

"Oh, Lord!" exclaimed Vance. "Am I to be made responsible for any part of this priceless lunacy? . . . True, I pried into the chap's emotions toward the lady; but that was before anything had come to light. I was bein' careful—tryin' to test each possibility as it arose."

"Well, that was a lucky question of yours, just the same." Heath turned back to Markham. "As I see it: Jessup was stuck on Odell, and she told him to trot along and sell his papers. He got all worked up over it, sitting there night after night, seeing these other guys calling on her. Then Skeel comes along, and, recognizing him, suggests burglarizing Odell's apartment. Skeel can't do the job without help, for he has to pass the phone operator coming and going; and as he's been there before, he'd be recognized. Jessup sees a chance of getting even with Odell and putting the blame on someone else; so the two of 'em cook up the job for Monday night. When Odell goes out, Jessup unlocks the side door, and the Dude lets himself into the apartment with his own key. Then Odell and Spotswoode arrive unexpectedly. Skeel hides in the closet, and after Spotswoode has gone, he accidentally makes a noise, and Odell screams. He steps out, and when she sees who he is, she tells Spotswoode it's a mistake. Jessup now knows Skeel has been discovered, and decides to make use of the fact. Soon after Spotswoode has gone, he enters the apartment with a passkey. Skeel, thinking it's somebody else, hides again in the closet; and then Jessup grabs the girl and strangles her, intending to let Skeel get the credit for it. But Skeel comes out of hiding and they talk it over. Finally they come to an agreement, and proceed with their original plan to loot the place. Jessup tries to open the jewel case with the poker, and Skeel finishes the job with his chisel. Then they go out. Skeel leaves by the side door, and Jessup rebolts it. The next day Skeel hands the swag to Jessup to keep till things blow over; and Jessup gets scared and throws it away. Then they have a row. Skeel decides to tell everything, so he can get out from under; and Jessup, suspecting he's going to do it, goes round to his house Saturday night and strangles him like he did Odell."

Heath made a gesture of finality and sank back in his chair.

"Clever—deuced clever," murmured Vance. "Sergeant, I apologize for my little outburst a moment ago. Your logic is irreproachable. You've reconstructed the crime beautifully. You've solved the case. . . . It's wonderful—simply wonderful. But it's wrong."

"It's right enough to send Mr. Jessup to the chair."

"That's the terrible thing about logic," said Vance. "It so often leads one irresistibly to a false conclusion."

He stood up and walked across the room and back, his hands in his coat pockets. When he came abreast of Heath he halted.

"I say, Sergeant; if somebody else could have unlocked that side door and then rebolted it again after the crime, you'd be willing to admit that it would weaken your case against Jessup—eh, what?"

Heath was in a generous mood.

"Sure. Show me someone else who coulda done that, and I'll admit that maybe I'm wrong."

"Skeel could have done it, Sergeant. And he did do it—without anyone knowing it."

"Skeel! This ain't the age of miracles, Mr. Vance."

Vance swung about and faced Markham. "Listen! I'm telling you Jessup's innocent." He spoke with a fervour that amazed me. "And I'm going to prove it to you—some way. My theory is pretty complete; it's deficient only in one or two small points; and, I'll confess, I haven't yet been able to put a name to the culprit. But it's the right theory, Markham, and it's diametrically opposed to the sergeant's. Therefore, you've got to give me an opportunity to demonstrate it before you proceed against Jessup. Now, I can't demonstrate it here; so you and Heath must come over with me to the Odell house. It won't take over an hour. But if it took a week, you'd have to come just the same."

He stepped nearer to the desk.

"I know that it was Skeel, and not Jessup, who unbolted that door before the crime and rebolted it afterward."

Markham was impressed.

"You know this—you know it for a fact?"

"Yes! And I know how he did it!"

CHAPTER 25

Vance Demonstrates

Monday, September 17; 11:30 a.m.

Half an hour later we entered the little apartment house in 71st Street. Despite the plausibility of Heath's case against Jessup, Markham was not entirely satisfied with the arrest; and Vance's attitude had sown further seeds of doubt in his mind. The strongest point against Jessup was that relating to the bolting and unbolting of the side door; and when Vance had asserted that he was able to demonstrate how Skeel could have manipulated his own entrance and exit, Markham, though only partly convinced, had agreed to accompany him. Heath, too, was interested, and, though supercilious, had expressed a willingness to go along.

Spively, scintillant in his chocolate-coloured suit, was at the switchboard and stared at us apprehensively. But when Vance suggested pleasantly that he take a ten-minute walk round the block, he appeared greatly relieved and lost no time in complying.

The officer on guard outside of the Odell apartment came forward and saluted.

"How goes it?" asked Heath. "Any visitors?"

"Only one—a toff who said he'd known the Canary and wanted to see the apartment. I told him to get an order from you or the district attorney."

"That was correct, Officer," said Markham; then, turning to Vance: "Probably Spotswoode, poor devil."

"Quite," murmured Vance. "So persistent! Rosemary and all that. . . . Touchin'."

Heath told the officer to go for a half-hour's stroll; and we were left alone.

"And now, Sergeant," said Vance cheerfully, "I'm sure you know

how to operate a switchboard. Be so kind as to act as Spively's under-
study for a few minutes—there's a good fellow. . . . But, first, please
bolt the side door—and be sure that you bolt it securely, just as it was
on the fatal night."

Heath grinned good-naturedly.

"Sure thing." He put his forefinger to his lips mysteriously, and
crouching, tiptoed down the hall like a burlesque detective in a farce.
After a few moments he came tiptoeing back to the switchboard, his
finger still on his lips. Then, glancing surreptitiously about him with
globular eyes, he put his mouth to Vance's ear.

"*His-s-st!*" he whispered. "The door's bolted. *Gr-r-r.* . . ." He sat
down at the switchboard. "When does the curtain go up, Mr. Vance?"

"It's up, Sergeant." Vance fell in with Heath's jocular mood. "Behold! The hour is half past nine on Monday night. You are Spively—
not nearly so elegant; and you forgot the moustache—but still Spively.
And I am the bedizened Skeel. For the sake of realism, please try to
imagine me in chamois gloves and a pleated silk shirt. Mr. Markham
and Mr. Van Dine here represent 'the many-headed monster of the
pit.'—And, by the bye, Sergeant, let me have the key to the Odell
apartment; Skeel had one, don't y'know."

Heath produced the key and handed it over, still grinning.

"A word of stage direction," Vance continued. "When I have departed by the front door, you are to wait exactly three minutes, and
then knock at the late Canary's apartment."

He sauntered to the front door and, turning, walked back toward
the switchboard. Markham and I stood behind Heath in the little alcove, facing the front of the building.

"Enter Mr. Skeel!" announced Vance. "Remember, it's half past
nine." Then, as he came abreast of the switchboard: "Dash it all! You
forgot your lines, Sergeant. You should have told me that Miss Odell
was out. But it doesn't matter. . . . Mr. Skeel continues to the lady's
door . . . thus."

He walked past us, and we heard him ring the apartment bell.
After a brief pause, he knocked on the door. Then he came back
down the hall.

"I guess you were right," he said, quoting the words of Skeel as
reported by Spively; and went on to the front door. Stepping out into
the street, he turned toward Broadway.

For exactly three minutes we waited. None of us spoke. Heath had
become serious, and his accelerated puffing on his cigar bore evidence
of his state of expectancy. Markham was frowning stoically. At the end

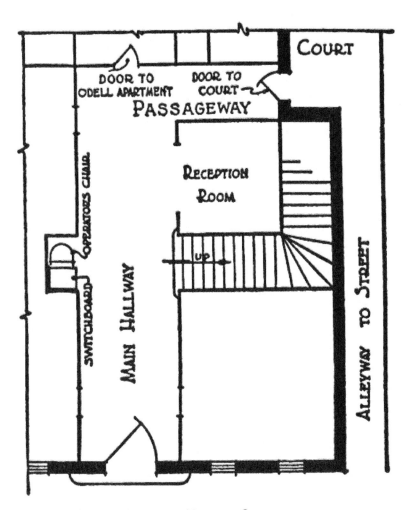

COURT

DOOR TO
ODELL APARTMENT

DOOR TO
COURT

PASSAGEWAY

RECEPTION
ROOM

OPERATOR'S CHAIR

SWITCHBOARD

MAIN HALLWAY

UP

ALLEYWAY TO STREET

WEST SEVENTY-FIRST STREET

of the three minutes Heath rose and hurried up the hall, with Markham and me at his heels. In answer to his knock, the apartment door was opened from the inside. Vance was standing in the little foyer.

"The end of the first act," he greeted us airly. "Thus did Mr. Skeel enter the lady's *boudoir* Monday night after the side door had been bolted, without the operator's seeing him."

Heath narrowed his eyes but said nothing. Then he suddenly swung round and looked down the rear passageway to the oak door at the end. The handle of the bolt was in a vertical position, showing that the catch had been turned and that the door was unbolted. Heath regarded it for several moments; then he turned his eyes toward the switchboard. Presently he let out a gleeful whoop.

"Very good, Mr. Vance—very good!" he proclaimed, nodding his head knowingly. "That was easy, though. And it don't take psychology to explain it. After you rang the apartment bell, you ran down this rear hallway and unbolted the door. Then you ran back and knocked. After that you went out the front entrance, turned toward Broadway, swung round across the street, came in the alley, walked in the side door, and quietly let yourself into the apartment behind our backs."

"Simple, wasn't it?" agreed Vance.

"Sure." The sergeant was almost contemptuous. "But that don't get you nowhere. Anybody coulda figured it out if that had been the only problem connected with Monday night's operations. But it's the rebolting of that side door, after Skeel had gone, that's been occupying my mind. Skeel might've—*might've*, mind you—got in the way you did. But he couldn't have got out that way, because the door was bolted the next morning. And if there was someone here to bolt the door after him, then that same person could've unbolted the door for him earlier, without his doing the ten-foot dash down the rear hall to unbolt the door himself at half past nine. So I don't see that your interesting little drama helps Jessup out any."

"Oh, but the drama isn't over," Vance replied. "The curtain is about to go up on the next act."

Heath lifted his eyes sharply.

"Yeah?" His tone was one of almost jeering incredulity, but his expression was searching and dubious. "And you're going to show us how Skeel got out and bolted the door on the inside without Jessup's help?"

"That is precisely what I intend to do, my sergeant."

Heath opened his mouth to speak but thought better of it. Instead, he merely shrugged his shoulders and gave Markham a sly look.

"Let us repair to the public atrium," proceeded Vance; and he led us into the little reception room diagonally opposite to the switchboard. This room as I have explained, was just beyond the staircase, and along its rear wall ran the little passageway to the side door.

Vance shepherded us ceremoniously to chairs and cocked his eye at the sergeant.

"You will be so good as to rest here until you hear me knock at the side door. Then come and open it for me." He went toward the archway. "Once more I personate the departed Mr. Skeel; so picture me again *en grande tenue*—sartorially radiant. . . . The curtain ascends."

He bowed and, stepping from the reception room into the main hall, disappeared round the corner into the rear passageway.

Heath shifted his position restlessly and gave Markham a questioning troubled look. "Will he pull it off, sir, do you think?" All jocularity had gone out of his tone.

"I can't see how." Markham was scowling. "If he does, though, it will knock the chief underpinning from your theory of Jessup's guilt."

"I'm not worrying," declared Heath. "Mr. Vance knows a lot; he's got ideas. But how in hell—?"

He was interrupted by a loud knocking on the side door. The three of us sprang up simultaneously and hurried round the corner of the main hall. The rear passageway was empty. There was no door or aperture of any kind on either side of it. It consisted of two blank walls; and at the end, occupying almost its entire width, was the oak door which led to the court. Vance could have disappeared only through that oak door. And the thing we all noticed at once—for our eyes had immediately sought it—was the horizontal position of the bolt handle. This meant that the door was bolted.

Heath was not merely astonished—he was dumbfounded. Markham had halted abruptly, and stood staring down the empty passageway as if he saw a ghost. After a momentary hesitation Heath walked rapidly to the door. But he did not open it at once. He went down on his knees before the lock and scrutinized the bolt carefully. Then he took out his pocket knife and inserted the blade into the crack between the door and the casing. The point halted against the inner moulding, and the edge of the blade scraped upon the circular bolt. There was no question that the heavy oak casings and mouldings of the door were solid and well fitted, and that the bolt had been securely thrown from the inside. Heath, however, was still suspicious and, grasping the doorknob, he tugged at it violently. But the door held firmly. At length he threw the bolt handle

411

to a vertical position and opened the door. Vance was standing in the court, placidly smoking and inspecting the brickwork of the alley wall.

"I say, Markham," he remarked, "here's a curious thing. This wall, d'ye know, must be very old. It wasn't built in these latter days of breathless efficiency. The beauty-loving mason who erected it laid the bricks in Flemish bond instead of the Running—or Stretcher—bond of our own restless age. And up there a bit"—he pointed toward the rear yard—"is a Rowlock and Checkerboard pattern. Very neat and very pretty—more pleasing even than the popular English Cross bond. And the mortar joints are all V-tooled. . . . Fancy!"

Markham was fuming. "Damn it, Vance! I'm not building brick walls. What I want to know is how you got out here and left the door bolted on the inside."

"Oh, that!" Vance crushed out his cigarette and re-entered the building. "I merely made use of a bit of clever criminal mechanism. It's very simple, like all truly effective appliances—oh, simple beyond words. I blush at its simplicity. . . . Observe!"

He took from his pocket a tiny pair of tweezers to the end of which was tied a piece of purple twine about four feet long. Placing the tweezers over the vertical bolt handle, he turned them at a very slight angle to the left and then ran the twine under the door so that about a foot of it projected over the sill. Stepping into the court, he closed the door. The tweezers still held the bolt handle as in a vice, and the string extended straight to the floor and disappeared under the door into the court. The three of us stood watching the bolt with fascinated attention. Slowly the string became taut, as Vance gently pulled upon the loose end outside, and then the downward tug began slowly but surely to turn the bolt handle. When the bolt had been thrown and the handle was in a horizontal position, there came a slight jerk on the string. The tweezers were disengaged from the bolt handle and fell noiselessly to the carpeted floor. Then as the string was pulled from without, the tweezers disappeared under the crack between the bottom of the door and the sill.

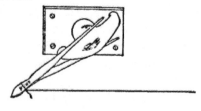

"Childish, what?" commented Vance, when Heath had let him in. "Silly, too, isn't it? And yet, Sergeant dear, that's how the deceased Tony left these premises last Monday night. . . . But let's go into the lady's apartment, and I'll tell you a story. I see that Mr. Spively has returned from his promenade; so he can resume his telephonic duties and leave us free for a causerie."

"When did you think up that hocus-pocus with the tweezers and string?" demanded Markham irritably, when we were seated in the Odell living room.

"I didn't think it up at all, don't y'know," Vance told him carelessly, selecting a cigarette with annoying deliberation. "It was Mr. Skeel's idea. Ingenious lad—eh, what?"

"Come, come!" Markham's equanimity was at last shaken. "How can you possibly know that Skeel used this means of locking himself out?"

"I found the little apparatus in his evening clothes yesterday morning."

"What!" cried Heath belligerently. "You took that outa Skeel's room yesterday during the search without saying anything about it?"

"Oh, only after your ferrets had passed it by. In fact, I didn't even look at the gentleman's clothes until your experienced searchers had inspected them and relocked the wardrobe door. Y' see, Sergeant, this little thingamabob was stuffed away in one of the pockets of Skeel's dress waistcoat, under the silver cigarette case. I'll admit I went over his evening suit rather lovin'ly. He wore it, y'know, on the night the lady departed this life, and I hoped to find some slight indication of his collaboration in the event. When I found this little eyebrow plucker, I hadn't the slightest inkling of its significance. And the purple twine attached to it bothered me frightfully, don't y'know. I could see that Mr. Skeel didn't pluck his eyebrows; and even if he had been addicted to the practice, why the twine? The tweezers are a delicate little gold affair—just what the ravishin' Margaret might have used; and last Tuesday morning I noticed a small lacquer tray containing similar toilet accessories on her dressing table near the jewel case. But that wasn't all."

He pointed to the little vellum wastebasket beside the escritoire, in which lay a large crumpled mass of heavy paper.

"I also noticed that piece of discarded wrapping-paper stamped with the name of a well-known Fifth Avenue novelty shop; and this morning, on my way downtown, I dropped in at the shop and learned that they make a practice of tying up their bundles with purple twine. Therefore, I concluded that Skeel had taken the tweezers and the twine from this apartment during his visit here that eventful night. . . . Now, the question was: Why should he have spent his time tying strings to eyebrow pluckers? I confess, with maidenly modesty, that I couldn't find an answer. But this morning when you told of arresting Jessup and emphasized the rebolting of the side door after Skeel's departure, the fog lifted, the sun shone, the birds began to sing. I became suddenly mediumistic; I had a psychic seizure. The whole *modus operandi* came to me—as they say—in a flash. . . . I told you, Markham old thing, it would take spiritualism to solve this case."

CHAPTER 26

Reconstructing the Crime

Monday, September 17; noon

When Vance finished speaking, there was several minutes' silence. Markham sat deep in his chair glaring into space. Heath, however, was watching Vance with a kind of grudging admiration. The cornerstone in the foundation of his case against Jessup had been knocked out, and the structure he had built was tottering precariously. Markham realized this, and the fact played havoc with his hopes.

"I wish your inspirations were more helpful," he grumbled, turning his gaze upon Vance. "This latest revelation of yours puts us back almost to where we started from."

"Oh, don't be pessimistic. Let us face the future with a bright eye. . . . Want to hear my theory?—it's fairly bulging with possibilities." He arranged himself comfortably in his chair. "Skeel needed money—no doubt his silk shirts were running low—and after his unsuccessful attempt to extort it from the lady a week before her demise, he came here last Monday night. He had learned she would be out, and he intended to wait for her; for she had probably refused to receive him in the custom'ry social way. He knew the side door was bolted at night, and, as he didn't want to be seen entering the apartment, he devised the little scheme of unbolting the door for himself under cover of a futile call at half past nine. The unbolting accomplished, he returned via the alleyway, and let himself into the apartment at some time before eleven. When the lady returned with an escort, he quickly hid in the clothes closet, and remained there until the escort had departed. Then he came forth, and the lady, startled by his sudden appearance, screamed. But, on recognizing him, she told Spotswoode, who was now hammering at the door, that it was all a mistake. So Spotswoode ran along and played poker. A

415

financial discussion between Skeel and the lady—probably a highly acrimonious tiff—ensued. In the midst of it the telephone rang, and Skeel snatched off the receiver and said the Canary was out. The tiff was resumed; but presently another suitor appeared on the scene. Whether he rang the bell or let himself in with a key I can't say—probably the latter, for the phone operator was unaware of his visit. Skeel hid himself a second time in the closet and luckily took the precaution of locking himself in. Also, he quite naturally put his eye to the keyhole to see who the second intruder was."

Vance pointed to the closet door.

"The keyhole, you will observe, is on a line with the davenport; and as Skeel peered out into the room he saw a sight that froze his blood. The new arrival—in the midst, perhaps, of some endearing sentence—seized the lady by the throat and proceeded to throttle her. . . . Imagine Skeel's emotions, my dear Markham. There he was, crouching in a dark closet, and a few feet from him stood a murderer in the act of strangling a lady! Pauvre Antoine! I don't wonder he was petrified and speechless. He saw what he imagined to be maniacal fury in the strangler's eyes; and the strangler must have been a fairly powerful creature, whereas Skeel was slender and almost undersized. . . . No, *merci*. Skeel wasn't having any. He lay doggo. And I can't say that I blame the beggar, what?"

He made a gesture of interrogation.

"What did the strangler do next? Well, well; we'll probably never know, now that Skeel, the horrified witness, has gone to his Maker. But I rather imagine he got out that black document box, opened it with a key he had taken from the lady's handbag, and extracted a goodly number of incriminating documents. Then, I fancy, the fireworks began. The gentleman proceeded to wreck the apartment in order to give the effect of a professional burglary. He tore the lace on the lady's gown and severed the shoulder strap; snatched her orchid corsage and threw it in her lap; stripped off her rings and bracelets; and tore the pendant from its chain. After that he upset the lamp, rifled the escritoire, ransacked the Boule cabinet, broke the mirror, overturned the chairs, tore the draperies. . . . And all the time Skeel kept his eye glued to the keyhole with fascinated horror, afraid to move, terrified lest he be discovered and sent to join his erstwhile *inamorata*, for by now he was no doubt thoroughly convinced that the man outside was a raving lunatic. I can't say that I envy Skeel his predicament; it was ticklish, y'know. Rather! And the devastation went on. He could hear it even when the operations had passed from out his radius of vision. And he himself was caught like a rat in a trap, with no means of escape. A harrowin' situation—my word!"

Vance smoked a moment and then shifted his position slightly.

"Y'know, Markham, I imagine that the worst moment in the whole of Skeel's chequered career came when that mysterious wrecker tried to open the closet door behind which he was crouching. Fancy! There he was cornered, and not two inches from him stood, apparently, a homicidal maniac trying to get to him, rattling that thin barricade of white pine.... Can you picture the blighter's relief when the murderer finally released the knob and turned away? It's a wonder he didn't collapse from the reaction. But he didn't. He listened and watched in a sort of hypnotic panic, until he heard the invader leave the apartment. Then, weak-kneed and in a cold sweat, he came forth and surveyed the battlefield."

Vance glanced about him.

"Not a pretty sight—eh, what? And there on the davenport reclined the lady's strangled body. That corpse was Skeel's dominant horror. He staggered to the table to look at it, and steadied himself with his right hand—that's how you got your fingerprints, Sergeant. Then the realization of his own position suddenly smote him. Here he was alone with a murdered person. He was known to have been intimate with the lady; and he was a burglar with a record. Who would believe that he was innocent? And though he had probably recognized the man who had negotiated the business, he was in no position to tell his story. Everything was against him—his sneaking in, his presence in the house at half past nine, his relations with the girl, his profession, his reputation. He hadn't a chance in the world.... I say, Markham, would *you* have credited his tale?"

"Never mind that," retorted Markham. "Go on with your theory." He and Heath had been listening with rapt interest.

"My theory from this point on," resumed Vance, "is what you might term self-developing. It proceeds on its own inertia, so to speak.—Skeel was confronted by the urgent problem of getting away and covering up his tracks. His mind in this emergency became keen and highly active; his life was forfeit if he didn't succeed. He began to think furiously. He could have left by the side door at once without being seen; but then, the door would have been unbolted. And this fact, taken in connection with his earlier visit that night, would have suggested his manner of unbolting the door. . . . No, that method of escape wouldn't do—decidedly it wouldn't do. He knew he was likely, in any event, to be suspected of the murder, in view of his shady association with the lady and his general character. Motive, place, opportunity, time, means, conduct, and his own record—all were against him. Either he must cover up his tracks, don't y'know, or else his career as a Lothario was at an end. A sweet dilemma! He realized, of course, that if he could get out and leave that side door bolted on the inside, he'd be comparatively safe. No one could then explain how he had come in or gone out. It would establish his only possible alibi—a negative one, to be sure; but, with a good lawyer, he could probably make it hold. Doubtless he searched for other means of escape, but found himself confronted with obstacles on every hand. The side door was his only hope. How could it be worked?"

Vance rose and yawned.

"That's my caressin' theory. Skeel was caught in a trap, and with his shrewd, tricky brain he figured his way out. He may have roamed up and down these two rooms for hours before he hit on his plan; and it's not unlikely that he appealed to the Deity with an occasional 'Oh, my God!' As for his using the tweezers, I'm inclined to think the mechanism of the idea came to him almost immediately—Y'know, Sergeant, this locking of a door on the inside is an old trick. There are any number of recorded cases of it in the criminal literature of Europe. Indeed, in Professor Hans Gross's handbook of criminology there's a whole chapter on the devices used by burglars for illegal entries and exits.* But all such devices have had to do with the locking, not the bolting, of doors. The principle, of course, is the same, but the technic is different. To lock a door on the inside, a needle, or strong slender pin, is inserted through the bow of the key and pulled downward with a string. But on the side door of this house there is no lock and key; nor is there a bow in the bolt handle.—Now, the resourceful Skeel, while pacing nervously about, looking for something that might offer a suggestion, probably espied the tweezers on the lady's dressing table—no lady nowadays is without these little eyebrow pluckers, don't y'know—and immediately his problem was solved. It remained only to test the device. Before departing, however, he chiselled open the jewel case which the other chap had merely dented, and found the solitaire diamond ring that he later attempted to pawn. Then he erased, as he thought, all his

---

* The treatise referred to by Vance was *Handbuch für Untersuchungsrichter als System der Kriminalistik*

fingerprints, forgetting to wipe off the inside doorknob of the closet and overlooking the hand mark on the table. After that he let himself out quietly and rebolted the side door the same as I did, stuffing the tweezers in his waistcoat pocket and forgetting them."

Heath nodded his head oracularly.

"A crook, no matter how clever he is, always overlooks something."

"Why single out crooks for your criticism, Sergeant?" asked Vance lazily. "Do you know of anybody in this imperfect world who doesn't always overlook something?" He gave Heath a benignant smile. "Even the police, don't y'know, overlooked the tweezers."

Heath grunted. His cigar had gone out, and he relighted it slowly and thoroughly. "What do you think, Mr. Markham?"

"The situation doesn't become much clearer," was Markham's gloomy comment.

"My theory isn't exactly a blindin' illumination," said Vance. "Yet I wouldn't say that it left things in pristine darkness. There are certain inferences to be drawn from my vagaries. To wit: Skeel either knew or recognized the murderer; and once he had made good his escape from the apartment and had regained a modicum of self-confidence, he undoubtedly blackmailed his homicidal confrere. His death was merely another manifestation of our inconnu's bent for ridding himself of persons who annoyed him. Furthermore, my theory accounts for the chiselled jewel case, the fingerprints, the unmolested closet, the finding of the gems in the refuse tin—the person who took them really didn't want them, y'know—and Skeel's silence. It also explains the unbolting and bolting of the side door."

"Yes," sighed Markham. "It seems to clarify everything but the one all important point—the identity of the murderer."

"Exactly," said Vance. "Let's go to lunch."

Heath, morose and confused, departed for police headquarters; and Markham, Vance, and I rode to Delmonico's, where we chose the main dining room in preference to the grill.

"The case now would seem to centre in Cleaver and Mannix," said Markham, when we had finished our luncheon. "If your theory that the same man killed both Skeel and the Canary is correct, then Lindquist is out of it, for he certainly was in the Episcopal Hospital Saturday night."

"Quite," agreed Vance. "The doctor is unquestionably eliminated. . . . Yes: Cleaver and Mannix—they're the allurin' twins. Don't see any way to go beyond them." He frowned and sipped his coffee. "My original quartet is dwindling, and I don't like it. It narrows the thing down too much—there's no scope for the mind, as it were, in only two choices. What if we should succeed in eliminating Cleaver and Mannix? Where would we be—eh, what? Nowhere—simply nowhere. And yet, one of the quartet is guilty; let's cling to that consolin' fact. It can't be Spotswoode and it can't be Lindquist. Cleaver and Mannix remain: two from four leaves two. Simple arithmetic, what? The only trouble is, this case isn't simple. Lord, no!—I say, how would the equation work out if we used algebra, or spherical trigonometry, or differential calculus? Let's cast it in the fourth dimension—or the fifth, or the sixth. . . ." He held his temples in both hands. "Oh, promise, Markham—promise me that you'll hire a kind, gentle keeper for me."

"I know how you feel. I've been in the same mental state for a week."

"It's the quartet idea that's driving me mad," moaned Vance. "It wrings me to have my tetrad lopped off in such brutal fashion. I'd set my young trustin' heart on that quartet, and now it's only a pair. My sense of order and proportion has been outraged. . . . I want my quartet."

"I'm afraid you'll have to be satisfied with two of them," Markham returned wearily. "One of them can't qualify, and one is in bed. You might send some flowers to the hospital if it would cheer you any."

"One is in bed—one is in bed," repeated Vance. "Well, well—to be sure! And one from four leaves three. More arithmetic. Three! . . . On the other hand, there is no such thing as a straight line. All lines are curved; they transcribe circles in space. They look straight, but they're not. Appearances, y know—so deceptive! . . . Let's enter the silence, and substitute mentation for sight."

He gazed up out of the great windows into Fifth Avenue. For several moments he sat smoking thoughtfully. When he spoke again, it was in an even, deliberate voice.

"Markham, would it be difficult for you to invite Mannix and Cleaver and Spotswoode to spend an evening—this evening, let us say—in your apartment?"

Markham set down his cup with a clatter and regarded Vance narrowly. "What new harlequinade is this?"

"Fie on you! Answer my question."

"Well, of course, I might arrange it," replied Markham hesitantly. "They're all more or less under my jurisdiction at present."

"So that such an invitation would be rather in line with the situation—eh, what? And they wouldn't be likely to refuse you, old dear—would they?"

"No, I hardly think so. . . ."

"And if, when they had assembled in your quarters, you should propose a few hands of poker, they'd probably accept, without thinking the suggestion strange?"

"Probably," said Markham, nonplussed at Vance's amazing request. "Cleaver and Spotswoode both play, I know; and Mannix doubtless knows the game. But why poker? Are you serious, or has your threatened dementia already overtaken you?"

"Oh, I'm deuced serious." Vance's tone left no doubt as to the fact. "The game of poker, d'ye see, is the crux of the matter. I knew Cleaver was an old hand at the game; and Spotswoode, of course, played with Judge Redfern last Monday night. So that gave me a basis for my plan. Mannix, we'll assume, also plays."

He leaned forward, speaking earnestly.

"Nine-tenths of poker, Markham, is psychology; and if one understands the game, one can learn more of a man's inner nature at a poker table in an hour than during a year's casual association with him. You rallied me once when I said I could lead you to the perpetrator of any crime by examining the factors of the crime itself. But naturally I must know the man to whom I am to lead you; otherwise I cannot relate the psychological indications of the crime to the culprit's nature. In the present case, I know the kind of man who committed the crime; but I am not sufficiently acquainted with the suspects to point out the guilty one. However, after our game of poker I hope to be able to tell you who planned and carried out the Canary's murder."*

Markham gazed at him in blank astonishment. He knew that Vance played poker with amazing skill and that he possessed an uncanny knowledge of the psychological elements in the game; but he was unprepared for the latter's statement that he might be able to solve the Odell murder by means of it. Yet Vance had spoken with such undoubted earnestness that Markham was impressed. I knew what was passing in his mind almost as well as if he had voiced his thoughts. He

---

* Recently I ran across an article by Doctor George A. Dorsey, professor of anthropology at the University of Chicago, and author of *Why We Behave Like Human Beings*, which bore intimate testimony to the scientific accuracy of Vance's theory. In it Doctor Dorsey said: "Poker is a cross-section of life. The way a man behaves in a poker game is the way he behaves in life. . . . His success or failure lies in the way his physical organism responds to the stimuli supplied by the game. . . . I have studied humanity all my life from the anthropologic and psychological viewpoint. And I have yet to find a better laboratory exercise than to observe the manners of men as they see my raise and come back at me. . . . The psychologist's verbalized, visceral, and manual behaviours are functioning at their highest in a poker game. . . . I can truthfully say that I learned about men from poker."

was recalling the way in which Vance had, in a former murder case, put his finger unerringly on the guilty man by a similar process of psychological deduction. And he was also telling himself that, however incomprehensible and seemingly extravagant Vance's requests were, there was always a fundamentally sound reason behind them.

"Damn it!" he muttered at last. "The whole scheme seems idiotic. . . . And yet, if you really want a game of poker with these men, I've no special objection. It'll get you nowhere—I'll tell you that beforehand. It's stark nonsense to suppose that you can find the guilty man by such fantastic means."

"Ah, well," sighed Vance, "a little futile recreation will do us no harm."

"But why do you include Spotswoode?"

"Really, y'know, I haven't the slightest notion—except, of course, that he's one of my quartet. And we'll need an extra hand."

"Well, don't tell me afterwards that I'm to lock him up for murder. I'd have to draw the line. Strange as it may seem to your layman's mind, I wouldn't care to prosecute a man, knowing that it was physically impossible for him to have committed the crime."

"As to that," drawled Vance, "the only obstacles that stand in the way of physical impossibilities are material facts. And material facts are notoriously deceivin'. Really, y'know, you lawyers would do better if you ignored them entirely."

Markham did not deign to answer such heresy, but the look he gave Vance was most expressive.

CHAPTER 27

A Game of Poker

Monday, September 17; 9 p.m.

Vance and I went home after lunch, and at about four o'clock Markham telephoned to say that he had made the necessary arrangements for the evening with Spotswoode, Mannix, and Cleaver. Immediately following this confirmation Vance left the house and did not return until nearly eight o'clock. Though I was filled with curiosity at so unusual a proceeding, he refused to enlighten me. But when, at a quarter to nine, we went downstairs to the waiting car, there was a man I did not know in the tonneau; and I at once connected him with Vance's mysterious absence.

"I've asked Mr. Allen to join us tonight," Vance vouchsafed, when he had introduced us. "You don't play poker, and we really need another hand to make the game interestin', y'know. Mr. Allen, by the bye, is an old antagonist of mine."

The fact that Vance would, apparently without permission, bring an uninvited guest to Markham's apartment amazed me but little more than the appearance of the man himself. He was rather short, with sharp, shrewd features; and what I saw of his hair beneath his jauntily tipped hat was black and sleek, like the painted hair on Japanese dolls. I noted, too, that his evening tie was enlivened by a design of tiny white forget-me-nots, and that his shirtfront was adorned with diamond studs.

The contrast between him and the immaculately stylish and meticulously correct Vance was aggressively evident. I wondered what could be the relationship between them. Obviously it was neither social nor intellectual.

Cleaver and Mannix were already on hand when we were ushered into Markham's drawing room, and a few minutes later Spotswoode arrived. The amenities of introduction over, we were soon seated comfortably about the open log fire, smoking, and sipping very excellent Scotch highballs. Markham had, of course, accepted the unexpected Mr. Allen cordially, but his occasional glances in the latter's direction told me he was having some difficulty in reconciling the man's appearance with Vance's sponsorship.

A tense atmosphere lay beneath the spurious and affected affability of the little gathering. Indeed, the situation was scarcely conducive to spontaneity. Here were three men each of whom was known to the others to have been interested in the same woman; and the reason for their having been brought together was the fact that this woman had been murdered. Markham, however, handled the situation with such tact that he largely succeeded in giving each one the feeling of being a disinterested spectator summoned to discuss an abstract problem. He explained at the outset that the "conference" had been actuated by his failure to find any approach to the problem of the murder. He hoped, he said, by a purely informal discussion, divested of all officialism and coercion, to turn up some suggestion that might lead to a fruitful line of inquiry. His manner was one of friendly appeal, and when he finished speaking, the general tension had been noticeably relaxed.

During the discussion that followed I was interested in the various attitudes of the men concerned. Cleaver spoke bitterly of his part in the affair, and was more self-condemnatory than suggestive. Mannix was voluble and pretentiously candid, but beneath his comments ran a strain of apologetic wariness. Spotswoode, unlike Mannix, seemed loath to discuss the matter and maintained a consistently reticent attitude. He responded politely to Markham's questions, but he did not succeed entirely in hiding his resentment at thus being dragged into a general discussion. Vance had little to say, limiting himself to occasional remarks directed always to Markham. Allen did not speak but sat contemplating the others with a sort of canny amusement.

The entire conversation struck me as utterly futile. Had Markham really hoped to garner information from it, he would have been woefully disappointed. I realized, though, that he was merely endeavouring to justify himself for having taken so unusual a step and to pave the way for the game of poker which Vance had requested. When the time came to broach the subject, however, there was no difficulty about it.

It was exactly eleven o'clock when he made the suggestion. His tone was gracious and unassuming; but by couching his invitation in terms of a personal request, he practically precluded declination. But his verbal strategy, I felt, was unnecessary. Both Cleaver and Spotswoode seemed genuinely to welcome the opportunity of dropping a distasteful discussion in favour of playing cards; and Vance and Allen, of course, concurred instantly. Mannix alone declined. He explained that he knew the game only slightly and disliked it; though he expressed an enthusiastic desire to watch the others. Vance urged him to reconsider but without success; and Markham finally ordered his man to arrange the table for five.

I noticed that Vance waited until Allen had taken his place, and then dropped into the chair at his right. Cleaver took the seat at Allen's left. Spotswoode sat at Vance's right; and then came Markham. Mannix drew up his chair midway behind Markham and Cleaver.

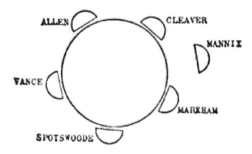

Cleaver first named a rather moderate limit, but Spotswoode at once suggested much larger stakes. Then Vance went still higher, and as both Markham and Allen signified their agreement, his figure was accepted. The prices placed on the chips somewhat took my breath away, and even Mannix whistled softly.

That all five men at the table were excellent players became obvious before the game had progressed ten minutes. For the first time that night Vance's friend Allen seemed to have found his milieu and to be wholly at ease.

Allen won the first two hands, and Vance the third and fourth. Spotswoode then had a short run of good luck, and a little later Markham took a large jackpot, which put him slightly in the lead. Cleaver was the only loser thus far; but in another half-hour he had succeeded in recovering a large portion of his losses. After that Vance forged steadily ahead, only to relinquish his winning streak to Allen. Then for a while the fortunes of the game were rather evenly distributed. But later on both Cleaver and Spotswoode began to lose heavily. By half past twelve a grim atmosphere had settled over the party; for so high were the stakes, and so rapidly did the betting pyramid, that even for men of means—such as all these players undoubtedly were—the amounts which continually changed hands represented very considerable items.

Just before one o'clock, when the fever of the game had reached a high point, I saw Vance glance quickly at Allen and pass his handkerchief across his forehead. To a stranger the gesture would have appeared perfectly natural; but, so familiar was I with Vance's mannerisms, I immediately recognized its artificiality. And simultaneously I noticed that it was Allen who was shuffling the cards preparatory to dealing. Some smoke from his cigar evidently went into his eye at that moment, for he blinked, and one of the cards fell to the floor. Quickly retrieving it, he reshuffled the deck and placed it before Vance to cut.

The hand was a jackpot, and there was a small fortune in chips already on the table. Cleaver, Markham, and Spotswoode passed. The decision thus reached Vance, and he opened for an unusually large amount. Allen at once laid down his hand, but Cleaver stayed. Then Markham and Spotswoode both dropped out, leaving the entire play between Vance and Cleaver. Cleaver drew one card, and Vance, who had opened, drew two. Vance made a nominal wager, and Cleaver raised it substantially. Vance in turn raised Cleaver, but only for a small amount; and Cleaver again raised Vance—this time for an even larger sum than before. Vance hesitated, and called him. Cleaver exposed his hand triumphantly.

"Straight flush—jack high," he announced. "Can you beat that?"

"Not on a two-card draw," said Vance ruefully. He put his cards down to show his openers. He had four kings.

About half an hour later Vance again took out his handkerchief and passed it across his forehead. As before, I noted that it was Allen's deal, and also that the hand was a jackpot which had been twice sweetened. Allen paused to take a drink of his highball and to light his cigar. Then, after Vance had cut the cards, he dealt them.

Cleaver, Markham, and Spotswoode passed, and again Vance opened, for the full amount of the pot. No one stayed except Spotswoode; and this time it was a struggle solely between him and Vance. Spotswoode asked for one card; and Vance stood pat. Then there followed a moment of almost breathless silence. The atmosphere seemed to me to be electrically charged, and I think the others sensed it too, for they were watching the play with a curiously strained intentness. Vance and Spotswoode, however, appeared frozen in attitudes of superlative calm. I watched them closely, but neither revealed the slightest indication of any emotion.

It was Vance's first bet. Without speaking he moved a stack of yellow chips to the centre of the table—it was by far the largest wager that had been made during the game. But immediately Spotswoode measured another stack alongside of it. Then he coolly and deftly counted the remainder of his chips, and pushed them forward with the palm of his hand, saying quietly, "The limit."

Vance shrugged almost imperceptibly.

"The pot, sir, is yours." He smiled pleasantly at Spotswoode and put down his hand face up, to establish his openers. He had held four aces!

"Gad! That's poker!" exclaimed Allen, chuckling.

"Poker?" echoed Markham. "To lay down four aces with all that money at stake?"

Cleaver also grunted his astonishment, and Mannix pursed his lips disgustedly.

"I don't mean any offence, y' understand, Mr. Vance," he said. "But looking at that play from a strictly business standpoint, I'd say you quit too soon."

Spotswoode glanced up.

"You gentlemen wrong Mr. Vance," he said. "He played his hand perfectly. His withdrawal, even with four aces, was scientifically correct."

"Sure it was," agreed Allen. "Oh, boy! What a battle that was!"

Spotswoode nodded and, turning to Vance, said, "Since the exact situation is never likely to occur again, the least I can do, by way of showing my appreciation of your remarkable perception, is to gratify your curiosity. I held nothing."

Spotswoode put down his hand and extended his fingers gracefully toward the upturned cards. There were revealed a five, six, seven, and eight of clubs, and a knave of hearts.

"I can't say that I follow your reasoning, Mr. Spotswoode," Markham confessed. "Mr. Vance had you beaten—and he quit."

"Consider the situation," Spotswoode replied, in a suave, even voice. "I most certainly would have opened so rich a pot, had I been able to, after Mr. Cleaver and you had passed. But since I nevertheless stayed after Mr. Vance had opened for so large an amount, it goes without saying that I must have had either a four-straight, a four-flush, or a four-straight-flush. I believe I may state without immodesty that I am too good a player to have stayed otherwise...."

"And I assure you, Markham," interrupted Vance, "that Mr. Spotswoode is too good a player to have stayed unless he had actually had a four-straight-flush. That is the only hand he would have been justified in backing at the betting odds of two to one. You see, I had opened for the amount in the pot, and Mr. Spotswoode had to put up half the amount of the money on the table in order to stay—making it a two-to-one bet. Now, these odds are not high, and any non-opening hand smaller than a four-straight-flush would not have warranted the risk. As it was, he had, with a one-card draw, two chances in forty-seven of making a straight-flush, nine chances in forty-seven of making a flush, and eight chances in forty-seven of making a straight; so that he had nineteen chances in forty-seven— or more than one chance in three—of strengthening his hand into either a straight-flush, a flush, or a straight."

"Exactly," assented Spotswoode. "However, after I had drawn my one card, the only possible question in Mr. Vance's mind was whether or not I had made my straight-flush. If I had not made it—or had merely drawn a straight or a flush—Mr. Vance figured, and figured rightly, that I would not have seen his large bet and also have raised it the limit. To have done so, in those circumstances, would have been irrational poker. Not one player in a thousand would have taken such a risk on a mere bluff. Therefore, had Mr. Vance not laid down his four aces when I raised him, he would have been foolhardy in the extreme. It turned out, of course, that I was actually bluffing; but that does not alter the fact that the correct and logical thing was for Mr. Vance to quit."

"Quite true," Vance agreed. "As Mr. Spotswoode says, not one player in a thousand would have wagered the limit without having filled his straight-flush, knowing I had a pat hand. Indeed, one might also say that Mr. Spotswoode, by doing so, has added another decimal point to the psychological subtleties of the game; for, as you see, he analyzed my reasoning, and carried his own reasoning a step further."

Spotswoode acknowledged the compliment with a slight bow; and Cleaver reached for the cards and began to shuffle them. But the tension had been broken, and the game was not resumed.

Something, however, seemed to have gone wrong with Vance. For a long while he sat frowning at his cigarette and sipping his highball in troubled abstraction. At last he rose and walked to the mantel, where he stood studying a Cézanne watercolour he had given Markham years before. His action was a typical indication of his inner puzzlement.

Presently, when there came a lull in the conversation, he turned sharply and looked at Mannix.

"I say, Mr. Mannix"—he spoke with only casual curiosity—"how does it happen you've never acquired a taste for poker? All good businessmen are gamblers at heart."

"Sure they are," Mannix replied, with pensive deliberation. "But poker, now, isn't my idea of gambling—positively not. It's got too much science. And it ain't quick enough for me—it hasn't got the kick in it, if you know what I mean. Roulette's my speed. When I was in Monte Carlo last summer, I dropped more money in ten minutes than you gentlemen lost here this whole evening. But I got action for my money."

"I take it, then, you don't care for cards at all."

"Not to play games with." Mannix had become expansive. "I don't mind betting money on the draw of a card, for instance. But no two out of three, y' understand. I want my pleasures to come rapid." And he snapped his thick fingers several times in quick succession to demonstrate the rapidity with which he desired to have his pleasures come.

Vance sauntered to the table and carelessly picked up a deck of cards. "What do you say to cutting once for a thousand dollars?"

Mannix rose instantly. "You're on!"

Vance handed the cards over, and Mannix shuffled them. Then he put them down and cut. He turned up a ten. Vance cut and showed a king.

"A thousand I owe you," said Mannix, with no more concern than if it had been ten cents.

Vance waited without speaking, and Mannix eyed him craftily.

"I'll cut with you again—two thousand this time. Yes?"

Vance raised his eyebrows. "Double? . . . By all means." He shuffled the cards and cut a seven.

Mannix's hand swooped down and turned a five.

"Well, that's three thousand I owe you," he said. His little eyes had now narrowed into slits, and he held his cigar clamped tightly between his teeth.

"Like to double it again—eh, what?" Vance asked. "Four thousand this time?"

Markham looked at Vance in amazement, and over Allen's face there came an expression of almost ludicrous consternation. Everyone present, I believe, was astonished at the offer, for obviously Vance knew that he was giving Mannix tremendous odds by permitting successive doubling. In the end he was sure to lose. I believe Markham would have protested if at that moment Mannix had not snatched the cards from the table and begun to shuffle them.

"Four thousand it is!" he announced, putting down the deck and cutting. He turned up the queen of diamonds. "You can't beat the lady—positively not!" He was suddenly jovial.

"I fancy you're right," murmured Vance; and he cut a trey.

"Want some more?" asked Mannix, with good-natured aggressiveness.

"That's enough." Vance seemed bored. "Far too excitin'. I haven't your rugged constitution, don't y'know."

He went to the desk and made out a check to Mannix for a thousand dollars. Then he turned to Markham and held out his hand. "Had a jolly evening and all that sort of thing. . . . And, don't forget: we lunch together tomorrow. One o'clock at the club, what?"

Markham hesitated. "If nothing interferes."

"But really, y'know, it mustn't," insisted Vance. "You've no idea how eager you are to see me."

He was unusually silent and thoughtful during the ride home. Not one explanatory word could I get out of him. But when he bade me good night he said, "There's a vital part of the puzzle still missing, and until it's found, none of it has any meaning."

CHAPTER 28

The Guilty Man

Tuesday, September 18; 1 p.m.

Vance slept late the following morning and spent the hour or so before lunch checking a catalogue of ceramics which were to be auctioned next day at the Anderson Galleries. At one o'clock we entered the Stuyvesant Club and joined Markham in the grill.

"The lunch is on you, old thing," said Vance. "But I'll make it easy. All I want is a rasher of English bacon, a cup of coffee, and a croissant."

Markham gave him a mocking smile.

"I don't wonder you're economizing after your bad luck of last night."

Vance's eyebrows went up. "I rather fancied my luck was most extr'ordin'ry."

"You held four of a kind twice and lost both hands."

"But, y' see," blandly confessed Vance, "I happened to know both times exactly what cards my opponents held."

Markham stared at him in amazement.

"Quite so," Vance assured him. "I had arranged before the game, d'ye see, to have those particular hands dealt." He smiled benignly. "I can't tell you, old chap, how I admire your delicacy in not referring to my rather unique guest, Mr. Allen, whom I had the bad taste to introduce so unceremoniously into your party. I owe you an explanation and an apology. Mr. Allen is not what one would call a charming companion. He is deficient in the patrician elegancies, and his display of jewellery was a bit vulgar—though I infinitely preferred his diamond studs to his piebald tie. But Mr. Allen has his points—decidedly he has his points. He ranks with Andy Blakely, Canfield, and Honest John Kelly as an indoor soldier of fortune. In fact, our Mr. Allen is none other than Doc Wiley Allen, of fragrant memory."

"Doc Allen! Not the notorious old crook who ran the Eldorado Club?"

"The same. And, incidentally, one of the cleverest card manipulators in a once lucrative but shady profession."

"You mean this fellow Allen stacked the cards last night?" Markham was indignant.

"Only for the two hands you mentioned. Allen, if you happen to remember, was the dealer both times. I, who purposely sat on his right, was careful to cut the cards in accordance with his instructions. And you really must admit that no stricture can possibly attach to my deception, inasmuch as the only beneficiaries of Allen's manipulations were Cleaver and Spotswoode. Although Allen did deal me four of a kind on each occasion, I lost heavily both times."

Markham regarded Vance for a moment in puzzled silence and then laughed good-naturedly. "You appear to have been in a philanthropic mood last night. You practically gave Mannix a thousand dollars by permitting him to double the stakes on each draw. A rather quixotic procedure, I should say."

"It all depends on one's point of view, don't y'know. Despite my financial losses—which, by the bye, I have every intention of charging up to your office budget—the game was most successful. . . . Y' see, I attained the main object of my evening's entertainment."

"Oh, I remember!" said Markham vaguely, as if the matter, being of slight importance, had for the moment eluded his memory. "I believe you were going to ascertain who murdered the Odell girl."

"Amazin' memory! . . . Yes, I let fall the hint that I might be able to clarify the situation today."

"And whom am I to arrest?"

Vance took a drink of coffee and slowly lit a cigarette.

"I'm quite convinced, y'know, that you won't believe me," he returned in an even, matter-of-fact voice. "But it was Spotswoode who killed the girl."

"You don't tell me!" Markham spoke with undisguised irony. "So it was Spotswoode! My dear Vance, you positively bowl me over. I would telephone Heath at once to polish up his handcuffs, but, unfortunately, miracles—such as strangling persons from across town—are not recognized possibilities in this day and age. . . . Do let me order you another croissant."

Vance extended his hands in a theatrical gesture of exasperated despair. "For an educated, civilized man, Markham, there's something downright primitive about the way you cling to optical illusions. I say, y'know, you're exactly like an infant who really believes that the magician generates a rabbit in a silk hat, simply because he sees it done."

"Now you're becoming insulting."

"Rather!" Vance pleasantly agreed. "But something drastic must be done to disentangle you from the Lorelei of legal facts. You're so deficient in imagination, old thing."

"I take it that you would have me close my eyes and picture Spotswoode sitting upstairs here in the Stuyvesant Club and extending his arms to 71st Street. But I simply couldn't do it. I'm a commonplace chap. Such a vision would strike me as ludicrous; it would smack of a *hashish* dream. . . . You yourself don't use *Cannabis indica*, do you?"

"Put that way, the idea does sound a bit supernatural. And *yet*: *Certum est quia impossibile est.* I rather like that maxim, don't y'know; for, in the present case, the impossible is true. Oh, Spotswoode's guilty—no doubt about it. And I'm going to cling tenaciously to that apparent hallucination. Moreover, I'm going to try to lure you into its toils; for your own—as we absurdly say—good name is at stake. As it happens, Markham, you are at this moment shielding the real murderer from publicity."

Vance had spoken with the easy assurance that precludes argument; and from the altered expression on Markham's face I could see he was moved.

"Tell me," he said, "how you arrived at your fantastic belief in Spotswoode's guilt."

Vance crushed out his cigarette and folded his arms on the table.

"We begin with my quartet of possibilities—Mannix, Cleaver, Lindquist, and Spotswoode. Realizing, as I did, that the crime was carefully planned with the sole object of murder, I knew that only someone hopelessly ensnared in the lady's net could have done it. And no suitor outside of my quartet could have been thus enmeshed, or we would have learned of him. Therefore, one of the four was guilty. Now, Lindquist was eliminated when we found out that he was bedridden in a hospital at the time of Skeel's murder; for obviously the same person committed both crimes—"

"But," interrupted Markham, "Spotswoode had an equally good alibi for the night of the Canary's murder. Why eliminate one and not the other?"

"Sorry, but I can't agree with you. Being prostrated at a known place surrounded by incorruptible and disinterested witnesses, both preceding and during an event, is one thing; but being actually on the ground, as Spotswoode was that fatal evening, within a few minutes of the time the lady was murdered, and then being alone in a taxicab for fifteen minutes or so following the event—that is another thing. No one, as far as we know, actually saw the lady alive after Spotswoode took his departure."

"But the proof of her having been alive and spoken to him is incontestable."

"Granted. I admit that a dead woman doesn't scream and call for help and then converse with her murderer."

"I see." Markham spoke with sarcasm. "You think it was Skeel, disguising his voice."

"Lord no! What a priceless notion! Skeel didn't want anyone to know he was there. Why should he have staged such a masterpiece of idiocy? That certainly isn't the explanation. When we find the answer it will be reasonable and simple."

"That's encouraging," smiled Markham. "But proceed with your reason for Spotswoode's guilt."

"Three of my quartet, then, were potential murderers," Vance resumed. "Accordingly, I requested an evening of social relaxation, that I might put them under the psychological microscope, as it were. Although Spotswoode's ancestry was wholly consistent with his having been the guilty one, nevertheless I confess I thought that Cleaver or Mannix had committed the crime; for, by their own statements, either of them could have done it without contradicting any of the known circumstances of the situation. Therefore, when Mannix declined your invitation to play poker last night, I put Cleaver to the first test. I wig-wagged to Mr. Allen, and he straightway proceeded to perform his first feat of prestidigitation."

Vance paused and looked up.

"You perhaps recall the circumstances? It was a jackpot. Allen dealt Cleaver a four-straight-flush and gave me three kings. The other hands were so poor that everyone else was compelled to drop out. I opened, and Cleaver stayed. On the draw, Allen gave me another king, and gave Cleaver the card he needed to complete his straight-flush. Twice I bet a small amount, and each time Cleaver raised me. Finally I called him, and, of course, he won. He couldn't help but win d'ye see. He was betting on a sure thing. Since I opened the pot and drew two cards, the highest hand I could possibly have held would have been four of a kind. Cleaver knew this, and having a straight-flush, he also knew, before he raised my bet, that he had me beaten. At once I realized that he was not the man I was after."

"By what reasoning?"

434

"A poker player, Markham, who would bet on a sure thing is one who lacks the egotistical self-confidence of the highly subtle and supremely capable gambler. He is not a man who will take hazardous chances and tremendous risks, for he possesses, to some degree, what the psychoanalysts call an inferiority complex, and instinctively he grasps at every possible opportunity of protecting and bettering himself. In short, he is not the ultimate, unadulterated gambler. And the man who killed the Odell girl was a supreme gambler who would stake everything on a single turn of the wheel, for, in killing her, that is exactly what he did. And only a gambler whose paramount self-confidence would make him scorn, through sheer egotism, to bet on a sure thing, could have committed such a crime. Therefore, Cleaver was eliminated as a suspect."

Markham was now listening intently.

"The test to which I put Spotswoode a little later," Vance went on, "had originally been intended for Mannix, but he was out of the game. That didn't matter, however, for, had I been able to eliminate both Cleaver and Spotswoode, then Mannix would undoubtedly have been the guilty man. Of course I would have planned something else to substantiate the fact; but, as it was, that wasn't necessary. . . . The test I applied to Spotswoode was pretty well explained by the gentleman himself. As he said, not one player in a thousand would have wagered the limit against a pat hand, when he himself held nothing. It was tremendous—superb! It was probably the most remarkable bluff ever made in a game of poker. I couldn't help admiring him when he calmly shoved forward all his chips, knowing, as I did, that he held nothing. He staked everything, d'ye see, wholly on his conviction that he could follow my reasoning step by step and, in the last analysis, outwit me. It took courage and daring to do that. And it also took a degree of self-confidence which would never have permitted him to bet on a sure thing. The psychological principles involved in that hand were identical with those of the Odell crime. I threatened Spotswoode with a powerful hand—a pat hand—just as the girl, no doubt, threatened him; and instead of compromising—instead of calling me or laying down—he outreached me; he resorted to one supreme coup, though it meant risking everything. . . . My word, Markham! Can't you see how the man's character, as revealed in that amazing gesture, dovetails with the psychology of the crime?"

Markham was silent for a while; he appeared to be pondering the matter. "But you yourself, Vance, were not satisfied at the time," he submitted at length. "In fact, you looked doubtful and worried."

"True, old dear. I was no end worried. The psychological proof of Spotswoode's guilt came so dashed unexpectedly—I wasn't looking for it, don't y'know. After eliminating Cleaver I had a *parti pris*, so to speak, in regard to Mannix; for all the material evidence in favour of Spotswoode's innocence—that is, the seeming physical impossibility of his having strangled the lady—had, I admit, impressed me. I'm not perfect, don't y'know. Being unfortunately human, I'm still susceptible to the malicious animal magnetism about facts and appearances, which you lawyer chaps are continuously exuding over the earth like some vast asphyxiating effluvium. And even when I found that Spotswoode's psychological nature fitted perfectly with all the factors of the crime, I still harboured a doubt in regard to Mannix. It was barely possible that he would have played the hand just as Spotswoode played it. That is why, after the game was over, I tackled him on the subject of gambling. I wanted to check his psychological reactions."

"Still, he staked everything on one turn of the wheel, as you put it."

"Ah! But not in the same sense that Spotswoode did. Mannix is a cautious and timid gambler as compared with Spotswoode. To begin with, he had an equal chance and an even bet, whereas Spotswoode had no chance at all—his hand was worthless. And yet Spotswoode wagered the limit on a pure bit of mental calculation. That was gambling in the higher ether. On the other hand, Mannix was merely tossing a coin, with an even chance of winning. Furthermore, no calculation of any kind entered into it; there was no planning, no figuring, no daring. And, as I have told you from the start, the Odell murder was premeditated and carefully worked out with shrewd calculation and supreme daring. . . . And what true gambler would ask an adversary to double a bet on the second flip of the coin, and then accept an offer to redouble on the third flip? I purposely tested Mannix in that way, so as to preclude any possibility of error. Thus I not only eliminated him, I expunged him, eradicated him, wiped him out utterly. It cost me a thousand dollars, but it purged my mind of any lingering doubt. I then knew, despite all the contr'ry material indications, that Spotswoode had done away with the lady."

"You make your case theoretically plausible. But, practically, I'm afraid I can't accept it." Markham was more impressed, I felt, than he cared to admit. "Damn it, man!" he exploded after a moment. "Your conclusion demolishes all the established landmarks of rationality and sane credibility.—Just consider the facts." He had now reached the argumentative stage of his doubt. "You say Spotswoode is guilty. Yet we know, on irrefutable evidence, that five minutes after he came out of the apartment, the girl screamed and called for help. He was standing by the switchboard, and, accompanied by Jessup, he went to the door and carried on a brief conversation with her. She was certainly alive then. Then he went out the front door, entered a taxicab, and drove away. Fifteen minutes later he was joined by Judge Redfern as he alighted from the taxicab in front of the club here—nearly forty blocks away from the apartment house! It would have been impossible for him to have made the trip in less time; and, moreover, we have the chauffeur's record. Spotswoode simply did not have either the opportunity or the time to commit the murder between half past eleven and ten minutes of twelve, when Judge Redfern met him. And, remember, he played poker in the club here until three in the morning—hours after the murder took place."

Markham shook his head with emphasis.

"Vance, there's no human way to get round those facts. They're firmly established; and they preclude Spotswoode's guilt as effectively and finally as though he had been at the North Pole that night."

Vance was unmoved.

"I admit everything you say," he rejoined. "But as I have stated before, when material facts and psychological facts conflict, the material facts are wrong. In this case, they may not actually be wrong, but they're deceptive."

"Very well, *magnus* Apollo!" The situation was too much for Markham's exacerbated nerves. "Show me how Spotswoode could have strangled the girl and ransacked the apartment, and I'll order Heath to arrest him."

"'Pon my word, I can't do it," expostulated Vance. "Omniscience was denied me. But—deuce take it!—I think I've done rather well in pointing out the culprit. I never agreed to expound his technic, don't y'know."

"So! Your vaunted penetration amounts only to that, does it? Well, well! Here and now I become a professor of the higher mental sciences, and I pronounce solemnly that Doctor Crippen murdered the Odell girl. To be sure, Crippen's dead; but that fact doesn't interfere with my newly adopted psychological means of deduction. Crippen's nature, you see, fits perfectly with all the esoteric and recondite indications of the crime. Tomorrow I'll apply for an order of exhumation."

Vance looked at him with waggish reproachfulness and sighed. "Recognition of my transcendent genius, I see, is destined to be posthumous. *Omnia post obitum fingit majora vetustas.* In the meantime I bear the taunts and jeers of the multitude with a stout heart. 'My head is bloody, but unbowed.'"

He looked at his watch and then seemed to become absorbed with some line of thought.

"Markham," he said, after several minutes, "I've a concert at three o'clock, but there's an hour to spare. I want to take another look at that apartment and its various approaches. Spotswoode's trick—and I'm convinced it was nothing more than a trick—was enacted there; and if we are ever to find the explanation, we shall have to look for it on the scene."

I had got the impression that Markham, despite his emphatic denial of the possibility of Spotswoode's guilt, was not entirely unconvinced. Therefore, I was not surprised when, with only a half-hearted protest, he assented to Vance's proposal to revisit the Odell apartment.

CHAPTER 29

Beethoven's Andante

Tuesday, September 18; 2 p.m.

Less than half an hour later we again entered the main hall of the little apartment building in 71st Street. Spively, as usual, was on duty at the switchboard. Just inside the public reception room the officer on guard reclined in an easy chair, a cigar in his mouth. On seeing the district attorney, he rose with forced alacrity.

"When you going to open things up, Mr. Markham?" he asked. "This rest cure is ruinin' my health."

"Very soon, I hope, Officer," Markham told him. "Any more visitors?"

"Nobody, sir." The man stifled a yawn.

"Let's have your key to the apartment. Have you been inside?"

"No, sir. Orders were to stay out here."

We passed into the dead girl's living room. The shades were still up, and the sunlight of midday was pouring in. Nothing apparently had been touched; not even the overturned chairs had been righted. Markham went to the window and stood, his hands behind him, surveying the scene despondently. He was labouring under a growing uncertainty, and he watched Vance with a cynical amusement which was far from spontaneous.

Vance, after lighting a cigarette, proceeded to inspect the two rooms, letting his eyes rest searchingly on the various disordered objects. Presently he went into the bathroom and remained several minutes. When he came out he carried a towel with several dark smudges on it.

"This is what Skeel used to erase his fingerprints," he said, tossing the towel on the bed.

"Marvellous!" Markham rallied him. "That, of course, convicts Spotswoode."

439

"Tut, tut! But it helps substantiate my theory of the crime." He walked to the dressing table and sniffed at a tiny silver atomizer. "The lady used Coty's Chypre," he murmured. "Why WILL they all do it?"

"And just what does that help substantiate?"

"Markham dear, I'm absorbing atmosphere. I'm attuning my soul to the apartment's vibrations. Do let me attune in peace. I may have a visitation at any moment—a revelation from Sinai, as it were."

He continued his round of investigation and at last passed out into the main hall, where he stood, one foot holding open the door, looking about him with curious intentness. When he returned to the living room, he sat down on the edge of the rosewood table and surrendered himself to gloomy contemplation. After several minutes he gave Markham a sardonic grin.

"I say! This *is* a problem. Dash it all, it's uncanny!"

"I had an idea," scoffed Markham, "that sooner or later you'd revise your deductions in regard to Spotswoode."

Vance stared idly at the ceiling.

"You're devilish stubborn, don't y'know. Here I am trying to extricate you from a deuced unpleasant predicament, and all you do is to indulge in caustic observations calculated to damp my youthful ardour."

Markham left the window and seated himself on the arm of the davenport facing Vance. His eyes held a worried look.

"Vance, don't get me wrong. Spotswoode means nothing in my life. If he did this thing, I'd like to know it. Unless this case is cleared up, I'm in for an ungodly walloping by the newspapers. It's not to my interests to discourage any possibility of a solution. But your conclusion about Spotswoode is impossible. There are too many contradictory facts."

"That's just it, don't y'know. The contradic'try indications are far too perfect. They fit together too beautifully; they're almost as fine as the forms in a Michelangelo statue. They're too carefully coordinated, d'ye see, to have been merely a haphazard concatenation of circumstances. They signify conscious design."

Markham rose and, slowly returning to the window, stood looking out into the little rear yard.

"If I could grant your premise that Spotswoode killed the girl," he said, "I could follow your syllogism. But I can't very well convict a man on the grounds that his defence is too perfect."

"What we need, Markham, is inspiration. The mere contortions of the sibyl are not enough." Vance took a turn up and down the room. "What really infuriates me is that I've been outwitted. And by a manufacturer of automobile access'ries! . . . It's most humiliatin'."

440

He sat down at the piano and played the opening bars of Brahms's *Capriccio No. 1.* "Needs tuning," he muttered; and, sauntering to the Boule cabinet, he ran his finger over the marquetry. "Pretty and all that," he said, "but a bit fussy. Good example, though. The deceased's aunt from Seattle should get a very fair price for it." He regarded a pendent girandole at the side of the cabinet. "Rather nice, that, if the original candles hadn't been supplanted with modern frosted bulbs." He paused before the little china clock on the mantel. "Gingerbread. I'm sure it kept atrocious time." Passing on to the escritoire, he examined it critically. "Imitation French Renaissance. But rather dainty, what?" Then his eye fell on the wastepaper basket, and he picked it up. "Silly idea," he commented, "—making a basket out of vellum. The artistic triumph of some lady interior decorator, I'll wager. Enough vellum here to bind a set of Epictetus. But why ruin the effect with hand-painted garlands? The aesthetic instinct has not as yet invaded these fair States—decidedly not."

Setting the basket down, he studied it meditatively for a moment. Then he leaned over and took from it the piece of crumpled wrapping paper to which he had referred the previous day.

"This doubtless contained the lady's last purchase on earth," he mused. "Very touchin'. Are you sentimental about such trifles, Markham? Anyway, the purple string round it was a godsend to Skeel. . . . What knickknack, do you suppose, paved the way for the frantic Tony's escape?"

He opened the paper, revealing a broken piece of corrugated cardboard and a large square dark-brown envelope.

"Ah, to be sure! Phonograph records." He glanced about the apartment. "But, I say, where did the lady keep the bally machine?"

"You'll find it in the foyer," said Markham wearily, without turning. He knew that Vance's chatter was only the outward manifestation of serious and perplexed thinking; and he was waiting with what patience he could muster.

Vance sauntered idly through the glass doors into the little reception hall, and stood gazing abstractedly at a console phonograph of Chinese Chippendale design which stood against the wall at one end. The squat cabinet was partly covered with a prayer rug, and upon it sat a polished bronze flower bowl.

"At any rate, it doesn't look phonographic," he remarked. "But why the prayer rug?" He examined it casually. "Anatolian—probably called a Caesarian for sale purposes. Not very valuable—too much on the Oushak type. . . . Wonder what the lady's taste in music was. Victor

Herbert, doubtless." He turned back the rug and lifted the lid of the cabinet. There was a record already on the machine, and he leaned over and looked at it.

"My word! The Andante from Beethoven's C-Minor Symphony!" he exclaimed cheerfully. "You know the movement, of course, Markham. The most perfect Andante ever written." He wound up the machine. "I think a little music might clear the atmosphere and volatilize our perturbation, what?"

Markham paid no attention to his banter; he was still gazing dejectedly out of the window.

Vance started the motor, and placing the needle on the record, returned to the living room. He stood staring at the davenport, concentrating on the problem in hand. I sat in the wicker chair by the door waiting for the music. The situation was getting on my nerves, and I began to feel fidgety. A minute or two passed, but the only sound which came from the phonograph was a faint scratching. Vance looked up with mild curiosity, and walked back to the machine. Inspecting it cursorily, he once more set it in operation. But though he waited several minutes, no music came forth.

"I say! That's deuced queer, y'know," he grumbled, as he changed the needle and rewound the motor.

Markham had now left the window and stood watching him with good-natured tolerance. The turntable of the phonograph was spinning, and the needle was tracing its concentric revolutions; but still the instrument refused to play. Vance, with both hands on the cabinet, was leaning forward, his eyes fixed on the silently revolving record with an expression of amused bewilderment.

"The sound box is probably broken," he said. "Silly machines, anyway."

"The difficulty, I imagine," Markham chided him, "lies in your patrician ignorance of so vulgar and democratic a mechanism. Permit me to assist you."

He moved to Vance's side, and I stood looking curiously over his shoulder. Everything appeared to be in order, and the needle had now almost reached the end of the record. But only a faint scratching was audible.

Markham stretched forth his hand to lift the sound box. But his movement was never completed.

At that moment the little apartment was filled with several terrifying treble screams, followed by two shrill calls for help. A cold chill swept my body, and there was a tingling at the roots of my hair.

After a short silence, during which the three of us remained speechless, the same feminine voice said in a loud, distinct tone: "No; nothing is the matter. I'm sorry. . . . Everything is all right. . . . Please go home, and don't worry."

The needle had come to the end of the record. There was a slight click, and the automatic device shut off the motor. The almost terrifying silence that followed was broken by a sardonic chuckle from Vance.

"Well, old dear," he remarked languidly, as he strolled back into the living room, "so much for your irrefutable facts!"

There came a loud knocking on the door, and the officer on duty outside looked in with a startled face.

"It's all right," Markham informed him in a husky voice. "I'll call you when I want you."

Vance lay down on the davenport and took out another cigarette. Having lighted it, he stretched his arms far over his head and extended his legs, like a man in whom a powerful physical tension had suddenly relaxed.

"'Pon my soul, Markham, we've all been babes in the woods," he drawled. "An incontrovertible alibi—my word! If the law supposes that, as Mr. Bumble said, the law is a ass, a idiot.—Oh, Sammy, Sammy, *vy worn't there a alleybi!* . . . Markham, I blush to admit it, but it's you and I who've been the unutterable asses."

Markham had been standing by the instrument like a man dazed, his eyes riveted hypnotically on the telltale record. Slowly he came into the room and threw himself wearily into a chair.

"Those precious facts of yours!" continued Vance. "Stripped of their carefully disguised appearance, what are they?—Spotswoode prepared a phonograph record—a simple enough task. Everyone makes 'em nowadays—"

"Yes. He told me he had a workshop at his home on Long Island where he tinkered a bit."

"He really didn't need it, y'know. But it facilitated things, no doubt. The voice on the record is merely his own in falsetto—better for the purpose than a woman's, for it's stronger and more penetrating. As for the label, he simply soaked it off an ordin'ry record, and pasted it on his own. He brought the lady several new records that night, and concealed this one among them. After the theatre he enacted his gruesome little drama and then carefully set the stage so that the police would think it was a typical burglar's performance. When this had been done, he placed the record on the machine, set it going, and calmly walked out. He had placed the prayer rug and bronze bowl on the cabinet of the machine to give the impression that the phono-graph was rarely used. And the precaution worked, for no one thought of looking into it. Why should they? . . . Then he asked Jessup to call a taxicab—everything quite natural, y' see. While he was waiting for the car the needle reached the recorded screams. They were heard plainly: it was night, and the sounds carried distinctly. Moreover, being filtered through a wooden door, their phonographic timbre was well disguised. And, if you'll note, the enclosed horn is directed toward the door, not three feet away."

"But the synchronization of his questions and the answers on the record. . .?"

"The simplest part of it. You remember Jessup told us that Spot-swoode was standing with one arm on the switchboard when the screams were heard. He merely had his eye on his wristwatch. The moment he heard the cry, he calculated the intermission on the record and put his question to the imagin'ry lady at just the right moment to receive the record's response. It was all carefully figured out before-hand; he no doubt rehearsed it in his laborat'ry. It was deuced simple, and practically proof against failure. The record is a large one—twelve-inch diameter, I should say—and it requires about five minutes for the needle to traverse it. By putting the screams at the end, he allowed himself ample time to get out and order a taxicab. When the car at last came, he rode direct to the Stuyvesant Club, where he met Judge Redfern and played poker till three. If he hadn't met the judge, rest assured he would have impressed his presence on someone else so as to have established an alibi."

Markham shook his head gravely.

"Good God! No wonder he importuned me on every possible oc-casion to let him visit this apartment again. Such a damning piece of evidence as that record must have kept him awake at night."

"Still, I rather fancy that if I hadn't discovered it, he would have succeeded in getting possession of it as soon as your *sergent-de-ville* was removed. It was annoyin' to be unexpectedly barred from the apart-ment, but I doubt if it worried him much. He would have been on hand when the Canary's aunt took possession, and the retrieving of the record would have been comparatively easy. Of course the record constituted a hazard, but Spotswoode isn't the type who'd shy at a low bunker of that kind. No, the thing was planned scientifically enough. He was defeated by sheer accident."

"And Skeel?"

"He was another unfortunate circumstance. He was hiding in the closet there when Spotswoode and the lady came in at eleven. It was Spotswoode whom he saw strangle his erstwhile *amoureuse* and rifle the apartment. Then, when Spotswoode went out, he came forth from hiding. He was probably looking down at the girl when the phonograph emitted its blood-chilling wails. . . . My word! Fancy being in a cold funk, gazing at a murdered woman, and then hearing piercing screams behind you! It was a bit too much even for the hardened Tony. I don't wonder he forgot all caution and put his hand on the table to steady himself. . . . And then came Spotswoode's voice through the door, and the record's answer. This must have puzzled Skeel. I imagine he thought for a moment he'd lost his reason. But pretty soon the significance of it dawned on him; and I can see him grinning to himself. Obviously he knew who the murderer was—it would not have been in keeping with his character had he failed to learn the identities of the Canary's admirers. And now there had fallen into his lap, like manna from heaven, the most perfect opportunity for blackmail that any such charmin' young gentleman could desire. He doubtless indulged himself with roseate visions of a life of opulence and ease at Spotswoode's expense. When Cleaver phoned a few minutes later, he merely said the lady was out, and then set to work planning his own departure."

"But I don't see why he didn't take the record with him."

"And remove from the scene of the crime the one piece of unanswerable evidence? . . . Bad strategy, Markham. If he himself had produced the record later, Spotswoode would simply have denied all knowledge of it, and accused the blackmailer of a plot. Oh, no; Skeel's only course was to leave it and apply for an enormous settlement from Spotswoode at once. And I imagine that's what he did. Spotswoode no doubt gave him something on account and promised him the rest anon, hoping in the meantime to retrieve the record. When he failed to pay, Skeel phoned you and threatened to tell everything, thinking to spur Spotswoode to action. . . . Well, he spurred him—but not to the action desired. Spotswoode probably met him by appointment last Saturday night, ostensibly to hand over the money, but instead, throttled the chap. Quite in keeping with his nature, don't y'know. . . . Stout fella, Spotswoode."

"The whole thing . . . it's amazing."

"I shouldn't say that, now. Spotswoode had an unpleasant task to perform and he set about it in a cool, logical, forthright, businesslike manner. He had decided that his little Canary must die for his peace of mind; she'd probably made herself most annoyin'. So he arranged the date—like any judge passing sentence on a prisoner at the bar—and then proceeded to fabricate an alibi. Being something of a mechanic, he arranged a mechanical alibi. The device he chose was simple and obvious enough—no tortuosities or complications. And it would have succeeded but for what the insurance companies piously call an act of God. No one can foresee accidents, Markham; they wouldn't be accidental if one could. But Spotswoode certainly took every precaution that was humanly possible. It never occurred to him that you would thwart his every effort to return here and confiscate the record; and he couldn't anticipate my taste in music, nor know that I would seek solace in the tonal art. Furthermore, when one calls on a lady, one doesn't expect that another suitor is going to hide himself in the clothes press. It isn't done, don't y'know. . . . All in all, the poor johnny was beaten by a run of abominable luck."

"You overlook the fiendishness of the crime," Markham reproached him tartly.

"Don't be so confoundedly moral, old thing. Everyone's a murderer at heart. The person who has never felt a passionate hankering to kill someone is without emotions. And do you think it's ethics or theology that stays the average person from homicide? Dear no! It's lack of courage—the fear of being found out, or haunted, or cursed with remorse. Observe with what delight the people en masse—to wit, the state—put men to death and then gloat over it in the newspapers. Nations declare war against one another on the slightest provocation, so they can, with immunity, vent their lust for slaughter. Spotswoode, I'd say, is merely a rational animal with the courage of his convictions."

"Society unfortunately isn't ready for your nihilistic philosophy just yet," said Markham. "And during the intervening transition human life must be protected."

He rose resolutely and, going to the telephone, called up Heath.

"Sergeant," he ordered, "get a John-Doe warrant and meet me immediately at the Stuyvesant Club. Bring a man with you—there's an arrest to be made."

"At last the law has evidence after its own heart," chirped Vance, as he lazily donned his topcoat and picked up his hat and stick. "What a grotesque affair your legal procedure is, Markham! Scientific knowledge—the facts of psychology—mean nothing to you learned Solons. But a phonograph record—ah! There, now, is something convincing, irrefragable, final, what?"

On our way out Markham beckoned to the officer on guard. "Under no conditions," he said, "is anyone to enter this apartment until I return—not even with a signed permit."

When we had entered the taxicab, he directed the chauffeur to the club.

"So the newspapers want action, do they? Well, they're going to get it. . . . You've helped me out of a nasty hole, old man."

As he spoke, his eyes turned to Vance. And that look conveyed a profounder gratitude than any words could have expressed.

CHAPTER 30

The End

Tuesday, September 18; 3:30 p.m.

It was exactly half past three when we entered the rotunda of the Stuyvesant Club. Markham at once sent for the manager and held a few words of private conversation with him. The manager then hastened away and was gone about five minutes.

"Mr. Spotswoode is in his rooms," he informed Markham, on returning. "I sent the electrician up to test the light bulbs. He reports that the gentleman is alone, writing at his desk."

"And the room number?"

"Three forty-one." The manager appeared perturbed. "There won't be any fuss, will there, Mr. Markham?"

"I don't look for any." Markham's tone was chilly. "However, the present matter is considerably more important than your club."

"What an exaggerated point of view!" sighed Vance when the manager had left us. "The arrest of Spotswoode, I'd say, was the acme of futility. The man isn't a criminal, don't y'know; he has nothing in common with Lombroso's *Uomo Delinquente*. He's what one might term a philosophic behaviourist."

Markham grunted but did not answer. He began pacing up and down agitatedly, keeping his eyes expectantly on the main entrance. Vance sought a comfortable chair and settled himself in it with placid unconcern.

Ten minutes later Heath and Snitkin arrived. Markham at once led them into an alcove and briefly explained his reason for summoning them.

"Spotswoode's upstairs now," he said. "I want the arrest made as quietly as possible."

"Spotswoode!" Heath repeated the name in astonishment. "I don't see—"

"You don't have to see—yet," Markham cut in sharply. "I'm taking all responsibility for the arrest. And you're getting the credit—if you want it. That suit you?"

Heath shrugged his shoulders. "It's all right with me . . . anything you say, sir." He shook his head uncomprehendingly. "But what about Jessup?"

"We'll keep him locked up. Material witness."

We ascended in the elevator and emerged at the third floor. Spotswoode's rooms were at the end of the hall, facing the Square. Markham, his face set grimly, led the way.

In answer to his knock Spotswoode opened the door and, greeting us pleasantly, stepped aside for us to enter.

"Any news yet?" he asked, moving a chair forward.

At this moment he got a clear view of Markham's face in the light, and at once he sensed the minatory nature of our visit. Though his expression did not alter, I saw his body suddenly go taut. His cold, indecipherable eyes moved slowly from Markham's face to Heath and Snitkin. Then his gaze fell on Vance and me, who were standing a little behind the others, and he nodded stiffly.

No one spoke; yet I felt that an entire tragedy was somehow being enacted, and that each actor heard and understood every word.

Markham remained standing, as if reluctant to proceed. Of all the duties of his office, I knew that the arrest of malefactors was the most distasteful to him. He was a worldly man, with the worldly man's tolerance for the misfortunes of evil. Heath and Snitkin had stepped forward and now waited with passive alertness for the district attorney's order to serve the warrant.

Spotswoode's eyes were again on Markham. "What can I do for you, sir?" His voice was calm and without the faintest quaver.

"You can accompany these officers, Mr. Spotswoode," Markham told him quietly, with a slight inclination of his head toward the two imperturbable figures at his side. "I arrest you for the murder of Margaret Odell."

"Ah!" Spotswoode's eyebrows lifted mildly. "Then you have—discovered something?"

"The Beethoven Andante."

Not a muscle of Spotswoode's face moved; but after a short pause he made a barely perceptible gesture of resignation. "I can't say that it was wholly unexpected," he said evenly, with the tragic suggestion of a smile; "especially as you thwarted every effort of mine to secure the record. But then . . . the fortunes of the game are always uncertain."

His smile faded, and his manner became grave. "You have acted generously toward me, Mr. Markham, in shielding me from the canaille; and because I appreciate that courtesy I should like you to know that the game I played was one in which I had no alternative."

"Your motive, however powerful," said Markham, "cannot extenuate your crime."

"Do you think I seek extenuation?" Spotswoode dismissed the imputation with a contemptuous gesture. "I'm not a schoolboy. I calculated the consequences of my course of action and, after weighing the various factors involved, decided to risk it. It was a gamble, to be sure; but it's not my habit to complain about the misfortunes of a deliberately planned risk. Furthermore, the choice was practically forced upon me. Had I not gambled in this instance, I stood to lose heavily nevertheless."

His face grew bitter.

"This woman, Mr. Markham, had demanded the impossible of me. Not content with bleeding me financially, she demanded legal protection, position, social prestige—such things as only my name could give her. She informed me I must divorce my wife and marry her. I wonder if you apprehend the enormity of that demand? . . . You see, Mr. Markham, I love my wife, and I have children whom I love. I will not insult your intelligence by explaining how, despite my conduct, such a thing is entirely possible. . . . And yet, this woman commanded me to wreck my life and crush utterly those I held dear, solely to gratify her petty, ridiculous ambition! When I refused, she threatened to expose our relations to my wife, to send her copies of the letters I had written, to sue me publicly—in fine, to create such a scandal that, in any event, my life would be ruined, my family disgraced, my home destroyed."

He paused and drew a deep inspiration.

"I have never been partial to halfway measures," he continued impassively. "I have no talent for compromise. Perhaps I am a victim of my heritage. But my instinct is to play out a hand to the last chip—to force whatever danger threatens. And for just five minutes, a week ago, I understood how the fanatics of old could, with a calm mind and a sense of righteousness, torture their enemies who threatened them with spiritual destruction. . . . I chose the only course which might save those I love from disgrace and suffering. It meant taking a desperate risk. But the blood within me was such that I did not hesitate, and I was fired by the agony of a tremendous hate. I staked my life against a living death, on the remote chance of attaining peace. And I lost."

Again he smiled faintly.

"Yes—the fortunes of the game. . . . But don't think for a minute that I am complaining or seeking sympathy. I have lied to others perhaps, but not to myself. I detest a whiner—a self-excuser. I want you to understand that."

He reached to the table at his side and took up a small limp-leather volume. "Only last night I was reading Wilde's *De Profundis*. Had I been gifted with words, I might have made a similar confession. Let me show you what I mean so that, at least, you won't attribute to me the final infamy of cravenness."

He opened the book, and began reading in a voice whose very fervour held us all silent:

"'I brought about my own downfall. No one, be he high or low, need be ruined by any other hand than his own. Readily as I confess this, there are many who will, at this time at least, receive the confession sceptically. And although I thus mercilessly accuse myself, bear in mind that I do so without offering any excuse. Terrible as is the punishment inflicted upon me by the world, more terrible is the ruin I have brought upon myself. . . . In the dawn of manhood I recognized my position. . . . I enjoyed an honoured name, an eminent social position. . . . Then came the turning-point. I had become tired of dwelling on the heights—and descended by my own will into the depths. . . . I satisfied my desires wherever it suited me, and passed on. I forgot that every act, even the most insignificant act of daily life, in some degree, makes or unmakes the character; and every occurrence which transpires in the seclusion of the chamber will some day be proclaimed from the housetops. I lost control of myself. I was no longer at the helm, and knew it not. I had become a slave to pleasure. . . . One thing only is left to me—complete humility.'"

He tossed the book aside.

"You understand now, Mr. Markham?"

Markham did not speak for several moments.

"Do you care to tell me about Skeel?" he at length asked.

"That swine!" Spotswoode sneered his disgust. "I could murder such creatures every day and regard myself as a benefactor of society. . . Yes, I strangled him, and I would have done it before, only the opportunity did not offer. . . . It was Skeel who was hiding in the closet when I returned to the apartment after the theatre, and he must have seen me kill the woman. Had I known he was behind that locked closet door, I would have broken it down and wiped him out then. But how was I to know? It seemed natural that the closet might have

451

been kept locked—I didn't give it a second thought. . . . And the next night he telephoned me to the club here. He had first called my home on Long Island and learned that I was staying here. I had never seen him before—didn't know of his existence. But, it seems, he had equipped himself with a knowledge of my identity—probably some of the money I gave to the woman went to him. What a muck heap I had fallen into! . . . When he phoned, he mentioned the phonograph, and I knew he had found out something. I met him in the Waldorf lobby, and he told me the truth: there was no doubting his word. When he saw I was convinced, he demanded so enormous a sum that I was staggered."

Spotswoode lit a cigarette with steady fingers.

"Mr. Markham, I am no longer a rich man. The truth is, I am on the verge of bankruptcy. The business my father left me has been in a receiver's hands for nearly a year. The Long Island estate on which I live belongs to my wife. Few people know these things, but unfortunately they are true. It would have been utterly impossible for me to raise the amount Skeel demanded, even had I been inclined to play the coward. I did, however, give him a small sum to keep him quiet for a few days, promising him all he asked as soon as I could convert some of my holdings. I hoped in the interim to get possession of the record and thus spike his guns. But in that I failed; and so, when he threatened to tell you everything, I agreed to bring the money to his home late Saturday night. I kept the appointment, with the full intention of killing him. I was careful about entering, but he had helped me by explaining when and how I could get in without being seen. Once there, I wasted no time. The first moment he was off his guard I seized him—and gloried in the act. Then, locking the door and taking the key, I walked out of the house quite openly, and returned here to the club.—That's all, I think."

Vance was watching him musingly.

"So when you raised my bet last night," he said, "the amount represented a highly important item in your exchequer."

Spotswoode smiled faintly. "It represented practically every cent I had in the world."

"Astonishin'! And would you mind if I asked you why you selected the label of Beethoven's Andante for your record?"

"Another miscalculation," the man said wearily. "It occurred to me that if anyone should, by any chance, open the phonograph before I could return and destroy the record, he wouldn't be as likely to want to hear the classics as he would a more popular selection."

"And one who detests popular music had to find it! I fear, Mr. Spotswoode, that an unkind fate sat in at your game."

"Yes. . . . If I were religiously inclined, I might talk poppycock about retribution and divine punishment."

"I'd like to ask you about the jewellery," said Markham. "It's not sportsmanlike to do it, and I wouldn't suggest it, except that you've already confessed voluntarily to the main points at issue."

"I shall take no offence at any question you desire to ask, sir," Spotswoode answered. "After I had recovered my letters from the document box, I turned the rooms upside down to give the impression of a burglary—being careful to use gloves, of course. And I took the woman's jewellery for the same reason. Parenthetically, I had paid for most of it. I offered it as a sop to Skeel, but he was afraid to accept it; and finally I decided to rid myself of it. I wrapped it in one of the club newspapers and threw it in a waste bin near the Flatiron Building."

"You wrapped it in the morning Herald," put in Heath. "Did you know that Pop Cleaver reads nothing but the Herald?"

"Sergeant!" Vance's voice was a cutting reprimand. "Certainly Mr. Spotswoode was not aware of that fact—else he would not have selected the Herald."

Spotswoode smiled at Heath with pitying contempt. Then, with an appreciative glance at Vance, he turned back to Markham.

"An hour or so after I had disposed of the jewels, I was assailed by the fear that the package might be found and the paper traced. So I bought another Herald and put it on the rack." He paused. "Is that all?"

Markham nodded.

"Thank you—that's all; except that I must now ask you to go with these officers."

"In that case," said Spotswoode quietly, "there's a small favour I have to ask of you, Mr. Markham. Now that the blow has fallen, I wish to write a certain note—to my wife. But I want to be alone when I write it. Surely you understand that desire. It will take but a few moments. Your men may stand at the door—I can't very well escape. . . . The victor can afford to be generous to that extent."

Before Markham had time to reply, Vance stepped forward and touched his arm.

"I trust," he interposed, "that you won't deem it necess'ry to refuse Mr. Spotswoode's request."

Markham looked at him hesitantly.

"I guess you've pretty well earned the right to dictate, Vance," he acquiesced.

Then he ordered Heath and Snitkin to wait outside in the hall, and he and Vance and I went into the adjoining room. Markham stood, as if on guard, near the door; but Vance, with an ironical smile, sauntered to the window and gazed out into Madison Square.

"My word, Markham!" he declared. "There's something rather colossal about that chap. Y'know, one can't help admiring him. He's so eminently sane and logical."

Markham made no response. The drone of the city's mid-afternoon noises, muffled by the closed windows, seemed to intensify the ominous silence of the little bedchamber where we waited.

Then came a sharp report from the other room.

Markham flung open the door. Heath and Snitkin were already rushing toward Spotswoode's prostrate body, and were bending over it when Markham entered. Immediately he wheeled about and glared at Vance, who now appeared in the doorway.

"He's shot himself!"

"Fancy that," said Vance.

"You—you knew he was going to do that?" Markham spluttered.

"It was rather obvious, don't y'know."

Markham's eyes flashed angrily.

"And you deliberately interceded for him—to give him the opportunity?"

"Tut, tut, my dear fellow!" Vance reproached him. "Pray don't give way to conventional moral indignation. However unethical—theoretically—it may be to take another's life, a man's own life is certainly his to do with as he chooses. Suicide is his inalienable right. And under the paternal tyranny of our modern democracy, I'm rather inclined to think it's about the only right he has left, what?"

He glanced at his watch and frowned.

"D'ye know, I've missed my concert, bothering with your beastly affairs," he complained amiably, giving Markham an engaging smile; "and now you're actually scolding me. 'Pon my word, old fellow, you're deuced ungrateful!"

CPSIA information can be obtained
at www.ICGtesting.com
Printed in the USA
BVOW08s1656020218
506817BV00001B/39/P

9 780857 064264